PERICLES AND ASPASIA

A Story of Ancient Greece

Yvonne Korshak

ISBN 978-1-959182-21-4 (paperback)
ISBN 978-1-959182-22-1 (hardcover)
ISBN 978-1-959182-23-8 (digital)

Caryatid Imprint

Printed in the United States of America

For Bob and Karin

CONTENTS

And yet, somehow,
we resemble the immortals,
    whether in greatness of mind
        or nature, though we know not
    to what measure
day by day and in the watches of the night
        fate has written that we should run.
—Pindar, 465 BC

Every golden age is as much a matter of disregard as of felicity.
—Michael Chabon, 2000

PROLOGUE

Head Down into Darkness

Running out the anchor line, the pirates babbled to one another, and in the tangle of their barbaric language, Aspasia listened for one word—*Athens*. It lit up the darkness in her mind, like the single glint her eyes fixed on above the distant gray-green hills. That had to be the tip of Athena's spear shining all the way from the Acropolis—her father had promised they'd see it from the water. Or was it only some stray signal light?

"Athens." She heard it again.

She took a deep breath and held on to it—practicing.

The captain would tie her up in the morning before heading in. He always did, and he planned on selling her in Athens. Her and the book scrolls.

It would have to be tonight.

The line slackened abruptly. The men jerked back to set the anchor.

It was deep enough for a dive. And her family had a kinsman in Athens. Two things on her side.

Plus, another she clutched like a pearl from the discarded shells of someone else's oyster bake: they had no idea she could swim or they would have tied her up each time they'd dropped anchor.

The watch swung his lantern to test it against the breeze. She flattened under the glaring eye. She could count on his falling asleep—they always did. Not like Greeks. She lizarded to the edge. The water far below was black in the shadow of the ship. A plank

1

creaked. She froze. No noisy jump. It would have to be a dive. Head down into darkness. She'd never dived at night.

Fill your lungs and lock the gates and necessity will lift you to the surface, her father had instructed.

Hold to the principles.

But this deck was higher than Chin Rock.

And the hull bulged between the deck and the waterline.

She trembled, shaken again by the memory of the tremor of the boat when they threw her father over and his head cracked against that massive hull. It had been—she linked her fingers in sequence—four days. She had fallen asleep with her cheek pressed to a scroll. A sudden jolt. Had they hit a log? Where was Axiochus? Her father always sat near when she slept. In terror, she'd run to the side and saw him in the water, his head cracked open, his brains bobbing like brine scum. His back and feet, tied at the ankles, blurred beneath the waves. Weighted down and sucked in, his body left a small depression, like a navel, for the water to fill.

The captain had put his fat arm around her shoulders as if to comfort her. Then his hand reached to her breast. He'd squeezed her nipple, a hornet sting.

He must have felt the pounding of her heart—and heard it as she did. Her body inside was already too known to him.

The men were watching.

Her father's head, heavy with all he had learned, had jarred the ship.

She hated the swollen hull, feared cracking her skull.

Far beneath, the waves flipped like minnows.

Then do you want to be sold?

With his shaved face and head, the captain was more naked than any human being on earth. In instructing her in the pleasures of men, he explained in broken Greek that he was protecting her from the barbarous crew.

And raising the price he'd get for her.

Knowing a few words doesn't make a man Greek—he was as barbarian as the rest of them.

If only I could set up the dive standing to get past that hull . . .

The watch's snort startled her.

2

Standing was too risky.

She'd wait for his snores to even themselves.

Although the moon was small and it was high time to start off.

Her eyes narrowed, searching for Athena's spear where the dark sky met the darker land.

A snort, a cough.

Water looks thicker in the dark.

If only they'd anchored closer in.

Or if only I . . .

She frowned to rein in her thoughts. All the *if-only*s had floated off with her father's brains.

The watch had slept several breaths-worth.

She bid goodbye to the scrolls—not to her father. He after all . . .

Curling her body over the edge, she hung there like a sucking bug.

She breathed deeply, locked the gates.

Closed her eyes. Opened them.

Took another deep breath.

An interrupted snore.

No more starting over.

She fought the air—a bundle twisting out of itself, wrenching free of flatness, and spiraling head down.

Keep the gates closed.

She hit. The blow, the noise and the cold conspired for her breath.

But she pruned her face.

Would her head meet a stone? She flattened her palms.

Her lungs insisted on air. Expanding her ribs, she fooled them. Not yet.

Going deeper, she pacified her lungs with imitated breaths.

She slowed against the water.

Now. Her chest an iron door, she arched upward.

Her being drew into the pocket of her lungs.

She crashed the surface—afraid. Was her snort louder than the waves?

She swung her head around. The ship was dark. She was landward. And beyond the ship's shadow.

She kept to small, quiet breaths, listening.

Still no light. Good—it was time the gods did her a favor.

She surrendered to a long deep breath—silent within her ribs.

Face up, she floated.

Her garment squeezed her limbs.

Her muscles refused to do what was necessary.

She argued with them.

She shoved her chiton off her slippery shoulders easily but peeling off the linen clinging to her hips and legs was like working a knot. She circled her neck for a rest. Her hands moved under water switching tasks—buoying her and working at the wet, flat slices of the fabric.

They'd pull her in like a fish. Gagging.

She turned herself into the shape of an eye and spun under the water, making a complete turn—porpoises do it.

Part of the hem floated loose. She spun around again—the fabric tightened like wool on a spindle. She breathed in fear. The boat was farther away. She swung her head around—so was the shore.

Swim.

My legs.

Free your legs.

Shoulders leading, she made a slow porpoise turn. An edge uncoiled—a tail. The shore was more distant. She shoved. The fabric drifted off, smaller.

Only the black ship interrupted the waves.

She kicked from the hips, as her father taught her.

Her breath was tight. She listened for his voice: "Open your mouth wide."

A girl must never open her . . .

"Raise that shoulder."

Her arms grew heavy.

"Forearm loose."

The briefest rest and the shore grew distant.

Forearm loose, mouth wide . . .

At dawn they'd see her missing.

4

Faster.

But her arms were heavier.

The waves were noisier. Higher against her face.

The shore ahead was blurry.

Her fingers brushed stones. Stay low.

She pulled herself in on her hands.

The water let go. Immediately Earth pulled her down—true everywhere, evidently.

Earth is flies and sharp, cracked shells with rotting creatures. *Only at low tide.*

Earth ground her ribs, pelvis and knees into the stones.

They say that vagrant men, thieves, scapegoats roam the beaches. Naked and white, she was a beacon. She snaked toward the bushes.

The East was still dark. She twisted around on her hip—so was the ship dark, but how long could good luck hold? They'd drop the skiff. She'd seen how fast they rowed after a big fish.

Athena holding her spear was somewhere west, beyond the dark and bushes.

Her hands, elbows, knees and heels pushed against the stones and sand. *Worms move faster.* She tried to force the thicket. Her hands closed on thistles. There was the slim beginning of light, no more than a haze . . . Her heart sped like when they murdered her father. Each loud beat of her heart forced more unwelcome blood into her head like a dagger.

She lowered her forehead to the sand. Her teeth chattered. Her arms wrapped around her chest, her hands gripping her shoulder blades. Tears squeezed from her closed lids. *If only . . .*

A prick—a stab. Poisoned!

She sat up fast, dizzy.

No snake. No bite mark.

If only. She shook her finger as her father did when he arrived at a philosophical point. *If-onlys not allowed.*

A fresh breeze crossed her face, a passenger on the rising tide. She breathed it in deeply.

Less stink. Fewer flies.

Water flowing? If it was there before she hadn't heard it.

Not the on-and-off, yes-and-no of lapping waves. Steady. A stream. She stood up and ran toward the sound.

She took long steps over the slippery rocks, eyes down, her ankles stiff with guiding her feet, her toes clutching where they could. The woods hid the bright stain in the eastern sky but remembering it, she sped up, her arms tilting and shifting like birds' wings. When the stream deepened, she took to the side, clinging to bushes to make a turn but was forced back into the pooled water. How long could her heart keep up that bird-like flutter?

She spotted something white at the base of a broad stone—a chiton. The wrong side of the stream but she breasted over and snatched it—why not? Hadn't the girl who'd washed it left it out all night to get wet a second time?

Where would she get shoes and a head scarf?

She heard men's voices, thin and distant, calling across the water.

The path in front of her would lead to whoever owned the chiton.

She waded against heavy water back to what she had come to think of as *her* side, holding the chiton above her head; she headed for a collapsed slope—no moss—pulled herself onto the bank, pulled on the damp garment, and stoop-ran along the deer path.

The sun was behind her: that meant that Athena's spear was somewhere ahead.

At first, she skirted the habitations and outbuildings, but soon there were too many to evade. She stopped behind a copse and pinch-shaped the drape of her chiton that had partly dried. She pulled her hair into a twisted hank and poked the end into the middle; it uncoiled. Should she use twigs for pins? What a way to enter a city. She divided the hank and yanked the two sections into a knot behind her ears. She had no head scarf and most odd—and most noticeable because the chiton was too short for her—no sandals. Her bony ankles and long feet stuck out. She was sunburned. Bruised. Dusty. She was hungrier than she'd ever felt—that probably showed, too. People would take her for a crude country girl, or a waif.

And which city was she approaching? By the depth and angle from which she'd glimpsed the spear point from the water, she'd gauged it was Athens. But what if it had just been a signal? Or a mirage? She could have been meandering like the curving river near her home in Miletus. Those city walls ahead might be Port Piraeus where the crew, by now, might be roaming the streets. And the captain, angry as Ares because he lost his prize. *Or whoever his war god is.* Her mind's eye saw his hairless face, grimacing.

She sat on a fallen tree trunk and, to avoid meeting the eyes of strangers, fit a stone to her palm and set about smoothing her fingernails. With her eyes focused on her hands, she could decide herself whose gaze to catch. And listen for a Milesian accent.

More people were passing in both directions. Some were returning to the city from their farms and some were returning to their farms after a day of buying and selling in the city. They had places to go. But she was no animal—to spend another night in the open.

A shadow, the edge of a skirt, and the aroma of sausage in a covered basket at the level of her nose—the last made Aspasia raise her eyes faster than she'd intended.

"I notice your sandals slipped off." The girl's accent wasn't Milesian.

"Sometimes sandal straps break," Aspasia replied. She was far taller than this girl, but the girl had yellow hair. "Are you heading for Piraeus?"

"No, Athens." The girl nodded toward the city walls. "Why, are you going to Piraeus?"

"Athens. But unfortunately . . ." Aspasia looked around, "I left my headscarf somewhere." Her eyes came to rest on the basket.

Sitting next to Aspasia on the log, the girl unwound the cloth covering it. "I'll need it back though."

Was this girl simple—lending what she might never see again? Accepting the scarf, Aspasia spotted two large coins between the sausage and some figs. *And letting others see her drachmas.*

Though how simple could she be to get her hands on those coins?

"Are you on your way home from a visit?" Aspasia asked.

"Yes, and he gave me some other things, too." Chewing, the girl handed a fig to Aspasia.

Aspasia bit off the tough end. Many people ate the whole thing but she didn't.

The girl stood up and tucked the coins in her cheek.

No sausage for the moment.

"Rhodia's expecting me." The girl shook twigs from her chiton. "What's your name?"

"What's yours?"

"Silky."

What kind of a name—

"Do men just call you that."

Silky lowered her eyes.

Aspasia had never met a hetaira, but she knew one thing about them—they were the kind of women who made their living by pleasing men.

"If you need a place," Silky continued, "I'm sure Rhodia would take you in. She always needs girls."

And this Silky took her for one of them. How not, a girl alone, sitting beside a path?

"Silky, do you know anyone living in Athens from Miletus?"

"The girls are from everywhere—I'm from Megara. I'm sure someone—"

"Someone who really lives here, a man with a household."

"There's a Hippodamus from Miletus—all the girls know him. He had me to his symposium, but he doesn't want a woman for his own." Silky brought her mouth close to Aspasia's ear. "Not even a wife."

"Lead me to Hippodamus' house, Silky."

"I told you my name but you didn't tell me yours."

They say everyone bargains in Athens. "Aspasia." *Be fair.* "From Miletus."

"How did you get here, Aspasia?"

"Let's find Hippodamus' house."

Silky eyed her and shook her head. "You have a bruise on your cheek." Aspasia's hand went to her cheek. "And a cut above your eye. Your chiton doesn't cover your knees. And you're barefoot—you'd better stay close to me."

The city wall looked sturdy and the stones were laid in even courses, like a good weave, at least along this stretch. And they kept the base clear of weeds. Perhaps Athens would live up to her reputation, or some of it.

"Silky, when you're in Athens, can you see Athena's spear point shining from wherever you are?"

"I've seen the whole Athena—she's on the Acropolis."

"I mean can you see it everywhere in the lower city? Can you see it from where Hippodamus lives?"

"I don't remember. Here's the gate—hold my basket handle tight so we don't get separated."

A mob—like Poseidon's wave—came toward them.

"The Assembly must have just let out," Silky said.

"We can wait until they're all through the gate."

"I'm already late and you want me to show you Hippodamus' house." Silky pushed to the side so they could follow a thin current entering the city.

"Grab it, Aspasia!"

A man had snatched Silky's sausage. Aspasia lunged for it but drew back as she felt a pain across her toes. Someone's boot had come down on her foot. The sausage was gone.

Silky wiped tears from her eyes.

Did this mean she wouldn't show her the way to Hippodamus?

The current moving their way thrust them through the gate into the city. Silky led them to an inset in the wall, out of the crowd. Aspasia bent down to check her foot, already turning blue—didn't she have enough bruises already? She brushed off the mud. Memory forced itself through the pain. She straightened her back and turned from the wall. Locating the tall hill and searching with her eyes, she found at its top the spark of light. Now she was certain—that shining point was Athena's spear.

CHAPTER 1

Buying and Selling

She was pouring wine into General Pericles' cup for the third time that evening but, without the glance she was hoping for, he brushed her hand away, engaged in discussing port taxes. And then she heard him say, "That rowdy Phoenician ship finally sailed off."

How she had longed to hear those words! Her heart jumped but her hand held steady.

She set the pitcher down softly, hoping one of the men would ask, "Have all the Phoenician ships left port?" But they went on to grain storage rates.

So she was left with *that rowdy Phoenician ship*.

"Rowdy" – not much to go on.

"Phoenician" – yes.

"That." Her hand went to her chin. "That" sounded like there'd been one, which meant that now there were none. Almost certainly.

In the morning, Aspasia sailed out to the Agora on the word "that."

For three weeks, she hadn't dared enter the Agora where all the buying and selling took place. Now she paused to look in all directions.

No pirates.

But the noise slammed at her ears like when she broke the surface after that long, underwater swim. The shouts of vendors, the tip-tap of a bootmaker, the braying of a donkey, the rumble of cart wheels, water sloshed on stone, a man's sudden laugh, the pebbly roar of giving and getting . . .

She checked Phidias' map, sweat glued to her palm. Phidias helped her with money. *Think it right, Aspasia*—she sold him what he wanted of her. But Phidias was better than most men since he made beautiful sculptures. He was even making one of her—well, he called it "Athena," but anyone could see it looked like her. On the map, Phidias had drawn a heavy circle around the bookseller's stall. Her gold, of course, was gone, but the Phoenician ship's captain would sell her books where he could get the best price. Athens was famous for its love of learning. Therefore, the books were here.

If the Athenians loved learning so much, somebody might have bought them already—she quickened her pace.

Bypassing the apples, pears and pomegranates, she felt a tug on her chiton, lost her breath and spun around, twisting the material out of his hand.

Thanks to Zeus it wasn't the Phoenician captain.

"How much, young lady?"

A curved back had been part of her disguise, just in case. Now she drew herself up tall, noticing the fine silver pin—it looked like a long grasshopper—that fastened his cloak at the shoulder.

He cocked his head toward the large building behind them. "There's a painting in there of our greatest battle."

Thin hairs circled the bald head like mold on a fig. But what man doesn't have something wrong with him? Phidias was bald. People said that General Pericles had an overlarge head—she couldn't see it because he wore his helmet all through the dinner last night which was peculiar enough.

A fast check of her map. The bookseller was past the fabrics and dyes.

The old man's glance drifted sidewise. "We chased those Persians all the way to the sea and burned their ships—I led the brigade that trapped them—" He shook away the memories. "It's all in the painting. Now let me see your face. I'm sure you're prettier than men fighting."

Prettier than men fighting. He knew Sappho's song so he was an aristocrat. But—she took a closer look—his pin had tarnished in the turns. He may have been a great man when he led a brigade but now the servants ignored him.

And the books were waiting.

She turned, evading the old man's grasp that landed on her arm like a bug. She swung past the linens and veered around the dyes. A drachma for a sun umbrella? Things cost more here than in Miletus where she came from. She took in on the run the location of the skin whitener and strode past tweezers (three drachmas!) and nail smoothers and—stopped short. There, near the edge of the Agora, under a shady oak, was the bookseller's stall.

A man's broad back blocked her view of the table.

She stepped sidewise.

The man's palm curved around a tied book scroll as if he already owned it. She moved in closer. He reached for another and the scroll rolled off the table.

The squares and triangle on the goatskin cover—her father's Pythagoras—into the dust!

She went for it but the seller got there first. "Get away from here." As if *she'd* thrown it down.

She didn't move. Her father had engraved the three squares to fit the right triangle. No other man, except the philosopher Pythagoras himself, would have the intelligence to do that.

And there was Broad Back, unrolling Pythagoras, flattening the coiled scroll against the table, waiting for another book. His clean fingernails meant money.

He rolled the new book back and forth under his palm.

She took a pace forward. At a nod from the seller, the buyer blocked her view. His untrimmed hair straggled past his shoulders, but the noise his coins made when he shook them onto the table alarmed her. She slipped her coins from her cheek to her hand. All those drachmas Phidias had laid on her open palm had seemed heavy when he'd agreed on the extra. They were nowhere near enough to keep the customer from leaving with Pythagoras secure between his elbow and his ribs.

Her book was gone. Like her father. Like brine foam.

"I told you to go," the seller said. "Shoo."

Shoo was a high wave. She stood strong. He'd probably never had a woman buying his books.

Her hand went to her chin—*too serious too soon if her drachmas were to cover any distance.* She played her fingers over the scattered manuscripts as Broad Back had done. The gods had forgotten to paint the seller—no color in his hair, eyes, or skin. That kind of skin burns easily; a sun umbrella leaned against his table.

"I suppose you're here to buy a book."

Sarcasm. She rattled the drachmas in her palm. "Several interest me."

"For a friend?"

"Perhaps."

It wasn't one of hers but she uncoiled the book Broad Back had palmed. The seller didn't stop her.

She scanned the script a moment, then read aloud, "For a day can bring all mortal greatness low, and a day can lift it up." She nodded slowly to show thoughtfulness. "How true."

"Sophocles," he said.

"Of course."

"How'd you learn to read?"

"My father. Do you have a lot of customers?"

"Everyone knows I have the best selection in Athens."

"That man here seemed to think so."

"He knows books, he writes plays himself, Euripides."

She skeined in the name of the man who had bought her book.

"Does he win first prize for playwrights?" She knew the answer: Sophocles won first prize.

"He will someday."

Money for books but not for the barber. If he didn't care about the opinions of others, he wouldn't be winning any prizes. "Sophocles is famous where I come from."

"Euripides will be famous when he starts winning. Here's his *Daughters of Pelias.*"

She didn't pick it up. "Do you have any Ionian poets?"

"I specialize in plays. But recently I bought . . ." He thumbed through his books and came up with Sappho. "From a dealer on Lesbos."

14

Liar. It was her Sappho. With its beautiful Ionian script. Scrolling through, she found her favorite wedding song. "Raise high the roofbeam, carpenters . . . the bridegroom comes like Ares . . . far taller than a tall man—" She looked up. "What about Homer?" It had to be here.

He drew a book from a rack and, with a practiced spin, rolled it open. "I happen to have an *Odyssey*."

She looked at it sidewise, as at the sun, to keep her eyes dry. Her father had taught her to read with the scroll that the seller now was holding in his pale hands.

Scrolling through, he found his place, tapped it with a long forefinger and, though he had no lyre, sang about Helen of Troy's magic potion that soothed all grief and pain. "No one that swallowed this, dissolved in wine . . ."

The voice of this bleached man was so deep he could sing Homer at a festival. That was something right about him.

". . . could shed a single tear that day . . ."

No, she would not let tears fall down her cheeks. "Nice book."

But, eyes closed, he pushed on, ". . . even for the death of his mother and father . . ."

He'd gone right to it without knowing anything about her. Had his mother and father died? Or was he guessing about her?

He jerked a thumb toward shelves behind him. "There's the rest of it. Would you like the set?"

"I would, but it's too . . . heavy to carry."

The book rolled shut with a snap. "Then we're done."

"How long have you had this *Odyssey*?"

"I bought it two days ago from a Phoenician. It'll go fast."

The Phoenician captain. Here. She plucked her veil higher over her nose as if this pale boy might see her with the captain's eyes. It had its good effect—he thought she was leaving.

"I can give you a good price. The Phoenician was in a hurry to sell—sailing out the next morning."

The next morning . . . She'd heard it twice now. The pirates were gone! Two points make a straight line. Joy made her bold.

She wagged a finger at him. "Never mind your good price, I want your best price."

15

"Ordinarily, I'd take thirty drachmas for a set like this."

Thirty. For balance, she squeezed her large five-drachma piece. She'd been excited when Phidias had dropped it in her palm and topped it with three smaller ones.

"I'll let you have it for twenty-eight."

Broad Back would snatch it at his next go-round, or that General Pericles with his twenty-eight or thirty—they said he liked to read.

"The script is disappointing." It felt like betraying a friend but she had her reason.

The seller watched her fiddle with her coins.

"Twenty-five?"

"I don't have twenty-five with me."

Tight lines formed from the corner of his mouth to his nose. He wasn't as young as she'd thought. "Do you have twenty-five drachmas anywhere?"

"No."

He scooped the books out of reach. "Good I grabbed that Pythagoras."

Now he took her for a thief. But he had her Homer.

"I came to buy them." She opened her palm to show him her drachmas—and there was Phidias' charcoal, grimy map. She flicked it away and then, with her pink fingernail smoothed to an oval, circled the edge of each coin slowly; his eyes followed her finger like a cat follows a fly.

"I used to have these books, more than you have but . . . I had to leave them behind in Miletus." At least she could let him know that she came from a city as good as any among the Greeks.

"You live in town?"

She nodded.

"With your family?"

"Friends."

He smoothed his white eyebrows. "If you have a room, I'll give you the Sappho."

"I'd prefer the *Odyssey*."

At last color came to his face—indignant red. "It's a four-scroll book, copied in Chios!"

She waited. They had something in common.

"Impossible," he spat out. "I have the local playwrights copied here, but these are foreign poets. Imported."

"I'm imported, so I'm more valuable too." Cleverness was worth a try but he came back with, "Athens is swamped with foreign women."

True. Silky, who lent her the sandals, was foreign. Some weren't even Greek.

He was setting the books—her books—into their cubbyholes.

How easily he was put off. But he had her *Odyssey*, and she had a room.

"I told you to go away."

He waved over her head, as if to an approaching customer.

"I'll take the Sappho."

"I'll bring it with me."

He bolted the door and grabbed his sun umbrella but was in too much of a hurry to bother opening it. She took a quick look back to make sure he was following her. His fine physique was silhouetted against the sun; his bleached skin looked darker against the brightness. As her friend Silky would say, "At least that's something."

* * *

"Don't tell me that's your mirror." He poked the bronze fragment with his walking stick.

She snatched it and stuck it behind the pitcher.

"And what's this?" His fingers were on her cup.

Hands on his wrists, she drew his arms around her ribs and pressed his palms to the small of her back. There's always something to overlook about a man.

"It doesn't bother you that I'm so pale?" Anxiety had turned his deep voice reedy.

"You're well-proportioned." Her gaze locked on the few white hairs on his chest.

"So I've been told. Could you please remove your veil?"

No sense fiddling with the knot. She pulled the veil over her head and fluffed her dark curls.

He smiled. "I knew you weren't hiding behind there because you were ugly."

He unfastened her belt, and—thanks to Artemis—wasted no time. After, he spun his forefinger around his head as if awarding himself a laurel crown.

"You're my first girl."

Palm up, she waited for *Sappho*. As she took it, he bent and landed a kiss on the book—he'd been aiming for her hand.

Picking up her veil, he fingered the fringe. "I'm Dion, son of Philetarus of Rhamnous."

"I'm Aspasia, daughter of Axiochus of Miletus."

"The philosopher?"

She felt less alone in Athens. "Not everyone knows his teachings—"

"So, Aspasia. That's how you know how to read." He bumped the legs of the chair closer.

"Shh!" Her finger flew to her mouth.

He laughed. "So your friends let—"

"Dion, leave now." He made no move.

"I told you to go." She held back on adding "shoo"—Homer was on her mind.

He shrugged and reached for his umbrella.

"Dion, leave me that sun umbrella and I'll come to see your books again."

"Not included."

The boy—the man—must still have been on the stairs when her cousin Hippodamus, who owned this house, clanged his bronze bracelet against her door.

"How much?"

"Not money exactly—"

"*Exactly* what? You don't live here for nothing—you owe me rent!" His eyes dropped to the *Sappho* on her lap and his fingers flew to his mouth. He stood for a moment, warming to an idea, winked at her, and hurried out.

CHAPTER 2

Sacred Prostitutes

"*. . . Darling, don't stop now, stop now . . .*"
That song from last year's festival. And he was here for business.
"General Pericles, may I take your helmet?"
"No, just the cloak."
"*. . . don't stop now, stop now . . .*" high-pitched laughter topped the refrain.

His cousin Cleinias' house, he should have known there'd be girls.

The drinking and singing stilled when Pericles came into the room. Then, as if swept by a rip current, everyone sped back into motion—toward him. Hippodamus wagged his tablet as if signaling from prow to stern—*I'll look at your plan, Hippodamus*—while Phidias shook his head vigorously, "no." Damon straightened his knees, brushing off crumbs. Cleinias—his kinsman and as much a general as he was—lunged forward, checking his embrace short of his spiky, seal-like whiskers, while Socrates toasted "General Pericles," then smiled as if the words brought some new thought to mind. Only Herodotus remained seated.

How to end this autocratic nonsense? Pericles cleared his throat and found the note: "*Darling, don't stop now, stop . . .*"

Everyone laughing. How delightful—it was as good as winning a unanimous vote.

"I came here tonight to raise my cup—"

The plump girl with yellow hair ran up with a brimming cup.

"—to Cleinias, who will lead our army against the rebels."

"To victory!"

Cleinias twirled a finger through his awry whiskers. "Your toast is a surprise, Pericles, since you spent today arguing against me in the Assembly."

Though there are no unanimous votes.

"I was arguing against what you *proposed*, Cleinias, not against you." *Why are men deaf to the difference?*

"The fact is you're my kinsman and you piled reason on reason. You let me down."

Pericles set aside his cup. "I presented my reasons for opposing a military campaign in winter—"

"I know your reasons. I don't need to hear them again."

"The only way I could let you or anyone down is if I saw danger ahead and stayed silent. We all sail on the same ship, Cleinias."

"Calm down, Cleinias," Damon said. "After all you won."

Then General Pericles must have lost a vote. Aspasia was surprised—she'd thought that he won all of them. But it didn't change her mind about making him notice her.

Pericles rested his palms on his kinsman's shoulders. "If holding different opinions turned friends into enemies, there'd be no friends."

Phidias raised his cup. "To Cleinias, who'll bring us a victory!"

"To Cleinias!"

The girls applauded.

Hippodamus had told Pericles that one of these girls did it for a book. *Which one?*

Cleinias snapped his fingers at the girl folding her pipes. "Play something elevated for General Pericles."

Pericles hoped it was the plump one. "Do you know the song 'Violet Crowned Athens'?" he asked. Yellow hair like hers was rare among the Greeks. Though some people say that Helen of Troy . . .

Cleinias hummed along with "Violet Crowned Athens," nodding with the rhythm. It was time for Pericles to move on to his next piece of business.

"Let's have a look at your plan for the Acropolis, Hippodamus."

Hippodamus pulled a chair toward Pericles' couch. "I drew it in wax to show I'm open to your ideas, Pericles. I can change anything you don't like."

Pericles raised an eyebrow toward the blond girl, but Hippodamus merely set the tablet flat between Pericles' facing palms.

So it was a guessing game. The tall girl came to refill his cup. He'd seen her around—she was so thin her belly lay behind her hipbones instead of in front of them.

"Here's the position of our *new* Athena temple on the Acropolis—our Parthenon." Hippodamus tapped the tablet with his straight edge. Pushing past the silence, he added, "You may not understand it immediately. It takes a planner like me or an architect to understand a plan."

"Or a sculptor," Phidias said.

It was exciting to view the Acropolis in a way ordinarily open only to the birds—or the gods. Locating the rectangle on the right, Pericles ran his finger its full length. "Here, I see clearly the Parthenon temple, but . . . Hippodamus, there's no indication of the old Athena temple with the shrine to Erechtheus across the way." He tapped the empty space.

The tall girl stretched her neck for a look.

"This is a new plan. The old temple won't square with it, so I erased it."

Erased it . . . "Phidias, have you looked at this?" Pericles tilted the tablet toward the sculptor, whose opinion was first with him.

"I told Hippodamus—eliminate that temple and you'll have us all thrown out of Athens!"

Hippodamus shook his head. "It's old fashioned and you know it, Phidias."

"That temple is dedicated to our city's goddess," Pericles said.

"Perhaps he doesn't care since it's not *his* city's goddess." Socrates smiled.

Not his city's . . . The Athenians never miss a chance to let you know who belongs here, Aspasia thought. Hippodamus was her cousin and from her city.

"And I don't want to be voted into exile—" Phidias thumbed his large front teeth, clicking the nail—"not until I finish my great work on the Acropolis!"

"That old temple is in my way."

"It's in the man's way." Damon, Pericles' advisor, grinned tight-lipped behind his palm.

"Silence." Cleinias tapped his table. "I didn't invite you to this symposium to argue about lines scribbled in wax—though I know, I know, it's important," he added to forestall further interruptions. "But I planned a special treat, Herodotus will read from his history of our war against Persia—"

"But my vision for the Acropolis—"

"Shh, Hippodamus." Cleinias' finger was to his lips. "Silky, that's enough 'Violet Crowned.'"

Silky. Pericles circled his thumb to his fingers . . . *soft, smooth, rustling, perfumed . . .*

Manuscript in hand, Herodotus took the chair with the curved back in the center of the room.

"It's been years since we fought in Egypt," Cleinias said. "Read about that."

"We only made to the Delta," Damon said. "Herodotus has been south into the land of the elephants."

"What took you so far, Herodotus?" Socrates asked.

Looking at Socrates and then beyond him and the mahogany couches and painted wine stand of the brightly lit room, Herodotus' eyes narrowed as he peered into the past. "I was fleeing Persian tyranny in my city . . . "

He's known tyranny—that's why he didn't stand with the others when Pericles came in, Aspasia thought. *But he should know Athenian generals aren't tyrants.*

". . . and I also wanted to know how we came to fight the Persians. Why did they invade Greece when they already held Egypt and Mesopotamia?"

"Everyone wants more," Damon said.

Damon's direct way of speaking his mind made him an invaluable advisor, Pericles thought, though he overlooked complexities.

"The fact is not everyone tries to conquer their neighbors," Cleinias said.

"Well then, Herodotus, what did you learn?" Socrates asked.

"By going backward in time one can arrive at the reason for things."

"That's obvious—just start at the root," Socrates said.

Since Pericles never noticed her pouring wine, maybe this would do it. Aspasia raised a finger. "No, *not* just at the root. Herodotus showed us that history is like a river fed by many streams."

It was as silent as when Pericles had first arrived.

Cleinias shook his head. "Since when are girls *us?*"

This must be the one. Pericles watched Aspasia set herself on Phidias' couch and pull up her knees. *Where did Phidias find this talker?*

"Aspasia!" Phidias tightened his fingers around her arm. That grip would leave white fingerprints.

Pericles leaned forward—these women shouldn't have to put up with that. But Phidias relaxed his hand and Aspasia—she had a real name—withdrew her arm.

Herodotus nodded. "Just as traveling through one country led me to the next, so I followed Ariadne's thread farther and farther back into the past. As she said."

As she said! They all heard it! Every man among them. Aspasia didn't even glance at Phidias. But did her eyes briefly shift toward him? Pericles wondered.

"Why or how—the fact is Persia invaded Greece and we won," Cleinias said.

Socrates smiled. "So then, Cleinias, you think only facts matter?"

"Victory matters," Cleinias said. "Let's hear about the Battle of Marathon. Socrates might learn something."

Herodotus read about the Athenian victory at Marathon that stopped the Persian invasion in its tracks. The Athenians sent their best runner to Sparta for help but, though he'd run halfway through Greece, the Spartans refused to send their army.

"It was the wrong phase of the moon for them." Again, Damon's thin grin.

"The fact is we chased the Persians into the sea ourselves," Cleinias said.

"And set their ships on fire." The way everyone had gone right to it, Aspasia figured she had the right battle, so she took a chance.

How would a foreign girl, in her teens, know about the Battle of Marathon? Pericles eyed her over his cup. A small bump interrupted the slope of her nose—no Helen of Troy here.

"'The Athenians counted six thousand and four hundred dead Persians,'" Herodotus read.

"And one hundred and ninety-two Greeks." Phidias thumbed his teeth.

The eyes of the Athenians filled with tears—sorrow and pride. Six thousand, four hundred to one hundred and ninety-two—and they all knew their ratios.

Cleinias, his cheeks rosy under his whiskers, held up his cup for more. "If—"

"If. Cleinias, I thought you only dealt in facts," Socrates said.

Why did this impertinent young man get invited? Aspasia wondered. *He's not even good looking.*

"—the Persians had won, we'd be under their thumbs today, don't you think, Pericles?"

"I can tell you this—you Athenians would never have developed democracy." Herodotus tapped his book with his long finger. "I know Persian domination—I was born to it."

"It's hard to imagine, but he's right," Damon said. "We'd never have had the chance, don't you agree, Pericles?"

Pericles, caught up on the word "never," finally said, "Without democracy in Athens, there'd be no democracy anywhere in the world."

"Pericles' family has always fought against tyranny," Herodotus said.

Socrates raised an eyebrow. "Herodotus, don't stop now but—"

"Don't stop now, stop now," the blond girl sang out.

"—let's hear Pericles' family's *un*democratic story."

"Old gossip," Damon said. "Remove that from your book, Herodotus."

"More wine!" Cleinias clapped his hands. "Let's have something amusing! Read about the sacred prostitutes."

"Not again." Herodotus sighed. "Everyone always wants to hear about the sacred prostitutes."

"Oh, come on, Herodotus. We listened to the war," Hippodamus said.

With a resigned shrug, Herodotus scrolled to the place, cleared his throat and read, "'The Babylonians have a very shameful custom. Every woman must once in her life visit Aphrodite's precinct and give herself to a stranger.'"

Cleinias surrendered to familiar amazement with open palms.

"I'd bet the rich pay to exempt their daughters." Damon had a squeaky laugh.

"The Babylonians take this matter seriously." Herodotus looked up from the scroll. "It's true that the rich often arrive in covered carriages so they don't have to mix with the others more than necessary, but once the girls are there, they all take their station—"

"Now *that's* democracy," Phidias said.

Damon shook his head. "He said 'so they don't have to mix with the others.' That's *not* democracy."

"Don't interrupt Herodotus." Cleinias circled his finger. "Girls, wine."

Aspasia let Silky pour the wine.

"There's a lot of coming and going while the men are looking to choose a woman," Herodotus said. "And once a woman has taken her place, she has to stay there until a stranger throws a coin in her lap and takes her with him outside the sacred area."

"Aspasia would bring something to read," Hippodamus said.

It was certain—the *skinny* one was the reader. Pericles felt disappointed, not that it was anything to him.

"It must be a silver coin," Herodotus said. "And the woman can't refuse it."

Cleinias shook his head. "The Babylonians are uncivilized."

"Lawless," Damon said.

Socrates raised an eyebrow. "But Damon, since the woman *must* go with the *first* man who throws her a coin that *must* be silver, can we truly say they're lawless?"

"That doesn't sound like law to me," Damon said. "Who voted for these laws? What city passed them?"

"It's just custom," Hippodamus said.

"It's clearly a religious law." Socrates said. "Herodotus, you must correct what you wrote there from *custom* to *religious law*."

"Oh well then, if it's only a religious law—"

"*Only* a religious law,'" Socrates said. "So then, Damon, do you think . . . ?"

"They're all barbarians." Phidias drained his cup.

"You can't put their laws on the same level as ours," Damon said. "Don't you agree, Pericles?"

"And the women . . . well, we all know what the women are," Cleinias said.

No. Aspasia didn't want another evening spinning into low talk about women—especially with General Pericles here who was said to be so elevated, even if he did know the words to that song. "The philosopher Heraclitus teaches that to gods, all things are beautiful, good and just." She brushed away Phidias' hand. "Let me be."

How had Phidias taken that? Pericles checked the sculptor's face—inscrutable.

Aspasia continued. "Heraclitus says it's men who suppose that some things are unjust and others just. Therefore—"

Therefore. Could it be this woman knows logic? Pericles asked himself.

"—perhaps in the gods' eyes, the sacred prostitutes are beautiful, good, and just."

Damon grinned. "And I suppose you're think you're 'sacred' when you—"

"But, my dear Aspasia, we are men," Socrates said. "*Therefore*, some things *seem* more just to us than others."

"The men are sure to choose the women who *seem* most beautiful." Phidias hand crossed his bald head. "What happens to the rest?"

Herodotus said, "Some wait in the precinct three or four years."

"Aspasia would be picked first." Phidias squeezed her shoulder.

Socrates lifted his cup. "To Aspasia, always picked first."

It was rude but there was an upside—they were toasting her, not Silky.

Pericles took in the hard-looking shin, the bare instep, long toes—thin as a sponge diver. In a woman like that, the breasts are a surprise.

Toasts followed to Cleinias' victory against the rebels, to the battle at Marathon, to historical inquiry, to the Babylonians, though when somebody was drunk enough to raise his cup to the Persians, nobody seconded.

Hippodamus leaned in toward Pericles. "I suppose you've figured out which is the book lover."

He had.

* * *

Aspasia was thumbing through *Sappho* the next evening when she heard a scratching at her door. So late?

"He said, 'With Pericles' compliments.'"

She grabbed the box from the old woman and unfolded the cloth. Inside lay a four-scroll book. She carried the top scroll to her oil lamp and read the first words of Homer's *Odyssey. Sing, O Muses!* Her copy! She examined the other scrolls—that bookseller might have put the best on top . . . but no, all four were in the same familiar hand from which she'd learned to read! She clutched the scrolls to her chest—hers again.

She ran downstairs, hitting the wall on the turn, but by the time she got there, he had gone.

CHAPTER 3

Finding a Way

She dipped her head and bit off a thread.

Four days and nothing more happened.

Should she write to thank him? Then he'd know she could write. But a letter from a girl would embarrass him. But by giving her the book, hadn't he opened himself to more?

She dumped the skein into her wool basket.

Why would a man give a girl something for nothing?

True, some Assembly speakers gave things away to curry favor, like letting anyone passing by pick their pears. But a book? Phidias said Pericles disdained vote buying, and anyhow, women didn't vote and what a stupid line of thought that was—she wasn't even an Athenian citizen.

He had no plan to see her then or ever. It was either just a kind thought or a joke. And by now he'd forgotten about it.

Though her father always said politicians have good memories.

And Phidias, who worked for him—or for the city—said Pericles liked to get a lot for his money.

She gazed at her *Odyssey* scrolls, coiled like seashells, as if the answer to her questions—as if Pericles—were inside.

Bits of wool stuck to her lips. What could she weave with all that yarn in her basket?

Silky claimed her lover was Pericles' friend, but Aspasia hadn't visited her because she didn't want to be mistaken for one of Rhodia's girls. Anyhow, everyone liked to claim a connection to Pericles.

On the other hand, would a girl of so few words like Silky have exaggeration in her?

At Rhodia's, Silky's first words were "He's going to marry me!"

A lover who would marry a hetaira . . . ? "What good luck!"

Silky nodded, unblinking, unwilling to close her eyes to the picture in front of her.

"But you belong to Rhodia."

"He's promised to buy me out."

"For how much?"

"We're going to ask her tonight."

We. From a Silky.

"When an Athenian marries a foreigner, his sons can't be citizens," Aspasia said.

"He says that architects travel for their jobs so it doesn't matter."

An architect.

"Silky, don't tell me you really believe you'll only be with him, all the time?"

"When he pays Rhodia." Silky ran the buffer over her nails.

"When will the wedding be?"

"He's saving up. He's building a temple for Pericles."

The name in her mind stirred a spin in her breast.

"Which temple?"

"Remember Hippodamus' tablet?"

"You mean . . . on the Acropolis?"

Silky nodded with pride.

Aspasia kissed Silky's cheek, inhaling the scent of a better perfume than what drifted off Hippodamus. Her architect could have put those drachmas toward paying Rhodia.

"It must be hard to wait until tonight."

"And Ictinus will be late. He's measuring for the Parthenon."

There was one thing Aspasia knew about how Phidias spent his time: he was forever on the Acropolis.

"Silky, let's go see Ictinus now." Phidias wouldn't be embarrassed—she'd been there with him before, though at night. But he or Ictinus might mention her unusual daytime visit to Pericles. *Some*thing might happen from it.

Silky shrank back. "We're not allowed."

"Get your sun umbrella."

"We'd be in the way."

"It's as large as the Agora up there. Don't you want to see Ictinus?"

"We'd interrupt his work. Ictinus hates that."

"We'll be careful not to bother him." Aspasia tossed Silky's nail buffer onto the couch. "Just a quick look around."

Balancing their sun umbrellas on their shoulders, they picked their way up the twisting path. Pebbles rolled under Aspasia's high-soled sandals—too short, but Silky was kind to lend them. It was a long time since Aspasia had walked arm in arm with a woman. She closed her eyes for a moment and thought of her mother. Past the switchbacks, a sudden brisk wind tossed grit at their faces and knocked their umbrellas sideways.

Ahead, the Acropolis swelled upward, its new bronze statues shining amid broken stones—like a child learning to speak but so far getting only some of the words right. Tallest of everything on this high hill was the bronze statue of Athena—the high, bright tip of her spear had shown Aspasia the way to Athens. Phidias said she was the Athenians' war goddess and he should know since he'd built the statue. But in this city that continually reminded her she was foreign, Aspasia counted this Athena as her friend. To let the goddess know she was visiting, Aspasia ran her fingers along the fence that surrounded her.

Beyond the fence was a clutter of downed stones.

"That stinky smell's from over there." Silky poked an elbow toward some ruins to their left.

Smoldering was on the wind, although Olympiads had passed since the Persians had burned the Acropolis—stealing everything they could first and knocking down everything else.

"In Miletus, after the Persians ruined our city, we didn't leave shattered temples around like this—we rebuilt and . . . "

Far ahead and to the right, Pericles stood on a stone platform, his arm extended, pointing—like the stone sculpture of the man in the Agora who tells the whole world the true length of a cubit—you just have to measure from the center of his chest along his outstretched arms to the tips of the fingers.

"That's him." Silky tilted her head toward the wiry young man squatting beside the platform. At the far end, Phidias was holding up a stick, his bald head suntanned.

Silky tugged Aspasia's cloak. "Ictinus will be angry. I'm going down."

But Aspasia was already stepping forward.

Phidias grinned as they approached. Ictinus, his cheek pressed to the stone, was squinting along the edge of the platform. The visor of Pericles' helmet shadowed his face. *Did he never take that helmet off?* He wore it raised and at a tilt as he had at Cleinias' symposium—not set for war.

"Welcome, on behalf of the gods," Phidias said.

"We're interested in how you're setting up this great work," Aspasia said. "We won't interrupt—we'll just watch."

"It *is* a great work." Phidias' gesture swept beyond the platform which was the foundation of the Parthenon, taking in the breadth and depth of the plateau.

"We'll sit on this step." A workman shouted and Aspasia sprang up. Her face grew hot under her sun umbrella—she must have looked foolish jumping up and hoped Pericles hadn't noticed.

Ictinus spat at a rock. "You're blocking his sightline."

"Here." Phidias blew dust from the top of a broken capital nearby. Once—before the Persians—that marble capital had sat like a crown atop a tall column. "Pericles, Ictinus and I are of one mind, we must broaden the Parthenon."

"That's a costly revision," Pericles said.

"If we don't, my gold and ivory statue of Athena will be crowded."

"You should have thought this out before I went to the Assembly for funds."

"We had old architects and were working with what we had on hand. You've hired this new, young architect now, and, Pericles, I'm going to build you a statue of Athena—all gold and ivory, *think* of that, Pericles—and taller than our city walls."

Pericles raised his eyes toward the birds.

"Olympia claims theirs is the greatest temple in the world," Ictinus said. "We have to be wider than Olympia."

"With rebellion in Boeotia, this is an inconvenient time to ask for more building funds." Pericles stroked his beard.

"On the other hand—"

"I know on the other hand better than you ever will, Ictinus," Pericles said. "If we had to wait for peace everywhere, we'd never do anything."

He stepped back several paces. "Here's what I say: widen the temple—make sure it's wider than Olympia. Figure the costs. I'll get the money."

At that moment, the sun, reaching under his helmet's visor, cast a particularly bright beam across his handsome face. *The certainty.*

"There's another point," Phidias said. "Since we're widening the temple, obviously the columns, too, must be broader. We have to scrap these old column drums." He pointed to the round sections of worked marble, arranged in rows face-up, magnets for the full glare of the sun. You could fall asleep on them—each was broader in diameter than most men are tall. Piled one on another as they were meant to be, the individual column drums would form into tall columns for a stately temple.

Scrap them? Aspasia's hand was to her chin. *How many men had spent how many sweaty days and consumed how much bread, wine, cheese, and drachmas from the Athenian treasury to quarry, transport and cut these massive stones?*

Pericles frowned at Phidias. "I went to the Assembly with your assurance that we'd use these old column drums. I got the funds on that basis; it's written in stone."

"We're building you a grander temple." Phidias thumbed his teeth.

"These column drums have been lying around since we beat the Persians." Ictinus kicked one.

"I will not tell our voters first one thing and then another."

"They'll do whatever you—"

"Add additional columns to fill in the space, but one thing is certain: these old drums must be used." Pericles glanced at the sundial.

"It can't be done," Ictinus said.

"Find a way." Pericles laid a smack on a drum that must have stung his palm. Aspasia had expected he'd only use words.

He started toward the gates. Aspasia gasped—it had happened fast. She'd been lucky to find him here and now he was leaving because of some columns.

"In Miletus, the temples have many columns." Her voice sounded too loud.

"You hear that, Pericles?" Phidias shouted. "She's not only a philosopher, she's an architect!"

"The Ionians have no rules," Ictinus said.

Pericles had slowed his step. Aspasia took the opportunity to defend Ionia.

"Our temples are as beautiful as yours. The proof is—" Pericles half turned at the word *proof.* "Men come from all over the world to see them." He might be disappointed it wasn't a mathematical proof but maybe it would satisfy him.

Ictinus spat. "Men can do whatever they want where she comes from."

"That's why everyone wants to go there," Phidias said.

"I said—"

Silky touched her arm. "Shh, they're teasing you."

"Keep to the point," Pericles said. "Why not fill in the space with additional columns?"

"Eight's never been done," Phidias said.

"Never been done is not a reason," Pericles said.

That was a new one—never been done not a reason. Aspasia's hand went to her chin.

"It's not in our Doric style, although . . . " Ictinus' hand was to his forehead. "I did see an eight-columned Doric temple in Sicily."

"They play as loose with the rules there as in Ionia," Phidias said.

Ictinus had turned to sketching columns in the dirt. "Eight columns, all the same dimensions and too thin for the temple's breadth, would be monotonous."

"In Miletus—"

"Shh!" Ictinus hushed her like a snake. "On the other hand . . . "

33

Pericles eyed the sundial.

"Suppose . . . just suppose we use the old columns, all right, but we make the new ones not just more of the same size, but thicker."

Hands on knees, Pericles bent over the sketch. "Different widths?"

"Larger radiuses," Ictinus corrected him.

"But wouldn't that look careless or . . . unfinished?"

"Not the way I'd do it. I'd place the more massive columns at the corners. That way, I avoid monotony and at the same time make the building look stronger."

"You know how to reach Pericles' liver," Phidias said. "He loves to get more than one thing for his efforts."

"Always worried about their money's worth, that's the voters in our great democratic Assembly." Ictinus spun out a long, curved foundation under the sketched columns.

"As they should be," Pericles said. "But Phidias, will it work?"

Phidias bent over the sketch. "Since he's setting the thinner columns between the new ones, at least you could tell the Assembly we'd use them all. As for will it work . . . "

"I'll also lean the corner columns inward." Ictinus was overstriking his lines, his stick raising dust.

"Inward? Why?" Another check of the sundial. "I must know your reasons but I'm off to celebrate my son's name day. Don't want to be late—my oldest son, you know."

"How old's that kid now?" Phidias asked.

"What about the money?" Ictinus shouted.

"I need a detailed plan," Pericles called over his shoulder. "My boy's fourteen."

Phidias invited Aspasia and Silky to his workshop to celebrate Ictinus' novel solution, but Rhodia expected Silky back. Since Aspasia's reason to stay had departed, she was ready to go too.

Descending the Acropolis, her mind circled back to when Pericles had first started to leave. Sure, he was in a hurry because of his son's name day but he'd come back after she'd called out—because of his concerns about the columns. Still, she hadn't plucked a wrong note.

CHAPTER 4

Name Day

Pericles hurried across the courtyard, the puppy Argos leaping at his knees. Euangelus, his steward, poured water over Pericles hands. Shaking off the drops—no time for a towel—Pericles took the last wreath in the basket.

His wife of fifteen years, Aristocleia, did not look at him when he reached them, making clear to his household what she thought of his being late. As always, though, he was drawn to look at her, seeking the pleasure of beauty. For their son's name day, she had spread five gold chains fanlike from above both ears, widening over the crown of her head to capture the dense abundance of her piled curls. Her gown and slippers were embroidered with roses. Fifteen years and his two sons and she looked like a young woman. It was easy to believe, as people said, that even after all that time had passed, Hipponicus still yearned for her.

Their older son, Xanthippus, and little Paralus stood on either side of her like columns of uneven height, as if she were a goddess in her temple. Xanthippus, the fourteen-year-old, looked freshly oiled, his hair slicked back, as if he had just made it back in time from wrestling at the palaestra, or more likely from riding his horse too fast in the hills. Pericles felt proud of his handsome son, near to manhood, his sleek muscles bronzed from the sun, although he was short, like his mother. Paralus, well, at six he was still too young to know well. A servant held out a wicker tray filled with dates and figs and decorated with ribbons. Taking Xanthippus' hand, Pericles walked with him to the altar where they set the fruits in front of the small, ancient clay statue of the Great Mother holding her child on her lap. Aristocleia and Paralus and then the others of the household followed, everyone placing a date or a fig or two at the altar.

"My son, since this is your name day, we should think about the grandfather whose name you carry, my father Xanthippus. You never knew him, but he is a great hero. He fought valiantly at the Battle of Marathon, but then Athenians sent him away for three years, for wrong reasons—"

"Not very grateful," said Xanthippus.

"Were you born then?" Paralus asked.

"Of course I was born. I was eleven years old."

"When your father was away, did you miss him a lot?" Paralus asked.

Aristocleia shook his arm. "Shh."

"Yes, we missed him. But despite everything, he never stopped loving his city, so when the Athenians, desperate for his leadership, called him back, he fought for them again. He won another great victory—"

"—and freed the Greeks of Ionia from the Persians in a battle at Mycale."

Xanthippus' singsong imitation of a repeated lesson approached sarcastic.

Pericles noted his son fiddling with his tunic. "And where is Mycale?"

"In Ionia."

The image of the Ionian girl arrived in his mind. That bold girl—she had the temerity to appear on his son's name day. He set aside the thought. He knew how to rid himself of distractions.

"Of course Mycale's in Ionia, but exactly where?"

"Opposite—" Xanthippus looked toward the ceiling. "Lesbos."

"Samos," Pericles said. "Opposite Samos. And that victory, along with the one on our mainland the same day, ensured our freedom from Persian domination. It opened the way for us to develop our democracy and—"

"—without democracy in Athens, there'd be no democracy anywhere in the world."

"That's exactly right, my son! Now, Xanthippus, I have a gift in honor of your name day." Pericles took a package from Euangelus.

Xanthippus was scowling before he'd pulled off the wrapping. "I told you I wanted a hunting knife with an iron blade."

Aristocleia smiled as always with only one side of her mouth, her lips drawn together as if trying to hear a soft noise. She would have made a poor model for a comic mask. Now, after everyone noticed her amusement, she covered her mouth with her hand.

Pericles frowned. "Herodotus wrote the story of our war with Persia in this book. You'll find your own name written inside—Xanthippus—think of that!"

As Aristocleia raised her cup to toast Xanthippus, her gown slipped from her shoulders, exquisite as Aphrodite's, and flowed like the water that slid over her naked breasts when she allowed him to watch her bathe. It was wonderful to possess a gem of a woman. It made a man feel beautiful and godlike himself, briefly. It was unforgettable, which was fortunate since it hadn't happened since Paralus was born. Or it would have been easier for him if it had been forgettable. Nor was he an Ajax to force himself on a woman.

Would the Milesian girl bathe for him? She was so thin.

"Aristocleia, join me for dinner in the andron."

"The andron—what a surprise, Pericles—I thought that was only for men. Anyhow," she raised her tiny hand, "I've already eaten."

"My sister sent in honey cakes from the country—"

"We got started so late, it's already turning dark and I'd like to catch the last light in my rose garden." She turned before he could say more, hooked her thumb under the edge of her gown, flipped it back to her shoulders, and went with Paralus and Xanthippus to her garden.

After dinner, Pericles set about reviewing the week's household expenses with Euangelus but the image of Aristocleia's pretty shoulders and breasts came to rest over his columns of numbers. How fruitless. Aristocleia said—to anger him—that forcing her to leave Hipponicus and marry him came to the same thing as doing an Ajax, but of course it wasn't. Anything to keep him at a distance.

Only Aristocleia would say it was the same.

Euangelus, would you say that . . .

Not a question to ask a servant. Instead, he told him to bring the torch.

On several occasions to discuss plans for the city, he had visited Hippodamus in his andron—the room in the house reserved for men (and hetairas, if the host had paid for them). It was exciting to reach the inner part of another man's house, even if it was only to follow a girl who rented a room in it. Should he seize her wrist in the usual way as they crossed the court? On the Acropolis, he'd thought she'd seen too much sun for a woman but in the courtyard, under the moon, her face, neck and arms were as pale as the moon goddess. Allowing himself to imagine it was the moon goddess leading him upward was a way of climbing to the second story.

Aspasia lit an oil lamp. Where, in this tiny room, was he to put his cloak? His battle tent was bigger than this. She took the cloak, folded it, and laid it over a box.

But Homer on a shelf reassured him that she was rare. Skinny but unusual. Never had he known a woman who read books. On the table were flowers and a pitcher of wine. Had she expected Phidias? He could give her more drachmas than his sculptor.

"May I take your helmet?" It sat at the same high tilt as on the Acropolis that afternoon.

"In a moment."

But her long fingers were already reaching up. He drew back, his neck stiff as a column. "In a *moment*," he repeated. He was here to have things the way he wanted them.

But she already knew what was wrong. Reaching for the helmet, she'd been startled to see Pericles' forehead through the helmet's eyeholes. So far up. In the wrong place. It scared her. With the helmet at that high tilt, the eyeholes should be empty. His forehead was way too high. And of course, the dome of his head had to be even higher. He was not normal. Quickly she looked aside.

That's why he's here. Men think that for the money, a hetaira will accept anyone, no matter how peculiar.

She felt keenly disappointed.

Was it because he was abnormal? or because that was why he was here?

Still, knowing gave her a slight edge on him.

She poured them each a cup of wine, anonymous in its pottery pitcher.

Dionysos emboldened them both.

"Do you think, Aspasia, that you are beautiful, good and just, like the Babylonian prostitutes?"

Was this sarcasm? Or was he genuinely interested, or just smoothing the furrows? She just said, "Yes," and pushed on to what was in her mind. Indoors, in her room, was no place for a helmet. It was absurd. And she was curious to see what that head really looked like.

"Do you think, General Pericles, that you can remove your helmet?" She shoved the cups and pitcher on the table close together to make room.

The wine had reached his fingertips, but he hesitated.

"Think." She raised her pointer finger. "Your helmet will fall off in making love and clatter onto the floor—what a joke Hippodamus will make of that!"

Think. He smiled inwardly. And she had a point. He lifted the helmet from his head and set it on the table.

Yes, it was a big head. His face was as handsome as if carved by a sculptor and he had a well-shaped beard and expertly trimmed hair, just as a man should. But above that, his forehead didn't stop. Instead, his head rose and kept rising until the top where, under his curly hair, it rounded off like a sea cucumber. She wished she could trim away all that extra part the way Phidias squeezed off extra clay or chiseled away superfluous marble on his way to making a perfect figure.

What a surprise, Pericles thought, to hold a woman so tall that her eyes are opposite yours. Where would she come up to on him without those high-soled sandals? When would he find out? She pressed her bony ribcage against his chest. Spartan girls exercised naked, but she wasn't Spartan, brief in speech and barely educated. She was from Ionia, spoke well, read poetry, and said things he didn't expect. She was refined but also somewhat . . . what was the word . . . ? Bathing for him would be the least of it.

He unpinned her chiton; it bunched around her ankles like waves swilling on the beach. Oh Pericles, that was no bolt of Zeus. He stood in the presence of a goddess. Only it wasn't the moon goddess; this was Aphrodite. And Hippodamus had said something about Aspasia emerging from the sea like Aphrodite . . . but never mind.

He gripped her wrist with his thumb and forefinger and led her to the small, hard couch—he might replace the couch. He pressed himself against her, but she held him at a distance. Oh, no, his huge head. But these women were supposed to do whatever you wanted—

She passed her hand over his shoulder, then his chest. He closed his eyes. Slim female fingers were gliding over his hip. When had that happened before?

When the warmth of her back permeated his hand, he realized he was holding her. How long since he had *held* anyone with whom he made love? How long since he'd made love to anyone he thought well of? How long since—

Thinking could come later. After all, he was paying for it.

The abandon of this important man, whom all of Athens viewed as restrained, excited Aspasia. His famous head rested on her cushion—and without a helmet. Yes, it was as bulbous as a squash. Or a melon. But every man has something one has to get past. True, it was worse than Phidias who was bald because bald isn't abnormal. It was more like Dion who had no color—an unpleasant tremor crossed her breast.

No wonder he always wore his helmet. Without it, he'd never be elected General. In a dim light, one could overlook the swollen shape of the head that decided, among other things, how much tribute to levy against her own city.

But—she looked again—this was wrong in the unpainted Dion way. Although Dion might have looked all right when he came out of the womb. Not this one, though. Why had they let him live? How had this man survived his first day? He must have been their first son and they couldn't be sure of having another. Or, the way families go, they figured another boy might not come out any better.

The next evening, he sent word that he could not see her, and sent a gift. When since coming here had she felt so elated? Her thoughts flew to Herodotus: "As she said"—what a moment that was!

But now, word and a gift. She decided that sending word said more about his view of her than the gift. Still—a gift: she unfolded the packet left by a messenger and a pair of earrings slipped onto her table. From each thin wire hung a silver circle with three silver beads dangling from the loop like tiny rays. She put on the earrings and checked her mirror. The circles filled in the slope under her cheekbones. The earrings were so becoming, she felt he was sending another message—that when he chose them, her face was in front of his eyes. His remote awareness of her stirred a spinning behind her breast, whipping up a vortex. Tomorrow night, if Pericles came, she'd wear them for him.

If not, they belonged to her now and she could wear them with someone else.

CHAPTER 5

Whose Money?

If not, they belonged to her now and she could wear them with someone else.

That, unexpectedly, became a topic at the next meeting of the Athenian Assembly.

As Pericles climbed the Assembly hill that morning along with multitudes of Athenians pressing upward, opposite the easy path down nature provides for water and stones, he felt proud of the fortitude of men and of his own strength. He was ready for the battle—not of muscle but of words—against Thucydides, his rival, his nemesis, the whetstone against whom he sharpened the blade of his oratory and the precision of his thinking.

It would be pleasant to have no rival, but he felt a nub of gratitude toward Thucydides for those last two points. He was sure, though, that Thucydides felt no nub of gratitude toward him, and he took pride in the difference, because it was why he would win—in the long view. As for today, he knew that Thucydides would be out in full sail against the proposed additional funds for the new Parthenon columns and he felt as prepared to defend his proposal as Heracles— Stop! It's hubris to compare oneself to a god—and dangerous. Pericles felt as prepared as the famous athlete Lugadamis.

"There's Pericles!" Simon the Bootmaker grabbed Xenon's arm.

"I don't turn my head for a man who chases prostitutes." Xenon the Barber was spit-cleaning his tunic of the red dye that the police used to lasso Athenians into the Assembly—nobody got away with spending Assembly Day drinking wine in the Agora if the police could get their wet ropes on them.

"You'll never get that red stuff off," Simon said.

"I know." But the angry barber continued rubbing.

Simon tongued his cobbler's nail from one corner of his mouth to the other. "I don't believe that gossip about Pericles."

"And the worst is she's a *foreign* prostitute."

"Pericles wouldn't waste time on women. And he made a rule against foreign prostitutes."

"It doesn't stop him—he's there every night," Xenon replied. "Epimedes says he's buying out his jewelry shop."

"That proves you're wrong! Everybody knows Pericles doesn't spend so much as an obol he doesn't have to."

"Oh yeah? Then how come yesterday he bought a bracelet that coils around a woman's arm like a snake—like he's got a grip on her arm."

Simon sucked on his cobbler's nail.

"Face it, Simon. Your great man Pericles is no better than anybody."

The sturdy cobbler's nail wiggled up and down several times before settling back in a corner of Simon's lips. "Seen right, Xenon, there's no harm in it. We don't elect him for what he does with his nights." He looked away. "Big crowd."

The sun was past its zenith when the President of the Council came to Pericles' proposal. He banged his gavel: "To the proposal to provide funds for quarrying and transporting marble for additional columns for the Parthenon temple. Who wishes to speak?"

Thucydides arose. A wrestler past the age of competing in the games, Thucydides now trained others—not that he needed the money. Approaching the bema, that stone platform where speakers stood to address the Assembly, he slanted backward, as if the massive muscles of his shoulders and neck hadn't left room for his head to sit directly on top. But when he began to speak, he pressed his full weight forward.

"When I was a boy, taking for oneself what belonged to others was called stealing. When our enemies do it, we still call it that but

43

now, when we do it, we give it a new name. We call it 'assessing tribute from our allies.'"

"He always starts off with the old days," Simon whispered.

"Theft is theft," Xenon replied.

"Like most bad habits, this one crept up on us," Thucydides continued. "After we were victorious against the Persians, we set up a common treasury to which all the allied cities of our Athenian League contributed voluntarily. We did this for one reason: to ensure the safety of Greece against the continuing Persian menace. The money was there to protect all of us—whatever move Persia might make—and since Apollo's own island, Delos, is sacred to all Greeks, we housed the money there. But we Athenians were not satisfied with the protection of the god Apollo, no, and pretending to be worried about the safety of the treasury, we forced our allies to agree to move the treasury to—Athens."

"We had the right!" someone shouted out.

"We transferred the silver intended for the common defense to Athens although—" Thucydides shook a finger toward the interruption, "—although we had no right to it."

"We chased the Persians out of Greece!"

Thucydides shook his head and sent a firm look toward to the Executive Council member presiding over the full Assembly that day, who banged his gavel.

"That was the first insult to our allies. Meanwhile, the Persians—because of some so-called secret agreement or more likely by a rational assessment of their own interests—have not attacked us again. Instead, they have *avoided* Greek territory. This deprives us of our only excuse for controlling League funds—security against the Persians. And who was behind sequestering the League's funds in Athens?—Pericles! The same Pericles who now urges us to spend those funds on our city, our temples, our public buildings and ourselves.

"For, after removing the funds from Delos, here's the second insult—that Athens uses funds collected for the common defense for her own purposes having nothing to do with defense. We call it tribute, but the allied cities of our League know what to call it—*theft*."

"When you come right down to it . . . " Xenon whispered.

"My Athenians, we have squandered the reputation for virtue our fathers earned for us in the war against Persia, all in the name of democracy. And the result is we have rebellion on our hands. Consider the rebellion in Boeotia. Once, Boeotia's prosperous, well-ordered cities were in the hands of oligarchs but we Athenians are democrats—"

"That's right, Thucydides. Democrats!" someone called out.

"—and we oppose oligarchies, not trusting governments of a few well-educated, disciplined, trained men—"

"Rich men like you!"

"—who can afford the responsibility of governing. So we drove the oligarchs out and replaced them with democratic governments because, our leaders told us, the Boeotian people would love democracy and democratic governments would be friendly allies for Athens. But their oligarchs have returned from exile—as they always do. And now that they're back in power, it turns out that the Boeotians aren't grateful at all for the democracy we've installed. In fact, Boeotia has revolted against us, and other rebellions are sure to follow. We'll be sucked into them like a whirlpool. Because the Greek cities who were once our allies now believe they're victims of tyranny—yes, open tyranny—as they see Athens claim for itself the money raised for the purpose of common security."

"Tyranny!" someone called out.

"And the worst insult of all is that we lavish this ill-gotten tribute wantonly, with besotted abandon, on marble temples and gold goddesses—listen to me, Athenians"—there was a nervous stir in the crowd—"for that's exactly what we're doing."

"It's civic construction!" Pericles recognized Damon's voice—quick to see where Thucydides was going.

"It's temples for the gods!" some other friend called out.

"I say—" In the rising excitement, Thucydides pounded one fist against the other. "I say we're adorning our city like some vain woman, the kind of woman who'll trade sex for gold."

The crudity linked to Athens—Pericles winced, and others felt the same. Some called out angrily. Some rose to their feet. Others smirked. Thucydides waited it out until shocked silence took over.

"We Athenians are like bewitched lovers, decorating this kept woman, this whore for that's what she is, with gaudy extras, gilding her, hanging her round with precious stones and ornaments and—since Pericles is so fond of numbers—with temples costing us hundreds of talents of our treasure."

Xenon the Barber poked Simon. "Think Pericles gets it?"

"Gets what?"

"About that girl." The bootmaker didn't answer. "That girl, the whore," Xenon said. "Everybody *else* here gets it but you, Simon. He's buying stuff for the *girl*. That's who gets the gaudy extras."

"Thucydides is trying to confuse us, Xenon. You know what Pericles says, focus on the logic."

"That's what I'm doing and when you come right down to it, Thucydides made some very logical points." Xenon's shake of his head fell between a thought and a warning. "How can Pericles possibly answer Thucydides?"

Those who loved Pericles, those who didn't, and those who hated him were united in wondering that as Pericles reached the bema. He had his answer but rage had imprisoned his words. Thucydides the filthy-mouthed. If any thought he'd missed the reference to Aspasia and to himself—he hadn't. To so degrade Athens. And Aspasia. He would never tell this to the lovely girl, *the talker, the reader* as he thought of her, who greeted him with a full-mouthed kiss. For more time, he glanced over some papyrus sheets he had with him, folded them, pulled them out again, and tucked them in his cloak. He made a quick prayer to Zeus and raised his eyes to four thousand men who had one question, *How can Pericles answer Thucydides?*

"Thucydides has falsely accused the Athenians of theft," Pericles began. "For that, he'll be lucky to escape your wrath and prosecution because the truth is this: Athens has nothing in her possession that does not belong to her and nothing that is not hard-earned.

"I ask you this question: to whom does money belong?"

"Our allies who contributed it!" someone called out— Thucydides' claque.

"Here is the answer." Pericles raised his teaching finger. "Money belongs to those who receive it, so long as they perform the service for which they're paid."

46

"Theft!" someone shouted.

"And I ask you again: who here or anywhere would dare to say that we Athenians have not fulfilled our responsibility? There is no one—not in Athens, not among our allies, not among our enemies, and not among the Persians—no one, I say, who can show that we have ever failed to perform the service for which we are paid—the defense of Greece."

"Sure not among the Persians!" someone shouted.

"Theft!"

"We Athenians have swept the Persian ships out of the Greek sea, at great benefit for commerce. Yes, Thucydides, the Persians have avoided Greek territory, and what a glory for us—what a contrast to the past! *Greek* territories rest in *Greek* hands. Do I have to remind you that was not always true? Thucydides calls that theft, but I call it courage and devotion to duty."

"Courage and devotion to duty!"

"Courage!"

"Duty!"

"So long as we maintain the freedom of our allies from foreign domination, so long as we shield from barbarian attacks those very allies who do not produce so much as one horse—" (the thumb) "one ship," (pointer finger) "or one archer, hoplite or sailor" (three more fingers) "in their own defense, but provide nothing but money, we are under no obligation to provide them, or anyone else, with an account."

He saw the nods, the relaxed shoulders, the shared grins and glances. He heard the soft chorus of men sighing in relief.

"I told you he'd have an answer," Simon whispered to Xenon.

"No, you—"

"Once Athens has equipped herself adequately with ships and weapons of war, she has every right to employ—"

"Theft!"

There was a scuffle but Pericles didn't see who was ejected from the Assembly.

"—our city has every right to employ her wealth to rebuild the temples and civic buildings plundered and burned by the Persians.

And it is our duty to rebuild them in a manner that honors the gods and ourselves."

"Thief!" A new voice.

He was about to ask, *Who among us hasn't seen that*—? but veered off from a question. Better to frame his point to avoid a hostile answer. "And we all have seen that our building projects enrich every Athenian citizen. They're stimulating all the crafts we're famous for and setting every hand into motion. And, Athenians, when they are complete, they will remain a glory to us for all time. That's how we will repay our single outstanding debt—the one we owe the gods."

"I still don't see why you need to pour out money for new columns?" someone called out. "The old columns are sitting on the Acropolis—use those!"

"We are using the old columns for the wider Parthenon as you can inspect yourself in the plans that the Executive Council posted," Pericles replied. "We must have additional columns for the broader temple, but take note, Athenians—we are using local marble so that every drachma spent will go to Athenian suppliers and laborers."

"Where's Ictinus hiding?" the son of the old war hero Cimon, wanted to know. "We need the architect here to explain these technical points."

"He's working on behalf of all of us, laying out our magnificent new Hall of Mysteries for the goddess Demeter at Eleusis."

"You see! You see! That's what I mean! Pericles is breaking the backs of all of us, rich and poor, building, at Eleusis, in the Agora, on the Acropolis." Thucydides' face flushed with anger.

"Order." The Presiding Officer banged his gavel.

"We won't pay for your thousand-talent temples!" Thucydides shouted.

Pericles had planned to speak for the new columns of the Parthenon that day but had ended up demonstrating to the Athenians the logic behind their empire. Good—it was a lesson they loved to hear and needed to have repeated. Soon, though, they would vote. He wanted to leave off with a thought that would ensure his proposal would win—*and* lift their minds from Thucydides' muck. *Theft . . . lavishing wantonly . . . vain woman . . . bewitched lovers . . . besotted abandon . . .*

Thucydides' attempt at public ridicule was vivid, vulgar, and unforgettable. Pericles could not allow his political opponent to stain his honorable reputation with salacious hints. Nor did he want the Athenians deciding how to vote to think that funding the new columns for the Parthenon meant bedecking a whore. And Aspasia— it pained him for that lovely girl to be dragged into the political slime—not that Thucydides had spoken of her in so many words but everyone knew.

To knock that wrestler Thucydides off the sand, he would use the man's own words.

"Yes, we Athenians are passionate lovers of our city." Pericles turned toward his rival. "I hope that includes you, Thucydides, although your disparaging words about Athens make me doubt it."

Taking the breath of readying for the long jump, Pericles raised his arms in a wide arc. Beyond that broad embrace, the Athenians could see the Agora, the Acropolis, the Hill of the Muses, and all the way to the new fortification walls, including the one he had built, the one they called Pericles' wall. "Athenians, fix your eyes on the greatness of our city. We are not besotted. We are devoted, and for the best of reasons. Athens is strong, wise, beautiful . . . " what had he left out? ". . . and sacred. And in all ways worthy of our gifts and of our love."

He paused to let them think about love and the city.

Pericles, as the speaker facing the audience, had his back to the Acropolis on the next hill over, while those listening to him faced the Acropolis. Now he spun around so that they all were looking at their sacred hill as one.

"See it with me," he said. "The broader temple will settle atop the Acropolis like a ship riding the crest of the toughest wave." Gesturing from his shoulder through his fingertips, he painted for them the Parthenon yet-to-come.

They looked from the top of their windy hill across to the windy Acropolis. Some were with him in glimpsing white sails, high masts, and shimmering brightness, while others saw broken stones and charred buildings.

Whichever way they think about it, let them vote right!

While the Athenians were caught in their common gaze and private thoughts, he stepped away from the bema.

The lovers of Athens voted to fund the new columns for the Parthenon.

Simon turned to Xenon as they descended the hill in the early dark of winter. "Now you see what I was talking about. Athens fulfills her duties to our allies and Pericles fulfills his duty to all of us, to the Demos—what else he does is his own business."

"Pericles—what's on those papyrus sheets you had with you?" someone called.

"Another time."

CHAPTER 6

The Island

He had his columns. Next, the roof. Stimulated by Thucydides' powerful arguments, proud of his fast change of tack, and just plain glad for winning, Pericles strode toward Hippodamus' house. Wait until she heard—he'd skip the part about the vain woman. Damp wind crossed his face but Aspasia would have the house comfortable for him. Up to now, he'd only found time to visit her after everything, very late, but she'd prevailed upon him to dine with her tonight. They would spend a long evening together. He would lie back, and she would read to him from the scrolls he'd given her.

The smell of roasting lamb filled the house. Aspasia, wearing a new gown, came forward and greeted him with a kiss. By Zeus, what a contrast! When he stopped by his own house to change into a clean himation for the evening, his servant Euangelus and the puppy Argos had greeted him. His courtyard was dark and his sons and Aristocleia were nowhere in sight. As Pericles bathed and oiled his body, Euangelus had briefed him on an arrangement he had worked out with a farmer to harvest olives on Pericles' country estate: it was beneficial to both the farmer and Pericles who would receive his fair portion of the profits. In taking care of business for him, Euangelus freed Pericles to take care of the business of the city.

Hippodamus was busy these days laying out a residential suburb of Piraeus Port—thanks to Pericles—so Aspasia had prepared to entertain Pericles in the andron. She led him to the couch, where she'd set out striped, tasseled cushions. He saw in her new dress—and had he seen those sandals before?—and in her necklace, her bracelet, the almond scent in her hair, the cushions, and the brightness of the room her new prosperity and took satisfaction in knowing that he was responsible for it. Though with so many lamps, she may have been spending too much money on oil.

He smiled. That afternoon he'd said that money was the property of those who receive it so long as they perform the service for which they're paid. She did more. And thinking of it that way, so did Athens do more than necessary for their allies. He'd say that next time.

"What are you smiling about?"

"I'm smiling because I'm here with you."

"Please take off your helmet."

He hesitated—the room was bright. Last spring, a comic playwright had called him "our cucumber-headed Zeus," and he had held to his seat in the theater. He had no trouble keeping his face impassive in any situation, but he heard the laughter.

Now all that Athenian laughter meant less than how one woman felt about his large head. Of course, he knew when he took her in his arms that her evident pleasure in his company was inspired by his family status, his wealth, and his high position; he expected as much and found it pleasing. And he could tolerate that her physical passion for him might be in part feigned—that would be her skill. But he could not bear to think that his deformed head stifled her desire . . . or worse: disgusted her. He couldn't go through the rest of the evening, which he'd so keenly anticipated, without knowing. But he couldn't humiliate oneself by asking directly. How, then, to tease out her thoughts?

"If I leave my helmet on, I'm dressed properly as Ares, the god of war, to be the lover of Aphrodite. And you, Aspasia, are surely Aphrodite."

"But you're not the god of war. Here's the proof: Ares would certainly support the campaign against those northern rebels but you're against it. No, there's only one god you can be—the king of the gods. Since I first met you, I've thought of you as Zeus."

"You must have heard Phidias' joke—Athena born from Zeus' head, swollen with carrying his daughter as a mother carries a child in her womb."

"I thought of you as Zeus when I first met you—before I heard the joke."

"Do you mean that night at Cleinias' house, you already thought of me as Zeus . . . so to say?"

She'd met him before that but why complicate the matter? Not allowing herself to hesitate, she lifted the heavy helmet from his head and put it on a bench. Then she ran her hand—forcing it to the full palm—over his forehead and along the top of his head through to the curve of his neck.

He followed the path of her hand in suspense but felt no fingertips. Well, he wouldn't go to war over fingertips. How can one ever truly know the mind of another?

The sudden softness of his kiss surprised her—a "gift kiss," she named it.

She took the platters from the old woman, sauced the lentils and sliced the fatty joint—it wasn't even a festival day. She poured into their cups an old wine with an exceptional bouquet that he could not identify but, busy as he was recounting to her the struggle with Thucydides in the Assembly, he did not pause to ask about it. There was so much to talk about and such a wealth of pleasures at hand that he let flow the sudden profusion of excitement and delights.

She listened as he described the angry outbursts and recounted Thucydides' attack that went all the way to comparing Athens to some vain woman whom Pericles was lavishly adorning . . . By Hades, he hadn't meant to mention that! The reference to her was obvious and insulting. She'd been dragged into public ridicule because of him. Was she angry? Did she hate him? Her face was impassive.

After a long moment, she refilled his cup. "What did you say to that?"

He could make amends for the insult. All he had to do was let her know of the positive twist he'd given to Thucydides description— turning the so-called vain woman into his own ideal of the greatness of Athens for which all Athenians felt an intense ardor. But he didn't want to give her that much either. It might lead her to make more of his ardor for her than he meant. She was a hetaira—if not the cheap whore he'd first met. And what exactly was the difference . . . ? Never mind about that—speaking about the Athenian empire was safer.

"You must realize, Aspasia, that most of our allies provide nothing in their own defense, no ships, no army, no navy, no cavalry—your city Miletus included. What do they do instead? They pay us money, leaving it to us to defend the whole of Greece. And what do they get? What matters most, Aspasia. Results. We protect them against foreign invaders. It's quite simple though Thucydides and his 'Little Athenians' have trouble understanding it. Money belongs to those who do what they're paid for. We don't owe any accounting."

His fist came down hard. "Look at our achievements! We liberated the Greeks and we've kept them free. What more could anybody want?" The resurgence of the oligarchs in Boeotia to the northwest and their rebellion against Athens cast a shadow on his excitement. "What more?" he added.

But Athens as a lavishly adorned vain woman rang in her mind. Was she hearing in those words the end of their time together? Not soon but when she was no longer a novelty in his life and the sexual urgency had abated. Would he cut her loose because she weakened him politically? She had to remain interesting.

"I hope you won't mind but . . . " He nodded for her to go on. "I'm not sure you said everything needed."

"Obviously I did. We won by a huge, well, ample majority."

"That's wonderful." When she hesitated, he urged her to continue. With her, there might be something useful.

"They're men, and as the philosopher Heraclitus taught, they're going to want to believe that what they do is beautiful and just—not just good for business."

"True. I told them they owe the buildings to the gods."

"Did you bring in that they are bringing honor to themselves?"

"Yes, to their glory—I did."

"So, since the Athenians benefit, I think they'd like to hear from you that the Athenians are, like the gods, uniquely worthy."

"To equate men with the gods—that's hubris. That's all my enemies need to shoot me down."

"Oh no! Not equally worthy to the gods but—" How to draw that line? "That they take the prize among men."

He regarded this pretty young woman sitting on the couch he'd bought for her, her chin resting thoughtfully on her hand, her attention now earnestly fixed on matters of his political strategies. How knowing she was, and how practical. He'd never seen anything like it. In the brief time since he'd met her, he'd become so used to recounting to her at night his struggles of the day that it seemed they hadn't completely transpired until he told her about them. Certainly, in going over them with her, new aspects emerged that he had overlooked amid action.

"You have as much of Athena in you as you do Aphrodite."

This was the first time he had ever spoken to her about her character. The unexpected disclosure filled her with a sense of joy—of triumph—like the vibration in a strummed cithara.

She had brought her scrolls of Homer's *Odyssey* to the andron. Now they sat reading together on the couch, thigh to thigh.

"You know which is my favorite scene in the *Odyssey*?" Pericles asked.

"The escape from the Cyclops' cave?"

"A great story, but not what I'm thinking of."

"Knowing men, it's probably the one where Odysseus lingers for a year—'shares the fine bed,' as Homer puts it so coyly—with that witch Circe on her island."

"I don't think it's Circe who bewitches Odysseus."

"Oh? Then who?"

"Nausicaa, the princess of the Phaeacians."

"I love that part, too, or at least the beginning."

"Read me some of it. It would be as good as if you played the lyre."

Pericles reached for his cup on the low table beside their couch, sipped the dark wine that, like the wine Odysseus found in the cave of the Cyclops, had no name, and lay back on the cushions, his eyes closed. Aspasia rolled through the scrolls.

She read how Odysseus was stripped of everything he had—the soldiers who had followed him, his raft, which was only a few logs lashed together, and his clothes. He swam, naked in the sea, for two days and nights, thinking he would die.

On the morning of the third day, carried high by a great wave, he spotted an island, but the coast was rocky and offered no place to land. Another wave thrust him toward the shore, where he would have been dashed to death but, encouraged by Athena, he clung to a rock as the huge wave swept past him, only to be hit by its backwash and flung back to sea.

But with the aid of Athena, Odysseus' luck turned. The once impenetrable shore suddenly provided a welcome. He reached the mouth of a river.

Aspasia fell silent. Opening his eyes, Pericles saw hers filled with tears.

He leaned forward and seized her to his chest. "My dearest Aspasia, what's the matter?"

She said nothing, but he felt in her trembling shoulders her attempt to control her tears.

Then he knew why she was crying. She, too, had been at sea, had, in her short life, lost everything, had, in a way, been tossed back and forth by the waves—though she was vague about the details. Like Odysseus' hands, her lovely hands knew what it was to cling to a rock and be stripped of their skin.

Though he held her firmly, the trembling turned into a shudder—yet his cheek to hers told him she didn't have a fever. What could he say? When his sister had cried as a child, he used to distract her with a pun, but that would be disrespectful for a grown woman. Nor could he refer to the past that was making her weep, for that would insult her and turn her from him.

"Aspasia, Odysseus found the mouth of the river."

His warm breath touched her ear. Still, though, the tears continued to well in her eyes.

"Aspasia, I'm glad you came to Athens."

Immediately the tears stopped. His words carried the weight of his caring for her, for while he talked readily about politics, like any man he didn't speak easily about what he felt within. Her burden lightened. Pericles was glad she had come to Athens. Although a foreigner, she felt like an invited guest, not a citizen.

That his words soothed her brought Pericles relief, pleasure, and a sense of power. Never had he, who moved all of Athens through his eloquence, brought to a woman a smile of joy such as was forming on Aspasia's face—certainly not to his wife.

"Aspasia." He started to pull her toward him. He wanted to kiss her.

She felt embarrassed. First, she hadn't controlled her tears, and now they'd dried up fast and she was smiling like a fool. It was undignified. She busied herself rearranging the scroll, took a deep breath, and in a calm voice continued with the story.

Odysseus dragged himself onto the land and he kissed the earth, not forgetting to return to the sea the magic protective veil given him by a goddess. He piled up leaves for a bed beneath two olive trees and fell asleep.

Meanwhile, Nausicaa, daughter of the king of the island, had the idea (inspired by the goddess Athena) to make an outing from the palace to the shore with her girlfriends to wash clothes. Her mother prepared a picnic, and Nausicaa and her girlfriends rode to the shore where, after laying the washed clothes out to dry, they bathed in the river and rubbed themselves with the oil her mother had sent along in a golden jar. After lunch, they played a game of catch. They were all pretty girls but Nausicaa was the tallest and most beautiful.

Aspasia used to do just this in Miletus—swim, play ball, eat basket lunches—although she'd certainly never had to do laundry. But Athenian girls weren't allowed out. She was about to comment on this but thought better of it. He might think she was criticizing Athens.

When she paused, Pericles said, "Now you're coming to my favorite part."

Aspasia read on. A ball, thrown wild, splashed into the river and the girls cried out, waking Odysseus who, hearing their voices, wondered whether he was among people who would help him or cause him more trouble. He emerged from the woods naked, covering himself with a leafy branch. "'Then he advanced on them like a mountain lion who sallies out, defying wind and rain in the pride of his power, with fire in his eyes, to hunt down the oxen or sheep or pursue the wild deer. Forced by hunger, he will even attack flocks in a well-protected fold. So Odysseus, naked as he was, made a move toward those girls with their braided hair; necessity compelled him.'" The girls, frightened of the naked man, ran away—but not Nausicaa. Either she wasn't afraid or, if she was, she didn't show it. She stood her ground.

Aspasia smiled. "I know why you like this part, you like to think of Odysseus coming out of the woods like a lion naked in the midst of all those young girls."

"Of course. Didn't you know I'm really a lion?"

First Zeus, now a lion.

"Oh?"

"Just before I was born, my mother dreamed she'd given birth to a lion. She used to call me 'my lion.'"

"But you're not savage like a lion."

"I've never been as hungry as Odysseus."

"Odysseus wasn't savage either. You have the strength of a lion. That was the meaning of your mother's dream." *Or was it?*

She sipped her wine to moisten her throat and returned to the story.

Odysseus implored Nausicaa to help him, telling her with sweet and cunning words that she was as beautiful as a goddess and he wished that she might receive her heart's desire. And he already knew what that was: "'a husband and a home, and the blessings of harmony.'"

She agreed to guide Odysseus to the palace, instructing her friends to give him clean clothes and to help him bathe, although he bathed himself, not wanting young girls to see him naked. How beautiful he was after his bath. The brine was washed away from his back and broad shoulders, his skin was rubbed with olive oil, and he had clean clothes. Athena had enhanced his beauty, "'and from his head caused bushy locks to hang thick as the petals of a hyacinth in bloom.'" As he sat thus by the ocean, Nausicaa admired him and said to her friends, "'I wish I could have a man like him for my husband, if only he were content to stay and live here.'"

"She didn't just mean 'a man like him,'" Aspasia said. "Nausicaa loved Odysseus."

"Odysseus thought Nausicaa was like a goddess in beauty and stature and shapeliness. He said it filled him with awe to look at her, that she was like a sapling of Apollo's palm tree."

"But he was speaking there with cunning, maybe he didn't mean all he said."

"I think he saw her that way. But do you know what Odysseus liked best about Nausicaa? It wasn't her beauty."

"What?" She hoped it was something in herself.

"It was her bravery. She hadn't run from him when he emerged from the sea and stood before her naked."

"He held up the branch, so he wasn't entirely naked."

"He had nothing but himself, he was only Odysseus. And you, Aspasia, are brave like Nausicaa."

Yes, she was brave. "And you are wise like Odysseus."

She could easily imagine herself the daughter of a king and queen—she felt something of Nausicaa in herself—but it was difficult to think of Pericles, who had everything, as a suppliant.

"But you're not like Odysseus in that you haven't lost everything."

"I'm naked before you in that you know so much of me that no one else knows. You know my strategies because I tell them to you, and when I don't, you see through to them anyhow. And tonight you even stole away my helmet. To Athens I may seem, at times, like Zeus"—it was true, after all—"but with you I'm Odysseus."

Pericles watched her as she started to read about Nausicaa guiding Odysseus to the palace.

"Aspasia, I cannot spend another moment close to you and not hold you in my arms."

He stretched forward and pulled her toward him. Homer slipped from her lap. As she leaned to pick up the expensive scroll, he gripped her arm and, drawing her to his chest, closed his eyes to the twirling spirals of the mosaic floor. He pressed his lips to hers and felt the fullness he'd noticed the first time he saw her. Her fingers pushed aside his himation and touched his chest. In this way, too, he was naked with her. He felt within himself the savagery as well as the strength of the lion, and in the midst of his pleasure felt proud of the wildness of his feelings. It was as if they swam together in Odysseus' tumultuous sea, unalone, and after pulling themselves onto the beach, lay down together in the sun. He'd waited all his life for this.

"Aspasia," he said after a time, "when I was a boy, we had an amphora at our country house painted with the scene of Nausicaa looking surprised when she first saw Odysseus holding his branch, his hair and beard uncut from his time in the ocean. I used to look at that picture and wonder if I would ever find Nausicaa." And how she'd feel about his deformed head if he did find her.

She was silent.

"You are my Nausicaa."

He meant it kindly, she knew.

After a moment she said what she knew he was waiting to hear. "My Odysseus."

He gathered his cloak. "And now, I must set sail from the island of the Phaeacians."

Like a sunflower and a vine growing upward together, Pericles and Aspasia rose from the couch, stepped from the bright andron, and walked with arms linked through the short corridor that now was dark and gripped by the winter chill. At the door he turned and encircled her in his arms. He felt he could never leave hold.

She shook her curls. "Good night, my Odysseus." He had to feel free to go or he wouldn't come back.

He looked at her with surprise. "Good night, my Nausicaa."

Still, he hesitated, so she helped him.

"Good night, my lion."

Alone, Aspasia stood by the door, stirring the charcoal in the brazier, watching the gray lumps that still held the shape of live wood chunks flatten to powder.

My lion. He was his mother's lion. Would he be her lion? It was the foolish kind of thought that she didn't usually permit herself.

Zeus' bolt grazed her, bringing its shocking light.

That's how his mother, Agariste, kept her son alive.

The child came from her womb with a huge head. She could hear the argument between his mother and father—

"Our son's head is not *deformed. It's big like a lion's head. Remember that dream I had—"*

"No, Agariste, I don't remember any dream. He has a deformed head. If you won't have done with him, I will." He reaches for the baby.

She clutches the infant to her breast. "It's true. I told you, Xanthippus, just a few days ago I dreamed I'd give birth to a lion."

To hold out against General Xanthippus, and after what must have been an exhausting birth, pushing out first that head.

She must have had the strength of a lion.

Aspasia shivered. Wrapping her arms around herself, she walked back to the warmer andron and picked up the fallen *Odyssey*. She didn't have to read the scroll to know the end of the story. After impressing the Phaeacians with his athletic prowess and tales of his adventures, Odysseus sailed home to Ithaca and to his wife Penelope, with whom he spent the rest of his life.

Nice for them.

But where did that leave Nausicaa? Homer never bothered to say what happened to her. Aspasia's hand went to her chin. Poor Nausicaa.

Homer wasn't telling that story about you, she reminded herself firmly.

The wind set the flame in his man's torch flickering but Pericles strode forward through the unsteady light. Odysseus went home to a loving wife. Chilly gusts whipped at his cloak, but like Odysseus' magic veil, the warmth of Aspasia and the evening they'd spent kept the cold at bay.

CHAPTER 7

Hazardous Terrain

Herodotus said the Egyptians built their greatest buildings for a few men—palaces and tombs for their kings.

"What about their temples?" Pericles had asked him.

"Most don't get past the temple courtyard, although if you're important, you can get to the second gate. Only the priests—oh, did I say kings are priests?—reach the holy room deep inside."

What a contrast to Athens! On his way to the Assembly, Pericles passed the construction site for the new temple of Hephaistos, the god of crafts, a blacksmith god not too proud to stand before the blazing furnace forging iron—the god for men who made things. Pericles gauged the vitality of his city by the audible pulse of hammers, the steady rasp of files, and the thick abundance of stone chips, ropes, beams, and strewn planks: it was in excellent health. Pericles had intended to introduce at this Assembly a new kind of building, a closed, roofed hall where all Athenians could hear music free of distractions and in any weather. It had not been done before. They'd love it.

But disappointing news from Generals Cleinias and Tolmides fighting the rebels in Boeotia forced him to postpone that plan. In mounting their military campaign to rescue the Boeotian democracies from the oligarchic rebels, the Athenians had counted on the Boeotian democrats for help but they hadn't gotten it. The Athenians were on their own in Boeotia.

So Pericles reluctantly had to set aside his vision of a music hall—he felt like a thick-necked horse jerked into a turn. Instead, he had to argue in the Assembly for yet more money and military reinforcements for Boeotia—for a land campaign, in the middle of winter, that he had opposed from the start.

Stepping away from the bema that day, Pericles glanced toward the Agora and saw from above, like a workman on the tallest scaffold, a column capital lowered into place in Hephaistos' still-unroofed temple. On the next hill over, workmen were raising the new columns for the Parthenon. The progress on the buildings was a bulwark for his spirit against the disheartening news that the democrats had not come over to the Athenian side. Turning his eyes southward, with a jump of his heart he located Hippodamus' house.

As Pericles descended the hill at the close of the Assembly, Damon, his trusted advisor, instead of congratulating him on winning the vote on reinforcements for Boeotia, came at him with, "You're heading toward her house again. Don't you realize that the whole city is talking about your visiting the same woman every night."

Damon was sounding like Pericles' brother Ariphron and Pericles didn't enjoy it from either one of them. "As long as a man participates in public life and obeys the laws, Athenians will tolerate what he does in private."

"But you're going beyond the law—your own law," Damon said. "You just passed a law to prevent Athenian men from consorting with foreign women."

"That law is about the *children* of foreigners married to Athenians—they can't be citizens, but it doesn't stop a man from . . . "

Damon's thin-mouthed smile. "From what?"

Pericles preferred not to use the word *consorting*. "It was my law and I know its intent. Damon, don't ever again tell me that I don't obey the laws."

The conversation with Damon made him feel at risk, but was he worried about the Athenians' opinion of him or Aspasia's? Heading toward Hippodamus' house, Pericles felt for the small package tucked in his cloak, assuring himself that he hadn't forgotten it.

After greeting him with a kiss, Aspasia asked how the Assembly had responded to his call for reinforcements for the army in Boeotia.

She always met him with questions. He thought it was unusual among lovers, but he looked forward to them: at last, he got to say all of it. There were always more reasons for and against a motion than he could include in a speech without confusing the listeners or boring them. Aspasia followed every thread attentively—or was that just her skill?

"I'll tell you, but first I have a gift for you."

Drachmas were easy but giving her only drachmas had not satisfied him. He had first sent Euangelus to choose gifts for her but, having trained his steward for thrift, he had created a Euangelus unprepared for buying bracelets and perfume. Instead, he had to call in the craftsmen or visit the shops himself—either way people talked. But drachmas were only ordinary compensation for the pleasures of the night. They couldn't begin to pay for the joy, now his best companion, that accompanied him during the day.

Thus he had given Aspasia a silver mirror with a small statue of Aphrodite for the handle so that when you grasped the mirror, your fingers encircled the love goddess. A tiny statue of winged Eros, Aphrodite's son, was attached with so narrow a silvery bridge that he seemed to be flying above her shoulder, taking off to spread his gift of passionate desire through the world.

Pericles, a recipient of Eros' gift, had on this night brought with him a silver necklace with a pendant that would fall between her breasts in the place his thumb liked to go, and he watched her open the parcel and slip the chain over her head waiting for that moment. He leaned forward to adjust the silver chain into a smooth oval, feeling the warmth of Aspasia's skin beneath his fingertips. The necklace still wasn't quite symmetrical—he repositioned the pendant which fell into place as he intended, and he ran his thumb along the inner curve of her breast. They gazed at their combined reflections in Aphrodite's mirror, his hand on her breast, and together admired the new necklace.

"How did the Assembly respond to your call for reinforcements for Boeotia?" she asked.

He smiled. The way she held to her questions was enough to make a man think she was genuinely interested. "When things are going well, the people can't believe a reversal is possible."

"Do they believe things are going well then?"

"Our marching armies haven't met resistance. The generals report that they have sold as slaves the few rebels they've captured."

No resistance—but there had been armed conflict. "What about the Boeotian democrats?"

"They're giving us no support whatsoever." He cracked his knuckles—she'd never seen him do that before.

"Why not when you're on their side?"

"I take it the democrats up there fear Athens as much as they fear their own aristocrats."

Was there a paradox stirring? "But if you win, you'll set them up again with democratic governments. Why do they fear Athens?"

"They must fear Athens."

When she was puzzled, she looked even younger than her nineteen years.

He spoke gently. "The point is, Aspasia, you don't rule an empire by being loved."

After a moment, she nodded. "Then it means that they don't fear Athens enough or they'd have—"

Enough. He drew her nearer. "Do I rule you by love or by fear?"

"You don't rule me like one of your allied cities. You persuade me as you do the Athenians by what you say and by looking as handsome as Zeus when you say it." She then commented that since the Athenians had dealt with the rebels they had captured by selling them into slavery, the Boeotians would now surely fear them sufficiently.

Pericles corrected her: enslaving captives would strengthen the Boeotians' will to resist. It would nourish among democrats a patriotic hunger for their city's independence that can overcome a preference for democracy. Furthermore, Pericles opposed in principle Greeks enslaving other Greeks. In any case, Athens should focus her resources on islands, not mainland territories like Boeotia. Anyhow, he had maintained from the outset that this invasion was ill-timed because of the winter weather.

Too many reasons, Aspasia thought. Listening to him, you'd think that the Athenians had lost the battle, not captured a city. "Are you sorry for the Athenian success?" she asked.

Up to that moment, she had never seen him confused. She was uneasy, especially because *she* had confused him.

"Sorry? For success?"

"What I meant is . . . since you opposed this campaign from the beginning . . . "

He felt his best companion flee. "How can you believe that I could regret Athenian success?"

"I didn't believe—of course I—"

"And could say it?"

Well, *he* had poured on all those reasons. "I meant that, if the expedition failed, they'd agree more with your policy that Athens can't hold these vast mainland territories."

"How can you imagine that I'd care more about my public position than the good of my city? I thought you were a woman of understanding."

She *was* a woman of understanding, and she was frightened. She drew nearer, but the curving strokes of her palm met the column of a neck hard as stone.

"You sounded troubled and I misunderstood."

"I devote my life to Athens."

"I—"

"I'd rather be wrong than see Athens suffer adversity, if it came to it."

She cast around for something to say. "Everybody knows you place the city before your own benefit."

"Then how can you have so poor an opinion of me as to think that I could want failure for Cleinias, my kinsman, and Tolmides, another fine general, and the Athenian soldiers, marching in wintry weather—Aspasia, do you realize they have *snow* up there?"

She was so relieved that he did care about her opinion that she plunged forward. "I didn't mean failure, I just thought that . . . " How by Hera could she finish this sentence without digging herself in deeper?

But now that she'd broached it, Pericles asked himself whether he could use failure as an argument. Would it give him a freer hand? Could such a tack, in the future, carry the Athenians to his vision that Athens' true destiny was the sea? The thought brought cold unease.

His path and that of his city were one. If the two ever separated, it would mean that his city had strayed onto dangerous ground, but that would be equally true of him.

That's why the gods, while handing him a mixed bag physically, had endowed him with an extraordinary ability to persuade others. He didn't need the city's failure—no more than he needed to hold the excessive force of a tyrant—to lead them in the right direction. Now if a political opponent, like Thucydides, were to fail . . . but that was another matter.

". . . a brief setback may stir the Assembly to vote for the additional reinforcements you advised," Aspasia said.

Even when a man is angry, surprise can tug out a smile.

He *had* been concerned about the Assembly's reluctance to double up on reinforcements.

"This much is true—I do worry that easy success will lead to overconfidence."

With the shallow breaths of uncertain relief, Aspasia remained silent. She, too, must beware of overconfidence.

As he left that evening, he flipped up the pendant and said, "For a moment I felt sorry I'd given you this necklace but you deserve it."

"What did I do to deserve it?" She really wanted to know.

"You understood me."

Which way did he mean she'd understood him? That a brief setback would loosen Athenian purse strings? Or—the big one—that military failure in Boeotia would make him stronger than ever in Athens? She was curious but didn't dare double back over that hazardous terrain.

A few nights later, Pericles was awakened by a messenger pounding on the door of his home. First check: no shaking of an earthquake—his thoughts skimmed past a tidal wave, a fire, a new rebellion among the allies, and landed hard on military disaster in Boeotia. Rushing to the Council Hall, he spotted men creeping through the streets close to walls, covering their faces with bloody rags as they disappeared into doorways. Their shame spelled catastrophe.

Many went home but the most stalwart of those returning from Boeotia and those who loved their city most ran immediately to the

Executive Council. The story was pieced together from what different men had seen with their own eyes, a mosaic with blank patches. As the Athenians approached their next target city, Orchomenos, they saw that it was more heavily fortified than the first city they had attacked, Chaeronea, which had fallen to them easily. It would take a siege to capture Orchomenos, and no interpretation of birds, no reading of innards and no seer can predict how long a siege will take. A winter siege—and the weather had become bitter cold.

The Athenians took stock: they had already won wealth and glory at Chaeronea and enriched Athena's treasury. And, as General Cleinias pointed out, even General Pericles, who opposed pouring resources into capturing vast tracts of land, would appreciate that they had secured a useful route to northern Greece. From generals to foot soldiers, returning home to enjoy the pleasures of their new wealth was far more appealing than waiting out a winter siege. While the generals were debating what to do, some refugees from Orchomenos arrived at camp and, claiming they were democrats, reported that while *they* were loyal to the Athenians, the other democrats had joined the rebellion and were ready to fight for their city's independence from Athens. As those reporting to the Executive Council all agreed, that tipped the scales toward abandoning Boeotia.

It was obvious to Pericles that the "refugees" who turned up at the Athenian camp were spies sent to discourage the Athenians from attacking Orchomenos. Taking them seriously showed bad judgment on the part of the generals—but the campaign had in any event ended in disaster, so he remained silent.

The generals seemed to have marshalled the army in good order for heading home, the thousand armed men marching in hollow-square formation with the baggage and supplies protected in the center. Tolmides led and Cleinias rode at the rear. The order was appropriate, Pericles thought—exactly what he would have done. What could have gone wrong? By all reports, the Athenians met no opposition and the scouts encountered only a handful of goatherds. Torrential rains that had troubled them near Orchomenos let up. Spirits rose the way they do when the sun comes out, even in winter. Some said the generals were planning for the army to take advantage of being in the region to visit the sanctuary of the Muses on Mount

Helicon, a detour off the road home. *No!* Pericles insisted in his mind, as if he'd been in charge. *No detours! Not with all that armor, baggage, and wealth.*

The Athenians had marched, up and down in heavy armor, for the better part of a day. Scouts reported that the plain ahead, entered through an old riverbed, was clear. The columns tightened ranks through the narrow passage. With their shields pressed together, the men stumbled forward, some tripping over the river boulders.

Then General Tolmides was hit in the neck by an arrow as he was about to enter the plain and fell dead from his horse.

Boeotians appeared on the hillcrests, hurling javelins and stones and raining down arrows. The first missiles did little damage since the troops were protected by their helmets and raised shields, but then the Boeotians, screaming their war cry, slid down, attacked the crowded Athenians from close range and killed a few with their spears. Some of the trapped soldiers turned to fight uphill with their swords. Those at the front tried to run toward the plain, but the Boeotians held them in the valley and forced them into uphill hand-to-hand fighting.

Cleinias rode forward to maintain the unity of the Athenian line but a javelin hit his horse in the chest and it stumbled forward. A Boeotian raised a spear to hurl at Cleinias and another grabbed his arm to stop him—a captured general is worth more than a dead one—but not in time. As Cleinias slid down to dismount, the hurled spear struck him under his upraised left arm, and he was dead. *Not Cleinias.* Pericles hand fell from his forehead to his eyes.

Pericles let others ask the obvious questions. *How could so large an enemy force group behind the hills without the army hearing it?* It was a windy day. *How could the enemy mass ahead of the army without scouts seeing them? Had the generals bribed goatherds to serve as lookouts?* No one knew.

But he knew. A gang of bandits should never have been able to rout the armed and trained Athenians. As the first shock was ground down by the repetition of testimony, it became clear to Pericles that the Athenian generals were at fault. They were dangerously elated by their victories and new wealth. Hubris had dulled their judgment. They had believed the word of fake refugees; they were thinking of visiting the Sanctuary of the Muses—a pleasure trip in hostile territory! These hadn't led to the critical misjudgments, but the high wave of hubris had lifted Tolmides and Cleinias above details. They had not used their scouts well; they had not reconnoitered carefully. Pericles' rage at the loss grew. It was a tragic waste. A thousand Athenians caught in a narrow defile—had the generals survived, he might have had to prosecute them. Prosecute his kinsman Cleinias? Impossible. Well, if he didn't, Thucydides would have stepped in. Then let him . . . what nonsense was he thinking? The generals were dead.

Someone was asking whether the bodies of the Athenians had been collected.

He would remind them that he had opposed the invasion from the start—but not now. Instead, Pericles asked whether the Boeotian "refugees" had died in the attack. A witness said they'd survived. He allowed himself to say he was not surprised.

CHAPTER 8

⌐⌐⌐⌐⌐⌐⌐⌐⌐⌐⌐⌐⌐⌐

Dust for Gold

What takes a man more courage than to tell a woman that her husband has died in battle, all the more when she is his own kinswoman? It's harder when there's no comfort of victory to offer. Through their errors, the generals had so wounded their city that, if they had survived, they would have been impeached. But, whatever Deinomache might hear from others, Pericles would not pile shame on grief. He could say without any doubt that Cleinias had been brave, so he told her about Cleinias' courage in riding up from behind and rallying the Athenian line.

But all she wanted to know was whether the body had been cremated in Boeotia. He told her that the embassy would return with the ashes in about fifteen days. As he was leaving, her fingers tightened on his arm in a grip that chilled him as if it came from the dead. Clearly, she was searching for Cleinias' physical substance.

The purification water by her door was scum. Deinomache refused to refresh it. At his next visit, she announced Cleinias' ashes must be buried not in the public cemetery but on their family's estate.

"Your husband would have wanted the honor of public burial." That Pericles knew as a certainty.

"He should lie beside our family's heroes."

"Public burial for those who die in battle is now the law."

"I don't care about the law!"

Not care about the law.

Pericles had proposed most of the new laws, and he was not responsible for Cleinias' death—had in fact tried to discourage the whole enterprise. But he held to the point.

"Your sons, as they grow older, will pass by the public memorial to their father. It will make them better men, and they'll point it out with pride to their friends."

"Cleinias died too soon."

No answer there.

He left, not dipping his fingers in the filthy water.

Cleinias with the seal-like whiskers. Although she'd met him only once, Aspasia was sorry he'd died. Cleinias, who was so interested in the Babylonian sacred prostitutes. She'd been in the man's house.

But why did he have to get killed just when Pericles seemed to be making her a regular part of his life? Now, as Athenians endured waiting for news from the embassy, uncertain about who was alive and who dead and about the surrender agreement, his visits were as short as with a man you'd meet on the street. He said he was occupied by concerns for his city and his family. When she expressed dismay at how drawn he looked, he said, roughly, "My well-being is not your concern."

She, too, had to wait it out.

Joy and grief took turns entering the city as liberated prisoners were followed by mule wagons carrying the ashes of the dead. Ten years earlier, the Athenians had taken control of all Boeotia except for the powerful city of Thebes. Now they had surrendered all they had fought for, and families who paid enormous ransoms for the return of their sons and husbands alive counted themselves lucky.

The families of the dead were to view the ash urns set up in state in a tent in the official cemetery outside the city. On the appointed day, Deinomache stepped out of her house, her hands fluttering up against the sun she hadn't seen for days. Beneath her veil, her hair was like a bird's nest in winter; she hadn't combed it since learning of Cleinias' death nor, Pericles thought, changed her gown. He was embarrassed to be seen with an unkempt woman. It dishonored Cleinias. Her mother and sisters pressed their knees together to make room for her in the cart.

Where were her sons, Young Cleinias and Alcibiades? No one had thought to prepare the children. *No one had thought . . .* what sad words for those two little boys. At their births, the Fates seemed to have showered them with the best gifts—to be sons of an Athenian general and a high-born Athenian mother. And now their father was dead and their mother . . . well, she seemed heedless. How abruptly everything had changed for the boys. Pericles shook his head, thinking how sudden it must have seemed to them, as when his own father had sailed off to another city, ostracized by the laws of Athens. Sudden change, sudden loss. Though his father wasn't dead at that time, thanks to Zeus.

Someone had gone in to get Alcibiades and Young Cleinias. Pericles and his brother Ariphron were their nearest kin—they'd take on the upbringing of these boys.

Walking beside the cart, Pericles held the hand of Alcibiades who skipped along chattering. Two more boys to raise, two new opportunities. Since their father was gone, he would himself influence them to become the best of men as he tried, always, with his own two sons. Not bothering to decipher the boy's childish lisp, he nodded, enjoying the feel of the small hand in his own, the tiny fingers interrupting his grief. Family mourners, friends of the dead, curiosity seekers, those wanting to be seen paying homage, women and their daughters glad of an honorable reason for an outing and boys let out of school all crowded out of the city through the Ceramicus Gate. In the crush, Alcibiades decided he wanted to be picked up. Pericles carried him a few steps before handing him to a servant.

Once in the tent, after staring at Cleinias' ash urn long enough for Pericles to shift his weight several times, Deinomache stretched out her hand. He raised his arm, ready for a struggle, but all she did was prop a clay figurine of a woman next to the urn. Pericles' offering was a jar filled with oil from his estate and painted with a sad picture, a young soldier, sitting near his own tomb and gazing at it thoughtfully.

Pointing to the line of cypress chests, Deinomache said in a loud voice, "I don't want him crowded in with all those other men. He should be buried on our own land and have his own monument!"

Pericles quickly leaned toward her. "Cleinias fought with these men. He wants to rest with them. He wouldn't want you to interfere with his lying beneath the monument that will describe their deeds."

She stood motionless.

Her uncertainty let him steer her from the urn. "His name will be known for all time—I've got the finest cutter in Athens carving the inscription. Be reasonable."

As they approached the cart, she said, "Some people talk of ash urns as if they had parts like a man. There's a foot, a belly, a shoulder, a neck, a lip." She tapped her finger against her wrist, keeping track. "But of course that's foolish."

How pathetic. But then he caught her looking at him slyly, as if to determine whether he thought she was being reasonable enough.

* * *

When the day for burial came, while families moved toward the cemetery, Dion, her bookseller friend, led Aspasia out of the city by another route and headed for a hill where she would have a good view. From a distance, the hill appeared desolate and brown, but as they began to climb, it turned out to be filled with children chirping like birds and climbing through the thickets. Aspasia and Dion settled themselves on the weathered stone of an old sanctuary of an unknown divinity and waited. She felt foolish since they were the only adults among many children, but how else could she see the ceremony?

She counted wagons as they pulled up, ten of them, one for each tribe.

"Last time they buried an extra chest empty for the ones they couldn't find," Dion said, "but this time they found everybody."

The ash urns in the open chests were stacked shoulder to shoulder—like the wine amphoras in the hold of the pirates' ship that brought her to Athens. Occasionally the sound of a rustling harness reached them.

Aspasia's cloak was too thin to keep out the cold. Dion wrapped his arm around her shoulders. From the pouch he'd hung on a branch, he took out some bread, cheese, and wine. Neither of them had eaten that morning. He covered a piece of bread with cheese for her. She took a swallow from his leather flask; he hadn't diluted the wine. Like other pleasant things Dion did, it had a sting to it, but it warmed her. It was kind of him to bring her here, and she told him so. He was Athenian and could have walked with the citizens.

The procession moved forward like a wounded animal dragging its haunches. The King Archon came first and the wagons next, followed by the mourners, those near the end held in place long after the front was underway.

Where would she find Pericles? From this distance, the marchers looked small. She sighted the tallest tree and concentrated on each person passing it. Dion ran his finger around her ear. It warmed her like the wine, but not wanting to lose her place, she brushed it away.

With his forearm to her cheek, he guided her line of sight. There was Pericles, whom she'd barely seen in weeks, at the front of his tribe. How could Dion know when his vision was so poor? She squinted—he must have spotted the metallic glint of the helmet. Near Pericles were women and children of different heights, some carried by servants, but one tiny woman walked next to him. That had to be his wife. Aspasia shouldn't have had that strong wine; she felt nauseated.

She forced cold air into her lungs and leaned forward, as if a couple of palms' widths closer could improve her view. Those were his sons, the youth and child walking beside the wife. She couldn't see from this distance if the wife was as beautiful as people said. As the crowd reformed opposite the speaker's platform, Pericles slipped his hand under his wife's elbow to help her up a grassy bank. Watching carefully, hand to chin, Aspasia decided his gesture was more than a formality; it had a tenderness to it. Pericles would never cup *her* elbow in that way—well, he might for the tenderness but not at a public event.

Tenderness only took you so far. There would always be his wife. Her mind went back to his hard anger when she misjudged his fierce devotion to Athens. *How can you imagine that I'd care more about my public position than the good of my city?* She'd tried to kiss him but he didn't budge. That hadn't lasted long—mostly he seemed as passionately devoted to her as he was to Athens. And while she was with him, she felt that she was not alone in this city, but that was only seeming. Nothing stopped him from changing toward her on any day, at any moment. From simply not coming to see her at Hippodamus' house. Easy for him. That would be the end of her hearing all the news first, his interest in what she had to say that was so like her father, the surprise gifts, the thrill of being desired by the most powerful man in Athens. It would end the drachmas.

The speaker's back was to them.

Aspasia, you need a plan.

"I'll tell you what he's saying," Dion said. "He's talking about Athenian heroes of the past. He's saying these men are like them. And he's urging everyone to be brave. What else is there to say? Aeschylus already wrote it in his play—Ares the war god is a tough money-changer."

She didn't like to admit ignorance but wanted to know more.

"Which play?"

"*Agamemnon.*"

Without words, the speaker's gestures lacked meaning.

"Is that all you know of it?"

Dion looked to the distance he couldn't see:

> For Ares, lord of strife,
> Who doth the swaying scales of battle hold,
> War's money-changer, giving dust for gold,
> Sends back, to hearts that held them dear,
> Scant ash of warriors, wept with many a tear,
> Light to the hand, but heavy to the soul . . .

His voice had taken on the resonance of a cithara's lowest tones.

She, too, was looking to the distance. "General Cleinias came back 'light to the hand, but heavy to the soul.'"

Dion nodded.

Two out of two generals died up there in Boeotia. That was another reason she needed a plan—Pericles might die in battle.

"Dion, would you go to war and risk coming back light to the hand?"

"How can you imagine anything else? The city comes first. What are you asking—would I go?" He sounded as angry as Pericles when she'd asked whether he regretted Athens' early success in Boeotia.

"Dion, you're not much like Pericles, but you remind me of him a little."

"I remind you of Pericles?" Dion's pale eyes opened wide and he leaned toward her.

It would probably be just a kiss of gratitude. Still, to keep him talking, she said, "But you don't go into battle like Pericles."

"They won't take me because I can't see well."

They hadn't moved from their spot and were feeling the cold. Dion offered her more wine which she sipped slowly, knowing its strength.

The cypress chests were lined up next to the trenches. Sobbing reached their ears.

"Familiar was each face," Dion said.

The chests were lowered. There was a stir. Pericles and several other men clustered around a woman with two little boys—she saw Pericles' brother Ariphron (who had nothing wrong with the shape of *his* head) and thought she recognized Pericles' friend Sophocles.

She leaned forward. "That must be Deinomache. Ariphron's got two boys by the hand—those must be her sons. Deinomache has caused Pericles trouble for weeks. She didn't want to attend these rites, but Pericles forced her, to honor Cleinias." Now *there* was something from the inside she could tell Dion. "Look—that smaller boy got away from Ariphron!"

"Now what's happening?"

Somebody ran up the hill to catch the child.

"They got him. You know, Dion, a little child like that—and they're going to be shoveling in the dirt over his father, maybe he didn't want to watch." Her hand went to her chin. "If he were my son, I might have kept him home."

Pericles had locked his hands around Deinomache's waist to keep her from falling—or leaping—into the trench. In the distance, she was as small as a fluttering leaf.

But if she hadn't wanted to honor her husband, why was she trying to throw herself into the trench? How would Pericles explain that?

They'd dragged Deinomache a safe distance away. Mourners dropped in their gifts and poured their drink offerings, tossing in the cups and pitchers. The piled dirt was shoveled over the graves, and seeds were pressed into the raw earth. Slowly, the families moved from the grassy ground.

Aspasia, chin resting on her hand, watched Pericles help his wife over the bumpy earth. She was so drawn to the plan that was forming in her mind that she didn't stir as Dion pressed close and kissed her cheek. Dion stood and spread his cloak out on the ground. Shouts and laughter came from children who couldn't be seen. He shook his fists for quiet.

"It would have to be fifteen drachmas," she said. She wasn't sure how much money she'd need but Athens was expensive—it was probably more than her father had brought with them from Miletus, stolen by the pirates.

"Fifteen! I'm your friend—it should be free for me. And Pericles gives you plenty, doesn't he?"

"He does, but I have a plan."

"A plan! What's your plan? All right, fifteen," he said when she didn't answer. "Just this once."

He reached for her hand. More laughter. He gathered some stones and hurled them toward the trees. Judging from a howl, one hit its mark. It grew quieter.

"I'm cold," she said.

"Have some wine. Here, wear my cloak."

"I want to go home now."

He didn't show his disappointment and tried to keep her warm beside him as they climbed their way out of the hill and walked back toward Hippodamus' house. By the time they got there, her teeth were chattering. It had been a hard day for Aspasia. She'd walked a far distance, been cold, and drunk that miserable wine. She'd watched the burial of the ashes. The phrase, *light to the hand, heavy to the soul,* would not leave her head. She'd seen a woman try to throw herself into her husband's grave. She'd barely seen Pericles for weeks and then she'd seen him cradling his wife's elbow in his palm. How would she ever raise the money for her plan? Her own soul felt very heavy.

"Another time."

* * *

Leaving the cemetery, Pericles asked Aristocleia to accompany him to the burial meal at Cleinias' house. She had, she asserted, fulfilled her duty by attending the public rites with him and now would do as she wished. Encircling the shoulders of her two sons within her cloak, she walked off with them toward the cart she had waiting on the far side of the hill.

Deinomache had smothered her house with the choking scent of burned rosemary and myrtle as if she were masking the smell of a real corpse. There was a wait for food. It was as if all day had been a matter of waiting. In fact, it seemed to Pericles as if the weeks since they'd learned of the disaster in Boeotia was one long wait.

Finally, the cooked eggs were brought in. Aware that his older brother, Ariphron, was about to start a round of toasts, Pericles spoke first so that he'd be free to get back to work. Holding an egg by the ends like a top, he said that since eggs contain the seeds of new life, they help people meet the apparent darkness of death. Then Ariphron raised his cup to Cleinias, their courageous and brilliant general. Courageous—that would have been praise enough. But brilliant? His brother didn't think things through. By accident of birth, Ariphron headed up the family but he, through genuine merit, had become one of the most influential men in Athens. That was democracy—he smiled at its virtues.

Then he set his cup on a table. He had fulfilled *his* duty.

At the door, he flicked a floating beetle from the water jar. Ictinus' architectural plans for the new Music Hall were on his table at home—he hadn't even unrolled them. He'd been neglecting his personal financial affairs. He'd better get home.

Or to Aspasia.

CHAPTER 9

Which Athena?

Splashing water on her face, Aspasia met him—like at the relays—on the run.

As she lifted off his heavy winter cloak, he drew from its folds a papyrus roll. A gift? No—

"I know what that is—you're going back to building that Music Hall!" That would be lucky for Silky, more work for Ictinus in town.

"And I've a new idea about it." She loved knowing things before others. "We'll have music contests to celebrate Athena's birthday at the Panathenaic Festival."

She nodded. "Contests stir men to do their best."

"I think that's the gift the gods favor most."

"*That's* what the gods want most—men doing their best?" She doubted it. "What about all the marble temples, the bronze statues, the fancy gold objects? Don't tell me they're wasted!"

"Those reflect men doing their best. Although I think the gods prefer artful things to athletic contests because they have more of mind in them. Anyhow . . . " He smiled because she knew his preferences. "I would if I were a god."

She put her finger to her cheek. Was music athletic or artful? The philosopher Pythagoras said there was a lot of mathematics to music. "I can see music has some mind in it."

"And I'll get that music hall built quickly. Since our losses in Boeotia, they're following my advice in everything—you were right about that, Aspasia. By the way, would you—"

"Wait! There's a contradiction in your idea about mind. What about all the animals we sacrifice to the gods?"

"I don't think the gods care much about the animals. Would you if you were a god? The smell of meat sizzling on the grills all day to whet appetites and then, when it's nicely cooked, we mortals take the meat for ourselves? By the way, Aspasia, all I've had to eat today is one egg."

She wanted only to do something for him. She jumped up to see what was in her pantry.

* * *

The Peloponnesians had completed their temple for Zeus at Olympia, near where they held the Olympic Games, some years back but had never managed to build the gold and ivory statue of Zeus to dwell within it. Pericles would not repeat that error: he had the Assembly guarantee funds for a gold and ivory statue of Athena—taller than the walls of most cities—as soon as work began on the Parthenon. The statue would be constructed on a wood framework sheathed in gold except for the face and hands which would be formed of ivory to give Athena the look of beautiful woman. Phidias the Athenian, the greatest sculptor alive, would design and construct it. If the Peloponnesians preferred their sculptor, Polycleitus of Argos, let *him* build their overdue Zeus.

But while Phidias was the expert in sculpture, *he* was an expert in knowing the mind of the Athenian voters, the Demos. Phidias had in the past incorporated into his works novel gestures, unlife-like proportions, and new ways of doing things. The sculptor was like a pathfinder who can move faster than his followers can keep up. When the Demos hadn't understood Phidias' reasons and were stirred up by Thucydides against anything that cost money, they'd bristled at what was new. Since Pericles had proposed the costly Athena, the Assembly made him accountable for the money. Ariphron claimed that Pericles would ruin the family fortune with all his civic "accountables" but Pericles didn't need to hear from his brother the meaning of accountable.

To keep a close eye on Phidias' plans, Pericles arranged to visit the workshop to see the sculptor's preliminary wax model for the gold and ivory Athena. Wax is easy to change—if adjustments are needed, let them be caught early. He climbed upward to the Acropolis with the yearning that he recognized with pride as a lover's yearning, now that he was a lover. He hoped to glimpse in Phidias' wax the actual gold and ivory Athena he longed to see in place, at home in the Parthenon.

Despite the lover that he was, when Aspasia had said she'd like to go, too, he'd said, "No."

No—that was the first time he'd said that word to her. He'd bridled when she'd implied that if the army failed in Boeotia, it might strengthen him politically, but that wasn't *no*. (And it turned out she was right.) He'd hardly seen her for weeks after the army's disaster but that wasn't a "no" either.

She had a good reason. "When I first came to Athens, Phidias was working in wax on an Athena for one of your allied cities, he called it his *young Athena* and I modeled for it. I'd like to see if he's cast it into bronze yet."

"It's impossible. I'm meeting there with three of my senior advisors to make an important decision."

Had he forgotten how good she was at decisions? "Who?"

"Sophocles, Anaxagoras, and Damon."

Damon hated her. Sophocles the playwright was Pericles' age-mate and friend so that made sense. Anaxagoras, well, she'd never met him but knew he was a philosopher—Pericles liked to say Anaxagoras was his teacher.

"Pericles, I'd be useful because I know Phidias' ideas about Athena—"

"What nonsense! There's no place for a woman among men making decision—not at the Council Hall, not at the Assembly and not on the Acropolis. A woman—and you a foreigner. In the midst of deliberations about important matters." He shook his head. "It's never been done."

"Never been done is not a reason."

He recognized his own words—he'd said them to Phidias and Ictinus about the additional columns on the Parthenon. That clever woman—fast as a runner at the turn, she'd circled tight and set them to her own purpose. And what a memory.

He enjoyed surprise, she knew. Noticing his behind-the-hand smile, she pressed on. "I'd like to see if Phidias kept something of me in that young Athena he was working on."

"Our gold and ivory Athena must be a grown woman, not a girl."

"Yes, and I want to be sure Phidias designs it right." *Get to the point, Aspasia.* "Oh, Pericles—you *know* I often have good ideas."

The gold and ivory Athena was the most important thing in the world to him. Well, there were other things. He thought of his sons. His new musical hall came to mind.

Aspasia's full gaze was on him.

What about Aspasia? He saw her most nights and when he missed a night, she was in his thoughts. But could he count something so new to his life as important?

She was waiting, excited.

For instance, if he had to choose between her and the gold and ivory Athena . . . ? What nonsense!

She did have good ideas.

Pericles frowned at a thought. "Damon and the others won't come if a woman's going to be there."

"Don't tell them ahead of time."

A good idea.

* * *

She followed the switchbacks up the hill, impatient with the slow pace of the house slave, Old Zoe—Aspasia no longer felt dignified running around Athens with Silky. She turned right at the tall bronze Athena that Phidias had built when he was much younger and, strumming her fingers along the fence, followed the foundation of the Parthenon, holding the edge of her gown above the dirt and planks, balancing her sun umbrella, covering her ears from the noise of sawing and hammering, with an arm across her nose to keep out dust. This was the first time she'd met Pericles during the day—she didn't count the time she and Silky had climbed to the Acropolis because he hadn't expected her.

She pushed aside the day-time curtain of Phidias' studio, sending specks of grit speeding through a sunbeam like startled fish. The four men huddled around a bench at the far end twisted around to look at her, turned toward one another, turned their backs to her and finally—thanks to Zeus—turned toward Pericles.

But what would he say to them? She held her breath in hopes of hearing the exact words he'd use to keep his advisors quiet and polite.

It was a vast space, but a few strides took Pericles from one end to the other to lift her cloak from her shoulders.

No words. He could surprise her, too.

She felt shaken as by a small earth tremor. She did not want to leave this man, ever.

She kept her cloak, however—this place was too big to heat.

As her eyes grew accustomed to the relative dimness—nothing is as bright as the Acropolis—she located the Athena she'd posed for in her days with Phidias, still in wax and in a corner. Did Pericles think it resembled her? Maybe not. Phidias had smoothed out the bump on her nose.

Phidias snapped his fingers. From behind the curtain that hid the small kitchen, Agoracritus, Phidias' apprentice, brought her a small cup with a red, thick juice. It was intensely sweet.

She didn't like having the men watch her sipping from the cup, especially Damon, whose narrowed lips looked like a robber had bound them with a length of string. Sophocles stared at her thoughtfully but she wished he'd look somewhere else. Anaxagoras circled his thumbs, now one on top and now the other, as if uncertain. Phidias—well, of course, Phidias grinned, but Pericles frowned and she thought she knew why. These men were here for business. She didn't want Pericles to be sorry he'd let her come. To lead their gazes, she turned toward the bench where Phidias had set out not one but four different wax statuettes of Athena.

Lined up like that, the statuettes looked like women waiting their turns to draw water at the fountain house, only instead of fiddling with their water pitchers, they fiddled with spears and helmets. Aspasia saw in the guano thick wax coating the bench

Phidias working hard and late on these wax goddesses—she had watched him labor well into the night on her own wax self still stuck in the corner—would he never cast it into bronze? Maybe the allied city that ordered it had decided not to pay up. Chalkboards powdery enough to compel a sneeze leaned against the bench.

"Time to work," Pericles said.

Sophocles passed along the Athenas on the bench, bending in and examining each of them as carefully as if he were planning a purchase, and paused in front of one of them.

"How thoughtful this one is, her neck turned, her head bent as she gazes at the helmet she holds in her hand." The playwright tried out the pose, staring at the helmet that he seemed to hold in his own hand. "She's thinking about war, and what it does to men."

Anaxagoras nodded. "Athena should be thoughtful because she's born from the Mind of Zeus—or so the stories tell us."

"By the gods, we don't want Athena without weapons!" Damon nearly shouted though they were all in easy earshot. "*This* one's Athena—brandishing her spear, gripping her shield, and *wearing* her helmet."

"Damon's right that she should hold her weapons and I'll prove it." Agoracritus waited for Phidias' nod to continue. "If Athena doesn't hold her weapons, people won't know who she is. Homer says that when Odysseus lands back home after his voyages and Athena appears to him without her weapons, he *does not recognize* her. There's your proof!"

"Good thinking." Sophocles pointed to a wax figure with her spear leaning against her shield. "This one might be a compromise because her shield and spear are near but resting on the ground. Phidias, could you put a helmet in her hand to gaze at?"

"She's our *war* goddess!" The bit jerked Damon's mouth. "Why not show her *wielding* her spear?"

Aspasia was little short of astonished that this important man did not get the point. "Because she's *already* victorious!" Immediately she regretted blurting out. Damon was forever advising Pericles to get rid of her.

But Sophocles was circling the wax Athenas murmuring, "wide of the mark." He looked up. "Phidias, if an intelligent man like

Damon didn't see it, you've missed the mark. I check every line I write against that measure. You must make it clear to your audience that she's victorious or they'll scratch their heads and shuffle in their seats and you won't win the first prize."

"It *is* clear," Phidias said. "Aspasia saw it."

Aspasia glanced at Pericles. Her elation matched the moment at Cleinias' house when Herodotus had told them that she was right. "*. . . as Aspasia said . . .* " These most important men were listening to her—surely there was nothing better in the world. And Pericles would be reassured about her.

Aspasia is quick but . . . "Sophocles is right," Pericles said. "We must have the Athena they're expecting, the one they'll recognize." He paused. "And also, it must be clear that she is victorious, as Aspasia said."

Aspasia cast her eyes down so as not to grin too broadly. *If only her father could know.*

What a day!

Feeling warmer, she shrugged back her cloak.

"I have an idea!" That bold apprentice again. "We can build a statue of Victory to stand next to Athena." Agoracritus looked at Damon with a high eyebrow. "That'll spell it out."

"We don't have enough space," Phidias said. To gauge the ultimate impact of the gold and ivory Athena, Phidias had built his workshop to be equal in size and proportions to the planned interior of the Parthenon. Now his long, bamboo jointed arms took in the full sweep.

"And a second statue would draw attention away from Athena," Pericles said.

Aspasia loved the silver mirror that he'd given her with winged Eros hovering over Aphrodite's shoulder. It would be convenient if she had that mirror with her but . . . "Here's what we can do—we can add a winged Victory as if she were flying above Athena's shoulder—like this." Her long fingers traced an arc over the head and shoulder of a wax Athena—she chose the one that was fully armed to appease Damon since she'd noticed his wince each time she'd said "we."

"Above Athena's shoulders . . . " Phidias eyed the high reaches of his studio. "She'd hit the ceiling."

"Well then, how would *you* include a Victory? Pericles asked.
"In gold."

"Not more gold!" Damon's mouth twitched.

"But waft on us the gift and gain of Victory divine . . . " Phidias went to humming Aeschylus' ode while his eyes tracked the wax Athenas, the kitchen curtain and some fragmentary marble statues leaning against the wall, until his gaze rested on a broken sculpture of a girl stretching her arm forward with a bowl resting on the flat of her hand; once that marble girl had offered the bowl as a gift to a god in a temple. A muscle in his cheek tightened. No one spoke.

This old statue of a girl, broken off below the knees, was propped against the wall like a cripple, Aspasia thought. Her curls coiled like snails' shells—that style was way out of fashion. The statue was as tall as a real girl (if you could put aside that she had no lower legs). Aspasia had seen Phidias drag broken statues like this out of the burned junk left behind by the Persians after they'd devastated the Acropolis. They were extremely heavy and she'd wondered why he bothered.

"Athena can extend her arm like this girl." Phidias swung his arm forward, palm up. "But instead of a bowl, a winged Victory could alight on her palm."

They looked at Phidias' work-roughed palm. Some among them could imagine a delicate, winged female figure perched on it.

"Don't you see—Athena is *offering* us Victory, her greatest gift—not a cup but Victory! The sculptor took a deep breath.

Sophocles broke the silence. "For a man of innovative ideas, it seems conservative for you to turn to an old statue for inspiration."

Was Victory or Wisdom Athena's greatest gift? Pericles had often thought about that question and held it undecided. But he had determined awhile back to encourage Phidias when he became excited because he was seeing beyond what others could see. Pericles rested a hand on Sophocles' shoulder. "My friend, you turn old stories into new plays."

"Just as Phidias will turn an old loss into a new Victory!" Aspasia said. Pericles nodded—she felt they were playing on the same team.

"Agoracritus—" Phidias cocked his head toward the broken marble statue.

The apprentice put his back to the lift to raise the girl.

Upright, she looked almost lifelike.

Damon shook his head. "No city has an Athena hand *holding* Victory in her hand."

"We'll be first," Pericles said.

Phidias squinted as if studying a ship emerging from beyond the horizon.

"The wind blows Victory's silk gown against her body, showing everything underneath that men love to see, like Aspasia's gown."

Phidias sketched the loose edges of the fluttering gown and Victory's wings swept back and upward.

"With the weight of a gold Victory on her palm, Athena's arm will break at the wrist." Agoracritus still held the marble girl against his back.

"No, a break would come at the elbow. But I'll support the arm with an interior iron rod."

"Inner strength," Anaxagoras said.

Phidias was raising chalk dust scoring new lines over old ones.

"Victory is our gift to Athena and she's Athena's gift to us." Pericles stroked his beard. "I like things that work two ways."

"And we're repaying Athena with interest because Victory is priceless," Aspasia said.

Pericles' smile was exciting.

"Women know nothing of interest," Damon said.

"Aspasia, you're perfect for Victory," Phidias said. "You can be my model."

She thought she'd be good for Victory. She'd had several herself. That she was standing here in an embroidered gown, conversing among the most powerful men of the most powerful city had to be counted a victory. And what's more they—some of them—listened to what she said. She'd moved on from being with a sculptor who worked for pay to a man who referred easily to "my country estate" (a voice inside her head whispered "partial victory"). She had an old woman to puff along behind her—that was a victory, though not one Phidias would include in a statue.

Leaving Phidias sketching, they crossed to the old Athena temple which was also a shrine to an ancient king, Erechtheus. It was the singed building that Silky had spotted when they'd come together to the Acropolis. The passage through the inner door and down the stairs was so narrow, Zoe couldn't make it and waited outside. It took time to recognize the olive wood Athena, stained from smoke. Her feet were shiny toeless lumps, her gown frayed by the fingers of reaching worshippers—no wonder she needed a new gown every four years. The wood had cracked along the grain in imitation of the cheeks of an old lady.

"Here, Aspasia, is Athena of the City." Pericles knew he'd get a response he'd enjoy.

"What city?"

"Athens," Sophocles said. "We love her. When the Persians came, she led us to safety."

We. Us. Not her. "Well, then, when Phidias finishes the new one in gold and ivory, *we* can give this one a proper burial," Aspasia said.

"Her priest, Dracontides, fought as hard as Thucydides against funding for the new Athena," Damon said. "For Dracontides, *this* is the real Athena."

Which *was* the real Athena? There was the large bronze Athena outside, the wax Athenas in the workshop, including the one in the corner like herself—and she was no goddess, no matter what pleasure it gave Pericles to say she was. Other cities had different Athenas, and Athena lived in all their temples, and up on Mount Olympus, and don't forget the new one they were building here in gold and ivory for the Parthenon.

"What does Athena really look like?" Aspasia asked.

"I'm sure she looks different to different people," Sophocles said.

Aspasia's hand went to her chin. "Homer says she has gray eyes. If we saw her, would we see her gray eyes?"

"Athena's Greek so I doubt it," Damon said.

"According to the philosopher Xenophanes, the Ethiopians think the gods are broad-nosed and black, and the Thracians say they have blue eyes and red hair," Sophocles said.

Anaxagoras rubbed Athena's worn-down toes. "Don't forget, Xenophanes *also* thought that if cattle and horses had hands and could draw, horses would draw the gods looking like horses, and cattle like cattle."

"He didn't mean that about the animals. He was just trying to make a point," Aspasia said. "But among men, which have the right idea about how the gods really look—us? the Ethiopians? the Thracians?"

"These aren't the right questions. Broad noses? Red hair? How would the gods seem to us?" With his right hand, and then his left, Anaxagoras brushed powdery stone dust off his shoulders. "The real questions are about being, not seeming."

She felt her face flush. Would Pericles think her a foolish woman, concerned only with appearances? She must try not to blurt everything in her head.

"'No man knows, or ever will know, the truth about the gods.'" Sophocles sought to calm the controversy with another of the philosopher's saying.

Aspasia knew her Xenophanes. "'But by seeking men find out better in time.'" So much for her resolve not to talk so much.

"One thing *is* certain: our Athena won't be made by a cow or a Thracian or an Ethiopian, but by a Greek who surpasses all others in creating images of the gods," Pericles said.

At a stony stretch on the way down, Pericles slipped his palm under her elbow. She caught her breath—it was just as he had taken his wife's elbow at Cleinias' burial. That was at an official event. Still, this was in sight of others. As Silky would say, "At least that's something."

Later, reflecting on the day, she recalled her father telling her about the Babylonians climbing their sacred mountain. They met their immortal gods on top, or so they claimed. She'd climbed up to the Acropolis a few times now and had found several Athenas, but none was the real one. Mainly there were mortals doing things in the best way they could.

CHAPTER 10

More Beautiful than the Fleet

Mathematics can be difficult. Money, for instance: this times that minus this plus that divided by something else equals—nobody knows but the shopkeeper. Ictinus needed so much time to calculate the measurements of the Parthenon and now the Temple of Mysteries he was building, way outside of Athens, that Silky rarely saw him.

But some mathematical questions are easy. Athens sends two generals to fight in Boeotia. Two are killed. How many come home?

Early that summer, a new rebellion arose, this time close to Athens and on an island, and Aspasia felt Pericles slipping from her fingers.

For all that pain it had cost Athens, Aspasia had been uncertain about the specific location of Boeotia, but a brutal geography lesson had taught her that Euboea was the island north of Attica—the pirate ship she'd escaped had made port in three Euboean cities. Until recently, the Euboean cities were democracies, friendly to Athens and members of the Athenian defensive alliance—just as all the world should be, according to Pericles. But the Euboean oligarchs had thrown out their democracies and were in rebellion against Athens. Aspasia knew that Pericles wouldn't sit this one out.

"Our policy abroad rests on two columns, our sea empire and democracy," Pericles told the Assembly. Thucydides retorted, "This rebellion is the earthquake Poseidon sent to shake down your columns," but on this issue his was a voice in the wind. Pericles' prestige was at its height because everyone recognized he'd been right about Boeotia. And Athenians had close ties with Euboea—only a narrow strait separated the island from Athens and the surrounding Athenian countryside called Attica and many Athenians summered their flocks on Euboea. The Assembly handed over to General Pericles supreme command of military operations, and he called up seven regiments.

Considering what she was up against, Aspasia had done well in Athens but that was largely because of Pericles. What he admired in her wouldn't pull in most men. She was too tall. She passed her finger over her nose—the bump was still there. He thought she was lovely but so did her father. If Pericles was killed, who would take care of her? And how would she complete the plan that had come to her mind that moment at Cleinias' burial when Aspasia had seen Pericles cup his palm under his wife's elbow? She had never confided her plan but kept it close to her heart, like a treasure. Also . . . Pericles said the Athenians had become used to grazing their flocks in Euboea in the summer. Well, she had become used to him thinking that everything about her was, somehow . . . beautiful.

Her fear that her general might be killed led her to do something that she despised in others: she asked questions to which she already knew the answers.

She said to him, as casually as she could, "You were so cautious about Boeotia. Why are you so determined to crush this rebellion in Euboea?"

"*Alpha*, it's essential that we support the democrats. *Beta*, our destiny is a sea empire. Euboea is an island. It's obvious."

Obvious. That hurt. But it didn't stop her from pushing.

"You're so powerful in Athens, why do you have to go yourself?"

"Obviously, controlling Euboea is too important for me to risk sending anyone else."

"Then why not take all ten regiments?"

"I need three to cover the south. I want to move from a consolidated base."

"If ten regiments go out, how will Athens be protected?"

"You ask questions like Deinomache." That put an end to them.

Did he see her as some crazy leaf in the wind like Cleinias' widow?

"I appreciate your concern for my safety." He sounded sorry for having spoken roughly. "Now I have a question for you. How long do you think I could maintain power in Athens if I was unwilling to lead the army?"

"But you gave them the right advice about Boeotia so—"

"That was yesterday, Aspasia."

"You do more than lead the army so I thought—"

"Nothing would play more into my enemies' hands than for me to set myself above the laws. A general holds the most important elected position in the city. What do generals do? Win battles, by land and by sea."

"They do other things. You—"

"I don't seek war, but I must fight to maintain power. In that, I'm like my city."

* * *

What fish, what meat, what fruit, what sweet, was good enough to be the last they might ever share? She bought a fish, then gave it to Zoe when she saw a better one. She gave that one to Euangelus and bought both quail and lamb.

From a packet of diplomatic correspondence and gifts from Persia, Pericles had selected rare yellow silk and asked her to wear it. Persia lacked democracy, but what a piece of cloth! Each thread was thinner but stronger than linen, or even Egyptian cotton—checked against her sun umbrella. Better than outlining a woman's shape like some drawing on a cheap drinking cup, the silk lay against the skin as if wet. The Milesians worked fabric well, but they had nothing like this. While she was arranging her belt around the clinging silk, a sealed jug of imported wine arrived as well as a package with instructions written in his own hand not to open it before he arrived.

When everything was prepared, she settled her hands on her lap. They trembled. Steadying them, she vowed not to reveal her anguish, in words or any other way. It was tempting but useless, or, as she reminded herself several times, worse than useless considering his pride and satisfaction at having gained full command.

During dinner, she moved slowly so as not to be surprised by any gesture or turn of phrase into showing her fear. He took her deliberateness in mixing the wine and water as special grace, and said she was beautiful in her yellow silk gown.

"You've given me many gifts and now I have one for you."

"Aspasia, a woman doesn't . . . "

She touched his lips with her finger to quiet him.

With an arm around her shoulders, he took a long time undoing the winding ribbon with his free hand and opening the small package. Together they bent their heads over the gift—a gold signet ring. He raised it to his eyes and examined the picture on the seal. Then, unwilling to release her, he brought her and the ring closer to the lamp. He saw Athena—*his* Athena—with her shield, spear, and helmet, and with a winged Victory alighting onto her hand. "Athena's gift," he murmured. The picture was engraved into the gold so that, when he concluded a message, he could press the ring onto sealing wax, leaving the tiny, raised sculpture of Athena and Victory as his seal. He rotated the ring to catch the light. He could see individual feathers in Victory's gold wings. It was, in perfect miniature, the Athena not yet completed for the Parthenon. Aspasia had found a way to give it to him early.

"Phidias must have made this."

"He did but I told him what I wanted on it." It was kind of Phidias to have come up with that bit of gold for her.

"It fills me with delight—and will help me wait until the large one is completed."

She knew the beauty of the workmanship would delight him—how could it not? But part of the gift—a mind part, as she thought of it—was how she'd arrived at the idea.

"I wanted it to be something small you could keep with you. Also, I figured that on campaign you'd be busy fighting or planning or arranging things so I asked myself, what could make you happy at a fast glance? Something having to do with the city. You're excited about all that's being built on the Acropolis and this little seal, since it pictures an important part, will bring the whole to you."

"It will."

"That's one reason I thought of it. But here's another. Sometimes you call me Athena, so in a way I'll be with you."

He closed his eyes, then opened them—trying out his imagination, she guessed.

"Aspasia, you've created magic. I'll be far from everything I most love, yet I will have everything I most love near me."

She caught his hand before he could slip the ring on his finger.

"Some Athenians say wearing a ring on one's finger is too Persian."

He appreciated her tact.

She strung the ring on a ribbon, lifted it over his head and guided it to the center of his chest.

After a few moments, he asked, "Aren't you curious about what I have for you?"

"Of course!" Admiring the ring, she'd forgotten to think of that.

Within the folds of the linen wrapping was a pendant of jasper with a picture carved into the yellow stone. A lean Odysseus, wearing a traveler's cloak and hat, stood in a deserted place—one small palm tree told you that—his foot up on a rock, his elbow on his bent knee, his chin resting thoughtfully on a tripod of fingers. He gazed seaward. She saw a whole world in it and yet, when she felt the slippery stone, the tip of her finger covered the picture. Pericles told her that the artist was from the island of Chios—that explained the Chian wine, sent in honor of their loyal island allies. Arching white lines ran across the yellow jasper, Odysseus and all, like waves in the sea.

He placed the pendant around her neck. "I will long to return to you as Odysseus longed for home."

He asked her to make him a promise.

Thanks to Athena it was he, not she, who was driven to seek a promise. It had taken self-control.

"I promise without even knowing what it is."

What had she said—asking for trouble, like something out of Aesop's stories? Where had her self-control gone?

"I don't know how long I'll be in Euboea. Probably weeks but perhaps months."

Would this be a promise she could keep?

"I will leave you money to cover your living and what you pay Hippodamus in rent, enough for six months even though it's not our custom to continue a campaign into winter."

She'd expected he'd do that but—thanks to Hera!

"But first, I want you to swear something to me."

Her heart shook. Was he going to make her his very own?

"I want you to swear by the god of the hearth that you will not return to Miletus while I'm away on the Euboean campaign and that you'll stay in Athens."

It was not what she'd hoped to hear. *By the god of the hearth . . .* that had a nice urgency to it but . . . *stay in Athens.* That was not equal to making her his very own, was it? No, it wasn't. He only wanted her to be available when he came back. And she had to stay in Athens. Was this a fair promise?

He was waiting for an answer.

"You certainly do like to move from a consolidated base."

He smiled but pressed the issue. "Then swear."

On the other hand, she had no intention of returning to Miletus. And Pericles had surprised her at every turn. "I swear."

"Say it all."

Still, she felt like holding back. She hoped he wouldn't notice. "I swear by the god of the hearth that I won't return to Miletus while you're away on the Euboean campaign."

He thought she understood him and agreed. But like any man around the law courts, he'd heard words uttered that let a person be true while being false. "Aspasia, I want to hear you say, *and I will remain in Athens.*"

His insistence reached her. Her finger circled the pendant he had given her with Odysseus longing to return. He hadn't said all she wanted but he was already planning his return, to her.

"And I will remain in Athens."

He held her at arm's length, gazing at her, at the saffron-colored gown and the jasper pendant. And then, in a soft voice, he sang,

> Some say a cavalry corps,
> some infantry, some, again
> will maintain that the swift oars

of our fleet are the finest
sight on dark earth; but I say
that whatever one loves, is.

The general singing a love song to her. She drew close, rested her head against his shoulder, reached up and stroked his curly beard. It felt softer than the silk.

He touched her breast, touched her waist, and raised a finger to her cheek.

Then he was gone.

She looked at the crumpled cushions where they'd sat.

Against those colorful cushions, a gray image arose of crazy Deinomache at Cleinias' burial. Deinomache's agitation wasn't as excessive as she'd thought. Aspasia's hand went to her eyes that were filling with tears.

Stop, Aspasia.

Alpha, he wants you to stay in Athens and, *beta*, even though he's a general, he thinks you're more beautiful than the fleet. Those were better thoughts for the days ahead.

CHAPTER 11

Necessary Expenditures

Thucydides said that rebellion among the Athenian allies was a hydra monster—every time the Athenians chopped off one head, it grew a couple more. Pericles was the only one who could argue against him well on that point.

Or could he?

Here is the urgent dispatch Pericles received on his arrival in Euboea.

> **From the Council of the Athenians**. *Our envoys report that the Boeotian cities and Corinth are urging the oligarchs in Megara to rebel against us, saying they can defeat us just as the Boeotians defeated us last winter, and promising aid in their fight for independence from Athens.*

Rebellion, Pericles thought—without help from Thucydides—was like a hydra. No sooner had he headed north to suppress revolt in Euboea than another rebellion threatened in the south. And in Megara, one of the most valued of Athens' allied cities—so strategically located! Megara sits on the only land bridge between central Greece and the vast land mass of southern Greece, known as the Peloponnese. You can't go by land from south to north, from Sparta to Athens, for instance, without crossing that isthmus. But the Megarian oligarchs hated the democracy the Athenians installed there, and even the democratic-leaning merchants chafed at Athenian port taxes, so to maintain control the Athenians had been forced to set up a garrison at Megara.

As Pericles' army, keen to re-take Euboea, poured down the ships' ladders, Pericles re-read the Council's dispatch. . . . *just as the Boeotians defeated us.* In the distance were the mountains of central Euboea. He took up his stylus to write the Council to send reinforcements to the garrison in Megara. . . . *rise in rebellion against us.* The very day he departed for Euboea, sedition arose in Megara. The timing pointed to a concerted effort by Athens' enemies, which meant that reinforcing the Athenian garrison in Megara might be insufficient. He must tell the Council to send General Andocides and his three regiments directly to Megara . . . though that left Athens undefended . . . but the distances were not great . . .

He checked the Council's dispatch. *Boeotian cities and Corinth* . . . only Athens' commercial rivals were named. Thanks to Zeus there was no mention of Sparta, though the timing . . .

The Athenian Council was debating these same questions when they learned that Megara was in full revolt. The Council sent out General Andocides with his three regiments immediately but they arrived too late—when they reached the gates, they learned the Megarians had massacred the entire Athenian garrison and taken over the city.

Andocides squeezed through a dispatch to Pericles: *Return to Attica with the army immediately. The Spartans*—Spartans! He scanned faster—*are at the isthmus*—The Isthmus! Pericles felt so hurried to get his army back to Attica that he had little patience to read the rest. *They'll re-provision and head toward Athens. We're stuck at Pegae on the coast—thousands of Spartans, their Peloponnesian allies, Megarians, and Boeotians surrounded us and we had to fight our way to this town which is still loyal to Athens, but our enemies hold the plain and our backs are to the sea.*

Attica emptied of its army and Sparta at the isthmus. The worst equation. The enemies had colluded, possibly setting their sights on an invasion of Athens itself—the hubris! Megara and Euboea were as much decoys as rebellions, pulling the army here, pulling the army there, and now Attica was wide open to attack.

While his eyes were still on Andocides' dispatch, the order arrived by fast boat from the Executive Council commanding him to return with his army to meet the Spartan army and their allies at Eleusis. As if he needed an order—he had already set in motion the return of the seven regiments to Attica, ordering essential repairs to be made to the transport ships and the provisioning of his regiments.

But they'd lose Euboea . . .

Hades!

He had to get back here as fast as possible.

His military withdrawal would fire the Euboeans with pride, confidence, and the certainty in the rightness of their cause as much as if they'd beat the Athenians in actual battle. The world at large would believe that Euboea had successfully challenged the Athenian alliance which would encourage other rebellions. The Athenians would look weak, not only to their Greek friends and enemies but to the enemies of all Greeks—the Persians. And when the Athenians returned to reclaim the territory, the Euboeans would be more determined than ever.

How fast could he return to Euboea? What is "as fast as possible" when you're facing the Spartan army? With much unknown, he couldn't predict the outcome of a land battle but there was one certainty: a battle and its aftermath would take time and he had no time to waste to get back to Euboea. Therefore he put his mind to avoiding battle.

* * *

Arriving at a border garrison near Eleusis, Pericles rode out to observe the Spartans from a secure position and to verify the reports of their vast numbers with his own eyes. He took Glaucon and a few bodyguards with him. Glaucon was the smartest young military commander in Pericles' own tribe—his leadership potential was worth developing. The territory was empty of citizens, farm families having fled the Spartans for protection within Athens' walls, taking with them what they needed most and burying valuable goods near their homes for when they returned. From a cautious distance, since Pericles' intent was to avoid any violent encounter that could lead to battle, he and Glaucon caught sight of red Spartan tunics in Athenian yellow fields of grain, a hateful sight that Pericles had never witnessed and would never forget. But he found out what he wanted to know: the Spartans were busy plundering the countryside, their animals were roaming freely and they were not yet preparing to cross the mountains toward Athens.

Glaucon commented, "The Spartans' greed gives us time."

Pericles was startled to hear the exact words that were in his own mind. Quickly he realized Glaucon meant time for Andocides and his men to return to Attica so that their combined regiments could, if necessary, face the Spartans in battle—which was not Pericles' plan. But he had sent a confidential message to the Executive Council and another to his steward Euangelus requesting items from his estate for his comfort in his military tent. He wasn't ready to divulge his plan to Glaucon until he had secured the Council's support and oath of secrecy, and also was certain that Euangelus understood the import of his message, so he just nodded and said, "True."

Since the Athenian commanders and their men believed Pericles was waiting for the arrival of Andocides' regiments so they could meet the Spartans at full strength, they complied with his order to hold to their tents the following day, although a skirmish occurred when Athenian scouts encountered a band of Spartans among the outbuildings of a homestead digging in fresh earth, probably thinking they'd find hidden silver, but the disorganized group fled at the approach of the Athenians.

* * *

Late that afternoon, when Glaucon arrived at Pericles' tent, he was startled by what he saw on entering and his fingers gripped his scabbard. "Why so lavish a military tent, Pericles? Have you gone mad?"

Pericles was startled by Glaucon's insubordination. He was also pleased to see the effect of glowing luxury on the young man, since he had another young man to impress that evening.

"And—" Glaucon swung his dagger toward Euangelus— "what's *he* doing here?" Everyone knew that on campaign, Pericles maintained simple furnishings, but Euangelus had set out a wagonload of fine household goods in the small tent and was perfecting his arrangements, hanging bronze lamps from the posts and setting striped wool cushions on two extra couches. The tent had become as luxuriously outfitted as in a play at the theater when the scene shifts from "Outside the walls of Troy" to "The Palace of King Priam."

Pericles had been uncertain how to broach it. Now he had an easy opening.

"I hope the young Spartan king is as impressed as you are, Glaucon."

Glaucon jerked his head around as if to see the king.

"Not yet but—hear me carefully, Glaucon—he will be here, along—I said listen to me—with his Uncle Cleandridas who advises him."

"Here?"

"Here, in this tent."

Glaucon's eyes circled the rich objects.

"Have you gone Persian, Pericles? Is this some bribery scheme?"

Again Glaucon got the words right, but opposite. Pericles eyed Glaucon's dagger, now pointed at him.

"Not the way you're thinking. *We* are going to offer *them* a sum of money."

Glaucon took his time. "And?"

"They will lead their army out of Attica. They will abandon this invasion. They will retreat to the Peloponnese. And—" he kept on it because he was excited, "—no more red Spartan tunics in Athenian yellow fields."

Glaucon tapped his lips with the flat of his dagger blade. "Why are you sure it will work?"

"We can't be sure but—"

"But if it doesn't work, we're no farther back than we were before we tried!"

Pericles nodded, glad Glaucon had gone from "you" to "we."

"Still . . . money." Glaucon shook his head. "It's not how Achilles fights in Homer's *Iliad*."

It was a relief that that Glaucon had not said more. Another man might have said, "It's shameful," but Pericles had chosen Glaucon for his realism. "Always think in terms of choices, Glaucon. Not Homer. We've dragged seven regiments back from Euboea, weakening our empire. I heard from the Council that they don't know the exact whereabouts of Andocides and his regiments who have encountered delays. I believe they will find their way out but we cannot count on them to fight the Spartans. Which means our seven regiments could confront the largest land army in Greece that would undoubtedly kill many of our men before we prevailed. That is, of course, if we prevailed, because if they prevailed, they would march on Athens and invade the city. Or we could . . . try it this way."

Glaucon nodded, then frowned. "Still, I don't see the glory in it."

"The glory is in saving our city. The glory is in saving Athenian lives. Now put that dagger away, Glaucon."

Pericles was going to add "When you find a greater glory than that, tell me." But he knew when to stop.

"What's my job?"

"To guard the silver when we show it to them." If needed, Glaucon and his dagger would be effective at close quarters. He positioned Glaucon at the entrance to the tent, and they waited for dark.

Pericles had arranged the clandestine meeting with the young king of Sparta and his uncle, with whose family Pericles had ties of guest-friendship going back generations. The two Spartans were certainly assuming that Pericles and the Athenians, with a large part of their army absent, would be making a conciliatory peace offer—a desperate effort to discourage a Spartan attempt to breach the walls of Athens. But Pericles had no conciliation in mind; instead, he had his bloodless solution for warding off the Spartan threat. The young king and his advisor, his Uncle Cleandridas, were in for a surprise: all they had to do was some quick thinking. Wouldn't Aspasia love to serve the wine—but he could not rule out danger, so Euangelus brought in the food, rinsed the fingers of his royal guests, and poured.

King Pleistonax of Sparta had only a light down on his cheeks. If the Spartans really planned to breach the walls and invade the city itself, wouldn't they have sent out the older of their two kings? But beyond guessing intentions, Pericles had seen their army with his own eyes. As he embraced Pleistonax and his uncle and advisor Cleandridas, he felt under his palms the coarse Spartan cloaks.

The boy's face expressed his wonder at Pericles' expensive, colorful, artistic objects. It was like the awe the Athenian soldiers felt when they captured the lavish tent the Persians left behind after the Battle of Marathon. It led them to admire their enemy—which is why he'd adorned his tent.

The large bowl in which Euangelus mixed the wine and water had a picture of the muscular, long-limbed hero Achilles stabbing the Amazon Queen. The young king's eyes fixed on the wound where the dagger plunged half a blade deep into her white breast and her blood, painted red as any Spartan's, spurted out.

"How lifelike."

"It is well painted," Pericles said.

"He's looking down and she's looking up—their eyes meet—they've fallen in love."

"Too late," Cleandridas said.

"You have excellent taste in painting for a young man, Pleistonax," Pericles said. "I'm going to give you this bowl so that when your wine is mixed, you'll remember the long guest-friendship between your family and mine."

"To the friendship of our families . . . What a wonderful cup," Cleandridas said.

"After dinner, I want each of you to keep your silver cup." Never mind pictures—Cleandridas was interested in the metal.

Pleistonax scanned the surroundings. "The base of that bronze lamp looks exactly like lions' paws, and lions are royal animals."

People said Spartans were slow-witted but this boy learned fast. Pericles smiled inwardly. Too bad that he could never tell this story. "You have a discerning eye," he said, but held back on offering the lamp. It had been in his family for generations, and the lamp wasn't going to matter one way or the other.

The mixture Euangelus dipped into their cups from the handsome bowl was ever more of wine and less of water.

"I've never talked to an Athenian before," Pleistonax said.

"You've fought against them, though," his uncle reminded him.

Pleistonax spun the dregs of his cup toward the stand of the bronze lamp—they hit with exactly the strong ping that can win a prize at a symposium. "Just shows, you can fight Athenians one day and drink with them the next."

Euangelus filled his cup.

"It can as easily go the other way," Cleandridas said.

"True, but I understand your nephew," Pericles said. "It's unfortunate that hostilities have driven a wedge between Athens and Sparta. Together we defeated the Persians, the mightiest empire in the world."

Pleistonax took another swallow. "We are the strong yolk-fellows of the Greeks."

"This enmity displeases the gods," Pericles said.

"Then we should come together in the name of peace."

"But to have peace, Athenians must stay out of our allies' territory," Cleandridas said.

"You are in our territory. But I'm sure you'll be leaving soon since it's not the will of the gods for you to remain. You've seen our powerful new fortification walls, you know that our army is a match for yours and that our navy is without equal."

"Boeotia and Euboea are shadowing you like storm clouds," Cleandridas said.

Pericles sipped his wine. "Do the Spartans study Homer as carefully as Athenians?"

"They don't know Homer there," Glaucon said.

"You there—you think we're barbarians?" Pleistonax twisted toward Glaucon, his hand to his dagger's sheath which was empty for the evening. One dagger allowed each side, and Cleandridas had it. "I know the *Iliad* from alpha to omega."

"I'm trying to remember . . . " Pericles said, ". . . near the end of the *Iliad*, what does King Priam pay Achilles in ransom for the body of his son, Hector?"

"Twelve robes, twelve mantles, twelve blankets, and twelve cloaks."

"Excellent! But isn't there something more?"

"Ten talents," Cleandridas said.

"Exactly ten talents of silver," Pericles said.

In the silence, Euangelus' hand hovered between the pitcher and the bowl.

"Ten silver talents." Pericles locked eyes with Uncle Cleandridas.

Glaucon's hand moved a thumb's width nearer to his dagger.

Pericles let a moment pass, then another. The Spartans needed time to set in balance the risks of accepting the offer and the joys of being rich.

Not as much time as he'd expected, though.

"When Priam loads his wagon with the ten talents for Achilles, he's warned that if robbers find out about all that silver, they'll steal it," Pleistonax said.

"It must remain secret," Pericles said.

"We could hide it in a cave like Odysseus!" Pleistonax said.

"Excellent! Alpha to omega on the *Odyssey*, too," Pericles said.

They'd arrived at the sticking point. Homer couldn't help them out here. Pericles knew it. So did Cleandridas who said, "If we return to Sparta without waging war, our countrymen will fault us for missing the opportunity to attack your city."

Cleanridas arose and paced the confines of the tent.

Our countrymen will fault us. Cleandridas had put the possibilities mildly. Prosecute? Fine? Exile? Execute?

Or—since they were high born—they might get away with it.

Cleandridas cleared his throat.

Pericles reminded himself that when his heart pounded loud to his ears, others couldn't hear it.

"You will have to swear to secrecy," Cleandridas said. "That guard by the entrance, too, and the wine-pourer."

"We must all swear to secrecy."

"How do we know such a treasure exists?" Cleandridas asked.

"Examine it." Pericles was so relieved, he almost smiled.

Pericles opened the chests. The Spartans spread out on the Persian carpet ten talents of silver bars of standard weight. Few men ever set eyes on, let alone possessed, ten silver talents. They were on their knees counting them like farmers chasing spilled apricots. Glaucon bent over for a look. Pericles masked his disdain.

They arranged to take a fifth of the silver with them, all they could conceal in a wagon. Another fifth would be delivered when the

Spartans had passed through the isthmus back into the Peloponnese. The largest part would be deposited outside their city in case the Spartans were "suspicious"—as Cleandridas put it to his nephew. They agreed on an abandoned house, situated on property owned by a guest-friend of both their families, in the central Peloponnese, near the coast. Nor in departing did Pleistonax and Cleandridas neglect to relieve their Athenian guest-friend of the wine mixing bowl and the silver cups. It would be known they had dined with Pericles, and gifts would be expected.

Pericles watched them bend their way out through the low opening of the tent. They left without voicing any concern for their allies. They were in too much of a hurry. He was glad he'd held back on the bronze lamp.

"Did you see that king's cloak?" Glaucon asked. "I wouldn't put that cheap wool on my dog."

"The Spartans hold themselves to living simply with everything shared which makes them hungrier for luxury than others." Even as Pericles uttered that common patter about the Spartans, he was thinking that greed was never scarce among men.

"Our squadron leaders train us to take advantage of the enemy's weakness—" Glaucon ticked them off on his fingers—"not enough archers, sick horses, few in number . . . "

"We used the enemy's weakness for our advantage—even if greed isn't on our training list of military weaknesses."

"But to betray their country." Glaucon looked disillusioned, almost as if he had betrayed his country. That's because he was very young.

"They betrayed their country and we saved Athenian lives. Consider, Glaucon, we would have been fighting head on with Spartans. I would say we saved easily . . . " Pericles stroked his beard several times . . . "a hundred lives. We saved our city, and we saved our Athenian empire." He clapped the boy—that is, the young man—on the back. "That was a good night's work, Glaucon."

"But wait—Pericles, how do you think those two will explain their military withdrawal when they get back to Sparta?"

Pericles saw several possibilities—he might go over them with Glaucon on the boat back to the fighting front. "We have no more time to waste on those traitors."

Glaucon raised a firm fist. "Back to Euboea!"

"Immediately."

It was Pericles' habit to enter financial transactions he had made for the city into his account scroll every night before retiring. At the end of the year, a Council committee would examine his financial activities on behalf of Athens, and each item would be scrutinized. Thucydides and his friends would be leaning in, hoping to find an error, zealous to charge him with embezzlement.

That night, he paused over his scroll, searching for a discreet way to enter the evening's business and the disbursement of ten talents of silver. What to write down? Certainly not the fact of it. He had sworn a holy oath of secrecy with the king and his uncle. Nor did he, nor the Council, want hostile powers to come looking for bribes from the large Athenian treasury. Also he was concerned that if word got out fast, his plan wouldn't work. Eventually, he supposed, people would guess, or know. So many people were already in on it—the Executive Council members, Glaucon, Euangelus—though Euangelus would never say a word—and surely the Athenians stationed to guard the Spartans' safe passage were already speaking of nothing else and making good guesses. But—he tapped the stylus to his lips—where the Demos and its audits were concerned, covert fund-handling could be more dangerous than dining with Spartans.

Bending his head to his tablet, he wrote:

To necessary expenditures, ten talents.

The sudden withdrawal of the Spartans made people believe Pericles could do anything. He held the thunderbolt of Zeus in his hand. It seemed to Aspasia, too, that he could do anything. The thought set into motion the spinning behind her breast that, traveling downward, met up with the new warm place. She heard a report that he was coming to Athens before returning to Euboea and could barely wait to tell him that she'd figured out how he'd brought about the Spartan withdrawal. Together they'd rejoice at his cunning and success.

A message arrived. Bouncing on tiptoes, she tore it open. His presence in Athens coincided with his younger son's name day so he would celebrate in the morning with his family and depart for Euboea immediately after. He would see her on his return. *On his return?* Her hand went to her chin. Could he really come to Athens without seeing her? At least briefly? She read the words again. A bolt from Zeus' thunderbolt hit her full square, searing her to ashes the way Zeus' thunderbolt had destroyed his mortal lover, Semele, and burned *her* to ashes.

By noon, Pericles was on his way back to Euboea. And Semele, Aspasia decided, had made one of the stupidest errors of all time. People told the story that when Zeus came to Semele with his thunderbolt, she mistook the god for her husband. Zeus—her husband! Hah! A woman who can't tell the difference between her husband and a god is not intelligent. The Athenians could call Pericles "Zeus" if they wanted. She knew he was a man. And being a man, he might or might not return. *Two generals died last winter in Boeotia—two for two.*

Pericles loved her as strongly as a man could love a woman, or so it seemed, but how strong was that? The flame that shot up like a campfire, brightening their corner of the Greek sea, would slip back to the glow that warms married men and women all their lives. But they wouldn't be married. He seemed not to notice the gossip raised by his enemies about his foreign hetaira—it amazed his friends and made her love him more—but when the physical urgency abated, would he start paying attention to the slurs and ridicule? His reputation was his currency. Damon hounded him like a Fury to push his point that she weakened him politically. She felt sick knowing that Damon was right, and since he was right, Pericles also knew it and in time would act on this knowledge. Wouldn't he?

He might. She felt for the smooth jasper on her chest. "My Odysseus."

Or he might not. Or he might become yet another general killed in battle. And that would put her—whatever the strength of a man's love—back to finding a living.

It was time to set into action the plan that had come to her during the burial of General Cleinias when Pericles took his wife by the arm and gently, she thought, cupped her elbow in his palm. Hippodamus was in Port Piraeus designing a residential district, but nothing stopped him from returning to Athens and setting himself up in his house again any time. He could evict her. Not that it was likely because she'd been paying rent, but that was the point—if she owned the house, she could be the one making money from it, not only now but when she was older and less beautiful. Preparing to depart for Euboea, Pericles had left her with handfuls of money. With that and what she'd saved, she thought she could buy Hippodamus' house. Seen in the right way, it was a necessary expenditure.

CHAPTER 12

Aspasia in Piraeus

Dion was talking about going to Piraeus to order some books from a ship's captain heading for Ionia and Aspasia told him she'd go along—first getting his assurance that this captain was *Greek,* not some barbarian thief like the one who'd brought her here. A perfect opportunity—she'd go to Piraeus with Dion and see how he managed his business *and* she'd meet up with Hippodamus at his inn and offer to buy his house. Two purposes for one trip—Pericles would like that. But he wasn't here to know it. He might not even live to know about that, or anything else.

Her mind sprang too fast to what Pericles would like. She should start practicing not to drift to that thought so readily, so she picked up her mirror. Seeing her own pretty face, she wondered again how he could have left without seeing her but, speaking into the mirror, she firmly told herself what she intended: *I have two good purposes for one trip, to learn about business and buy my house.*

She saw her plan as clearly as the path between home and the Agora and she was in a hurry, but Dion wouldn't leave until the next Assembly Day when the Agora would be empty and nobody would be buying books. That was lesson number one in how he managed his business. But to push forward on her plan, she bought for the smallest coin, an obol—Dion was always considerate—a blank scroll to list the contents of Hippodamus' house.

Silky couldn't call out how many cups were on a high shelf or how many blankets. She hadn't used her tricks—purposely, Aspasia

111

suspected—and now had been pregnant for some months. She couldn't reach or bend, in fact, she was useless. But Silky was also finding it hard to wait and having something to do might help her forget her discomfort. And Aspasia wanted someone to talk to and was curious how Ictinus felt about the baby.

Aspasia set out the mirror, earrings, arm bracelets, necklaces, and other jewelry, and took off her jasper pendant to count that, too. No, she would not sell the silver mirror with Aphrodite and Eros. It had inspired Phidias in his design for the gold and ivory Athena! She held the earrings to her ears. No. She would not sell Pericles' gifts. But she wanted a complete list. What exactly did she own?

Silky looked over the array. "How lucky you are to have the love of a great man."

"You're lucky, too. Ictinus is an excellent architect, and the city pays him well."

"I don't have that much jewelry."

"You may be luckier than me in one way."

"Oh, Aspasia, you could have a baby if you wanted one."

"Anyone can have a baby. But *you* have a man without a wife who says he'll marry you."

Silky drew her scarf across her face, but Aspasia saw she was hiding her smile out of kindness.

"Maybe you can find a man without a wife in Athens—"

Silky was so hopeful Aspasia felt sorry for her. She was a fool to think Ictinus would marry her, or he was the fool. If an Athenian man married a foreign woman, his children could not be citizens—that was the law. And why would any man lucky enough to be Athenian want to raise non-citizen children? Anyhow, she'd noticed Ictinus had been out of town a lot recently.

"They discourage Athenians from marrying women from other cities."

"Or—" Silky's eyes brightened. "You could go back to Miletus."

"I'll tell you what we'll do, Silky. I'll go back to Miletus and you go back to Megara."

"You know I couldn't go back now. Everybody would say . . . you know."

Aspasia watched Silky finger the edge of the scarf. "Do you think it would be different for me?"

"That's what I mean about a husband." It was hard not to love Silky when her blue eyes widened earnestly—Ictinus might follow through after all. "I'll have my own family and be out of the business. You should think about it too, and not let all this"—she circled her wrist—"all this Pericles be in the way." She ran one of Aspasia's bracelets up her own arm. "You already have enough things for a dowry—a smallish one."

"Anyway, I can't possibly go back to Miletus now. Pericles made me swear by the god of the hearth that I wouldn't leave Athens while he was away."

Silky looked impressed. "Well, at least that's something."

Aspasia took up her blank scroll and marked headings "Aspasia" and "Hippodamus" at the top. The lamps had always been there and belonged to Hippodamus, but the new couch and clothes chest went under "Aspasia." She and Silky discussed whether they should list under "Hippodamus" the floor mosaic in the andron with the spiral design and decided that it was part of the house.

Aspasia handed Silky a large cup. "Look what this cup does."

Silky peered in. "There's just a naked girl at the bottom."

Aspasia poured a measure of wine and water into the cup. "Do you still see the girl?"

"No."

"Now drink and turn the cup around. What do you see?

"The girl."

Silky just didn't catch on to things. Aspasia snatched the cup and took a sip. "Now look, Silky. We've gotten near the bottom and when I swirl the wine around her, the girl swims."

Silky shook her head. "Girls don't swim."

Aspasia swam—that's how she got here. "I had this cup made for Pericles. They painted it the way I told them."

Silky patted Aspasia's arm. "It's OK, Aspasia. He's very smart. He probably sees the girl swimming."

"Anyhow, I'm not going to squeeze in a *Pericles* column just so he can have this cup. I'm putting it under *Aspasia*."

Silky frowned. "Why have you been so annoyed with Pericles lately?"

If she told Silky she was angry at Pericles because he left without seeing her, Silky would be shocked. She'd say, "That's silly, Aspasia. He had to lead the army." Or she might say, "Be careful, Aspasia."

She let it go with, "I'm tired of doing everything on my own," something Silky would understand.

Pushed to the back of a top shelf was a cup with the words "I belong to Hippodamus" scratched on it the way workmen scratch their names on cups they bring to a worksite. She blew off the dust. Hippodamus wasn't a bad man. He always wanted money from her, but he'd been hospitable when she needed help. Still, she didn't want his name on things here.

"We don't need to list this. I'll bring it to him in Piraeus."

"Piraeus—? But you said Pericles made you swear you wouldn't leave Athens."

Aspasia's throat went dry.

"What's wrong, Aspasia?"

What exactly had Pericles tagged on to that oath? *I will remain in Athens.* It was amazing what trouble swearing things about the future could give you. Now, if he'd made her swear *I will remain in Attica* it would be easy—Attica took in the whole Athenian territory, Piraeus included.

"Piraeus is the *port* of Athens, Silky. It's almost the same thing."

Anyhow, all Pericles seemed to care about is that she'd be in Athens on his return.

Aspasia had never been on the Athens-Piraeus road before—she'd gotten to the city through the woods, and half-naked. She was proud of the contrast—she must have done something right! Bumping along in Dion's donkey cart, she watched cubit after cubit of Pericles' handsome, new fortification wall pass by—too bad she had to narrow her nostrils and look high above the clutter at the base of the wall, broken table legs jutting up through filthy blankets, sherds of cooking pots, frayed mats. When the country people who'd taken refuge here from the Spartan invasion returned to their homes, they'd abandoned their junk. If Pericles saw this, he'd get after the road commissioners to clean up the filth.

"Where's their pride and gratitude?" she asked.

Dion kept the cart to the center to avoid the smell.

As they neared the Piraeus waterfront, Aspasia finally dared open her lungs fully to a cool breeze. What a relief—like the deep breaths she took after locking her lungs under water. Walking the cart along the quay, they came to an abrupt halt as Dion struggled with the stubborn donkey. She turned away, resting her arms on a fence.

Past the broad bay was open water. She looked remembering, knowing clearly that there was no Aspasia in those waters swimming and pushed in by the waves but at the same time pleased to imagine she could see a girl's pale length—flickering in the swells, a white oblong moving toward shore. Imagined, but she couldn't take her eyes off her. Water is very continuous, she thought. Some of the low waves lapping this moment against the breakwater could have parted at her stroke back then. In fact, some of the waves may have rolled in all the way from the other side of the Greek sea . . . from Miletus.

An acrid smell pierced her reverie. A sailor coating the hull of the captain's ship with pitch was saying they'd find that captain at The Three Jugs, halfway down the street. For an obol, the sailor watched the cart and donkey.

They knew the place by the sign—three big, round breasts drawn in blue paint.

The bar was dim, hot from the kitchen, and smelled of sausage. The local divinity reigned from above the hearth—a carving of a woman naked to the waist with three big breasts painted blue. The carver must have seen the sculpture in the temple near Miletus of the goddess with a multitude of breasts lined up from neck to waist—Aspasia had seen them with her own eyes and they looked like breasts, no matter what stories about them the guide told visitors. That sculpture was a favorite joke among sailors. Aspasia knew a lot of sailors' jokes.

The captain, greasy bread in hand, waved his girl to the kitchen for more food. She was small-boned, with sharp clavicles and narrow shoulders but her hips and thighs were full. Phoenician? Aspasia wondered. Her straight hair was as black as the raw pitch on the ship and as glossy as the pitch would be when waxed. Or Egyptian? Her complexion was dark but under the nails her fingertips were pink. Probably nineteen—the same age as Aspasia. Like herself, the girl had traveled far.

"Doesn't understand a word of Greek but knows what's wanted."

The captain let the girl serve sausage to Dion and Aspasia, then pulled her to his couch.

What loss had landed her in Piraeus?

Aspasia pushed away her plate. Dion could have her sausage.

"Let's see here." The captain's calloused palm rasped across Dion's list. "Order for books, Ionian philosophers. Hmm . . . Thales . . . Anaximander—try to get one of his maps of the whole earth." The captain looked up. "Did this Anaximander really make a map of the earth?"

Dion nodded. "So they say."

"He did," Aspasia said. Both of those philosophers were from Miletus.

"I could use a map like that," the captain said.

Dion frowned. "Don't charge me for what you keep for yourself."

The captain returned to the list. "Axiochus. Now there's one I never heard of."

Never heard of her father—well, this was a captain who didn't have time for philosophy.

"He didn't write a lot but he was very wise," Dion said. "Bring back any scrolls you can find by Axiochus."

Loyal Dion. She pinched a soft piece of bread from the middle of the loaf.

Back to the list. "Heraclitus—"

"Heraclitus died fairly recently," Aspasia said. "His scrolls should be easy to find." Maybe she should go into the scroll business.

Dion and the captain estimated the cost.

It was a large part of what she'd brought with her.

"And my commission of forty percent," the captain said.

She started to figure the forty percent.

"And I'll need half my estimated commission in advance."

Half ahead of time! Aspasia lost track of her calculation. Why so much in advance? And how to stop the captain from just sailing away with it?

"What if you're robbed by pirates?" Dion said. "What if the ship sinks? I risk losing everything."

"So do I, every time I go out."

The girls, the house and what Silky called "the business" were safer, and she knew a lot about that, too. Silky had been at it a long time and could help her.

* * *

The orderly city plan Hippodamus had created for Piraeus led them right to the inn where he lodged, Mycerinus' Palace. They arrived in daylight but all the lamps were lit—how wasteful. Hippodamus came toward them with a broad smile and open arms.

"How fine you smell, Aspasia." She had rubbed her skin with an imported scent—given the cheap scents he used, it gave her an edge. "The kitchen is working on our supper, a stew of cuttlefish, eel, and sea urchin cooked with leek, parsley, garlic, and anise. I told them how to make it. I sent Hypanis for the sesame cakes."

Hypanis?

"He's Thracian—you'll see. Aspasia, wait for the cakes!" But she was already pulling out her list and the cup with Hippodamus' name on it she'd brought from the house. He was pleased to have the cup.

"But Aspasia—a hundred and sixty drachmas for eight cedar couches? Three bronze braziers, sixty drachmas? You've been taking lessons from that cheating god Hermes. How did you figure these prices?"

"I consulted friends."

Hippodamus laughed. "Who? That girl—what's-her-name —Slimy?"

It was not hard to guess that the boy coming toward them, head held high and with necklaces of blue stones swinging from his chest, was Hypanis. His eyes were blue as the stones. His red hair reflected onto the metal lamps, and as he lowered himself onto the couch, each muscle of his shoulders, belly, loins, and legs cast its own moving shadow. He helped himself to a cake—so did Dion.

But Aspasia and Hippodamus went back to arguing about the prices Aspasia had noted next to each item.

She had written down that she would offer eight hundred drachmas for the house—after all, it was a small house. In addition, she'd go as high as four hundred drachmas for all the furnishings— if he was still a little undecided, at just the right moment she could show him that he'd be getting a little extra above her price list.

"I will tell you seriously, Aspasia." Hippodamus fastened his eyes on hers. "I don't want the house or what's in it."

Dion's sharp elbow hit her ribs in a way she knew meant *Good!—you can offer less.* That was rational, but Hippodamus' hold on her gaze seemed to say that in ceding an easy point, he'd be asking for more.

"In that case, we'll have no trouble settling on a fair price." She tossed in a smile.

"I don't want a fair price."

She was confused, so she waited.

"I want a price that will give me what I want."

Oh. There was no way around it. "What do you want?"

"Hypanis."

"Hypanis!" She looked amazed to please him.

Hypanis' eyes were half closed, his legs draped over the cushions. The hair on his legs was red—she checked. Did he understand Greek?

She lowered her voice. "How much would that take?"

"Two thousand."

"Two thousand drachmas! Who owns him?"

"The owner of this place."

She drew back. "I'm not here to buy Hypanis. I can offer you eight hundred for the house and three hundred for the furnishings— that's well above the sum of the items but there are always little things . . . "

"That's a ridiculously small amount. And his owner doesn't want to sell. Hypanis performs."

"What does he perform?"

Hippodamus raised his forefinger.

Hippodamus' Piraeus stew came from the kitchen, bubbling.

Had Hippodamus planned these interruptions? She was sharing Dion's couch as once she had shared Phidias'. It was comfortable to be at a noisy drinking party again leaning against a man. Pericles didn't waste his time that way. Aspasia tipped her cup. The warmth of Dion's body through her silk gown sped the wine to her fingertips. Boys and girls piped shrill music, their cheeks puffed like owls.

Men costumed as satyrs cartwheeled off the platform as Hypanis, who had left their group, leaped onto it, his necklaces swinging. Now he wore a black wig. To the side, an actor of godly height in his platformed shoes and wearing a king's mask began to speak, his deep voice, silencing the music, the jokes, the seductions, and the business deals.

"At a famous shrine in Egypt," the actor began, "an oracle predicted that King Mycerinus had only six more years to live and would die in the seventh."

"You could do the actor's part," Aspasia whispered to Dion.

"Shh!" Hippodamus glared.

While the actor told the story in words, Hypanis and a dainty girl mimed it in dance. "Anguished at the thought of an early death, Mycerinus grieved for himself." Hypanis sat on the floor in despair, head to knees, covered completely by his cloak.

"Dion," Aspasia whispered, "that's exactly how Achilles grieves when his dearest friend dies."

Dion whispered, "You can't really believe Hypanis knows Homer."

"Shhh," Hippodamus hissed.

"But an idea came to Mycerinus." Hypanis' head emerged from the cloak. "He decided to stay awake night and day for the six years and decreed that all the lamps would burn constantly so there would be no nights, only days. Since he was king, his courtiers had to stay up all the time, too."

"That's why the lamps here are—"

Hippodamus spun around, finger to lips.

"By turning his nights into days, Mycerinus turned his six years into twelve"—Hypanis made an amazing, broad-legged leap in triumph, giving just enough time for a quick glimpse under his kilt, but he didn't do it twice, which was disappointing.

"Mycerinus filled his time with pleasures. He hunted gazelles in the desert and birds in the marshes. He feasted and drank the Egyptian beer." And then—a couch was shoved onto the platform—Hypanis beckoned the girl, who danced toward him with light steps. He drew her onto to his knee and kissed her, filled, it seemed, with physical desire. She covered her face with her forearm. But as his embraces persisted, she too became overwhelmed by desire. She put her arms around his neck, yielding increasingly to his caresses.

It was so like life. Hypanis tenderly lifted the girl and carried her away.

Despite dramatic appearances, however, Aspasia knew Hypanis would be rejoining Hippodamus.

Dion was running the edge of her gown between two fingers. Those who had a companion for love shared the desire they seemed to see in Hypanis and the girl, and the rest looked for a partner for the evening.

How did Mycerinus die? Aspasia tried to recall the end of the story.

"Isn't he a fine dancer?" Hippodamus asked with sure pride.

"Very believable." Hypanis was on his way back. If they didn't settle on a price for the house now, they'd miss their opportunity for the evening. "Hippodamus, I offered you eight hundred for the house and three hundred for the furniture. Accept my offer."

Surprisingly—since Aspasia thought him bewitched by Hypanis—Hippodamus answered in a businesslike tone. "You didn't take into consideration the mosaic in the andron. I had it made for the house, it's the best thing in it and alone is worth eight hundred drachmas."

"It's attached to the floor, it's not something separate to be paid for."

"Then add it to the price for the house, call it what you will, but I want eight hundred drachmas for it."

Hypanis was his new mosaic.

"You don't want eight hundred for the mosaic, you just want two thousand for Hypanis, and it's not worth it.

"But he is."

"I offered you eleven hundred, but the mosaic slipped my mind. I'll make it twelve hundred."

"Two thousand."

She looked at Dion, who shrugged.

"Hippodamus!"

"Two thousand."

"I don't have that, Hippodamus."

"Sell that pretty jasper."

Her fist closed around the pendant on her chest.

"Living at this inn is expensive." Hippodamus sighed. "And tiresome. I might have to return to Athens and take over my house."

Hypanis was crossing the court toward them.

"But we're both from Miletus."

"Two thousand." He smiled—the smile she'd seen when he told a nasty joke.

Dion put his mouth to her ear. "Say you'll give him the twelve hundred, plus thirty-five a month until the difference is made up."

"I never heard of that," she whispered back. It must be some odd way men knew for buying things.

He nodded. "See what he says."

Eight hundred. Divided by . . . "That'll take forever!"

"A couple of years." Dion raised an eyebrow in a way that suggested he thought Pericles might dig her out. "And if he doesn't," Dion spoke as if the unsaid had been said, "you'll have your house anyway."

"More than two years . . . " She put her chin on her hand.

"Anyhow, you said it's for when you're older."

The night was getting away from them, and she and Dion had to leave well before dawn so he could put in a full day selling.

"You sure came up with an unusual arrangement, Hippodamus."

Hippodamus rubbed his chin. He smiled at her—a friendly smile this time. "I hope by the end of it, I'll still want what I want."

"Then we agree?"

Thank the gods, he nodded his assent. Quickly, she extended her hand. He reached across and embraced her.

"One should never bargain with a woman." He sighed like a tragic actor, then smiled with satisfaction and settled back on his cushions as Hypanis returned. The young man had taken off his wig, but his kohl blackened lids made his eyes seem bluer than the gems around his chest.

"Oh, and Aspasia. Don't forget that foreigners aren't permitted, ordinarily, to purchase property in Athens. You'll need a special dispensation to buy a house."

Her heart missed a beat. She looked at Dion, who just shrugged. She looked around the room—was there anyone she knew here? Someone who might know about these dispensations. She turned to Hippodamus. "You should have told me that first."

"Oh, didn't you know? But don't be concerned. Pericles interceded for me. I'm sure he'll do the same for you."

In the small, second-floor room she'd taken for the night, feeling troubled and worried, she asked herself how she had come to depend on Pericles more now instead of less. And if he wouldn't intercede for her . . . well, he would. But not if he didn't come back. Could she find some other general to help her, or somebody else around the law courts? She was spending two thousand drachmas instead of twelve hundred. She'd made a complicated promise she didn't fully understand. Hippodamus should have told her about needing an important Athenian to intercede on the house. And did it make sense that Hippodamus was really planning to own Hypanis? With two years to go?

There was a tapping at her door.

She felt like a fool and now there was Dion at her door, wanting to stay the night.

With all that she'd be paying out, she'd have to cut down her expenses. And she'd been feeling so rich lately.

"Aspasia," Dion called out.

A night's lodging calling at her door.

"Shhh. Wait!"

She could ask him for extra—she'd helped him a lot with the ship's captain through her knowledge of philosophers.

She'd sworn to Pericles that she wouldn't return to Miletus while he was away. If he'd wanted her to promise more than that, wouldn't he have said so?

Or did he mean to leave it up to her? And what did that mean about her place in his life?

"Aspasia."

Pericles meant *this*, he meant *that*. She shook her curls, impatient with herself. There she was again, listening too hard to him.

Seen in the right way, she accomplished exactly what she planned for this trip. *Alpha*, she learned about running a business, more than she expected, and, *beta*, she'd bought a house. Her father would like to know she owned a house, just as they had in Miletus. And her mother . . . Well, her mother died so long ago she might not be able to see—in whatever way the dead can see—all the way to Athens.

Paying out money every month would be difficult, but it was nothing compared to diving down into darkness.

She yawned—and again louder so Dion could hear her through the door. The day had been as jammed full as a Piraeus stew. It was time for her to snuff out the lamp, no matter what some Egyptian king thought about that.

The money would be nice but—

"No," she called out. "I don't want to."

CHAPTER 13

Preparing

Looking down to the mirror, she tipped up her chin and admired the length of her neck. She was a woman who owned a house, almost. No more looking up to a mirror like a round-eyed puppy hoping for a biscuit. As for the legalities of the house—she'd come to feel sure that Pericles would work out the details.

Now that she had her backup plan in place, she saw in another, inward mirror, that she had underestimated the power of Pericles' love for her. How could she have put so much weight on that one time he had disappointed her—with the whole army waiting for him? She felt embarrassed to think of it—she would never tell him. Yes, he would come back to her if he survived. And he would survive because he had gone with a large army, not a pick-up force like they had in Boeotia last year. He would come to her home and embrace her—she was sure it would be his first night back in Athens. She checked the wall of the Altar of the Twelve Gods for official notices, going out early morning so the mid-summer sun, which pressed its light as well as its heat right through her sun umbrella, wouldn't darken her skin. Then she came home to work on her house.

She and Zoe scrubbed the stone floors, whitewashed the clay walls, polished the bronze lamps, scoured the cooking pots, oiled the wood furnishings including her loom upstairs, stuffed the couch cushions with new wool and—the hardest job—dug out the accumulation of ashes and grease in the cooking hearth down to the mud brick which they then cleaned with sand. Aspasia hired a man to repair those wood shutters that needed fixing and reinforce the enclosure in the courtyard around the chickens Zoe kept for eggs. Replacing the tiles on the roof could wait. She did not want to ever do this kind of work again, and when Silky, invited to admire, said, "I wouldn't do that all that scrubbing," Aspasia felt foolish. But who was the fool here? "These things must be taken care of when you own your house—" Aspasia's sweep of her arm took in the first story and the second—"as I do." She hadn't told Silky about the special way she was paying off Hippodamus—Silky wouldn't understand it.

But Silky kindly pretended not to notice Aspasia's short, chipped fingernails and her hands rough at the knuckles from scrubbing with salt and sand. Aspasia guessed she had time to repair that before Pericles' return but he might pull another of his surprises, so she went right to oiling her skin and shaping and buffing her nails—fingers and toes—until they looked like small seashells. She drew her thick hair to the back of her head and tucked it into a little pocket made of colored ribbons, the way the prettiest girls waiting in line at the water fountain were doing, but that made her face look thin. With an eye to the mirror, she pulled several curls forward to bounce around her cheeks. Perfect. Too bad Pericles wasn't here right now!

But he sent a package—she was elated to recognize the tiny image of Athena on Pericles' ring impressed into the seal. The thought of the soft wax and of his hands applying pressure to the ring she'd given him made him seem near. Inside was a length of deep purple cloth colored with the dye made from mollusks from the waters off Euboea, similar to what she'd seen in Ionia—it took a strong diver to reach those depths. Pericles was thinking of her. And how like him to seize an opportunity to obtain something rare and beautiful. Stroking the soft cloth, she remembered his saying that she was rare and beautiful. It was a large piece of cloth and she'd been thinking the chitons she'd been wearing were too girlish for her now, so she made it into a peplos-styled gown that fell to her ankles, with a loose fold flowing from her shoulders to her waist.

Now that she had time, she borrowed scrolls from Dion, usually plays but he also had a small selection of scrolls by philosophers, and she read them aloud to herself on the long afternoons when staying in from the sun. With a man like Pericles, education was as much a preparation for his return as a new hair style. But she loved books before she ever met Pericles.

One long afternoon, she was reading in her chair with the curved back, set to catch the slivers of light through the shutters which had to remain closed because of the heat. "The Ethiopians," she read, "say that their gods are broad-nosed and black, the Thracians that they have blue eyes and red hair . . . " She raised her eyes from Xenophanes, rolled her shoulders and stretched her neck. She already knew Xenophanes from *alpha* to *omega*.

The trouble was that the newest ideas hadn't been written down. Those who originated them spoke them aloud to interested friends. But for her to join a cluster of men under a tree in the Agora, where everybody did their newest talking, would darken her skin. It would be a "never-done-before" for sure, though not one Pericles would like. And, it occurred to her that, as a woman outside among men, she would divert the stream of the conversation, and she didn't want to interfere with what could be the birth of new philosophy. But she was falling behind in new learning.

Setting aside the scroll, she reached down to the floor to snag a piece of purple fuzz that had fallen on her freshly washed mosaic. The black and white curves in the whirling spiral design were dizzying, even in the dim light. It was a clever design for an andron where so much wine was consumed. It prompted intoxication. Looking around the room, her eyes settled on her four newly oiled cedar wood couches.

So she decided to invite Pericles' favorite philosophers to her home—a small symposium evening wouldn't put her out too many drachmas.

Pericles called Anaxagoras "his teacher" so she invited him, and since Pericles spoke highly of Protagoras, he was her second philosopher. She was worried about whether they would accept her invitation. It was bold. She felt an insult might come her way. On the other hand, she thought they might accept because she was connected with Pericles. They might think she could influence him in their favor, for some prize for instance.

Dion laughed when he heard about it and predicted neither of them would accept a dinner invitation from a hetaira, her own concern, but he may have said that because he was unhappy about missing the evening—his father had fallen from a donkey and Dion was leaving shortly to help on the farm, somewhere in northeast Attica. The next day, when he heard they both accepted her invitation, he said philosophers wandered around looking for people to listen to their teachings and were poor so they were probably hungry for a decent dinner. Maybe she and Dion were both right about the reasons the two philosophers were coming since Sophocles the playwright, a rich Athenian with no need to ingratiate himself with Pericles, turned her down. Aspasia thought of inviting Silky but she wasn't well and nobody wants a pregnant hetaira at a symposium. So she filled only three couches, and that with only one person to a couch, but it was a start.

After old Zoe had removed the food, Aspasia had her mix extra water into the wine so the conversation would stay serious. Since it was her house, she decided she could set the topic for the evening: *what is truth?*

"These days," Protagoras began, "it's the fashion to say that humans developed from a wild and savage state to our excellent way of life by acquiring skills—"

That wasn't on the topic but—philosophical inquiry should move freely. "I suppose you mean Prometheus and his gift of fire to men," she said.

Protagoras dismissed Prometheus with a wave of his hand. "Making fire, ploughing fields, smelting bronze, those skills everyone talks about these days—these are not first-rank skills—" He talked through her interruption. "The most important skills are city skills."

That didn't sound like philosophy.

"What's an example of a city skill?" she asked.

"The most important is speaking well in public to persuade others."

How insignificant compared with the philosophy she knew.

"*That's* what's most important?"

"And it doesn't come easily. Children must be educated for it from an early age."

"An early age . . . " Anaxagoras shook his head. "I hope you will give them some vacation time, Protgoras."

"Do *you* think city skills are the most important, Anaxagoras?" she asked.

"They are irrelevant for true understanding."

"Don't feed the girl that nonsense! I know you, Mr. Mind—mind, force of intellect—whatever you care to call it—sitting in one place out there somewhere in the aether contemplating your cosmic vortex."

"What's a cosmic vortex?" she asked.

Anaxagoras raised his teaching finger. "Mind, which is the finest and purest of all things, thrust the cosmos into a rotating motion like a whirlpool, a vortex that is—"

Aspasia looked down at her floor mosaic with its swirling design.

"All he talks about is his so-called vortex which—" Protagoras raised his teaching finger—"nobody's ever seen . . . "

"I'd expect a philosopher such as yourself, Protagoras, to know that Mind is the force of intellect at the heart of the cosmos." Anaxagoras cleared his throat. "As I was saying, Mind began it all with a small rotation but the rotation grows wider and wider still . . . "

". . . and nobody ever will."

Anaxagoras turned toward Aspasia as if speaking only to her. "Just look at the stars and you'll see the great cosmic rotation. Don't take that literally—it's just a glimpse of the obscure but it gives you the idea."

Protagoras shook his head. "This is Mesopotamian nonsense."

"You look puzzled, Aspasia," Anaxagoras said.

"If Mind is the finest and purest substance—"

"Not a substance."

"Oh, no, yes. If Mind is the finest and purest something, I don't see how it can shove anything as large and heavy as the cosmos into motion."

"Mind has all knowledge about everything and the greatest power," Anaxagoras said.

Immediately she thought of Pericles.

"Don't let this graybeard confuse you, Aspasia," Protagoras said. "Mind can only think, it doesn't do. Animals do. And men do even better than animals. Do men have claws, fangs, or outstanding speed, or any of the other means animals have for defending themselves?"

"N—"

"No. But do they survive?"

"Y—"

"Yes, they do. And have they gained mastery over all other species?"

"Yes." You had to answer fast with this philosopher.

He nodded. "And how is that possible?"

"Through their minds." Oh. That was too fast.

Protagoras smacked his forehead. "By cooperating with other men in the crown of human achievement—the city."

She hadn't meant to insult him, so she explained, "Philosophy is different where I come from."

"Miletus, isn't it? Examining nature, truth."

"And the fundamental substance of the cosmos," Aspasia said.

"I recall a recent Milesian philosopher," Protagoras said. "Axiochus—he thought water was the fundamental substance, I believe."

Aspasia had not felt such joy since—she ran through her best memories—*Pericles said he was glad she'd come to Athens.* She took a breath to maintain her composure.

"Axiochus of Miletus was my father."

"Your father. No wonder you have a reputation for asking questions." A better reputation than some she'd heard about.

After they'd left, Aspasia gazed down at her swirling mosaic. What artist had put together all those small stones into this fine design? Had he glimpsed the cosmic vortex? Or had he just seen a whirlpool somewhere? It must have been difficult to find so many stones, near to the same size and all totally black or totally white. "The best thing in the house . . . " Hippodamus said. It was hard to know why but, following the spirals with a turn of her head, she felt that the high value Hippodamus had placed on the mosaic was not unreasonable. It was a glimpse of . . . something important.

Slowly, without noticing what she was doing, she fluffed the cushions on the three couches. Protagoras hadn't persuaded her that city skills were a lofty philosophical inquiry, although speaking well in public was definitely useful—look at Pericles. But Anaxagoras' idea that there is thought or the force of intellect, he called it Mind, that set the cosmos in motion—that caused you to take a deep breath, stretch and look upward, like starting off the morning. While looking upward, it came to her—with a spin—why Pericles was so important to his city. He had a greater measure of mind than most men, *and* a greater measure of the ability to persuade others. The combination was unique—at least she couldn't think of anybody else like him in that. She couldn't wait to tell him.

Or else he knew and that's why they were his favorite philosophers.

Aspasia went to Rhodia's to show Silky her purple peplos and found her friend lying alone in her darkened room. Ictinus, busy with construction on the new Hall of Mysteries at Eleusis in the far western end of Attica, had not been to see her for weeks. Aspasia felt sorry for her. Silky had always been generous and done whatever Aspasia wanted—she especially remembered the loan of the high-soled sandals. It would be pleasant to have company during the long days indoors, and Rhodia was glad not to have to bother with Silky's pregnancy and to have one less mouth to feed.

At Aspasia's house, Silky spent much of her time resting on a couch, but they ate meals together and, when Silky was up to it, wove on the loom, taking turns guiding the shuttle and pushing each newly laid thread tight with the rest, and talking about their experiences and hopes. It was the first time since leaving Miletus that Aspasia felt she was in a real household, like a family. When news came that some Euboeans had captured and killed the crew of an Athenian warship, Silky shared Aspasia's fears, and when it turned out that Pericles was elsewhere and out of danger, she shared her joy. Or at least seemed to; you never can be sure how much someone else shares your joy.

One night, Aspasia heard scratching at her door. Was it Pericles? In the dark, her heart pounding with excitement, the objects around her coming into view, she realized that even if Pericles did find himself in Athens unexpectedly, he would have the old woman awaken her. Nor was it Zoe at the door, but Silky, hunched over in pain. She was ahead of her time—not surprising, given her size.

Calling out to Zoe, Aspasia helped Silky down the stairs and to a chair in the andron to be near the kitchen for heating water—she knew that much. With each pain, Silky squeezed Aspasia's and Zoe's hands. In between, they sponged perspiration from Silky's face and body and calculated many times over how far along in months the baby was and whether it had spent enough time in the womb to survive. Their best guess was it had.

The waters broke around noon. Late in the afternoon the pains came closer together and, judging from Silky's moans, had intensified, but Zoe assured Aspasia that everything was happening as it should. Now Zoe had Silky kneel on a stool and grasp the door frame while Aspasia supported her, and with each moan, Zoe urged Silky to push the baby out. Aspasia joined in, and they sounded as if they were cheering a runner at the games. When the head appeared, Zoe became excited and positioned herself to catch the baby. After one powerful push—surprising Silky still had that much strength— the rest of the baby sped out as if from a jug of bubbled wine. Zoe slapped the baby, who uttered a cry. Quickly she bit off the cord and tied it. Aspasia helped Silky to the couch. All their faces were wet with perspiration and tears of excitement.

Aspasia supported Silky's head and gave her a sip of wine.

"What is it?" Silky asked.

Zoe was sponging the baby. "It's a little boy."

"A boy, how wonderful! Let me see."

"Just a minute."

"*Before* you wrap him up." She raised herself onto her elbow. Her large eyes filled again, now with tears of sorrow.

"What's wrong with his foot?"

Aspasia peered over to look. The foot was twisted so that it looked upside down.

Zoe pressed her thumb into the arch.

"It's a little curved."

Silky brought her eyes near the foot as if she were reading a small script in a dim light.

"He won't walk right."

"He'll walk well enough." Zoe stroked Silky's hair.

He would shuffle along, his leg curved, his foot sideways. Aspasia averted her eyes from the image in her mind.

Silky pressed her palms together as if asking for a favor.

"Why did that happen?"

"Nobody knows." Zoe bent kindly to lay the baby across Silky's chest.

But Silky closed her eyes and pushed away the arms of the old woman that held the clean, wrapped, tiny baby.

When Zoe pressed the baby to Silky's cheek, she averted her head. She would not look at the baby and, despite Zoe's perseverance, would not hold it. Zoe walked around the room with the sleeping baby in her arms, watching the regular expansion of its nostrils, a movement so slight Aspasia would not have noticed it had Zoe not pointed it out. When the muscles of the baby's face became taut and its skin grew purple, Zoe joggled it back to sleep.

Aspasia sat down next to Silky and took her hand.

"Should I send for Ictinus?"

Silky shook her head. "Not until I'm beautiful again."

"But he'll want to know about the birth."

"He won't want to know about a baby with a bad foot."

"But if he saw the little baby and knew it was his—"

"He would say it *wasn't* his. I have to get rid of it or Ictinus definitely won't marry me."

Aspasia paused. "Perhaps he won't marry you anyway."

"I know." Aspasia was surprised at her ready agreement. "But I won't let a baby with a crooked foot ruin the chance that he might."

"But if he doesn't marry you in any case, it would be too late. The baby—you'd have already left your baby out there."

"Why raise a wrong baby?"

How wrong was it? "Zoe, let me see the foot," Aspasia said. Zoe eased the baby's leg from the linen. The foot curved inward and upward. The heel was on sideways. An unpleasant shiver went through Aspasia's breasts and shoulders. She didn't want to touch that foot. But it was right to try to fix it. It seemed one could just turn it. She reached out, touched the instep, then firmly grasped the tiny foot to twist it to where it belonged. Tiny, but it wouldn't move. Tough, as if it thought it belonged where it was. Screwed on wrong.

Pressing sideways and downward against the foot, Aspasia thought that Pericles' mother. Agariste would have kept the defective baby—the proof was Pericles.

But all Agariste had to do was face down her husband.

Unlike Agariste, Silky didn't come with a dowry.

Silky's life was hard. She didn't deserve the added burden of raising a baby who'd never be normal.

And why should the baby have to live with that burden? Did Agariste ask herself that question when she first looked at Pericles' swollen head? Had she averted her eyes? Not wanted to touch?

Questions, questions but the fact was Agariste protected his life. And Pericles had grown up to be not just a man, like his brother, but the leader of the Athenians.

With the little foot in her hand, Aspasia decided that to get rid of a baby was hubris because it implied an ability to predict the future. How ironic, Silky was the last person one would expect to act with hubris—how easily it can slip up on anyone. She explained to Silky that the outcome of her life was not known. Even with the child, she might marry Ictinus, or if not him then someone else. Or, having been born unlucky, the boy might come on some good luck. He wasn't headed for the Olympics, but how many men are? He might become a great leader instead—well, not without citizenship. But at least he might be able to take care of his mother in her old age.

Silky shook her head.

A fine idea came to Aspasia. "Hephaistos is an artist among the gods, and he has a misshaped foot. Ictinus is an artist, so he might want his son to become an artist."

"That was an injury. He wasn't *born* that way."

She urged Silky to at least send a message notifying Ictinus of the baby's birth and decide what to do depending on what he said, but Silky was sure that her best course was to rid herself of the baby and as quickly as possible restore herself to the way she was when Ictinus first loved her.

Aspasia sighed. To be certain of what's best for someone else is also hubris. Look how hard it is to be sure of what's best for oneself.

When it was dark, Silky asked Zoe to dress the baby in fresh linen. As Zoe wound the strip around the small form, Silky rolled a bronze bracelet from her arm and approached the baby for the first time to slip it between the turns of the cloth. Then she picked up the swaddled infant and left the house, taking with her a round clay pot, intact except for a chip along the edge of the lip. The pot would enclose the child and protect it for a little while. It would buy the child time, as Pericles had bought time for the Athenians by paying off the Spartans. They knew she'd leave the baby behind a rock or shrub on the far side of the river, near the old cemetery and the precinct of Heracles. After all, Heracles was born out of wedlock, and he became a god. Someone who wanted a child—even an odd one—might hear it crying and take it home.

Silky returned exhausted and passed the next several days without moving from her couch. She wanted to stay with Aspasia as long as she could so they didn't tell Rhodia. Since the pregnancy had ended early, Rhodia would think nothing of it if she didn't see Silky for a while. When she was stronger and her complexion less pale, they sent a message to Ictinus at Eleusis, telling him that the baby had come stillborn.

CHAPTER 14

A Moderate Course

Pericles knew well the exhilaration of military victory. In the years after the Persian wars, he had sailed under General Cimon, liberating Greek towns in Asia Minor from Persian garrisons, rooting out pirates, and—once they began—quelling rebellions among Athenian allies that balked at sending in their tribute. The Athenians had often placed him in command—the first time when he turned thirty, the youngest age at which one could be elected general. He'd fight when it was necessary, and with outstanding physical bravery. But he'd polished to a shine the impressive show of Athenian strength as an instrument of policy, and that was often all it took to achieve a military objective—he had taken Achaea that way—and the Assembly was as gratified as he at the Athenian lives saved.

Now he sat at his little writing table in the stern of the state ship, *Paralus*, drafting peace terms for the conquered Euboean cities. The reduction of Euboea that summer was among his greatest military triumphs. It was of critical importance, it was complete, and it was fast—the entire island pacified within a few weeks. His victory stood out like a sculpture carved in high relief against a sunken background of recent defeats: Boeotia (Pericles opposed that campaign), Megara, and the Spartan invasion of Athens (when Pericles rescued everyone by his "necessary expenditures").

Aspasia would say *good for Pericles though bad for Athens* except that she'd learned to hold her tongue on that disturbing contrast.

But Sparta, Sparta, Sparta. Pericles punched fist to palm three times. Rebellions among Athens' allies had become more frequent, all backed by Sparta. He—like all Athenians—was cloaked with the horror of the Sparta's near-invasion of Athens and the dread that it might happen again. How could he bridle the Spartans who commanded the strongest land army in Greece?

How could he get this clinging tiger off his back?

The answer was not military. Athens must sign a peace treaty with Sparta. Yes, a peace treaty with her greatest enemy. After their success in Euboea, the Athenians wouldn't be in the mood to hear it or think about making concessions, but he'd just led them to victory, so they'd listen. It would take time, however, to persuade the Athenians, elated by victory, that signing a peace treaty with the hated Spartans was the only reasonable thing to do.

To the more immediate matter, and a step in the direction of the Spartan peace treaty, he had also concluded that moderation was essential in dealing with the vanquished Euboean cities—except, of course, for Histiaia that had massacred an entire Athenian crew. The goal was not to wipe out the Euboeans but to keep them importing Athenian goods, providing Athens with grazing grounds and sending Athens the agricultural products she needed. The Euboeans must remain in the empire—yes, to count as allies. As an island, Euboea *belonged* in the Athenian Empire.

Opposite those seeking to punish and oppress Euboea, he'd have to face down Thucydides and his "Little Athenians" who'd be clamoring to relinquish their costly and hard-won control over the island—just give it up. Absurd.

Helmsman that he was, he would steer the course between Scylla's rock and the whirlpool of Charybdis—"My Odysseus," Aspasia would say. His thumb circled the engraved seal she'd given him. Images of her were woven through his thoughts like a bright ribbon in a girl's hair.

During the summer, with the benefit of objectivity offered by their separation, he had also worked out an agreeably moderate course regarding Aspasia. While no action was necessary, he was not at ease with their present arrangement. In fact, he felt nervous about it. No doubt his importance had a powerful hold on her, she loved him, and he took good care of her. But—he winced every time the thought pushed in—there was nothing to stop her from going to another man.

He was not the only wealthy, distinguished man in Athens. Perhaps none possessed all the qualities she admired in him, as she told him often, but everyone knew that a woman's deepest desire was to marry. If someone free to marry her came around, wouldn't that compensate for any qualities he might lack? Someone younger? More . . . well, call it handsome? Pericles looked for but found little comfort in the thought that an Athenian would be reluctant to have her as the mother of his children because of his citizenship law. She could easily find a husband among the resident foreigners. The fact was, she was so extraordinary a woman, so beautiful, so passionate, so skilled in the arts of love, so intelligent, so well read, so refined, that even an Athenian citizen might think it worth the consequences to have her with him, all the time, in his home.

Therefore, he'd come up with an idea to resolve the issue.

They were passing the old port, where the Athenians used to beach their ships before they'd built the fortified harbors of Piraeus. At the first sight of Athena's spear, shining from the Acropolis, cheers rose, echoing from ships across the water. Sailors stationed near Pericles glanced toward him—would he, with all his dignity, cheer, too? As he joined his voice to theirs, they shouted louder, and with broad, directed nods signaled their friends to notice: he was an aristocrat, he was a general, and he was with them. At a signal from the helm, the oars slowed for the easy passage to the military harbor.

Pride and excitement pressed the walls of his chest. The Acropolis and the Parthenon—soon he'd see the progress made on erecting those columns. Below it were the Agora and the Council Hall, where he would hammer out details of his Euboean treaties. And across the way, at the special Assembly, through the power of reason, persistence, and his knowledge of the crowd, he would argue down the opposition and persuade the Athenians to vote the way he knew was best for all of them, and for the long run. And beyond the Euboean treaties loomed belligerent Sparta. He would act quickly for peace while the wave of success was at its crest.

Thus it was late that night when he finally freed himself from the press of city business, and from all those who insisted on seeing him immediately, and made his way to Aspasia's—but then, he usually arrived late. He had a gift for her, a bronze oil bottle in the form of Eros. He also brought along his treaty draft since he thought it would interest her.

She was waiting for him as he expected, but as he fixed his eyes on her and drew her towards him, just as he had imagined doing for many weeks, he saw that the loved familiar had an unfamiliar outline. Had she grown taller, or filled out in her body—or both? Or was it her purple gown? Or her expression? She looked more like the sculpture of Athena that Phidias had once modeled upon her, as if the sculptor had seen into the future. He told her so but felt jealous that Phidias had been the first to recognize her queenly beauty. Was he worthy of this woman, whom the gods had so uncannily endowed with all their gifts?

Filled with joy at having her near, he said, "Some in the Council are opposing the treaty I worked out for Euboea."

What! It was so what she didn't expect that she almost laughed aloud. Did he think he had to talk himself into her arms?

She answered to get past the treaty talk fast and turn to what lovers who'd been separated should be doing. "The Athenians shouldn't oppose you since you've brought them a great victory."

"Their temper's hot for treating the rebels harshly and that, my darling Aspasia, is totally the wrong tack."

My darling Aspasia—she hadn't heard that for a long time. No, it wasn't that he thought he had to talk himself into her arms. He was impelled to argue the points of his treaty.

"But don't you have to make an example of rebels?" she asked.

He came back with an emphatic "Why?" He'd posed the same question in the Council meeting that afternoon—one word for strong effect.

"To deter others—like when Cleinias sold the Boeotian captives into slavery."

"And did that prevent the next rebellion? No." Her quick understanding delighted him—the Council members hadn't brought up Boeotia so he had to remind them.

She rested her chin on her hand—*that* hadn't changed, thanks to Zeus.

She asked the question to which, clearly, he'd led her: "Then how will you treat Euboea?"

His hand tapped his papyrus. "The moderation of my plan may surprise you." Her curls were tickling his ear as, heads touching, they took up the treaty oath. It was like reading the *Odyssey* together. He took her hand. But he had put so much thought into this, he wanted her to know about it too, so he guided her fingers to the papyrus. Reassured because he continued to rest his hand on hers, Aspasia bent her head to the papyrus, and he watched her read.

She looked up. "I'd think you'd at least get rid of the known rebels—it looks like you're not going to exile anyone from Euboea."

"Except Histiaians." He pointed to the place.

"I see right here—" she underlined with her fingertip—"that you're guaranteeing the Euboeans access to the Athenian Assembly within ten days. That's favored treatment!" Raising their linked hands to his cheek, she stroked it with the outside of her thumb. "Considering they'd kept my Pericles away from me for so long a time, I think you're treating the Euboeans very kindly."

He kissed her thumb. "As long as they, *his free thumb*, pay tribute and, *free forefinger*, adhere absolutely to our foreign policy like our other allies, they can have internal autonomy."

"Does that mean that for their own law cases, they can use their local courts?"

"I'm going to leave that question to the Assembly, Aspasia. It's best that I don't seem to be dictating everything."

His trust filled her with desire. He truly wanted to share his innermost thoughts with her. The Eros on her mirror winked at her, and she said, "You are the cleverest man in the world, Pericles, to work out one treaty to cover all the Euboean cities."

"Except for Histiaia because they killed an entire crew. That's not war, that's massacre. That's heavy to the soul. They will be exiled from their territory." He paused. "It happens, though, it will turn out to our advantage, though that's not why we'll do it."

"I know—that will give you a protected route to northern Achaea."

A rapturous smile spread across his face. How had he ever found such a woman?

"My darling girl, how do you know even where northern Achaea is?"

It was her turn to smile. "When you described how you took southern Achaea with no bloodshed, you told me where the other Achaea is."

"You're absolutely right. Now, how have the weeks passed for you?"

Most men would never ask, certainly not *before* making love. She'd leave out about Silky's baby.

"I own my house!"

"What? What house—this house?"

"I paid Hippodamus for it—in a special way. Will you help me make it legal?"

She'd become so confident and self-sufficient in his absence, it was a relief to know she needed him for something.

"Of course I'll take care of it." He needed to retrieve the initiative. "But I must say, Aspasia, that's not exactly how I expected you to use my money."

"Whose money?" She was actually shaking a finger at him. "It seems to me I remember someone saying something about money belonging to—"

It was so adorable a finger he seized it. She laughed but didn't stop.

"There are a couple of other things: *alpha,* Sophocles refused to come to my dinner, but with you here, I'm sure he will."

"What's *beta?*"

"Will you get Sophocles here for me?"

"Yes. And?"

"You're not going to like hearing this, but I saw a lot of garbage thrown out and left along the Long Wall."

That was all? "My new Long Wall—how dreadful. As soon as I turn my back."

"Some people have no city skills. Now, here's *gamma.* You are the best man in the city because you combine Protagoras' persuasive power and Anaxagoras' mind power."

This woman could tempt a man to hubris.

With his hold on her finger, he drew her nearer.

How do you say it to a woman?

Did you miss me? Too passive.

I missed you.

You were in my mind sometimes . . . much—most of the time . . .

Occasionally, speaking before the Assembly, his words ceased, as if jammed against fallen branches in a stream. To start the flow, he had learned to ask himself a simple question: *what do I mean exactly?*

"I longed for you, Aspasia."

"My Odysseus."

What do I mean exactly? "I want you with me always."

If an unmarried man—if Ictinus would say that to Silky, it would be one of the happiest days of her life.

She was silent.

"But I have a wife. A solution did occur to me, however, one that I think will be to your advantage and to mine. You are of an age to have a husband. You'd like to have a husband, I'm sure."

She said nothing.

"And children. I think it's important to look at all sides of a question, don't you?"

Before she could nod, he pulled a Protagoras. "Of course it is, because you appreciate that it's as important in one's personal life to use reason as it is, say, in matters of state. It's important in a marriage that the husband and wife get along well—like Nausicaa's parents. I know you're friends with Bi—Dion. You get along well with him. Why are you frowning?"

She managed to say, "Was I frowning?"

"You could marry Dion, Aspasia. I would pay for the wedding." He spoke quickly, as though she might interrupt. "Dion doesn't make a living that would support a wife like you, so I'll see to it you have everything you need and want. That would be only right, under the circumstances. I'll take the expenses of this house off your hands— or a larger one. You can have a child if you want, as I'm sure you do, or two. I will always love you, and care for you."

Rage shoved away desire. Did he think she could be traded among men? Bought and sold like some Piraeus dancing boy.

Her fist went to her lips. How could this have happened when she had been so warmed to him? She had felt so tender thinking of his missing her when he was away, so excited by his homecoming. She touched a cushion, looking for balance.

Waiting, he completed his thought. "We would be together always."

Together always—the thought penetrated the fog in her mind. This was different from Hypanis the dancing boy. But yet—to hand her over to another man. She had to slow him down so she could think.

"I can't believe that your wife would allow it."

"She wouldn't have to know about it."

"Everybody knows about it."

"Or, if she did, she wouldn't care, her interests lie elsewhere. She'll do what I say in this, as long as I leave her alone."

"She might change her mind."

"She won't change her mind."

She almost said *I'd never want a bizarre, pale child like Dion*, but glimpsed hazardous territory ahead. So she said, "Dion might not want to—if he married me, his children couldn't be citizens."

"Dion not want to marry you? That's ridiculous. Why are you making problems about this?"

"If I married anyone in Athens besides you—that is while really being with you—Dion would make sense."

"I knew you'd see it. And you do like him, don't you?"

"Pretty soon it would be like living with my brother."

"That's what I thought."

"There are minuses to it."

She could be more difficult than the Assembly.

"Protagoras believes that the father's qualities are important for a child's success in life. Dion isn't the kind of father I'd want for my children."

"I could be the father."

That had them walking around a new corner.

But what if the gods decided to fit his big head on her baby. It was not unlikely. Moaning like Silky but worse, she could die pushing it out. His mother had made it through, but Agariste hadn't known what was coming. Well, Aspasia hadn't known *this* was coming. She circled past her thoughts.

"But my children would never be citizens, even with Pericles for their father. Born out of wedlock and no city to call their own?" She was going to add that she wouldn't want that for her children but decided not to take it that far.

"Nobody would need to know they were born out of wedlock."

They'd know if he came out with a big head. "Setting things up that way with all those people is hubris."

"Who are 'all those people'?"

"You, me, Dion, Aristocleia, my children, your children—it assumes we know more about the future than we can."

"I thought you'd like the idea for the same reasons I do."

"You've painted a picture but a picture stays put. I think it's more like a play where things change as you go along."

He looked so disappointed it made her sad—and he had just come back from war—from winning one. She'd better watch out for hubris, too.

"Of course there are pluses to it."

"I knew you'd see that."

"We would always be together."

"My Aspasia." Immediately she felt his lips on hers, full and soft—his gift kiss. "Then you'll do it."

"No. I won't do it. You can't pin me down like Euboea."

He drew away and walked around the room, flipping his fingers over the backs of the gleaming couches. Arms crossed, he returned to her.

"Yes, I am trying to pin you down, but not like a colony. Don't get carried away by analogies."

"It's a perfect analogy—"

"Analogies are good for explaining but they don't prove anything. People take them too seriously."

"This is to that as that is to this—everybody knows that."

Say what you really mean. "You are not a colony to me. You are—"

She quieted her breath.

"It's hard to explain . . . "

"Try an analogy." She tried out her wry smile.

"You could be more respectful!" He stroked his beard. He felt he was opening his unshielded side to the enemy—but rejected that as a poor analogy. "Aspasia, with you, I've found a part of me that's always been missing."

She tried to keep them away, not wanting to give him an easy victory, but tears filled her eyes.

The softness, warmth and weight of her breast filled his palm. "I've imagined this for weeks," he murmured.

Thinking of her out there on the battlefield. In his tent. What more could a woman want?

Quite a lot, actually.

CHAPTER 15

The Rose Garden

She was incomparable and he had insulted her—he turned away from the thought but it stayed in front of him, so he watched to see if she was the same toward him as she had been before. He must have been desperate to come up with the idea of tying her down with marriage to Dion. Well, he still was desperate, but it was reassuring that she seemed to maintain an interest in his views on Athenian politics . . . *seemed to.* Though he had noticed that she seemed (there was that word again) more likely to challenge what he said. Well, that was very . . . stimulating.

"Back when my father was a boy, Sparta tried to destroy Athens exactly as they tried this summer," he told her. "They allied themselves with Boeotia and Euboea, just as now, and instigated a three-taloned attack." Withdrawing his hand from hers, Pericles contracted the three long fingers into a claw. "But we trimmed their talons one by one, and the eagle dropped its prey. Herodotus tells about it." His hand relaxed.

"I haven't heard that part."

"The bronze victory chariot with four horses on the Acropolis was made from a tenth of what we gained in those victories. Someday I'll show you what's written on the base."

Ever since she had refused to marry Dion, she felt relieved by any mention of their future.

"It was brilliant that you, as some say, bought peace from the Spartans from that young king and his uncle."

145

"'Some say.'" He laughed. *Brilliant* was reassuring. "But I didn't buy peace, I bought time."

Since he was a boy, Pericles had been fascinated by the way money, like a changeable goddess, could turn into anything, pleasure, for instance. It could even transform into something as amorphous as time—how convenient.

"You needed time to pacify Euboea without having the Spartans on your back, so you bought it."

"The money got us more than that." He hated the sound of what he was about to say, but it needed to be faced. "Athens was weak, Sparta was strong. There's no other way to say it when they were approaching our city gates and our ally was in revolt."

She always noticed when he cracked his knuckles since he did it so rarely.

"The win in Euboea evened the equation between Athens and Sparta," Pericles said. "Nobody wants to negotiate from weakness. By collecting Euboea back into our alliance we've leveled the scale pans. With that, I plan to negotiate a peace treaty that will last for twenty-five years."

"Since the last peace treaty with Sparta didn't work, I think it's foolish to think one will work this time."

He overlooked "foolish." "It did work, for almost five years—it just didn't work as long as intended. Five years of peace, Aspasia." He said those last words as if he were savoring a ripe pear.

She nodded. "If you look at it the right way."

"I do believe, Aspasia, that I am looking at it in the right way." He rose and stretched. "Now I want one that will work for twenty-five or thirty years."

She figured he meant for the rest of his life.

* * *

Pericles was at the Council House working with Archestratus, a young man he was teaching about politics. Archestratus, he'd decided, would make the motion covering legal arrangements for the Euboean treaties. The Euboeans would have the right of appeal to the Athenian courts for the most serious sentences, but which sentences should they include in that wording—death? exile? disenfranchisement? Pericles smelled the scented oil that his brother used. He looked up. "You can see I'm busy."

An oil bottle was suspended from Ariphron's neck, tied in the slipknot he'd invented which had been taken up by others in his favorite exercise palaestra.

"Sorry to impose on your precious time, but you're never home in the evenings."

"Did you come to discuss my evenings?"

Archestratus left.

"We have to discuss Cleinias' children." Ariphron smoothed back the hair over his temples—sure sign of an awkward moment. First one side then the other, just as their father had done. The jaw jutting forward as the palm presses back . . . With a helmet on his head, Pericles couldn't try out the gesture. "Both of those boys are badly behaved," Ariphron said.

"How can that be?—they have a strict Spartan nurse."

"These aren't ordinary children. Young Cleinias is stupid, even though he's the older of the two. He doesn't understand what he's taught, doesn't move like a normal boy—he can't even catch a ball."

"Can he throw one?"

"And the young one, Alcibiades, is willful, stubborn, insolent, arrogant, impertinent, and selfish."

"I take it he likes having things his own way."

"You think I'm exaggerating. Yesterday he's playing knucklebones in the street and a cart comes along when it's his turn to throw. The other boys run out of the way but Alcibiades tells the driver to pass right over him. The mules balk, the cart topples and everyone's screaming that Alcibiades will be killed. He's made himself the center of attention, as usual."

Pericles smiled at the child's anticipation of the actions of others. He remembered the boy's upturned face with its easy stream of chatter when they'd walked to Cleinias' burial, his small warm hand in his own.

"With training, willfulness can give way to outstanding achievement."

"He's a rogue," Ariphron said. "But I didn't come to discuss their characters. I came to say I don't want them anymore. We're joint guardians and it's time you took over."

"What about Deinomache—she's their mother after all."

"Hipponicus expressed an interest of marrying her—since his wife died, he'd prefer another woman of our family—but I had to let him know Deinomache hasn't been in her right mind since we buried Cleinias. She can stay with me—looking after her keeps my wife busy, and they grew up together. If her mind heals, we can see then about finding her a husband."

Pericles' heart quickened, but why? He was silent for a few moments. "I'll discuss it with Aristocleia in the next few days."

"You're as bad as Themistocles, heeding the judgment of women."

"It's no insult to compare me to the general who created the original Athenian navy."

* * *

Despite preparations for bringing the treaties to the Assembly, Pericles managed to leave the Agora earlier than usual that day. His wife wouldn't like the idea—and displeased, she could be very unpleasant—but he was impatient to discuss bringing Cleinias' boys into his house. He could do more for them than Ariphron, especially that bright one.

He found Aristocleia in her rose garden with Paralus. The air was sweet and still. It was a pretty place, and one he hardly ever saw. Though it was late summer, she had a profusion of flowers, sustained by the well he had built as a gift when they were first married. They had to dig down fifteen cubits. It was costly, but she'd brought a lot of money with her.

A wide vessel filled with water had been set above a thin clay pipe. Water dripped from the pipe and splashed into a basin beneath it where birds bathed—a clever device, one he hadn't seen before, although it resembled the water clock used to time speeches in the courts. At his mother's bidding, Paralus stopped feeding celery to his rabbit and rose to greet his father. Xanthippus, she said, was practicing boxing with friends at the palaestra. When Pericles told Paralus to leave the garden, he clung to his mother's neck.

"It's time to put Paralus in the care of a man," Pericles said.

"You object to the way he's been cared for?"

"Not at all. But he'll be seven years old and ready to start school."

"I'm touched by your concern for your son. I can't recall the last time you expressed interest in either Paralus or Xanthippus."

"I'm interested in them all the time. A man doesn't hover over children. I've been away fighting a war—I'd say you forgot that except that I don't think you noticed."

"I've just returned from festival of the Mysteries at Eleusis. The music, the dancing—I was up all night and I'm tired, so if you came here to argue, I wish you'd leave."

She was right. He'd allowed his anger with her to divert him from his purpose. No man could spoil his aim so easily.

"I'd like to bring in Cleinias' sons from Ariphron's. I would prefer now that they live here."

"Why?"

"I think I can influence the development of their intelligence and civic-mindedness."

"How lofty. It wouldn't have anything to do with Ariphron's refusal to keep them any longer? I suppose it wouldn't matter to you that Paralus hates Alcibiades though they're the same age, says he's selfish and spoiled. Yesterday he disrupted traffic so he wouldn't miss his turn at knucklebones. And he's the smart one of the pair."

"Paralus may not like him, but I've heard that, for all of this selfishness, Alcibiades is constantly surrounded by others. With proper discipline, he may develop into a genuine leader."

"For what, Big Head—"

"We agreed long ago that you'd stop—"

"For what *Pericles*—so that he can be killed in some town no one ever heard of? Neglect his family and nobody dare criticize him? So that the Demos can cut him down to size? Send him out of the country with an ostracism? Impeach him? They'll find a way, and all will be legal thanks to your wonderful democratic vote. That's what happens to leaders."

She sounded like the chorus of a drama even though, being a woman, she could never have seen a play performed, nor did she read them. She didn't understand what impelled a man to distinction. But she understood family matters.

"It's a responsibility we owe to Cleinias."

"You don't have to tell me what my responsibilities are because I've fulfilled them all. You forced me against my will to divorce Hipponicus, the father of my first son, so greedy were you to control my inheritance. Yet, at great danger to myself, I risked producing two sons for you, and"—she let her eyes linger on his head—"thanks to Hera, they both came out normal. Two legitimate sons, something your foreign whore can't offer. I've raised them properly. I've never dishonored you. I've made all appropriate sacrifices and satisfied all rites . . . for fifteen years. I've never failed to accompany you to a family festival, or burial—or a civic one when it was necessary."

"It's not true I forced you to divorce Hipponicus for personal gain. Ariphron pointed out the necessity to keep your estate in the family."

"The one time in your life you listened to your brother. *You're* the one with all the great ideas—aren't you, Pericles? Aren't you? You just got him to do the talking. The same way you get those little friends of yours to make speeches for you when it doesn't suit you to talk yourself."

"It was my duty to keep the estate intact."

"What an onerous duty! To marry a rich woman—and the most beautiful girl ever to weave Athena's peplos, some people say. As if Hipponicus, with his wealth, needed my inheritance. It'll go to my boys."

"As it should, as I was—"

"You may have fulfilled your duty, as you like to call it, but I have fulfilled mine better."

"How can you—"

"Because I had something to lose, and you had only gain."

In the stillness, he was aware of the birds splashing in the basin, the rabbit nibbling in his cage and the hands of Aristocleia fiddling with the gold chain around her neck.

"You made no attempt to like me."

"That was not my duty."

She spoke with the pleasure of one who had waited a long time to say exactly that. Many would say that to try to like one's husband was a duty, but he let the point slip by, in barter for something more important.

"I heard today that, since his last wife has died, Hipponicus is again seeking a wife from our family."

"I know."

Her expression was placid and her smile uneven—that single asymmetry in an otherwise perfect face.

"How do you know?"

"He told me. He was at Eleusis, too, celebrating the festival, pouring the potion of the Mysteries that does so well to—" the crooked smile—"free us from all sorrows."

Amid all her talk of fulfilling her duties, had she dishonored him? He walked to the watering device and peered into the top. Once again, he'd allowed her to divert him from his purpose.

Or had he?

He averted his face so she wouldn't see the sudden flush—he didn't like her to see emotion in him because he didn't trust her. He felt dizzy at the thought of great change.

How best to raise the issue?

"I think Hipponicus has never ceased to desire you for his wife."

"You think. I know."

She certainly was well informed about Hipponicus. Pericles was both amused and angry amidst his excitement.

"Yet, he and I have remained friends."

"He's very rich, and you have some influence in the city."

"Most women would be proud to be married to the most influential man in Athens."

"Hubris goes before a fall—as everybody knows but you."

Everybody knows—so predictable. With everything else, she bored him. He was glad he'd taken the moment to even the equation.

Still, he hesitated. He liked to put things together and build— plans, coalitions, temples. Before he spoke again, he wanted to reassure himself that breaking things apart was also sometimes necessary. Like expelling the Histiaeans from their territory.

"This might be a time for us to divorce. You can then marry Hipponicus again and live in his house."

It was easy to imagine the sarcastic comments running through her mind—about his head, about the past, about Aspasia—but she'd probably resist uttering them since that wasn't what she wanted most. In that way, they were alike.

He prodded her. "Is that agreeable to you?"

"What about my inheritance?"

"There are several factors. I will have our sons to care for. Eventually the estate will pass to them. This is family land and I want to manage it for them. I think Hipponicus will find that reasonable and will not insist on taking over control of your estate."

"But it would be his right."

"I'll discuss it with him."

"But would you let that stand in the way of my marrying him again?"

She was twisting her necklace one way then the other. Even as he enjoyed her agitation, he hoped the valuable chain wouldn't break. She wanted to shake him—except she didn't like touching him. He could set her mind at rest, but it was best not to reveal his intent; there was bargaining to do, and she seemed sufficiently in contact with Hipponicus to tell him.

"I said I'd discuss it with him."

"What about my dowry?"

"I'll turn it over to Hipponicus." Though, by Zeus, the richest man in Athens didn't need it. "That's the law."

"If I leave this house, Pericles, I wish for Paralus' sake you won't drag in Alcibiades and Cleinias."

"I'll hold Ariphron off for a while, but I can't guarantee they'll never live here. That would be true whether you were here or not."

He knew there was another she didn't want him bringing into the house, but she didn't dare say it.

She did say—couldn't resist saying, "You certainly have become willing all of a sudden to part with my money."

"Shall I take the matter up with Hipponicus?"

"How soon can you speak with him?"

"Within the next couple of days."

She lowered her head. Thick curls were piled on top, a few escaping from the bands holding them in place. When she spoke, it was with new words—words he had never heard from her.

"Thank you, Pericles."

* * *

"What about her estate?" Ariphron asked.

"It belongs to the boys."

"But you'll have to pay the dowry."

"I'll sell that upland piece I bought from Andocides."

"Our parents will haunt you."

"It's not family land. Nor contiguous."

"But to sell land for a woman." Ariphron palmed his temples. "Hard to believe a member of our Alcmaeonid family would do such a thing."

"I did what was right and necessary for our family—as you said then."

Ariphron raised his oil bottle to his nose and inhaled. "And I suppose you didn't want that beautiful woman?"

Pericles had many thoughts about that, but nothing he owed telling his brother.

"Don't take that girl into your house, Pericles." Ariphron shook his head sadly. "It'll break our sister's heart."

As if Ariphron ever visited her. "Calliope's in the country. It won't affect her one way or another."

"Then you *are* going to take her into your house."

Did he owe Ariphron an answer?

"Listen to me, Pericles. A man can keep his wife and have a woman, set her up somewhere. I think it's a waste of money, but some men want to do it that way. But not in your own household, with your children and servants. You know, you don't *always* have to do things differently from everybody else. People tend their own business. You tend the whole world's. Father dies, I take my money and outfit a warship, and what do you do? Put on a play. So much money for a play—and not everybody liked it. Why'd you do that, Pericles?"

He didn't owe him the answer for that either but liked the one that came to him.

"There are many warships, but only one *Persians* by Aeschylus."

"You hubristic—" palms over temples, jaw jutting forward. "Listen to me, Pericles . . . "

Not this time.

* * *

"I'm sure you had a good reason for passing that citizenship law against foreigners, but why, by all the gods, did you do it?" His Aphrodite was pouring cool wine for him later that evening.

Aristocleia had not yet moved out and Aspasia was already arguing her case. Well, he expected no less of her.

"The Athenians don't want to share the benefits of citizenship that come with our holding an empire. No one wants to share things of value, just as I don't want to share you with anyone."

There it was! A loving moment, a tender moment, a time that could change how they lived to the way she wanted.

And all she could think of were petty sarcasms. *Look who's talking. You don't want to share me with anyone, that's news.* They crowded in. *It's about time you figured that out.*

When he had brought up her marrying Dion, she had briefly seen a practical side to it. But it had left her furious. Bought and sold. No. She was a woman who had bought her own house. It had been harder to love him.

But this was no night to sound like Aristocleia, so she circled back to the Athenians.

"The fewer the slices, the larger the piece—that's your citizenship law."

Even that came out with an unintended sarcastic edge, but since it was a favorite subject, he didn't notice.

"Take for example the pay I established for serving on a jury," Pericles said. "It strengthens our democracy because without pay for jurors, only those rich enough to take the day off would be judging cases. But on the other hand, we can't spread our money too thin."

"But if there were more citizens, there'd be more cases and more juries. It would have worked out all right for everyone."

"We're already the largest city in Greece. Thucydides and his Little Athenians say that if we become any larger we'll cease to be a city."

"You believe Thucydides?"

"I think he may be right about this." Pericles rubbed his beard. "Up to now, the system I invented of sending Athenian citizens abroad to populate our cleruchies—like colonies but still a part of Athens—has let us to expand without putting it to the test."

"Of course you must check the citizenship lists to make sure nobody's here taking advantage of handouts, but there's one thing I do not understand. At all."

"Well, if Aspasia doesn't understand something . . . What?"

"I simply can't understand why you passed a law saying that if an Athenian marries a foreigner, their children can never be citizens . . . I mean, for instance, if Ictinus marries Silky."

"We must discourage Athenian men from marrying foreign women."

"General Themistocles' mother was a Thracian princess."

He smiled. "You've been studying up on it."

"And your great Uncle Megacles married Agariste of Sicyon."

"That's how the name Agariste entered our family." She probably had found out already, but he added, for the pleasure of hearing the words, "It was my mother's name."

"Then why did you propose the law?"

Young Megacles and the first Agariste, so long ago. To be as young as that Uncle Megacles was. He sighed deeply.

Aspasia couldn't tell if he sighed with regret over the citizenship law or annoyance at her questions.

To be there in ancient Sicyon with the other fine young men of Greece, their lives at the starting line, running, feasting, laughing, competing in the contest for the hand of that first Agariste. Surely he would have won the beautiful foreign girl when her father saw that he was most worthy. And according to Athenian custom, he would have been able to marry her—back then.

But he was way beyond the starting line. Again he sighed deeply. Who could have imagined when he passed that law that it would ever apply to him? That he would ever want to marry, or be free to marry, a foreign woman whom other men had loved, who came with no dowry, who in fact had nothing he hadn't given her himself?

Aspasia, stroking his cheek, repeated the question. "Why did you propose that law besides to please the citizens?"

As she brushed her fingers across his lips, he caught her hand and, kissing the open palm, breathed in a kind of rapture, like what he felt when he heard musical harmonies. He pushed aside thoughts of the past that were making him sad. Aspasia was near and he was alive and running.

"Building the empire cost Athenian lives. In a single year we fought in Cyprus, Egypt, Phoenicia, Halieias, Aegina, Megara. We lost almost one in ten of our fighting muster that year—*one in ten men*, Aspasia."

"But that hasn't continued—"

"Keep in mind I've settled thousands of Athenians abroad and that our settlers take their prize of Athenian citizenship to the new lands. It's one of my best inventions, the cleruchies. Our young men gain wealth and spread our power and ideas of justice at the same time. But you know how men are—"

She did.

"—far off they find wives in neighboring territories. We could easily have thousands of half-Athenians. And who'd be left to marry our Athenian women? They'd be helpless, unprotected." Hearing the stream of the old arguments in his own voice, he felt reassured about the necessity of his law.

"In other words, you passed the law because Athenian women needed husbands." Aspasia nodded enthusiastically. Anything to bring an end to the conversation, now that she could see its direction.

"It's not easy for an ordinary Athenian to buy bread for a household of spinsters and widows—mothers, sisters, aunts, cousins, servants and their children—and to provide dowries for all those daughters. But that's what was happening. Obviously it's the duty of Athenian men to marry Athenian women, and the law encourages that."

"Ordinary women do need a man's protection."

"Meanwhile, our merchants and sailors met up with more and more women from other cities—some are not even Greek. As Athens became richer and more powerful, marriage with an Athenian man, and Athenian citizenship for their children, became extremely attractive."

He stopped short of adding that some women traveled to Athens for that purpose. After all, she was here by accident, or . . . anyhow, no matter how she came, there wasn't another in the world like her. The law was not intended for her. It just happened to apply to any children she might have, which must be why she was pecking at it this evening.

What an odd piece of luck for him! The law had turned out unexpectedly to his personal advantage. He wanted to have Aspasia with him, in his house, always. But he had two citizen sons already—one and a backup. He didn't need more to mince his land to slivers, leaving none of them with enough to grow garlic. That would be unfair to his Athenian boys, and they'd hate him for it. But he held back from adding it to his list of good reasons. It would annoy her to no purpose. She was smart enough to figure it out for herself.

* * *

Shortly after, Damon sought him in his office in the Council Hall.

"I hear you sold that upland piece you just bought."

"You sound annoyed. Did you want to buy it?"

"I'm no rich landowner. People say you're going to take her in to live with you."

"That would be my business, not yours, not people's.

"Is it true?"

"I don't owe you an accounting."

"She's bewitched you."

"I thought you were beyond superstition."

"I'm not beyond practical thinking. Take her into your house and your reputation crumbles."

"Damon, pacify a large island and join it to the Athenian empire, then come and lecture me about reputation."

"Visiting a woman—that's understandable. But this." Damon shook his head. "You, the very man who taught us the value of Athenian citizenship. She doesn't even bring you property. You have to *sell* property—wish I had some to sell."

"Don't forget the most important reason. I'd lose an opportunity to strengthen my ties with an important Athenian family through marriage."

"I was getting to that."

"Fortunately I have two sons, and Teisander's daughter is already promised to my oldest. And as for Aristocleia, well, I'm tightening our connection to Hipponicus."

"The Athenians let you get away with Aspasia because you have an Athenian marriage and Athenian children."

"I lead them to victories and give them the best advice. That's what they care about—and they're right. That's what they *should* care about."

CHAPTER 16

The Gold Cups

After Pericles signed the contract for Aristocleia's marriage to Hipponicus, he felt like a ship awaiting a brisk wind. One day, returning home he had to squeeze himself against the wall of the corridor to make room for Aristocleia's boxes, lugged past him to a wagon sent by Hipponicus. Giving his wife away from his own home as if he were her father—Pericles was impatient for the end of a tiresome round of activities, continued with no concern for him.

And there was the pointed gossip and open amusement among Athenians stirred by the divorce and marriage. He knew that these days when his friends—or enemies—spotted him on the paths between his home and the Agora, their thoughts went first *not* to an issue of policy as he would have wished, but to his wife, to Aspasia, to whatever was happening behind closed doors. The word spread that Aristocleia and Hipponicus were arranging things as if this was a first marriage and Aristocleia was a virgin—which set off rills of mirth. Pericles' wife and the mother of his two sons a virgin—even he saw the humor in it.

Turning the corner toward home one night, he was surprised to see shiny leaves of olive and laurel branches above his door, catching the moonlight. Aristocleia had set out the foliage that announced her wedding too soon—she was in a hurry. As he considered that the leaves might wilt on the costly decoration, which he had paid for, he heard from within Aristocleia and Hipponicus—*singing*. He had never heard Aristocleia sing. Then laughter, more singing—you'd think it was a drinking party though Aristocleia, the daughter of an aristocratic Athenian family, had never set eyes on a symposium. He doubted she'd ever entered the andron.

Inside, the house seemed over bright at first—too many lamps and braziers burning at considerable cost. But as he surveyed the women sewing, weaving, cooking, cleaning, and arranging Aristocleia's gowns, he warmed to the full activity—like an autumn harvest. Even Deinomache sat near the women of the family, watching. He breathed deep to take in the smell of browned sesame seeds—cakes were baking and he thought of heading to the kitchen but what use?—the women would be saving the cakes for the welcoming reception. Three nights would bring the full moon, a wedding moon as Aristocleia and Hipponicus had planned. Despite the fifteen years they'd been apart since their first marriage, Aristocleia and Hipponicus moved as one in planning for this event. Laughing and planning. And, Pericles noticed, touching one another. Imagine! They cared for one another as he cared for Aspasia. He, too, had three more nights to wait; he, too, was in a hurry.

With the wedding one day away, Pericles sought out Ariphron at his home, concerned that his brother, who had made clear his disapproval of Pericles' divorce, might not show up. Ariphron told Pericles—with a wink and a nudge to Pericles' ribs—that his wife had seen Aristocleia that morning dedicate a gown to the patron goddess of virgins, Artemis, in her temple on the Acropolis. Pericles refused the show of amusement Ariphron was looking for, but his brother agreed to attend anyway. Ariphron was a man who stood by family—though Pericles never felt sure he would the next time.

Returning home, Pericles looked for his sons, thinking they might want to talk about the divorce or have some questions. He found Paralus in the kitchen licking honey from his fingers, and he assured the boy that he would still see his mother often—not only that, he could feed the puppies Hipponicus bred in his very large city house that had two courtyards. Pericles sent for Xanthippus who, he was told, was at the house of his older cousin Euryptolemus.

The boy looks like me, he thought, as his older son returned. In a glance so as not to make his son feel awkward, he took in the almond shape of Xanthippus' eyes and the long, firm, straight nose.

The fuzz on his son's cheeks would soon take on the shape and form of his own beard. A nicely shaped head—nothing there to joke about. He had his mother's rounded chin, her small lips—well, she was a pretty woman, those were good features, too. But he was short, like Aristocleia—too bad he had taken his height from her.

"My son, you are of an age to stand beside me and my brother when Hipponicus arrives to formalize your mother's new marriage."

Xanthippus slicked back the hair on his temples. "My cousin and I are going hunting and so I won't get back in time."

"Cousin Euryptolemus is attending the wedding."

After a moment, Xanthippus smiled—Aristocleia's crooked smile. It was a feature Pericles would have preferred Xanthippus hadn't inherited from his mother, but he knew it was a surrender.

The servant, Euangelus, did many things in his master's stead that Pericles, because of his absorption in the work of Athens, didn't have time to do himself. Euangelus ran his household in the city, often cared for Pericles' sons like a pedagogue, saw to the smooth maintenance of Pericles' country estate in Cholargos and worked out financial arrangements with the estate's tenant farmers. Now Euangelus had come in from the country to arrange the wedding party. Pericles returned from his office in the Council Hall the next day just in time to bathe and dress in fresh clothes and greet Hipponicus and his male relatives and friends.

They arrived at dusk, strolling ahead of Hipponicus' elegant cart, wreathed and wearing clean cloaks and smelling of perfumes, accompanied by a chorus of boys playing the pipes. Hipponicus' two sons had not come though they were both grown men. It was seemlier for the son Aristocleia had borne to Hipponicus during their first marriage to wait for the wedding party at Hipponicus' house. As for the other, he was only Hipponicus' bastard. Pericles, along with his brother, his oldest son, and their cousin Euryptolemus, welcomed the men attending Hipponicus, leading them into the courtyard where Aristocleia sat in the center of her women in a virgin's violet gown, her head bowed modestly, her diadem shining beneath her veil. Euangelus had Paralus by the hand.

Though this was not a customary wedding—the groom here had certainly set his eyes upon the face of the bride—the ritual was conducted as if it were. Servants placed the sacrificial baskets filled with the dried fruits and the few fresh fruits available in that season on the family altar. As Pericles poured libations and offered prayers, he noticed with a pang of his own sadness that Paralus' eyes were moist—he was relieved that Paralus did not embarrass him by crying openly, though Euangelus bent to pat the child's cheeks dry several times. Afterwards, when everyone was biting through the sesame crusts and sticking their fingers into the centers to get at the cheese, Pericles smiled—Paralus was licking honey off the top of his cake. Pericles decided that moment of sadness was like the salt in the cake. Paralus could visit his mother when he wished but Pericles would have him at home to guide him toward manhood. Without Aristocleia to coddle him constantly, as she had Xanthippus, Paralus might become a leader. And now for the wine—Hipponicus had chosen an outstanding vintage for the first toasts to the bride and groom, as good as any he would serve in his own home later that night. And it was particularly thoughtful of Hipponicus to select a wine from Mende, a loyal city of the Athenian alliance; it was Hipponicus' way of easing tension between them.

Pericles had done all that was right and necessary. He wouldn't accompany the wagon to Hipponicus' house for the feast nor sit through an evening of toasts that would continue long after the last drop of wit had been drained from them. Nor did he wish to be on hand when the marriage torches were lit within the wedding chamber.

Cousin Euryptolemus said, only half joking, that Pericles should attend the feast to receive the gold wreath Hipponicus would give each guest, but Hipponicus responded quickly that he'd give Pericles a wreath either way. Ariphron would receive his at Hipponicus' feast and—Hipponicus looked around—he had a wreath for Pericles' older son, too, but where had the young man gone? Not having an answer, Pericles just said he would give it to Xanthippus later. The wreath looked like it was worth quite a lot, though you could never be sure until you weighed the gold.

All in all, the matter had worked out well. It was as if he'd married off a daughter. His relationship with Hipponicus and his family was stronger than ever. Hipponicus was not the man his father had been—three times a winner in the Olympic chariot race and a brilliant diplomat. But it was a fine alliance.

Aristocleia took her seat in the cart and Hipponicus held his balance standing beside her as his pair of precision-trained, matched gray Macedonian mares with braided tails pulled the cart into motion just as the moon, round as a compass-drawn circle, rose above the roofs. Pericles could still hear the shrill pipes when he set off in the other direction.

As soon as he arrived at her house, he took Aspasia by the wrist and led her to the andron—the way a man leads a bride, the way Hipponicus would be leading Aristocleia into his house—to open the gift he'd sent that day. Not that this was a real wedding, but it pleased him to do it that way. His arms locked around her waist, his cheek pressed to her hair, he watched over her shoulder as she unwound the protective strips of linen. Inside was a wine cup of hammered gold.

She held it to the light. Inscribed around the foot were the words "I belong to Aspasia." It was like a workman's cup with a name crudely scratched into the clay, "I belong to Phidias" or "to Hippodamus," but Pericles had transformed it into something fine and golden. No, it wasn't a real wedding, but he had given up a great deal for her. He was putting at risk the lofty view the citizens had of him and giving Thucydides fodder for his nasty analogies. He'd even sold a piece of land for her, though it wasn't contiguous with his ancestral property.

"What a beautiful cup!"

Someday she'd like to see that ancestral property.

"There's more."

She kept unwrapping and found the second cup, exactly like the first, but inscribed, "I belong to Pericles." Two gold cups—expensive. With one for each of them—promising.

He broke the seal on the amphora he had sent in from the cave of his estate. She poured wine into both cups and, checking the writing on the foot, handed him the one with his name on it. But he reached for the other.

"*This* is my cup—the one that says, 'I belong to Aspasia.'"

163

It was dizzying, but she recovered quickly because she wanted to remember this moment forever.

"The one you're holding—read it aloud!" He was grinning.

"'I belong to Pericles.'"

"I wanted to hear you say it."

Linking their arms as in an χ, they drank from their cups.

* * *

As Pericles counted them, he had already spent more of his life without Aspasia than he had ahead of him. He felt grief over those lost years and was in a hurry for her to come to his house. He saw no reason to wait for another full moon since marriage for them was not possible, as he was sure she understood.

She understood very well. She understood Pericles' law to ensure that Athenian men married citizen women better than most citizen women understood it. And she knew that the child of a citizen with a foreign woman could not be an Athenian citizen. And beyond the laws, she doubted whether the leader of the Athenians would marry a hetaira in any case—Athenian or otherwise.

Although so far Aspasia had been fortunate in Athens, she did not totally trust Tyche, the goddess who presides over good fortune. True, Pericles had, *alpha*, divorced his wife for her, *beta*, was making her his very own, *gamma*, was taking her into his own home, *delta*, vowing to care for her always and, *epsilon*, loving her—five fingers for five letters of the alphabet, that was a lot. Seen in the right way, that was the most he could do for her. Tyche had been on Aspasia's side but the goddess of good fortune often changes her mind, so Aspasia didn't waste time moving to his household either.

She came "without a lot of noise in the street" as Pericles said, although all of Athens talked about it. Pericles enlarged a room for them facing the rose garden and had planted a young olive tree for Aspasia—they could see it from their window. She spread out the milky-colored carpet with the Milesian pattern that she and Silky had just taken off the loom. When Pericles said he'd asked Damon to sing his wedding song for them at the family altar, she didn't tell him that she disliked Damon—after all, it was a *wedding* song. But when Pericles said that she should sell her house because he provided everything she needed, she told him that she would keep her house. Even though his money had paid for it and he'd arranged for Aspasia to own it, still, she didn't want him to decide what she should do with it. She didn't *always* try too hard to please him—Pericles had learned that about Aspasia.

Instead she proposed a plan to Silky.

"I remember this cup with the girl swimming!" Silky said. They were sorting through Aspasia's possessions to decide what she would take to Pericles' house, and what she would leave in her house.

"I had that cup made for Pericles so it's coming with me. But I'm leaving a lot of good things for who'll be living here—my cedar wood couches, my lamps, the brazier for winter, and I'm leaving the mosaic in the center of the floor."

"Who will live here?"

"You! Shh . . . Let me finish—here's my idea. You can live here—hear me out!—and you can set up your own business. Your men friends could come here instead of to Rhodia's and you could keep all the drachmas they pay, not Rhodia."

"Rhodia would kill me!"

"Not the way I plan it. You see, at first you wouldn't quite keep all the money. You'd give a percent, I'd say twenty-five percent, to Rhodia. We have to ask what she—"

"I don't know percent."

"I'll help with that. Rhodia's commissions will add up so you'll buy yourself out of Rhodia's."

"Ictinus is going to buy me out." Silky's eyes filled with tears.

Ictinus hadn't visited Silky since before the baby. When Aspasia put her arms around Silky's shoulders, they were trembling. "It won't change anything if he does. This is just in case he doesn't. This is good for you, Silky, and good for me, too."

"Rhodia needs me at her place."

"Rhodia will like it because you'll be paying her money and not eating her food."

"I don't know how you learned mathematics, Aspasia, but I didn't. I don't percent, I don't add up, I don't commission. And I have to go soon. This was fun, like when we sorted everything out before that time you went to Piraeus, but it's not fun now."

Aspasia grabbed her arm. "Just think, Silky, in a little while you could keep all you earn. You'll live in this house. It will be good for your old age." Aspasia held to the thought that it could be good for her own old age, too, because Pericles' "always" might not be her "always." "And I won't charge you any rent until you pay off Rhodia."

"Rent?"

"Even after you've paid off Rhodia, I won't charge much."

After a few times of getting help from Aspasia about the numbers, Silky was happy to be earning her own money. Aspasia wasn't superstitious but it wouldn't hurt to share with Silky. Aspasia had herself fallen into very good fortune. So good that at the age of twenty years, she'd probably used up the whole life's portion of good luck that Tyche had allotted her. To make good fortune last—for herself and the child in her womb—would be up to her.

CHAPTER 17

The Perils of Peace

The Athenians were euphoric over having escaped a Spartan invasion and for their great win in Euboea. As the leader responsible for both wins, Pericles' prestige was at its height.

Past the elation of victory, though, Pericles' thoughts rotated around the great cost of the military campaign, in silver and in Athenian lives, that had gone to suppressing a rebellion in Euboea. And little new had been won in Euboea: the Athenians were where they'd been before. True, he had thwarted the Spartan invasion by bribing the Spartan king and his uncle but there was nothing to stop the Spartans from invading again. The Athenian alliance was popular but there was always some city or another resistant to paying tribute to Athens and ready to rebel. The Athenians could not have the Spartans invading Attica every time they needed to discipline an ally. Therefore, Pericles decided it was time to initiate his plan to negotiate a peace treaty with Sparta. He remembered that Aspasia had doubted the usefulness of a treaty when he had mentioned the idea to her, but that was while she was annoyed with him for suggesting she marry Dion and little he said seemed to please her. Now that he had brought her into his own home, he expected she would appreciate the usefulness of a treaty. Any woman with a child growing in her belly should welcome a guarantee of peace.

"Aspasia, I am prepared to tell the Athenians what they won't want to hear."

She smiled. "That never stops my Pericles. But what is it?"

"I will propose that we negotiate a peace treaty with Sparta to last thirty years . . ."

She opened her arms to the obvious. "Of course they'll want to hear about a peace treaty. By Hera, they'll love you even more for it!"

He smiled, amused that he had guessed correctly that she would now see the benefits of the treaty. But Aspasia's enthusiasm was not enough to pass a proposal in the Assembly.

"If they love me now, getting this treaty will use up some of that love. The Athenians are so elated by their victory in Euboea, they won't want to hear any talk of compromise. But the Spartans are on a strong footing—they came near to invading Attica—so it will be up to me to make it clear that we must have a peace treaty and that we're not going to get it without concessions."

She was silent, waiting to hear about concessions, so he pushed his point, as he would surely have to do when the time came to argue for the treaty before the Athenians in the Assembly. "You must face the fact that we can't have the Spartans ready to spring on Attica every time our army is drawn elsewhere."

She thought back to the frightening summer, to the Spartans advancing on Attica, to Pericles alone in a tent with two Spartans and a lot of silver. "I can see that a treaty will give Athens a free hand, that is if the Spartans will live up to it which I've always wondered—"

Well, she had wondered that in the past and, true, it was a real concern, still . . . "We cannot maintain our alliances without that peace treaty."

She sighed. "It seems the scale pan never slips down on Sparta's side."

"The Spartans learned from experience. When their serfs rebelled against them, it took years to pacify them. Sparta has maintained total military preparedness ever since so as not to have to fight those battles again."

"But everyone says Sparta is like living in a garrison bristling with spears."

"Of course I don't want Athens to be a narrow place like that. They never spend a drachma on anything but their military. Their music is boring—"

"*They'd* never build a Music Hall," she interrupted.

He was about to say that. Sometimes she tried too hard to please him. But that was far better than trying too hard *not* to please him—which he'd also known.

"That's obvious because Athens is the *only* city that has built a Music Hall. And you won't find any fine sculptures or paintings in their public buildings—they have no public buildings of note. You would hate it there, Aspasia, there's no point to discussing philosophy in Sparta. They don't have enough words to express ideas, and no curiosity either. And the worst is the state steals children from their families to train them in obedience and fighting. Instead of letting their bravery unfold naturally through love of their city as we do, they push a state-induced courage on them."

"I've also heard—" She was going to say that their laws force the parents to kill any child born imperfect. But no! Pericles wouldn't want to dwell on the death allotted to defective babies. He knew about that Spartan law but had skipped it.

He was looking at her, curious. "What else have you also heard?"

"Spartan women exercise naked like men."

He nodded. "The Spartans have terrible laws."

Which laws was he thinking about?

That winter, Athens and Sparta signed the Thirty Years Peace Treaty which divided Greece between them—land and sea. Sparta controlled the cities of the "Pelponnesian League" allied with her and Athens the islands and cities of her alliance. States not listed in the treaty were free to join either side in the future, which would make them party to the non-aggression pact with whichever side they joined. Among the concessions the Spartans extracted, the one hardest for Pericles was the Athenian surrender of southern Achaea—which he had captured and brought into the Athenian realm with no loss of lives.

Pericles diverted the Athenians from their preoccupation with the concessions by reminding them that, while Sparta was most powerful by land, the sea was Athens' domain. Ticking off the facts, newly calculated, from the papyrus he had to set aside awhile back, when filthy-mouthed Thucydides had managed to insult Athens, himself, and Aspasia before the Assembly, he listed for the Athenians, the numbers and capacities of their ships for war and transport. He described the numbers, training, experience, techniques, coordination, and discipline of their sailors. He praised the judgment, control and mastery of their helmsmen. He counted the shipyards of Piraeus, enumerated the ships undergoing construction, their capacities, and state of completion. He reminded them that their glorious Euboean campaign had secured a major source of ship timbers and mainsail posts. No state could match Athens in shipbuilding or manning a navy. In the realm of the sea they conceded to no power on earth.

* * *

Thirty years of peace ahead and Aspasia in his house. Thirty years of clear sailing—he recalled the small boat he had made of twigs when he was a child that he had set to sailing on the quiet pond behind the house in Cholargos. Pericles felt a contentment that brimmed to joy. His house that had once seemed hollow now seemed full. The numbers of his household had increased. Zoe (and her chickens) came with Aspasia. His wards Alcibiades and Young Cleinias came with their strict Spartan nurse, Amycla. Alcibiades brought his ferret which had to be separated from Paralus' rabbit, and after the ferret scratched the nose of Pericles' hunting dog, Argos, the dog knew to stay away, too.

Pericles felt that Aspasia would cast a benign influence on his whole household. Since she understood ambition in a man, she would be a better influence on his sons than Aristocleia. Young Cleinias and Alcibiades had the unfortunate fate of losing their father in their early years and being left with a mother with a disturbed mind. Aspasia would be the rational mother that they needed, while Pericles would shape their characters toward excellence the way only a father can, particularly the smart one, Alcibiades.

Aspasia smiled happily when Pericles said she brought good luck. As the baby within grew, she felt a glow of beneficence which she could imagine spreading to others. But, she thought, there certainly were a lot of little boys here. Paralus and his rabbit, Alcibiades and his ferret and Young Cleinias with his runny nose. Pericles' oldest, Xanthippus, spent his time with his age-mates exercising at the palaestra, riding his horse in the hills, and at night dining at his cousin's house; from the clatter he made when he came in late, she suspected too much drinking, and with hetairas on hand—Aspasia thought he was too young to have those tastes.

Four boys, and not one of them showed signs of aspiring to distinction. (She and Pericles differed about Alcibiades—where Pericles saw leadership potential, she saw a troublemaker.) Their lack of ambition was because of their mothers, Aspasia concluded. From what Pericles said, Aristocleia was just an ordinary woman, pretty as she was, and Deinomache was crazy.

Clearly neither one of those women was an Agariste who dreamed she gave birth to a lion before her son Pericles was born and, as Aspasia discerned, had gone on to fight for his life. Beyond admiring Pericles' mother, Aspasia felt that she and Agariste shared an understanding friendship—even though Agariste had died years before Aspasia had come to Athens. Not that Aspasia had dreamt of a lion or any other signifying animal since her child had begun to grow within her, but that wasn't necessary. The son—she felt sure it would be a boy—conceived by the daughter of Axiochus of Miletus and the leader of the Athenian democracy would surpass all those other boys crowding Pericles' house.

Along with ferret, rabbit, chickens and dog, that most exotic bird, a peacock, had recently joined the household menagerie. Pericles' friend Pyrilampes, whom he had dispatched to Persia as a negotiator years earlier, had returned with some peacocks, planning to sell eggs for profit, but he hadn't been able to develop a breeding population in the new habitat and so he'd finally sent to Persia for more birds. When they arrived, Pyrilampes offered Pericles several peacocks but for a politician, owed is better than owing, so he turned them down. Still Pyrilampes persisted until refusing them would be an insult, so Pericles accepted them, letting Pyrilampes know he would give them to their political allies—their wives and children would find them amusing as novelties. He had saved one for his own household.

"I suppose that the younger boys are enjoying the peacock," Pericles remarked to Aspasia.

"Paralus feeds him grain right out of his hand."

"Hmm, yes." It was touching that Paralus was a tender-hearted boy—still, the child did spend more time than necessary feeding animals.

"And Alcibiades ties rags to the edge of his tunic and struts around like a peacock with its tail dragging behind." She held back on saying he looked ridiculous—Aristocleia had opposed having Alcibiades in her household and Aspasia didn't want to sound like Pericles' former wife. So she just added, "The servants applaud him like a comic actor."

"Hmm, yes." The son of an Athenian general performing like a comic actor—he frowned and spared himself asking about Alcibiades' older but unintelligent brother, Young Cleinias.

* * *

With the Thirty Year Peace Treaty between Athens and Sparta signed, Pericles felt free to guide the funds previously soaked up by war toward peaceful purposes, particularly toward his building program. The Assembly assigned him the position of Magistrate with responsibility for the gold and ivory Athena, a task he had sought for himself that also made him accountable. If anything went seriously wrong in the vast constructions of the Parthenon or the gold and ivory Athena, the Athenians would vote him out of office as General and would likely prosecute him as well. But in large projects, concerns were bound to arise. When they pierced his dreams, Pericles climbed the Acropolis to voice them. That's how Pericles first came to hear the gossip about the peacocks.

Like olive pits on an unswept floor, Phidias and Pericles stood atop the massive, stone foundation that would bear the colossal Athena. Sunlight fell across the inner faces of the still unroofed marble walls of the Parthenon.

"Since the only light will be coming from the doorway of the temple, I'm worried that the gold and ivory Athena won't be bright enough for people to see the details," Pericles said.

Phidias stretched his arms, wrists turned, hands linked. His long fingers and large knuckles were like the shafts and joints of

Egyptian bamboo. The nails were split and chipped. The skin was rough—he'd been working up here all winter.

"I hear you got some peacocks."

Did Phidias want one of the birds? That could be managed.

"People say you're giving the peacocks to the wives of your political allies to seduce them."

Pericles reached back to touch his bulwark—integrity.

"As long as my friends don't say it, I'm not worried."

"I don't want to lose funds for the Parthenon because of some birds."

"They know I can't be corrupted so they try this."

"Ever since Aspasia." As if cleaning house, Phidias threw a pebble off the foundation.

"They don't get anywhere with that." Pericles tossed his own pebble over the edge. "But where'd you hear this gossip about—" Pericles shook his head at the nonsense of it—"seducing my friends' wives with peacocks?"

"They make sure I hear everything—protecting their jobs." Phidias nodded toward the workmen.

Pericles stroked his beard. Did this seduction rumor make him look corrupt or ridiculous? He wasn't sure but he knew it had to come from that dirty-mouthed politician. "Thucydides and his crew must be sending this around."

"Thucydides' ship has a new sailor—Pyrilampes."

Pericles' breath snagged like a sail on a branch. He had himself enabled Pyrilampes' diplomatic contacts with Persia in the first place and now he'd switched to Thucydides' camp, complete with dark gossip. Pericles cracked his knuckles.

Phidias' hand was on his shoulder, steadying him. "It's not news, Pericles—we know that when votes get in the way of Thucydides and his band of Little Athenians, they sneak around."

"Pyrilampes insisted I take the peacocks." Let Phidias pass that on to the workmen.

"He says you begged him to give them to you."

Pericles turned away and looked east, the brilliant sun hitting his face like a bold message sent directly across the ocean from Persia. The Persian king had bribed Pyrilampes to weaken Athens by undermining its leader. Pericles gave a quick thought to "maybe," but the coincidence in time and his knowledge of the ways of men made him certain.

He had already told Phidias the truth. He would not feed gossip with a denial.

To quiet his heart, Pericles breathed deeply. Score a point for King Artaxerxes of Persia. The gold and ivory Athena would score many more points for Athens.

"As I was saying, Phidias, the gold and ivory Athena must be well lit. Friends, enemies—everyone must feel her power. We need to fill the temple with torches, lanterns—"

"I'm going to double the light coming in from the doorway."

Double the light? Was this some new theory of nature?

"Is this about atoms—I've heard that talk among the young philosophers."

"See it as I do." Phidias' hands sketched a long rectangle extending from the statue toward the entrance. "Here's a pool of water. Light floods the goddess from the door *and* reflects up from the water. Twice the light. The shadows will vanish, *and*"—he pushed on before Pericles could interrupt—"the moisture will keep the ivory and wood underpinnings healthy. You know the cracks on those old—"

"How big a pool?"

"As long as our Athena is tall."

"That's huge!"

"But shallow—just deep enough to reflect light."

"How will you pay for it?"

"I figure out how to multiply light by two. You figure out how to multiply money."

Phidias' flat hand slid along the slant of the sun's rays . . . the path up, the path down.

With light *and* moisture, they'd be getting double value from the pool.

Had Aspasia heard the ugly gossip about the peacocks? If she believed he was seducing his friends' wives, would he lose her? No, because she was a hetaira, which was reassuring. But he might lose her love, which was equally bad. Had she seemed altered toward him that morning? She wasn't a hypocrite but didn't always say everything in her mind.

She hadn't heard so he told her the rumor and the truth of it together.

"There's a good way to look at it," she said. "You love the irony in Aeschylus' *Persians* where, after the Athenians beat them in war, it turns out the Persian queen doesn't even know where Athens is. Hah! Well, now the Persians know very well where Athens is—and think it's worth their gold to malign the great leader of the Athenian democracy!"

"Pyrilampes was my ally, but of course I know that betrayal . . . "

"It's a tribute to you—the Persians know how strong you are."

"Persia's our enemy sure as geometry but Thucydides' attacks on my integrity disgust me. He lies, Aspasia. He lies." He pushed aside his syrupy drink. "I save the city, win the war, and bring peace. Yet he slanders me."

He looked pale, possibly ill, so she held back from saying, "You spend more on temples and civic buildings in peace," although that's what Thucydides hated. Instead, she came up with, "In war rumors are *about* attacks and in peace they *are* attacks."

That was useful. He might find a place for that in a speech.

There was a scream from the other end of the house. Aspasia, careful to make no sudden movements, followed Pericles to the courtyard, where they found Alcibiades fighting with his nurse, Amycla. She was holding him down with her left hand and beating him with a broom pole. As Pericles and Aspasia came up, he twisted around and sank his teeth into Amycla's arm, eliciting another scream. Pericles pulled the boy away from the nurse, who leaned against the wall, sucking at the wound. Alcibiades beat against Pericles' chest with his fists until Pericles caught his wrists in his hands. In the abrupt silence, he heard Paralus weeping in the next room.

Holding firmly to Alcibiades, Pericles went to Paralus, followed by Aspasia and the nurse. Paralus sat on the floor, the peacock before him, lifeless. He wailed louder as they entered and pointed his finger at Alcibiades.

"He killed my bird." It was more fuss than needed for a bird. But as Pericles watched his son smooth the thin layer of feathers, damp with his tears, that covered the bird's body, he thought back to the dog his father had given him, Argos—the *first* Argos. He'd died as a casualty of the Persian invasion, though no one talked of dogs as casualties.

At the Persian onslaught, the entire population of Athens had evacuated to the island of Salamis in boats so crowded there was no room for dogs, but Argos, without hesitation, jumped into the water and swam after their boat. That memory was never far, nor was the sense of painful loss that came with it. But in Pericles' darker moments, he thought also of his dog's determination. Argos swam against the tumultuous waves all the way to Salamis. He made it! If ever there was an animal that knew what he had to do and had the persistence to do it, that was Argos. But as the dog dragged his body up onto the beach, his legs went soft and Argos crumbled to the rocks, dead. Wavelets rolled in over the dog's limp body. To assuage Pericles' grief, and perhaps his own, his father had built a fine tomb of stone, not mere wood, on the beach where Argos fell. The tomb was still in good order: on a recent official visit to Salamis, Pericles had checked.

Those thoughts were so familiar that they slipped through Pericles' mind fast squatting beside Paralus on the floor, his damp cheek pressed against his son's damp cheek as he stroked the child's back. But Paralus cried even harder.

Yet as Paralus wept over the bird, Pericles asked himself whether all these tears worth it for an animal that had been in the household two days? A bird, at that. Argos, now he was a hunting dog. Pericles had raised him from a puppy and trained him. After long days in the hills and woods, he and Argos had brought home partridge and hare. He wished Paralus would pull himself off the floor.

It was sad—children love animals the way a mother loves a child, Aspasia supposed. But these tears were going on too long for a seven-year-old boy. She looked away to spare Pericles embarrassment. And promised Pericles silently that *her* son would make his father proud.

After a last pat to Paralus' head, Pericles straightened up and, with a dark frown, sternly shook his finger at Alcibiades, whose buttocks were smeared with pitch as if he'd soiled himself. A few long feathers still adhered.

"I'm thorry, Pericles, but I didn't mean to kill him. I jutht wanted his feathers." Alcibiades lisped like a young child although he was nearly eight. "He could grow others and I couldn't grow any. It wathn't fair."

Pericles' hand rose to cover a smile but Alcibiades spotted his amusement.

"It wathn't democratic."

Pericles stifled a grin.

Amycla said Alcibiades should be required to remain at home for a month and eat only bread and water.

"He's not to miss a single day of school," Pericles said. "Instead, he'll be forbidden to play with his friends for the month."

Paralus interrupted his weeping to say he favored bread and water for Alcibiades. Pulling his son to his feet, Pericles took the opportunity to explain that a poor diet would cause a boy to grow up shorter and weaker than he was meant to be.

"Alcibiades is to have regular food during his punishment," he told Amycla.

"That isn't fair," Paralus muttered. "It isn't democratic." He tucked in his chin as if talking to the dead bird, not looking at his father.

Pericles didn't look at his son either.

Later, Pericles spoke to Aspasia about Alcibiades. "Even boys who don't like Alcibiades imitate him."

Pericles made too much of Alcibiades' leadership potential, Aspasia thought. She had her own pick—though he wasn't born yet.

Peacocks, betrayal, squalls at home. Thirty years of peace ahead—but no clear sailing. Pericles recalled that his little twig boat had often jammed up against a web of weeds. Each time he had plucked it out and set it back on a helpful current.

CHAPTER 18

∎∎∎∎∎∎∎∎∎∎∎∎∎

The Board Game

Some months before, Pericles had gotten the funds authorized from the Assembly for the ivory that Phidias would craft into the face and hands of Athena. The ivory was a day out from arriving in Piraeus and Thucydides had proposed that the Assembly postpone payment for the ivory indefinitely—and won by a large majority, persuading the Demos that the material was simply too expensive. One day before it would be in port—and payment suspended.

Coming home, Pericles was so angry he brushed past the new puppy, Argos, without giving him the usual pat on the head. It was rare for the Assembly to suspend action on a previous decision, he told Aspasia over her favorite board game. Aspasia, near to her delivery time, was large and heavy and, following the doctor's instructions, made slow movements, rested often, and developed an interest in quiet games.

"I don't see how you could lose a vote," Aspasia said. "It's as if they forgot you saved them from the Spartans and went on to win a whole island for them."

"Now they're saying I win too often." He counted his pieces for the game. "In my opinion, it's impossible to win too often . . ."

"I suppose they want to use marble instead of ivory for the face and hands." She was counting her pieces.

"Thucydides told them we should use *local* marble instead of ivory, corralling the votes of the marble workers." He shook his head. "*Marble.*" He said it as if marble were wood.

She skipped over that he had used that same argument as Thucydides in arguing for the Parthenon's new columns. She also skipped asking why Thucydides had pushed for "indefinite postponement" (which she'd never heard of), instead of just out-and-out canceling the payment—to dig so deep into the raw loss of the day would sting him. So Aspasia couldn't think of what to say. Instead, she moved her piece down one and over two on the multicolored board.

Pericles went on, though. "By using an indefinite postponement, he avoided the punishment that comes with contravening an Assembly decision but obviously it comes to exactly the same thing." He pondered the game board and moved a piece down two and over two. "On top of everything else, he's dishonest."

"I didn't know there's a punishment for reversing an Assembly decision." She moved a piece over three.

"Just think, Aspasia. In Piraeus Bay there'll be a shipment of ivory, of great worth for its rarity, beauty and for the long distances it's traveled. And he has us postponing payment." Pericles' hand hovered over a piece, then shoved it down four.

"Outrageous!" She moved a piece down one.

"Tell the Syrian ship captain who's bringing it to us, 'pardon us but you will have to wait indefinitely for your payment.' He'll curse the Athenians and unload it in the Peloponnese. I'll have to see to it he's paid one way or another. Olympia would welcome ivory for their gold statue of Zeus—especially if they're taking it from us." He moved over two, took a sidewise look at the board, and then down three.

Hard to know what to say. "I understand the elephant is the largest animal on earth." She moved up four.

"A city's no different from a man in that it trades on reputation. If we failed to pay, we'd harm relationships with merchants throughout the world. It will weaken our credit and weaken our city. Transactions with Athenians will seem more risky."

Aspasia felt she knew so much about risky enterprises that she couldn't stop from saying, "You'll end up paying higher interest that way." She winced—she'd been trying not to be the one to bring up anything unpleasant.

"Ivory is smooth, white, and pure but danger is hidden in its cost." He hesitated, then moved down two and one over. "Elephants die or men die."

At those morose words, she glanced up at him. Suddenly he looked tired and sad. She reached across the board to place her hand on his.

How drawn he looked. And he hated to lose. That large Assembly majority against him weighed heavily. And on what did he rest his certainty that the merchant would be paid? It would tire him more if he felt his unease was rubbing off on her.

"It's too bad you can't force them do what you want."

"Don't ever tempt me to hubris, Aspasia."

"I only meant—"

"Do you really think that when I lose a vote, I don't think of that?"

She wanted to say something safe and soothing but, as always, the only time she came up blank was when she couldn't speak what was in her mind.

He looked at her. "Who was your game partner this afternoon?"

"Dion." She studied the board and moved a piece up one.

"I could have used his vote in the Assembly." He moved a piece three to the left. "Who won?"

"I did, five to one. I always win from Dion."

"I think Dion lets you win."

"No! I'm smarter than Dion." She moved her piece two up. "But I don't suppose *you* would let me win."

"No, I wouldn't." He looked at the board. Most of her pieces were in his territory. He moved three up. "Why don't you teach Silky to play?"

She moved three over. "She won't learn, says it's a man's game. But Zoe's playing with me now."

"Your servant—how democratic of you." He moved down one and took her piece from the board.

She moved her fingers above the pieces, diagramming the possible moves left to her. "Oh look . . . *you* won!"

"So I have." His smile was back. "And I was certain that you'd win since you play every day. And you're so 'smart' as you say." He stood and stretched. "Last time I played, I was a young man onboard ship, with hours to pass and no command responsibilities."

"All that time ago. That's remarkable! You won from me even though you're out of practice."

Pericles put his hands on her stomach. She put her hands beside his. The baby kicked. He didn't seem as sad and that was thanks to her—not that he'd ever know. The thought that he'd never know made her smile to herself, like knowing about a hidden treasure, like the baby inside. She hated to lose every bit as much as Pericles did. But it was worth it.

CHAPTER 19

The Ivory

The wheat freighter from the Black Sea arrived in Piraeus at dusk the next day, giving Pericles two reasons to go to port: to greet the freighter and to work out with the merchant more time to pay for the ivory. He picked up a boat early and he and Phidias were on the water before the Piraeus Agora was full.

From a distance, the freighter seemed to span half the distance between the harbor breakwaters. Their boatman rowed them along its full length. Reports indicated that this year's harvest north of the Black Sea would be smaller than last year's, so it was a relief to see the freighter sitting low in the water, weighted with wheat.

"It's Pericles!" The words were hard to hear but they could see the men clustering starboard to catch sight of him.

"Pericles!"

"Hallo, Pericles!" The cry was picked up by the warships guarding the freighter, and the men in towboats joined in. Pericles' name crisscrossed the sun-shot waters of the bay.

He waved a broad arc. "Welcome home!"

"Welcome home!" Phidias and the rower shouted.

"If only these men had been there to vote," Pericles said.

"Come aboard, Pericles!" "See what we brought you!" came the calls. "Come aboard!"

Their rower, proud that Pericles had chosen his boat, was all for navigating through the dangerous web of ropes and small craft surrounding the freighter but Pericles wanted no delays. Early spring and rain a constant threat—those bushels of wheat had to be in his new warehouse by nightfall. The rower turned the boat toward the ivory merchant's ship, easy to spot since it was the only two-masted ship in the harbor. This merchant, a Syrian, dealt in the unusual. Pericles and Phidias climbed down after him to the hold.

Briefly sightless below after the glare, Pericles knew from the sound of waves slapping the hull that the hold was nearly empty. He'd use that to his advantage. Phidias fell to his knees, loosened the protecting goatskin, and kissed the polished tusk. Running his fingers along the exposed ivory, Pericles thought of Aspasia's long neck and tested the memory of her smooth skin. Already the ivory seemed to have taken on the living character of the goddess. With a lantern and his nose, Phidias inspected the length and checked the sawed surface for signs of flaws within. He ran the inside of his arm along the ivory, then his lips—to explain, he rasped his thumb across his palm.

The deckhouse, where they went to discuss business, was built of acacia wood—there was that spicy scent.

Pericles placed two flat palms on the table. "Payment for the ivory will be delayed briefly."

Fat as the drunken divinity Silenus, the merchant observed him through thick-lidded eyes. "I was shocked to hear that the great city of Athens would renege on a promise."

So fast? Spies must have told him—from Olympia? Corinth?

"Very shocked." The merchant rolled and unrolled the ends of his split beard around his thumb.

"Since you're so well informed, you know that it's merely a postponement. The Assembly will release the payment."

"You lost that vote."

"You'll have your money in three weeks."

"I need it now to restock." He'd twisted the ends of his beard into a single hank.

"Your hull is empty. You've plenty of money."

"For dinner plates. But I'm after your best olive oil."

"Start with dinner plates. You'll get your money in three weeks."

The merchant worked his beard. "Why should I believe you?"

"You have my word."

"Don't think you'll get to sell it at Olympia," Phidias said. "They've halted all work on their Zeus."

"Why in three weeks?"

"Our Festival of Dionysos is in three weeks."

"The tribute comes in and we all feel rich," Phidias said. "It changes everything."

"Sophocles and Euripides are both presenting plays," Pericles said. "I can guarantee you a token."

"Pericles—I can't believe you're promising *that*." Phidias moved confidentially close to the merchant. "It's almost impossible for foreigners to get tokens."

"No city matches our wealth," Pericles said. "We're your only buyer."

The merchant threw his arms apart, palms-up helpless. "I'll have to sail off to see who—"

Pericles could not bear to hear the end of that sentence. "That would be a great loss for Athens."

"The loss would go beyond Athens. The *world* is waiting to see Phidias' gold and ivory goddess." The merchant's concern sounded genuine. "But how will you change their minds? Not that you wouldn't be the man to do it," he added quickly, "but the Assembly has reversed its decision once, and I'm told it's unlikely they'll—"

"Not reversed."

They sipped their beer.

"I'm told also that you've lost other motions recently," the merchant said. "Of course I don't trust these accounts." He frowned, tucked back his chin, shook his head and brushed away invisible dust—all that to say that he didn't believe what people were telling him. The exaggeration made clear, however, that the Syrian's confidence in Pericles' ability to control the Athenians had wavered. And how many others' confidence? It was unjust. Athens was a democracy, nobody wins all the time. Pericles flushed with anger and felt pressed to assert his firm footing with the Assembly. But first he had to obtain the ivory. The merchant's elaborate politeness meant he hadn't given up on a successful business transaction—nor should he.

The ivory had originated south of the fifth cataract of the Nile, farther than Herodotus had traveled. It wasn't likely that a merchant holding so rare a commodity would hang around town for an uncertain payment, even for Sophocles and Euripides. Even in the Athenians' theater of Dionysos. Though if he did, he'd talk about it the rest of his life.

Or, if this Syrian did remain in Athens, he'd let out word that the ivory was available. Corinth had a large temple in the works—the Corinthians would enjoy buying Athens' ivory right out of Piraeus, though Pericles doubted they had the money. And Thebes—they'd prospered since expelling the Athenians from Boeotia. To lay hands on Athens' ivory would be another victory.

"Still, although it's merely a postponement, I can understand your concern for your investment," Pericles continued. "To set your mind at rest, I will guarantee personally the cost of the ivory."

The merchant looked confused.

Pericles clarified. "If the Assembly doesn't pay for it, I will purchase the ivory out of my personal funds."

Phidias raised his hands toward Pericles' chest as if arresting a fall.

"And a theater token."

"How do I know you have the money?"

"I have it. You have Pericles' word on that."

"How do I know you'll pay up when the time comes?"

"I'm known for my integrity."

"No doubt. But you must swear to it at the shrine of Zeus the Savior when we row in."

Pericles doubted the Assembly would let the burden fall on him. Still, he wouldn't let them know what he was promising the merchant. "I'll swear, and you must swear before Aphrodite of the Syrians to remain absolutely silent on the matter. You, too, Phidias, to Zeus." By day's end—since they'd gone together to both sanctuaries—they had all sworn before the Greek *and* the Syrian god.

In parting, the merchant pressed into Pericles' palm an amulet, carved in ivory with fine detail, of a bald, fat, naked, grinning man, squatting with his knees spread apart so that his genitals pushed forward. It had a loop at the top for wearing on a chain. "It will bring you luck in the Assembly."

Pericles refused the repellent gift but the merchant insisted.

"Take it. I'm protecting my investment."

Too valuable to throw away, too small to be re-carved, and too ugly to wear. He stuck it in a cabinet with his pens and inks, chalk and charcoal, behind a slate.

* * *

Coming from the market in the morning, Zoe complained to Aspasia about the rising cost of bread.

"Pericles' household will never go hungry," Aspasia said. But people *were* going hungry, Zoe told her, spending most of a day's wage to buy three loaves for their families.

That night, while they were eating honey-poached figs, Aspasia asked Pericles, "Does Athens ever grow enough grain for all Athenians?"

"We did in the past, I think. Otherwise, we'd have had a navy. Since we built our navy after the Persians attacked, I believe that in the early days we weren't dependent on imports."

"The navy was built to fight the Persians, not to import grain."

"But now we use over half our ships for wheat."

Aspasia licked honey from her fingers. "When I first came here, I heard that Athens' great General Pericles was leading a campaign to the Black Sea to secure a wheat supply. I hoped you'd return soon so I could meet you."

How like a woman, putting private concerns before civic duty, like the pale moon blocking out the life-giving sun.

"I made the Black Sea an Athenian lake—but I'll have to go again to keep it that way. More wheat grows there than anywhere except Egypt, but Persia controls Egypt."

"Euboea grows a lot of wheat."

"That's why we fought there last summer. It's our second largest supplier."

"I still don't understand why, if imports didn't concern leaders like Themistocles in the past, Pericles has to worry about them now. And wheat, wheat, wheat—you're always worrying about it."

"I'm sure you can figure that out."

"Here's an answer. Once the Athenians were a simple folk, content with barley which is all that grows here. Now because of their empire they've learned more about the world. They've become finicky and realized wheat tastes better than barley." She didn't like to sound like Thucydides harking back to the old days, but it was all that came to mind.

"Wheat *is* a better grain. Children grow taller on it. Your child will have only wheat bread." Pericles smiled. "But that doesn't account for forty freighters hauling wheat from the Black Sea alone."

Always *your* child.

"When you put it that way, it seems there must be more Athenians," she said.

"That's it of course. We've sustained huge losses in war, we've sent our men out to new colonies, and still our population swells— more women than men, unfortunately. If Themistocles were alive today, he'd have to import Black Sea grain. He couldn't rule the city otherwise."

She chewed slowly on a fig. The numbers of Athenian citizens increased but her own child, conceived here, growing in her belly, wouldn't increase their number because of Pericles' citizenship law. Because of the law passed by the child's own father. Talk about irony.

As his birth drew near, her speculations about her child's future became more insistent. He'd be a great man, of course, yet how was that possible given the obstacle of his lack of citizenship? Her son could never sit in the Assembly or Executive Council. He couldn't argue before the law courts or become a general like his father. By the gods, if only she'd met Pericles a few years earlier, that law would never have seen the light of day! She tossed away the stem end of the fig. With all his talk of Athens, Pericles didn't notice her sullen silence.

"Just think, Aspasia, until recently we saw our plays from temporary stands in the Agora, and anyone who wanted a seat got one. Our new theater is four times the size and all the seats are filled."

"Does everyone get a seat?" She guessed she wouldn't like the answer.

"Citizens do. Foreigners aren't always so lucky."

"Some foreigners come here just to see the plays. What about them?"

"They may get a token from a friend in town—I'll get one for that Syrian. Or they can sit outside on the grass."

That's what their son faced. A future outside. Forever on the grass.

That cursed law! Since Pericles had proposed it, could he reverse it? The situation for the city hadn't changed since the law passed—still too many women. But things had changed for him. Now he loved her. Now she was bearing his son.

She bit her inner lip to remain silent. She would ask him, but not now. Not while he was facing a restive Assembly, Thucydides' growing influence, and some of his friends switching their support. And on top of all that, there was the problem of the ivory payment.

Which, for all her confidence in him, had her worried. It was unlike him to act so impulsively. Maybe his exuberance over the sailors' greetings had sent him on to an extravagant promise.

"Piraeus does that to a man," she'd said when Phidias described what happened.

Phidias had replied, "Ivory does that to a man."

Pericles seemed sure he'd win on the Assembly's ivory payment—but how? She didn't want to seem lacking in confidence, or risk weakening his by asking. But one evening, when she looked in on his workroom after his brother had left, he beckoned her.

"Ariphron is worried that I'm risking a vast portion of my family fortune for the ivory."

And along with that vast portion, the well-being of your dependents. The boys—don't you even worry about your own sons? the servants, your sister. Our child. Me. She placed her fingertips on his table. "I understand that ivory is important—"

"My brother thinks we should use marble instead."

"But I *have* wondered why you gambled so much on an Assembly vote right after they dealt you a defeat."

"You sound like Damon."

Not wanting to sound like either Damon or Ariphron, she waited.

"I realized as soon as soon as I took my seat that I'd made a mistake. I'd told them they could afford the statue, but I didn't remind them why they wanted it. My mind was clouded because I was angry at having to go over it all again."

"Next time—"

"I'll tell them that to abandon the ivory would dishonor the goddess, incur her wrath and damage our credit with merchants."

"You told me you'd already said—"

"And I'll remind them that our colossal statue of Athena will fill our friends' hearts with awe and our enemies' livers with fear." He passed his thumb over the Athena on his pendant. "She'll inspire us to surpass the achievements of those who came before us."

"You'll persuade them with what you should have said the first time?" She winced—she hadn't wanted that to come out sounding like a question.

He'd heard it, too. "Surely you don't think I was wrong to guarantee the ivory payment. We must have it. The error was in what I left out. The Athenians recognize a compelling argument when they hear one."

If the Assembly was in a sober and deliberative mood. It could go quite the other way if it turned capricious and perverse, which Pericles thought the exception and she thought the rule. But he knew the Assembly from inside, which gave him a confidence in its judgment she couldn't catch up with. Still, what a lot of money that would be going off to Syria. He'd sold land to pay Hipponicus. Would he sell land for ivory? How long could he keep that up?

CHAPTER 20

The Citizenship Law

As the wheat harvest in the Black Sea region thinned, the freighters returned to Athens high in the water and wheat became expensive. What good was Pericles' huge, new, costly wheat warehouse in Piraeus if there was not enough to fill it? If there was not enough to eat?

Help came to Athens, and to Pericles, in the form of a large gift from Egypt.

In contrast to the north, the harvest in Egypt that year, particularly in the Delta, held by the rebel Psammetichus, turned out to be exceptionally rich. Years back, an earlier Psammetichus had dragged the Athenians into an uprising against Persia's control of Egypt—a failed attempt in which many Athenians were killed. This Psammetichus, however, held much land in the Delta as well as a determination to overturn Persian rule, and since he was anti-Persian, he considered himself an ally of Athens. Thus, in this year of scarcity, he made his gift to the Athenian citizens of a vast amount of wheat.

The news spread from the Council Hall to the farthest homesteads.

"When will it arrive?"

"Ten ships-worth!"

"Do we all get some?"

"Or only citizens?"

"I can only say what's written!" cried out a herald.

"Will resident foreigners get any?"

"What about large families—will we get more?"

That night, Pericles recounted for Aspasia, homebound and eager for news, the excitement the gift had caused.

"A crowd tore the notice from the hands of a government slave posting it at the Twelve Gods altar."

"Will the perpetrators be punished?"

"The Council decided that their actions were understandable and they were released."

"You didn't agree?"

"True, but it wasn't worth an argument."

"I've never known Athens to be this excited—mobbing heralds, grabbing notices. It's a great relief to have the grain shortage solved."

"See what other problem Psammetichus has solved for us?"

Most men could only hear his questions and think along, but she got to answer him directly. What a fortunate woman she'd become!

"Psammetichus restored their pride."

"Exactly. Most Athenians understand the necessity of the Peace Treaty but concessions make men feel weak—and we gave up a lot of territory."

"A huge amount of wheat can't be a simple gift. What does he want for it?"

"Psammetichus knows we're the only power capable of containing Persia, so it's like tribute."

"That's why the Athenians are so stirred."

"That, and they won't be hungry. Is that a new scroll?"

"A new *blank* scroll. Dion gave it to me so I could . . . " She uncoiled a couple of turns on the table for him and watched his face as he examined it.

"I see you've been writing the *Odyssey* into this scroll." He scratched his beard. "But why in such big letters?"

She gave him a moment to figure it out. "For the *baby*." He looked puzzled. "Because I think big letters will help the baby learn to read quickly."

He looked down at her, smiling. "That's a lucky baby."

* * *

The Council met to consider Psammetichus' letter closely. It was written in Egyptian, with a copy in Greek, and addressed to the Honored Council and to the Assembly. King Psammetichus, it said, having learned of the poor grain harvests in the Black Sea region, considered how he could assist the Athenians, great leaders in the fight against Persian tyranny. In his region where the Nile spreads into a thousand rivers before it pours into the sea, the harvest was plentiful. Therefore he would share the bounty with his Athenian brothers, requesting only that they arrange its transport, since he had no oceangoing cargo ships to equal the Athenians' nor the warships to protect them.

Both copies were passed among the councilors so that everyone could read the letter and take a look at the Egyptian picture writing which some had never seen.

Holding the letters to the light, Thucydides made much of examining Psammetichus' name written in a frame at the end of both versions, comparing its many small marks—none making sense to a Greek. Pericles drummed his fingers. One could see easily that they were identical. But when Thucydides announced that the king's name was indeed the same on both scrolls, council members applauded—no one else had thought of comparing the signatures line by line.

Score one for Thucydides. But in debate over whether the Council should recommend acceptance of the wheat, Thucydides, reminding them of the disaster Athens had suffered in Egypt under the earlier Psammetichus, urged them to avoid involvement with the new adventurer and reject the gift.

"Psammetichus asks nothing in return!"

"All we have to do is ship it here."

"Didn't you read the letter, Thucydides?"

"No, he only reads signatures!"

Everyone laughed, including Pericles. How easy it is to swim too far out on a wave of public approval.

After voting to recommend that the Assembly accept Psammetichus' gift, the Council turned to the harder question— how to distribute the wheat? Psammetichus clearly intended it for the citizens, but should that include women and children as well as men?

A starting point was to allow one allotment for each male head of a household, but that omitted many young men of fighting age—even married ones who had yet to leave their father's house.

Pericles took his turn holding the letter before the Council. Tapping the papyrus, he showed where Psammetichus had spoken of the Athenians as brothers. This demonstrated that he had in mind the Athenian men, and since he had addressed the letter to the Council and the Assembly, he was specifically referring to men old enough to vote. Pericles recommended, therefore, that the Athenians divide the wheat based on one allotment for each male citizen of voting age, with any excess to be sold and the proceeds given to the treasury of the goddess. There was a good precedent. Years ago, the Athenians had struck a rich vein in their silver mines, and the proceeds had been distributed this way.

When the Council voted to recommend his proposal to the Assembly, he was pleased but didn't give himself any points. It was too easy.

To the special Assembly called the next day to consider the recommendation, Pericles added, "According to my distribution plan, every adult male will carry away a basket full to the brim"—he gestured to show the contents of the baskets would be rounded above the top. Picturing ahead of time their own rounded allotments as well as their own rounded bellies, they all applauded with a sense of fellowship and joy worthy of a feast.

Some speakers felt the pounding of their heart when they went in front of the Assembly but for Pericles, the excitement came after. Now he felt the strong exercise in his chest he had learned to expect as a pleasurable reward for success. He would transform today's applause into a vote in favor of the ivory payment at the next Assembly.

It seemed that was the end of the matter, but it wasn't.

Thucydides rose.

"When the wheat arrives, and men arrive in Piraeus by the thousands with their empty baskets and their donkeys, how are we to know who are citizens and who are imposters? Lately everyone tries to pass himself off as a citizen. Pericles pushed us into paying everyone who serves on juries and on the Council and for other services we once did for our city freely, so now it pays to be Athenian.

"You may say that Pericles took care of sorting out citizens from foreigners in that citizenship law he passed a few years back. But he left it to the towns and kin groups to enforce it. Now, instead of looking into the parentage of each young man as he comes of age, they make examination day just another occasion for feasting. The result is that foreign men call themselves Athenian and foreign women bear our children." He stared at Pericles. "Brine infiltrates our clear Athenian springs." He spat.

"Therefore we must prepare a plan to verify the citizenship of those coming to collect wheat—no foreigners."

No one spoke against Thucydides because those who were certain of their citizenship had no reason to, and those who weren't didn't dare call attention to themselves. The Assembly directed the Council to work out procedures for distributing the wheat in time for the first shipments, expected in twenty days.

* * *

That many days later Pericles entered his house eager to share his news. "Aspasia!" Where was she? "Thanks to Zeus!" he called out. Why wasn't she there to greet him? Was the baby coming? Zoe said she was talking with Dion in the andron. Annoyed, he stood patting Argos before going to find her.

"Aspasia, the Council—"

Aspasia rose from her couch and came toward him with her arms open. The distress in her eyes frightened him.

She reached up to touch his beard. "Please help Dion. He's met disaster. Dion, tell Pericles."

Dion was paler than ever. He looked like he'd been crying—tears in a man made Pericles reluctant to hear his troubles, though he knew that Aspasia was level-headed.

"My name was crossed off the citizen list," Dion said.

This was indeed disastrous for any man. "I take it you went to claim your wheat allotment."

"Yesterday morning, I walked out to our farm to pick up my father. I hitched up our cart and put him in it to drive him to Piraeus—that way I could pick up both of our allotments and have a way to carry them home. My father didn't want to go, said it would rattle his bones to make the trip—he's very old. Fortunately for what happened, he's also deaf." Dion put his arm across his face to compose himself.

"Why didn't you go alone and pick up both allotments?"

"I heard you had to show up yourself or you wouldn't get any."

The Council hadn't specified that. Had Euangelus picked up his wheat for him? Or would he have to take time from more important matters to get it himself?

"Thucydides has threatened to prosecute any magistrate who wrongly gives out wheat," Dion said.

The sunspot, as Pericles had taken to thinking of Thucydides. Always in the way.

"There were so many carts and wheelbarrows in Piraeus it was hard to move around or learn anything," Dion continued. "I couldn't leave my father alone with the cart and donkey in that crowd. Finally someone from my town told me the wheat was being distributed according to tribes." Dion said proudly, "We are of the tribe of Cecrops . . . or, I was."

Irrelevant details made Pericles impatient, but they were helping Dion keep his composure. "Did you find the Cecrops table?"

"In front of the eastern warehouse, someone told me. Finally our turn came. Some of our tribesmen were around the record table—one from my town, an old friend of my father." Dion took a deep breath and looked up. The pale eyes were so red-rimmed that Dion's sadness crept into Pericles' breast. Even a man might weep to lose his citizenship.

"Perhaps if you tell me exactly what happened I can help you."

"I'm about to step forward and I hear my name called—but from behind. 'Dion!' I turn around. It's Cleon—the family owns land near us and they're trying to buy out my father—this Cleon has a straight line of thick black eyebrows and hair on the back of his hands. We're age-mates and during military training he mocked me for being pale, and later he said I used it as an excuse for avoiding active duty." Dion's voice grew stronger. "I wanted to go. My tribe never called me up."

"Dion has told me that he would willingly risk death for this city," Aspasia said.

"I have no doubt," Pericles said. "Go on."

"From the way he shouts 'Dion,' I know he's calling out my name for everybody to hear. Everyone in line, magistrates, police, they all turn to look. And when he has them all looking at us, he shouts . . . " Tears were welling up again.

"Tell Pericles what this Cleon said so he can help."

"Cleon shouts—" Again Dion stopped short, and when he spoke again, his voice had taken on a harsh, startling timbre. "'Dion's the bastard son of a foreign whore.'"

If he ever heard this Cleon speak, Pericles thought, he'd know the voice.

"Others clamber in," Dion said. "'Bastard.' 'Barbarian.' 'Son of a whore.' 'Persian spy.' 'Barley for bastards.'"

Like a comic chorus.

"'We've got you now!'" The Cleon voice again.

They ask me if Cleon's charge is true. I stay silent, so the magistrate checks to see if my name is on the tribe list, and it is. I'm safe. But then the magistrate calls over my father's friend and asks whether they say I'm legitimate in our town."

"'We put him on the town roll as a legitimate citizen when he came of age.'" An old voice from a northern town. Dion hunched his shoulders forward like an old man, his chin jutting.

"The magistrate said, 'That doesn't answer the question.'"

In the way Dion spoke those words, Pericles could hear the precise diction of a magistrate in the new democracy.

"'You think nobody knows what you do in those small towns,'" Dion continued in the magistrate's voice. "'But we must separate the wheat from the chaff, we must unmask foreigners. Dion, do you know the penalty for collecting wheat as an imposter?'"

Dion went back to his own voice. "To be sold into slavery by the Athenian state." The magistrate says he's arrested three non-citizens passing themselves off as citizens. If it's proved in court, they'll be sold. Suddenly the god Hermes puts a clever thought in my mind. I tell the magistrate I'm not picking up wheat for myself, but here to help my poor, aged father get his and carry it home for him."

Even in his misery, a note of triumph sounded in Dion's voice. "Cleon had nothing to say to that."

"That's where the matter stands—you took your father's wheat and went home?"

"Before I left the line, the magistrate crossed my name off his citizen list—I saw it with my own eyes."

"But Cleon offered no proof, so the magistrate was wrong to take your name off the list." Pericles stroked his beard. "Dion, are you in a position to appeal this action?"

Dion shook his head, then dropped his eyes. "Cleon's right."

"Then how did you become enrolled on your town's citizen list?"

Dion sighed. "My father's wife died giving birth to her first child, the women pulled it from her feet-first, dead."

Which was worse, feet-first or a large head? Aspasia wondered.

"My father took in a woman to help in the house—she was from Boeotia." Again, his eyes filled with tears. When I came of age, my mother was long gone. Back to Boeotia, I suppose. So, you see I am a bastard son of a foreigner."

Hopeless. But Dion was waiting. "I'm very sorry," Pericles said.

"Sorry about what, Pericles—that I lost my mother or that I'm a bastard foreigner?" No tears now—fast as an actor, Dion donned a new mask.

"But how did you come to be enrolled as a citizen?"

"I was my father's only child, so they put me on the list. What difference did it make to Athens? My father's Athenian—I love Athens!"

"There must be something you can do for him," Aspasia said.

"If he was accused wrongfully, I would have defended him and taken his case to court—at no cost to you, Dion. But he has no case."

"But surely an exception can be made—a special law passed? He's so much an Athenian. His father's a citizen."

"I won't place myself above the law, and by urging me to seek an exception for a friend, that's what you're asking me to do." Pericles didn't mention Dion was *her* friend, which would make seeking a favor for him even more dangerous.

"But he's lived here all his life, he's undergone Athenian military training, where else in the world would he be a citizen?" Aspasia was in tears.

Why by the gods was she so upset about this? It didn't really concern her. She was fond of Dion, but that didn't explain tears—she wasn't one to weep over the misfortunes of others.

Nor had she ever asked him to put himself at risk, even for herself.

"Why are you asking me to do what I can't do? You know I must uphold the law. It's my law, and I made it with good reason, although I regret that it falls heavily on Dion."

Usually his impatience was enough to draw her up short, but not this time. "There must be *some* way for a person to become a citizen who isn't born one."

"Of course. By distinguishing himself so highly on behalf of Athens that the Assembly awards him citizenship through a special vote. That path is open to Dion."

Aspasia felt the shock of diving into cold water. And she felt extremely alert.

"Has that ever happened?"

"During the Persian wars, the Plataeans helped us at the Battle of Marathon. They and their sons enjoy citizenship rights to this day."

"Surely I can find a way to so distinguish myself on behalf of the city that I'll be voted citizenship." The strain of his smile stretched Dion's lips thin.

"You'll think of something magnificent," Aspasia said. "Perhaps something having to do with books."

"If you do, I'll introduce the measure to the Assembly myself," Pericles said.

"I'm honored. And meanwhile . . . " There was that thin smile again. "I never attend the Assembly, I never sit in the law courts, and even bastard foreigners are permitted to fight for Athens, so I'll hardly notice the difference."

Shirking public responsibilities was no more to Pericles' liking than tears in a man. Still, Dion's helplessness troubled him. Was there some way he could help within the law? "Even though you're illegitimate, the law allows you to inherit from your father in the absence of legitimate heirs. If at the death of your father your inheritance is challenged, I'll defend your case."

"The likelihood that my father will die is considerably greater than that my achievements will impress the Assembly."

Her curiosity pressed her. "Is your father pale like you?"

Dion drew his cloak around him. "No."

The moment he'd gone, Aspasia turned to Pericles. "Our son will distinguish himself in so outstanding a way that the Athenians will have to vote him citizenship."

So that was her distress—he should have realized it. His eyes dropped to her belly. What was the relationship between the incomplete, alive thing in there and the grown man? Education plays its role. Chance plays another. There are many roles, many changes of scenery, even, one might say, an audience—not that it was a tragedy. Though it could not be said to be a comedy. She hadn't asked a question but was waiting for an answer.

"Of course he will."

Did he mean it or was he just comforting her?

He cleared his throat to attract her attention. "Aspasia, you may be pleased to know that the Assembly agreed with my arguments concerning the greatness of the goddess and voted to pay for the ivory."

"I suppose the arrival of the wheat helped."

"It did play a role—I told them it demonstrated our power."

General Pericles . . . he was always so distinguishing himself he could probably get voted citizenship a hundred times over.

CHAPTER 21

The One-Horned Ram

At Pericles' urging, the Assembly had authorized a carved marble frieze for the Parthenon that would show a scene from real life: Athenians bringing Athena her birthday gift, just as they did at the Panathenaic Festival. It was novel for the Greeks (although Pyrilampes the peacock dealer claimed he'd seen something like it in Persia). Phidias planned that the citizens—carved in relief—would seem to climb the Acropolis, circle the Parthenon to the holy east end, bringing Athena their gift as they would do when—soon—the temple was complete. The Athenians conducted this sacred Panathenaic Procession with special splendor once every four years but, Pericles told the Assembly, the marble images of true Athenians honoring their goddess would be there "all the time *and* for all time."

"Temples are for the gods," Thucydides said. "No city has the hubris to put her own citizens on a temple."

Phidias promised, "The Athenians will look like gods."

Having failed to stop the frieze of Athenians at its root, Thucydides tried again when the time came to allocate funds to transport marble blocks from the quarry. "Nowhere anywhere at any time have Greeks ever violated a holy temple with images of themselves." Thucydides slammed his fist into his palm. "This is impiety!"

He seemed to have made his points, but he carried on.

"Pericles is squandering the tribute of the empire to adorn the city as if it's his whore."

Somebody shouted, "Get it right, Thucydides, he's adorning the *temple*."

"He'll probably set her up in there!"

"With the kid!"

"He's diverted the proceeds of the empire for what's her name!"

"Milesia!"

The waters were black as Pericles rose to speak.

"Thucydides believes I've spent too much on Athena's temple." He pounded a fist into a hand like Thucydides. "Do you agree?"

"Too much . . . too much," sounded through the Assembly as if the Echo had abandoned Narcissus in the woods and sped in to support Thucydides.

Pericles waited until the sound died down—Echo's voice always thinned away.

"Fine. I won't ask you to finance any more of the temple. But I see only one way to do what must in fact be done. *I* will myself pay all further expenses, starting with moving the blocks for the frieze of Athenians to the Acropolis. Let the cost go not to your account, Athenians, but to mine. And naturally the inscriptions carved upon the building will stand in my name, since that would be only just."

Now murmurs surfaced, submerged, and reappeared in a wave of calculations.

"Would he really do it?" "He can't afford it." "Does he mean it?" "He said he'd pay for the ivory." "He spends his own money for the city all the time." "That's how he gets things done." "He doesn't have the money for the temple." "And the frieze." "And the statue." "The Alcmaeonids have immense wealth." "In land but not silver." "He's not as rich as Hipponicus."

"Pericles," someone called out, "we Athenians will build the temple!"

"Only tell us what's needed!"

"Let the work be a fine one!"

"And put our name on it!"

"We can afford it!"

"Together, we're richer than Hipponicus!"

It takes immense work to move a hunk of stone from a mountain along with its heedless companions and shape them into a temple worthy of men and gods.

* * *

"We won," he told Aspasia. He looked angry as Ajax.

"I'd think you'd be pleased to win." He'd lost a handful of motions recently which was particularly worrisome since the annual election for generals coming up soon. Thank the gods he'd beaten back Thucydides' challenge today. "How did the debate go?" she asked.

Not everything must be said. "They authorized the frieze this summer, and now this Charon comes in looking for an obol in the middle of the river Styx. It would be better if—"

"—if he drowned in the Styx. I don't know if it will cheer your heart but I can show you something interesting."

"That will cheer my heart."

In the courtyard, Philemon, the young groom from Pericles' country estate (rumor said he was Euangelus' son) sat cross-legged on the ground near the well with an animal lying across his knees. "I found this portent at Cholargos," Philemon said. Pericles bent in for a closer look at the newborn ram with one eye and a single horn. Paralus held a cup of water to the ram's lips, but the animal was heedless, dragging in each rasping breath through its narrow nose.

"A portent!" Alcibiades exclaimed. "Monthters have one eye. The Thyclops has only one eye in the thenter of his forehead. Think of it, Cleinias." Alcibiades looked cross-eyed at his older brother. "One eye."

General Cleinias' younger son was smart and the older one stupid but they both made too much noise, as Pericles and Aspasia had discussed. Still, smart was better than stupid.

"One eye! One eye!" Young Cleinias screamed, setting Zoe's chickens in their boarded-off coop clucking and flapping their wings so they rose, like a miniature dust storm, a hand's breath into the air.

His hands covering his ears, Pericles looked at Aspasia in mock sorrow. She smiled and covered her ears.

"Shh," Paralus stroked the animal's neck. "The ram is trying to sleep."

Philemon had brought the ram in from Pericles' estate in Cholargos—its mother would have nothing to do with it. Pericles knelt to study the animal closely. He'd never seen a one-horned ram although, he remembered, one-eyed sheep had been born in the neighborhood. How did nature create its odd inventions?

"It's not jutht a ram, Paralus—it's a portent. We need a theer to tell us what it means. Pericles, get us a theer."

People should know that not every oddity is a portent. Pericles recalled how, recently, when the moon had grown dark, everyone on the streets had rushed inside terrified as if the "portent" was a wild boar on the loose. But Anaxagoras and Pericles went outside. Pericles was curious; the philosopher was joyful to see the eclipse because he so cherished opportunities to observe natural phenomena. As the moon disappeared—and it *was* strange—Anaxagoras explained the natural cause of eclipses. "Ordinarily the moon is illuminated by the light the sun casts on it, but occasionally the moon moves into the earth's shadow, out of the sun's reach." He pointed up with excitement: "Now watch—the moon is moving out of the shadow of our own earth!" As the heavenly body emerged from darkness, first as a glow, then a sharp sliver, and finally almost full, it lit the philosopher's upturned face.

This was a good opportunity to open the children's eyes to natural causes—well, Paralus and Alcibiades. Young Cleinias wouldn't catch on.

"It's not a seer we need, Alcibiades, but a philosopher to explain the single horn because—" Pericles' teaching finger took an emphatic shake—"philosophers explain the reasons for things."

"But theers tell us what will happen in the future—that's better."

Pleased to side with Pericles and to quiet that nuisance boy, Aspasia said, "As a matter of fact, Alcibiades—" time to raise *her* teaching finger—"sometimes philosophers predict the future. Once Anaxagoras predicted a red-hot stone would fall from the sun and it did, on the day he said it would."

"Let's get Lampon the Theer here, too, and hear what both thay."

Lampon's and Pericles' families had been friendly since Pericles' family had built Apollo's temple at Delphi where the seer's family was influential. Still, Pericles hesitated—he'd seen often enough that with anyone who claimed special knowledge of the gods, things could go out of control.

"C'mon, Pericles, you always thay you welcome all points of view."

"That's a good idea," Pericles said. "We'll have both Anaxagoras and Lampon examine the one-horned ram."

Pericles sent Philemon after them, and for Xanthippus at the palaestra—it would be educational for his older son to hear Anaxagoras and anyhow, it was time for him to be home.

Philemon returned with Lampon. "Anaxagoras will be here when he's finished writing, Xanthippus after his wrestling match."

"The animal is too curled up to see him clearly," Lampon said. "Carry him to that bench."

"He's comfortable here," Paralus said.

"Paralus can't tell the difference between comfortable and nearly dead," Alcibiades said.

Pericles watched Philemon carry the animal across the courtyard with Paralus tagging along, stroking the ram's head. He didn't want to waste one of his short prayers to Zeus about it, but he hoped that moisture in Paralus' eyes wasn't about to turn to tears—he'd had enough of his son's crying over animals.

Lampon pushed aside the tight curls at the base of the horn to scrutinize the tough cone. He nudged the horn in a circle, and pressed his fingers under the short white hairs, feeling for other horn mounds. The single eye was too apparent to spend time on.

"This ram tells us that where there should be two, there is one."

"What's *that* thupppothed to mean?"

"Pericles and Thucydides are wrestling for control of Athens and soon power will fall into the hands of one man. The prodigy of the one-horned ram predicts that one man will be Pericles because the animal was born on his estate."

Pericles *knew* he shouldn't have given in to Alcibiades on "all points of view." This prophecy spelled trouble.

Aspasia wasn't smiling either.

This "prediction" was an arrow shot from Apollo's bow directly to Pericles' heart. It was as if Thucydides himself had aimed it, Pericles thought. Now Thucydides could—skip *could*—*would* use this prophecy as proof that Pericles planned on seizing one-man rule. It would feed the Demos' fear of tyranny. Worst of all, since action is stronger than fear, it would justify a vote of ostracism: they'd try to force Pericles to leave the city. Had Lampon fallen into Thucydides' league?

Pericles turned to Philemon. "Which ewe was ready to give birth?"

"None that we knew about."

Didn't know about the ewe? Pericles didn't have many ewes to track. Even Alcibiades was silent at that—with the rest of them.

"Where did you find him?"

"Inside the gate to our tower, across the way from that piece Glaucon just bought."

Glaucon's piece—Thucydides had recently sold it to Glaucon, the young officer of his own tribe whom he had himself elevated in rank—his aide at that most crucial moment when it had been necessary to bribe the Spartans. And yet . . . *across the way from Glaucon's property* . . . Had Glaucon gone over to Thucydides? Just how ambitious was Glaucon?

In a voice loud enough for the servants in the kitchen to hear, Pericles told Lampon that he had no desire to wield sole power in Athens. "And the proof is—" he slowed his speech for emphasis— "that I propose the motions that further our democracy in which power lies with all citizens." He had provided Lampon with words— like Sophocles writing for an actor. He hoped the seer got the point.

Lampon cast a glance upward. "One horn where two should be—one-man rule. Perfect logic."

Anaxagoras called from across the courtyard. "Lampon, you talk of truth but you love certainty."

Lampon spun around. "When I know the truth, I say it."

"Truth ha ha," said Alcibiades. "You should listen to the philothopher Thenophanes."

Lampon turned toward the gate. "I'm leaving this cave of points of view."

"Everyone here honors your wisdom." Aspasia's hand was on Lampon's arm.

"I especially honor the long friendship of our families, and the temple my family constructed for your family at Delphi," Pericles said. "Naturally, we built it for Apollo but . . . "

Lampon cocked his chin toward Anaxagoras. "I suppose *he* has a better explanation for the single horn."

Anaxagoras pushed the horn in all directions and felt for other horn mounds. "To understand the natural cause, we must look at the horn's root."

"Let's thee inthide."

"No!" Paralus' tears fell on the animal's neck.

Anaxagoras patted Paralus' trembling shoulders. "Don't feel sad. We're going to sacrifice him to Zeus."

"I don't want to sacrifice him!"

It's one thing to weep over a horse or a hunting dog but another to weep over a farm animal. And he felt sure that this one hadn't come from his farm but from Glaucon's. Had Thucydides' tentacles sucked in Glaucon? First peacocks, now a ram. What other weird animals awaited him?

"Good advice," Pericles said. "We'll sacrifice him to Zeus."

Anaxagoras smoothed Paralus' damp curls. "He'll be a gift to the gods. He'll have a better death than otherwise."

"Do you know what Heraclitus wrote, Paralus? 'Better deaths gain better portions.'" Aspasia doubted that Heraclitus had animals in mind, but Pericles wanted to get on with Anaxagoras' inquiry.

"And you're old enough to carry the water jar," Anaxagoras said.

"Theus won't want a blemithed animal."

Paralus sponged the ram and wound the ribbon around its horn. Pericles delayed until Xanthippus arrived—glossy with oil, still damp from exercise, his cloak open immodestly over his tanned, muscular chest. A dainty oil bottle hung from his wrist, tied with Ariphron's slipknot. Xanthippus made a quick apology for being late—his wrestling opponent had twisted an ankle, delaying their match. Xanthippus' carelessness, his luxury, and that expensive scent angered Pericles, but he was proud of his son's good looks and skill in sports.

"Did you win?"

"Three to none." Xanthippus ground down on a mouthful of grapes and spat out the skin and seeds. "My back never touched the sand."

The ram had to be carried to the altar—Lampon warned that Zeus would reject an unwilling victim, but Anaxagoras said the ram wasn't unwilling, just unable to walk.

Paralus sprinkled water over the animal, jumping back when the ram raised his head.

"He's nodding 'yes,'" Anaxagoras said.

But when Pericles drew the knife from the basket and brought it to the animal's throat, Paralus cried out, "No!" The chickens squawked. Paralus ran to Zoe, seated by the chickens, and pressed his face against her knees.

To be done, Pericles cut the ram's throat quickly. This was not an animal to eat. He'd send the carcass back to the country.

When the ram was bled, Anaxagoras cleaved the skull with the axe so it opened like a hinged mirror case. Less brain spilled out than Pericles expected. The brain's basin was dry and the brain itself was small and shaped like an egg but pointed at the ends. "An entire brain's worth of matter has gathered itself toward the center into a dense mass. Furthermore, here—" Anaxagoras pointed with his knife—"it's attached by one end to the precise place where the single horn is rooted. Thus—" Anaxagoras caught his breath—"the single horn resulted from the brain's stunted development."

The philosopher was close to tears of excitement over his discovery—a better kind of tears, Pericles thought.

Pericles knew that people pocketed summaries like packets of dried fruits from a wedding—small but they were remembered kindly. So he summarized: "Anaxagoras has shown that the cause of the ram's single horn lies in its development."

"By Theus, Pericles—your brain mutht be exthra thufficient."

That boy was quick as Aspasia—though a nuisance, she was right about that.

"What about the prophethy that Pericles will be a tyrant?"

"It's not about the future," Aspasia said. "It's just something nature did."

"I'm dithappointed, I want Pericles to have one-man rule . . . with his extra brains."

Aspasia put a finger to Alcibiades' lips.

Pericles steered Lampon by the elbow from the courtyard. Since the seer hadn't gotten the point the first time, Pericles told him, with as little show of emotion as he could muster, that he preferred that Lampon stay silent about his prophecy, placing a pouch in Lampon's hand—not the customary dried fruits.

Later, Aspasia said, "They didn't know you'd call in Lampon. And you wouldn't have if Alcibiades hadn't thought of it, and Alcibiades is a child—he can't be in league with Thucydides."

"It's a trespass on my land. It's disgusting. It was a grotesque creature with an odd head—an insult to me. Thucydides and his crew knew they could get something out of it one way or another." Or Glaucon knew.

CHAPTER 22

The Election for Generals

"Absolutely not, Pericles would never hold a mock sacrifice in his home." Simon the Bootmaker shook his head at the thought. "That would be impiety." He was tracing the customer's feet with a charcoal.

Thin hair fringed the customer's bald head like an old wreath that had slipped down over his ears. "But it's a certainty. *Alpha*, they didn't eat the ram, *beta*, Anaxagoras sacrificed a *blemished* animal which the gods hate."

"Anaxagoras—oh I know all about that philosopher." Xenon had left his barbershop in the care of his son. "He's telling everybody in the Agora that the sun is a hot lump of stone which means—" the barber raised his teaching finger—"the sun god Helios doesn't exist."

"That's Pericles' teacher for you," said the old man. He rotated a free ankle. "I happen to know that Anaxagoras doesn't believe in Zeus either."

"He does believe in Zeus!" Simon scraped his charcoal against the emery. "He just calls him by a different name. Mind."

"Thucydides calls this worship of Mind impiety," the customer said.

Simon's charcoal cracked. "Thucydides calls everything new impiety."

"That's true about Thucydides," Xenon said. "But still, I wonder—if Zeus is Mind, what are the other gods?"

"Apollo, Artemis, Aphrodite, Athena—out they go." The customer shook dust from the folds of his cloak.

Simon looked up abruptly. "If Pericles believed that, he wouldn't spend so much money on Athena's temple. Hah!"

"Take my advice." The old man slid past Simon's comment. "Don't vote in the next election for a general who takes lessons from philosophers."

"We vote for Pericles because he has more skill and experience than anyone running against him." With a light puff, Simon blew off the charcoal dust edging his outline of a foot.

"Of course Pericles has the most experience—he runs for every election and nobody else in his tribe stands a chance." To engage their attention to his next words, the old man slowly polished the grasshopper pin that held his cloak together at the shoulder. "Thucydides says that Pericles is aiming for one-man rule."

Simon had often observed Pericles change the subject in the Assembly when it suited him. "Polishing that fancy pin with your thumb like that will leave black tarnish in the turns."

The customer persisted. "Smart younger men in Pericles' tribe—Glaucon for example—don't have an opportunity to develop. I'll pay ahead for the boots." He shook drachmas into Simon's palm. "Remember," he said in leaving, "the one-horned ram came from Pericles' estate. That proves he's aiming for one-man rule."

Simon waited until the customer had gone. "You know, Xenon, I don't think that old guy really came here for boots."

"He has a point though—Pericles wins too often."

* * *

Dawn came without the sun on election day for generals, and the wind was damp—good weather for a farmer to mend tackle, craftsmen to catch up on orders, and sailors to head to The Three Jugs instead of making their way from Piraeus to Athens to sit on the Assembly's windy hill. But not good for a democrat. And if Pericles lost, he would fall from the power that enabled him to direct the course of his city to . . . being a citizen with one vote.

Pericles' eyes fixed on the Athenians entering the rope gates, set up tribe by tribe.

What was running through the minds of these citizens heading to their places? Were they recalling the trophies he'd erected in their name on the fields of battle? Were they thinking of the democratic reforms he'd passed for them? Of how he'd opened the secret deliberations of the aristocratic Areopagus council, with its vengeful investigations, into the light of the democratic courts? That he'd instituted pay for jurists so now even a poor man could afford to serve? That he'd instituted pay for attending the Festival of Dionysos so that everyone could attend the theater? That he'd opened to all the random lottery for political office so that now every citizen had a chance to hold a high position? Were they thinking of the wealth he'd brought them—a wealth for the Demos scorned by men like Thucydides who had all the wealth they could need? Were they remembering how he'd saved them from the Spartans? Of the thirty years of peace he'd guaranteed them? Were they thinking of how they'd cheered for him when these things were achieved? Were they thinking of the intelligence he'd brought to the tasks of the city? Of the risks he'd taken?

Many had come to vote for him, but many had come to see him fail as if they were attending a tragedy by Sophocles—with tokens he had himself provided.

Clustering to enter, Thucydides and his clot of followers knocked ropes to the ground. A frowning policeman set them back on their posts.

Sophocles brushed off a cinder. "Noisy."

"Thucydides tells them to shout when he arrives," Damon said.

"Thucydides isn't the man his cousin was," General Andocides said. "In the old days, General Cimon won battles and conquered territory for us, but Thucydides has won nothing."

"He doesn't have Cimon's charm," Teisander said.

"Nor his good looks," Sophocles said. "But he speaks well."

At the call for order, Pericles and Andocides took their seats at the front.

What would it feel like to lose his place in the front row?

It was after noon before the Assembly finished choosing religious officials. There were ten generals to elect and several candidates from each tribe. By law, each tribe's list was read aloud, though everyone already knew the names.

The herald proclaimed, "The Erechtheids."

Thucydides' Leontids would be fourth, Pericles' Acamantid tribe fifth.

A Council member of the Erechtheid tribe read his list of candidates. The names were repeated. Council members responsible for the separate tribal sections counted hands, and others recorded the totals.

"Perhaps we should save ourselves trouble and elect all our magistrates and officers by the lot, generals included." Andocides polished the handle of his dagger hidden under his cloak (weapons were not permitted).

"There's a reason generals are almost our only elected officials. Do you want to fight under a farmer who's served once in the ranks because his token falls into a slot?" Pericles asked. "Do you want the fate of Athens to rest in the hands of inexperience?"

"Even this way, the best candidates don't always win."

"The Demos usually makes the right choice." Knowing he said that often, Pericles forced himself to say it now.

"Well, at least if the Demos chooses wrongly with one general, there are nine other generals to share the load."

The recorders brought the totals from each tribe to the chief recorder, who tallied votes and presented the totals to the Presiding Officer, who announced the winning candidate. One general had been elected.

"The Aigeids."

The same procedure was repeated, and a second general was elected.

"The Pandionids."

When Andocides' name was called, Pericles twisted for a fast look behind. "You have it."

"We can't be sure until all the names are voted."

But when the Presiding Officer read off the result, it was as Pericles had said.

"From the Pandionids, Andocides is elected general."

Andocides flushed red, and his eyes shone. Reaching over, Pericles gripped his arm.

"The Leontids." Thucydides' tribe.

Pericles held to regular breathing.

"Diphilus."

They're looking for excitement—men miss war's urgency.

"Thucydides."

Hands surged like carp for bread.

Shortsighted. Small-minded. Stinking-mouthed. Selfish Thucydides.

A man who drops cut marble on the path for the weeds—

"Philo."

Only a summer's worth of marble, though—he can't stop the buildings.

"Hippon."

For all of Thucydides shortsighted, small-minded, stinking-mouthed, selfish, cheap gyrations, when it came to pay for serving on the juries, the vote was almost unanimous.

And as for Athens' power abroad . . .

"Phanus."

. . . while he had enlarged the navy, defended friends, established new cleruchies despite this cheap, shortsighted Thuc—

"From the Leontids, Thucydides."

During the Leontids tally, Sophocles had sauntered over and congratulated Andocides. To Pericles, he said, "Suspense and Pain are brothers."

"You came over here to find out how I feel in this critical moment."

Sophocles nodded.

"I want to do all I can to benefit your art but I'll keep that to myself."

"The Acamantids."

The silence had its own voice: they'd come for this one.

"Conon."

One might argue that being born into his tribe shouldn't prevent a man from rising to general.

"Macron."

He could argue that himself.

"Glaucon."

Arms brushed upward.

From the sound of it, he might have to make that argument.

"Epictetus."

The word was they were tired of him, or—Sophocles' precision—"They're tired of your success."

Simon had told him, "They fear you'll take over one-man rule."

"Some fools claim you favor the new gods of natural causes," Xenon had said.

Damon whistled through his teeth. "A, S, P, A . . . "

"Lycus."

All of it was true.

And none of it was critical.

"Antiphilus."

Without war, shipwrights were missing the business, despite that motion he'd pushed through for ten new warships. Sailors were missing the overseas pay.

At the call of his name, he assured himself that no one could see the blood push abruptly against his veins—though he'd heard his name uttered publicly more than any man, just as his mother had predicted in giving him the name Pericles—spoken of all around. Or was it the name that . . .?

"You may have it," Andocides said.

But Pericles saw the spaces between hands as an old mouth with a lot of missing teeth. He checked Ariphron—his brother was looking the other way, but his arm was up.

"From the Acamantids, Glaucon is elected general."

Glaucon. The sword Pericles gripped in his right hand took a direct hit from Zeus' lightning, shaking his arm so hard he nearly dropped it and blackening his mind—though in fact he held no sword. Glaucon—whom he'd taken under his wing in Euboea, taught him everything he knew. Pericles steadied his hand, arm, shoulder, chest, and flank—one by one was the best he could do. Then he reached to see if his helmet was still in place, as if he couldn't feel its weight with his eyes closed. He wished he could close his eyes.

Andocides leapt to his feet. "Glaucon's a good fighter but he's just a boy! You taught him everything he knows." His knuckles stretched to white. "I told you—the people can't judge merit."

The applause and the blood in Pericles' ears—either alone was as loud as the rupture of a sea wall.

"Macron."

Above the torrent, a thought hovered like a white-winged creature.

"Euaion."

They hadn't rejected his policies. They'd passed the Thirty Years Peace Treaty.

"Cleomelus."

Yes, and then blamed him for the concessions. Wanting makes men forget—

"Antias."

—that everything's linked.

It's the same with money. Pay the jurors? Don't lower the tribute.

"Nearchus."

His friends sped to him, racers at the pole drop, at the close of the Election Assembly. His arm burning from Zeus' bolt, torrents rushing through him, white-winged creatures circling above—but nevertheless, it was essential he speak. "Glaucon will make a fine general, just as father did in his time."

It had happened. Thucydides, his archrival, was a general. Glaucon, from his own tribe, was a general.

And Pericles was no longer a general. He was just a citizen with one vote.

And an idea.

CHAPTER 23

Eleven Generals

Running in, Philemon tripped against the lamp and knocked it over. "Pericles lost."

Aspasia had no game in her repertory to pull Pericles out of this defeat. He'd been rejected by his tribe. He would not sit with the generals. She could not bear to contemplate his disappointment. *Humiliated.* She closed her ears to the silent word.

"What happened to the lamp?"

She spun around and opened her arms. "Oh Pericles! I'm so terribly sorry . . ."

He set the lamp upright, checking that it was balanced on its three outwardly curved feet, shaped like lions' paws.

"There. That looks alright."

He was courageous, stalwart. But he was human. "Pericles, I'm sorry that you have had this . . ." *Don't say disaster* . . . "setback."

"I saw it coming." He sat, then lay on the couch. "The young men in my tribe need a chance. Plus . . ." He closed his eyes, and just when she thought he might fall asleep said, "I see it as an opportunity."

For paying more attention to his estates? Pericles the farmer? Not likely. "For what?"

"Something I have in mind. My friends will be here this evening. Do we have those cakes Calliope sent in?"

"The ones with the sauce."

"Serve those."

* * *

"Glaucon's too hot-headed," Sophocles said.

Andocides checked the shine on his dagger blade, looking into it like a mirror. "Too inexperienced."

"We have to remember that our young generals learn by serving with the older ones," Archestratus said.

One, thought Pericles.

"It's anti-Pericles and it's wrong," Andocides said.

"Only in that they feared he'd take over one-man rule." Damon's hand hovered above the cakes. "They didn't reject our policies."

"Jealousy aims its arrows high," Sophocles said.

Two.

"It doesn't help that the comic poets call him Zeus." Aspasia was measuring water into the wine.

"And you're his Hera." Breaking his cake in two, Damon spilled crumbs. "According to the comic poets."

A half.

Damon brushed the crumbs from his palms. "The main thing is we have too much peace!"

"There's no such thing as too much peace," Sophocles said. "You mean that differences among men emerge more in peace."

"Reasons, reasons. The point is that without Pericles on the Board of Generals, Thucydides will do a lot of damage," Teisander said. "If he blocks our trade agreements. I'll be too poor to marry off my girls."

"He'll cut loose our allies," Andocides said. "He'll cut the navy. He'll cut."

"The sailors will revolt," Archestratus said.

"Or sign up with our enemies," Andocides said.

"It'll finish pay for serving the city," Damon said. "And when I think of how hard we worked . . . "

Teisander reached over to clap Andocides' thigh. "As our elected general, you're going to have huge responsibility, Andocides."

"I'll do what I can, but how do we make sure Pericles gets back in next year?"

Damon's moistened finger retrieved some crumbs. "Glaucon might fail."

Aspasia was wiping wine from the bottom of the pitcher. "A failure for Glaucon would mean a failure for Athens and we must never hope for that."

Pericles rose, circled his chair and rested his fingers on the back of it. They turned to him for an answer, but he had decided the answer was going to come from them. He could start them off, though.

"*Alpha*," (thumb) "our laws call for our ten tribes to vote individually for their general, so that we have ten generals and, *beta*, (forefinger) "In our democracy, the laws rule."

He waited.

"I have an idea!" Andocides said. "We can watch how things unfold during the year and then bargain with some tribe that lacks a suitable candidate to . . . to lend us a generalship."

"No tribe will volunteer away its rights to our highest position," Sophocles said.

"And nobody would pay back," Damon said.

Pericles tapped the chair. "We must keep in our minds that the laws call for each tribe to vote individually for its general, so that we have ten generals, and in our democracy, the laws rule."

Aspasia flushed alert. It wasn't like Pericles to state the obvious—let alone repeat it.

"I have an idea!" Archestratus said. "We could change the law because Pericles' tribe should have *two* generals."

"To change the law—how radical." Sophocles passed the edge of his cup across his lips. "I'm amazed—how did you ever think of that, Archestratus?"

Aspasia checked—Sophocles was smiling behind his cup.

"This is no time to change the laws," Damon said. "Not with all this concern now about Pericles seeking one-man rule—and that cursed one-horned ram."

"You didn't hear me right. I propose having *two* generals from his tribe," Archestratus said. "That's nothing to do with *one*-man rule."

"We can't give Pericles' tribe anything we don't give the others," Damon said. "One man, one vote. One tribe, one general."

"What if *all* the tribes were allowed two generals?" Sophocles said.

"That would keep the tribes equal." Archestratus scratched his chin. "Pericles, what do you think?"

"It's democratic, but too many generals," Andocides answered.

"What can be the answer?" Pericles closed his eyes and put his hand to his forehead—it encouraged his own thoughts so it might encourage thoughts in others.

"If it's alright to ask a question when I don't have the answer," Teisander said, "why are we talking about two generals from your tribe when your tribe only needs one general? You don't need two men to command one tribal unit. They'd be in each other's way."

"The tribes don't need two generals," Archestratus said. "But Athens needs Pericles."

After a silence of puzzled agreement, Aspasia cleared her throat. "Why don't w—" She checked herself—it was not wise to say "we" in this discussion about generals—and began again. "Since, as you all so wisely say, Athens needs Pericles, I have a suggestion, though of course I'm not out there on the battlefield. But my thought is, since what you need is Pericles, and he's just one person, well, I see that there might be a logic in . . . " *Out with it, Aspasia.* "Why don't you just add on one additional general, and he would be Pericles."

"Nonsense!" Damon looked around for agreement on that from others. "She doesn't even know that Pericles and Glaucon are both from the Acamantids."

She saw no need to prove she knew who was who in Athens. "That's not what I'm saying. I'm suggesting that you let Glaucon command the Acamantids." They were looking at her not in annoyance, or surprise, or anger or condescension (except for Damon who managed to crowd all of that into his thin face). She took satisfaction is seeing that they wanted an explanation, and she went on. "The way I would have it, you would put Pericles in as general for everybody."

Sophocles smiled. "I think Aspasia means that we could elect one general from all the Athenians—"

"That's tyranny," Damon said.

"—while continuing to elect one general from each of the tribes."

She was surprised to get support from Sophocles—her idea must be excellent. She glanced at Pericles. He was smiling, too. But at her idea? Or because he was getting what he wanted?

"Yes! We'll vote for eleven generals," Andocides said.

"Good idea. Andocides," Archestratus said. "But we lose out unless Pericles is the man elected general from all the Athenians. How do we make sure he wins?"

"That's not a demo—"

"It may not be democratic enough for you, Damon, but we must have him in office."

Damon shook his head. "Pericles above all the other generals— well, he's a democrat. But if another man took that spot, it could lead to tyranny."

Pericles had no argument with Damon there. The new tribes were meant to break down the old divisions and create unity but too often produced the opposite—no surprise to Heraclitus. But if he tried to abolish the tribes, they'd have a revolution on their hands. One step at a time.

"It's not just that I'd be in office," Pericles said. "One general all the Athenians agreed on would unify the city."

"Am I hearing right?" Damon circled around to look directly into Pericles' face. "Have you forgotten you just *lost*?"

"We're talking about *next* year, right Pericles?" Archestratus asked.

Pericles nodded.

Damon shook his head. "How, when you've just been defeated, voted down, say it any way you want, can you possibly propose that the Demos votes to make you some new kind of general with more power than any of the others?"

"I see merit in the idea," Archestratus said.

"You'll inspire Thucydides' vile figures of speech," Damon said. "I can already hear him ranting about the homegrown cannibal Tyranny devouring his friends and neighbors—"

"Don't help Thucydides make a speech," Archestratus said.

"Damon, look at it this way—it's like our empire," Teisander said. "The cities of our alliance have autonomy, but at the same time we unify them. We're just first among equals. It's best for them and best for us."

"And like our empire it wouldn't be undemocratic," Andocides said. "All the generals would be in charge and one would have overall charge."

"Tied votes are always a problem—eleven generals get us out of that," Archestratus said.

"And think how efficient it would be in war," Andocides said. "By far more efficient. I can't wait to try it out."

"We're at peace and we'll remain at peace," Pericles said.

"We always have battles to fight," Andocides said. "I like my idea—we'll call him General from all the Athenians. What do you think, Sophocles?"

His idea? She had done everything but give it the name. She felt as if somebody had swiped a gold coin from her pouch. But she couldn't interrupt these men and say, "I thought of it first." Even Pericles never claimed, "I thought of it first." The hubris of it. And from a woman . . .

As Sophocles straightened his back preparing to speak, Aspasia hoped he'd remind them that she'd thought of it first. But Sophocles stayed to the matter at hand. "It solves how to have two generals from Pericles' tribe but there's no guarantee Pericles will win."

Those precious words, "*as Aspasia said*"—she wasn't going to hear them, not this time.

"Pericles will win," Andocides said.

"He didn't win today," Sophocles said. "Pericles, what will you do about Thucydides?"

But that didn't stop her from saying, "You have to get Thucydides out of the way."

"Don't you see, Sophocles—now there'll be room for Pericles *and* Glaucon. You may not want to propose it yourself, Pericles—the one-horned ram and all that—so I will," Archestratus said.

"I'll propose it!" Teisander said.

"*I'll* propose it!" Andocides said. "What about it, Pericles?"

"I'll think about it."

"What's there to think about?"

How to ensure a win, that's what.

CHAPTER 24

His Crown and Shield

From the Acropolis path, Pericles and Damon paused to look over the city, and hills and valleys of the countryside. But though they were on their way to see how Phidias had set up shop to work the ivory, Damon had politics on his mind.

"It's time we start planning for the election for that fancy new title you came up with—General from all the Athenians," Damon said.

It was an intrusion in his thoughts. "Damon, we're on our way to see Phidias' preparations to complete the gold and ivory Athena and all you can think of is politics."

Damon slapped his palms together—to warm them or to get ready for a fight. "The Athenians are restless. You lost an election because of too much peace."

That refrain of "too much peace" again. It was as if the Athenians had forgotten the losses of war as fast as women forget the pains of childbirth, or so they say. As if the benefits of peace had become taken for granted.

"Thanks to Zeus for the Peace Treaty!"

Still, Damon's view held a nub of truth. "Let's put it this way, Damon. What you call restless, I call enterprising. That's why we're going to cross the sea! I plan to establish the new colony in Italy that will capture the Athenians' imagination and spirit of—"

Pericles spotted Philemon, who stayed in town now as his houseman, running toward them up the hill against the wind.

Breathless, Philemon blurted out, "Aspasia's feeling the pains! Zoe's walking her around the room!"

Pericles started down the hill. "Have they sent for the doctor?"

"I don't know."

"Should she be on her feet? Damon, what do you think?"

"Probably—I'm not sure."

"It would be just like Zoe to think she can manage the delivery herself."

"I'm sure Aspasia will call in the doctor."

Turning into his street, Pericles' heart jumped—someone had already painted the front door with pitch.

The inner door to their rooms was locked. Of course. He thumbed his Syrian amulet for good luck. Dion's birth story flew about his mind like a panicked bat. What if the child came out feet first? Or if a large head stopped her up like a cork on a bottle—he averted his eyes from the thought.

He didn't need a third son—especially a bastard. It wasn't worth the risk of losing Aspasia even if, as she was certain, the child would turn out intelligent, forceful, and handsome. And a boy. But the deformed head might have just skipped his other boys, like a curse that hides underground for years before . . .

* * *

Beneath the table were two buckets of seawater. Mint was useful for ordinary cleansing, Zoe told Silky, but salt water was best for purifying a house after a birth or a death.

"Since birth and death are opposites, why do we use seawater for both?" Silky asked.

"Because the path up is the path down."

Silky looked disappointed. "Oh, Zoe, that has nothing to do with salt water."

Leaning on Silky's shoulder, Aspasia shuffled past the table with her cosmetics and her silver mirror, the cupboard with her jewelry, the clothing chests, the shelf with her books, and around the two couches—someone had removed the cushions from one and covered the other with linen. Pausing at the window, she looked out at the olive tree, and then continued past the two chairs where she and Silky sometimes sat spinning—the basket was half-full with balls of wool—past the brazier and the tables with the linens and blankets, the spoons, strainers, and herbs to the door. Then, with Silky at her side, she retraced her route. Her room began to seem both confining and very large, like the ocean of Odysseus. The familiar objects of her life were like islands in the water, landmarks of Odysseus' journey, as if she were in a world in which nothing existed beyond what she could see, and she wasn't certain she'd ever reach anywhere else.

The doctor set his stool between the door posts. He'd had a carpenter cut a hole out of the top so a woman could sit on it during the first part of delivery, to conserve her strength, he said, and then kneel on it when the baby was set to emerge.

Amycla fingered the smooth edge. "Spartan women don't need it."

The doctor ground leaves of lemon balm. Aspasia groaned. Zoe, pouring hot water through a strainer filled with chamomile, looked up. Aspasia, who had halted, continued on. The doctor emptied and refilled his water clock.

"For now she can rest on the couch." The doctor spooned four measures of olive oil over a spoonful of the lemon balm and mixed them in a bowl.

Silky and Zoe led Aspasia to the cushionless couch. Leaning on her elbow, Aspasia sipped the chamomile. She hadn't thought anything could make her feel better.

Abruptly she pushed the cup away, spilling the chamomile, and pressed her lips together. *They say any kind of baby hurts.*

The doctor checked the water level—higher than last time— and told Zoe to put the bowl with tarragon over the brazier. She acted quickly, making clear she didn't need the doctor to tell her what to do with tarragon. Setting the bowl beside Aspasia's couch, she squeezed the tarragon to a pulp through her fingers, covered a piece of linen with it, and gently pressed the warm mixture against Aspasia's hard belly. Aspasia sighed. In a moment she felt another pain. *Or which way it comes out.*

With Zoe and Silky supporting her, Aspasia began her walk again, pausing so often that the water in the clock had little time to sink below the rim.

"Do you feel warm?" the doctor asked.

"Of course she does," Amycla said. "It's hot as Hades in here."

As the doctor sponged Aspasia's forehead with cool water, she gripped his arm.

"Grip harder," he said.

They helped her kneel on the stool and Aspasia seized the post.

The doctor said, "You have a firm grip." She felt proud.

He knelt. "The baby's head is showing."

"What do you see!" Was that her scream?

"A smooth patch of the crown," Zoe said.

Head first was one thing to know.

A spasm. Gripping the post, she pushed hard—she felt less pain that way. No, it *was* hurting less.

"A beautiful head," Zoe said. *Beautiful but . . . Zoe always tried to bring comfort.*

"It looks like a bloody wet bat," said Amycla.

"A bat! What—" *Was it ugly? Bats have small heads.*

"She means a pretty little face," Zoe said.

Little.

Pain again—but it's alright because they allow you to scream when you're giving birth.

The doctor rose to his feet, rounded elbows, arms full. That new doctor Pericles had brought in was standing up—her baby was here! A sigh ran through her from the deep place where sighs are born.

She felt the arms of Silky, Zoe and Amycla lifting her off the stool.

"It's a boy," Zoe said.

The doctor cut the cord.

"I'll tell Pericles!" Silky started toward the door.

"Wait!"

"Wash him in wine as we do in Sparta," Amycla said. "If he doesn't die of convulsions, you'll know he's a strong child."

"Don't tell the doctor what to do," Aspasia said.

Zoe was applying lemon balm to her cuts and sponging her off. "We don't follow barbarous customs here."

"A bath in cold water will be sufficient." The doctor held the baby by his heels, examining him.

Zoe spun around. "Listen to that boy cry!"

"A perfect child." The doctor turned the tiny body on all sides. "He's meant to draw breath."

"A little Heracles," Zoe said, "born strong as he could be."

Aspasia raised herself on her elbow. *No lion head.* She thought of Pericles' short prayers and came up with one herself. *Thanks to Artemis!*

"*Now* call Pericles."

When he entered, Aspasia was leaning back against the cushions, eating pear jelly.

Pericles examined the baby on all sides, moved his limbs, and pressed his thumb into the baby's palm. By Zeus, if he didn't see his own features on a normal head. Nature was skilled at carving a likeness. He loved this child immediately. "He looks like an Alcmaeonid." Though he was dark like Aspasia.

An Alcmaeonid. She'd borne a son of the illustrious Athenian family, no matter what they had to say here about citizenship. An Alcmaeonid had to be a citizen somehow. In some way.

Zoe wrapped the baby in linen.

Amycla shook her head. "We don't bind Spartan babies."

"*Surely* you swaddled Young Cleinias and Alcibiades," Zoe said.

"Surely I did *not*."

"Now I know why they're growing up like barbarians." Zoe turned to the doctor as he was leaving. "Wait—why did you bring rue? You didn't use it."

"Since we believe that rue will encourage the beginning of a girl's monthly periods, I surmise that it also opens the womb. So when a woman spends a long day in painful labor to no avail, a small amount may speed things up."

Zoe snapped her fingers with emphatic regret. "Wish I'd known that when it was your time, Silky."

Tears flooded Silky's eyes.

Zoe lay the baby across Aspasia's chest and rubbed its mouth across her breast. They watched its tiny purple lips circle the nipple. When the baby started to suck, warmth spread from Pericles' chest and shoulders through his neck to his face. His eyes grew moist.

Pericles drew from his cloak a gift for the baby—twined snakes, wrought in gold, the sign of an ancient Athenian king whom Athena had reared as if he were her own child—some said he really was Athena's child.

Gently leaning over to kiss the top of Aspasia's hair, he said, "And this is the child of my Athena."

She seized his arm. "Have you thought about the name?"

Zoe placed the gold snakes under the crib cushion.

He sat back. "I have a few more days to decide."

"But have you put your mind to it?"

"Since the Athenians are eager to claim territory in the West, I could name him Italius."

"Be serious."

"I am being serious. Did you know that Themistocles called his daughters Italia and Sybaris?"

Zoe frowned. "Those are girls' names."

Aspasia lifted her face and looked into his eyes. "I know the name you really want."

"That's impossible, I've said nothing."

"Xanthippus is named after your father, but"—Aspasia's voice held the humor of one who asks while knowing the answer—"why did you name your second son Paralus? It's a most unusual name and doesn't run in your family."

"It's the name of our state ship, a perfectly good name."

"Paralus is a good name for a ship but an odd one for a child. I think you had another reason."

"What, then?"

"Paralus sounds a little like Pericles." He started to shake his head. "Not the same, but more alike than most names. You wanted to name your second son Pericles, but Aristocleia didn't."

"Paralus and Pericles don't sound alike to me . . . Aspasia, you're like the Delphic oracle in discerning what's hidden, though— Aristocleia did not like my name."

"And now you want to name this boy Pericles."

The baby made a small sound. Pericles watched her place her nipple back in his mouth. "Look how strong he is for a newborn." What a tactical mistake! But he couldn't help himself.

"That shows he'll grow to be forceful, intelligent and handsome, like his father. He should be named Pericles."

"No."

Zoe shuffled toward the door, pushing Amycla ahead of her.

"I want him to be named Pericles," Aspasia said.

An illegitimate child, and the son of a foreigner—with the name Pericles. No. He could never present this child to his brotherhood or register him in the Alcmaeonids' deme, the country town where the family had its roots and most of its property. This child would never be an Athenian citizen, barring, that is, some extraordinary event. And even if that did happen—highly unlikely to remote—he'd still be a bastard.

"It cannot be. In my family, names skip a generation or two. My father was Xanthippus and my son is Xanthippus. That's how we do it."

"Cleinias named his son Cleinias."

"They do it differently. Anyhow, that was his first son. I certainly would not have named my second son Pericles no matter what you say." He thought that should put an end to it. "Or a third."

Letting his inconsistency fly past, she raised her hands toward his face. "I've never asked you for anything, but now I'm asking for this."

Never asked him for anything. He had taken her from the streets and placed her in a fine home. His home. Surrounded her with beautiful objects, provided her with every luxury. Silver. Gold. Silks. He had sent her an astonishing piece of cloth, dyed purple, from Euboea. He paid money toward her house. He had divorced his wife to be with her. The citizens were aghast but he'd done it. How could she say that she'd never asked for anything?

Her fingers touched his chin. "I want you to name him Pericles more than anything in the world."

Well, what had she asked for?

She had refused to marry Dion. But that was refusing.

229

She was certainly happy when he said he'd help pay for her house, but she'd figured out how to do it herself. That little arrangement he'd pulled off so she could own it was nothing.

Hah! He could say *you asked me to intervene for Dion's citizenship.* But how petty that would be—she'd let go of it as soon as she'd seen why he couldn't do it.

He took his thoughts back to the beginning. She hadn't even asked for the *Odyssey.* Not that she didn't have her ways of getting what she wanted.

"I want no other name for him," she said.

"Why are you pushing this on me? I have days to decide."

He left and told Philemon to tie an olive sprig above the door of the house to let everyone know that a boy had been born.

* * *

In off moments, he tried to think of a name for the baby. A hero's name might console Aspasia for not naming him Pericles. He ran through names—Theseus—Ajax—Achilles—but they all met sad ends. Anyhow, that would be hubris. The names in his family were out—Cleisthenes, Megacles, and so on. By the time the baby's fifth day celebration came round, he had decided on the name "Hippocrates" as a compromise because it was used in his family and in other families as well.

The scent of lamb ribs braising with onions, cabbage leaves frying in oil, cheese imported from the Chersonese, crusted and baking, along with the clattering of cooking pots reached even their quiet room, where Pericles sat with Aspasia as she nursed the baby. Zoe came in to clean and oil her "little Heracles" for the ceremony. Humming, she wrapped him in a blanket with an embroidered picture of the Gorgon monster across his chest. The details traced in the threads were as precise as if they'd been painted by an artist's brush—the flat, ugly face, bulging eyes, snakes sprouting from the monster's head, fangs, a huge grinning mouth, and that disgusting, unwomanly beard.

Pericles leapt up.

"Take that hideous blanket off the child."

"I copied it from a cup and embroidered the Gorgon myself.'"

"Children are easily influenced. I want nothing frightening near him."

"It will protect him." Zoe tucked it under the baby's chin.

"Take the cloak away, Zoe," Aspasia said.

"But every child wears one. Even Athena wears the Gorgon on her breastplate."

"Let Athena wear the monster when she fights for us," Pericles said. "I won't have this child raised amid these superstitions. Do as I say." Zoe unwound the cloak. "Take it out of this room and out of this house."

"He doesn't need the cloak." Aspasia comforted Zoe but looked directly at Pericles. "He has Pericles to protect him."

Protect, protect, protect. Everyone wanted him to protect. He protected Athens. He protected the Parthenon's budget. He protected democracy—make that *democracies.* He protected his household. He protected Aspasia. He protected his sons—and Cleinias' sons. Nobody, however, protected him.

Except Agariste.

He could only imagine what had happened when he was born. His father turning him on all sides as the women averted their eyes from his overlarge head. Ariphron was too young to remember. And his sister wouldn't speak about it.

In war, Pericles had faced spears, swords and arrows, but he knew with a certainty that the moment of his birth was the nearest he had come to death.

"Have you decided on a name?" Aspasia asked.

"I've given it a good deal of thought."

How could he come out with Hippocrates?

He was silent for too long.

She smiled. "Remember, I told you it would be a boy."

He nodded.

"So now you'll believe me when I say he will grow to be intelligent, forceful, and handsome, just like his father."

What can a man say to those words, spoken by a woman he loves?

"But Pericles, I know the truth of things. I know that you won't be able to present this darling, beautiful little baby . . . " she kissed the baby on his nose . . . "to your brotherhood. I know that he'll be left out of your deme. He won't be permitted to exercise at the best palaestra."

"Who told you that?"

"Xanthippus."

Pericles cracked his knuckles.

"Those are what a father gives his sons and you won't be able to do that."

Of course, she was right. This boy was fated for a bad ticket at the theater.

His head rested on his hand, his brow furrowed. He looked so unhappy. "My Pericles." She reached out and touched his cheek. She would like to see him smile.

"But how lucky, how amazingly fortunate that there's one thing you can give him that nobody else can. You might say . . . a person could possibly even say it's better than all those other things."

But how could he hand over his own name to an illegitimate child?

"Your name, Pericles, will carry him through the rough seas."

"It's a name, Aspasia. It doesn't change the laws."

"It's the veil of the sea goddess that protected Odysseus."

"You may be overestimating the effect of my name."

"Maybe so." He was surprised that she shrugged. Then she raised her eyebrows and smiled. "But this much is certain. It's the best you can do for him."

That was true.

"You should be arguing cases in the law courts, Aspasia."

* * *

"God Whose Face We Do Not Know," Pericles raised his cup, "I pray that my household will be purified." He stood his distance, watching the poured libation set the flames to flare and spatter in approval. The blaze of the hearth heated the faces of everyone in his household, all scrubbed, crowned with myrtle wreaths and wearing the new cloaks and gowns Pericles had given them to honor the new child. Ariphron, evidently, didn't need a fine new cloak at no cost to himself—he'd turned down Pericles' invitation to attend the ceremony of Running-Around-The-Hearth.

Zoe held the baby high—for most, it was their first glimpse of the child who would share their home—and she circled the hearth slowly with him in her arms, the other women falling in behind: fat, short Zoe, tall, regal Aspasia, Silky, plump and pretty, and bony Amycla.

"Run, Zoe!" Alcibiades shouted. "You're thupposed to run around the hearth!"

"You're supposed to run, Zoe," Paralus echoed.

Young Cleinias jumped up and down. "Run, Zoe, run!"

Zoe maintained her stately pace.

"Zoe's too old to run," Xanthippus said.

Along with his new deep voice, Xanthippus had taken to smoothing back the hair on his temples as Ariphron did.

"Take off your clothes, Zoe," Alcibiades called out. "In this theremony you're thuppothed to run around the hearth naked!"

"You're supposed to take your clothes off," Paralus said.

Young Cleinias jumped higher. "Naked Zoe! Naked Zoe!"

Amycla left her place in line and hit Alcibiades across the mouth. His hand flew to his jaw and tears filled his eyes. Amycla stepped back in behind Silky.

The women moved faster while the onlookers clapped them to a faster pace. Not every woman circles the hearth after giving birth, Pericles thought. Under her gown Aspasia was near to the shape he loved—his familiar coast. At first he didn't notice that the women's path had become irregular and their steps were faltering.

They're dizzy! So was everyone else, from watching them—so was he. He grasped Zoe by the shoulder—she must not fall holding the child. He'd fathered three normal sons. He owed the gods something for that.

"I think we've gone round thirty times!" Silky was laughing and breathless. Even Amycla smiled as she shook her head to regain balance.

Pericles raised his hand and waited until they were quiet enough to hear him. "The god of running around the hearth,

Amphidromios, is surely in our midst tonight—we have proof of his presence." Everyone laughed knowingly. "And we've fulfilled his rite of running around the hearth with interest."

The laughter kept coming like the rills in a wake. He'd heard—and encouraged—laughter like that in the Assembly but couldn't remember such hilarity in his household.

"We'll enter Zoe in the running races at the Games this summer!" He turned and picked up an extra wreath.

"And the'll win!"

When Pericles set a wreath on Zoe's head, her cheeks were wet with perspiration and tears of laughter.

He looked at Aspasia holding the child on her lap, like the small, clay statue of the Great Mother directly behind her on the altar.

"The naming ceremony is five days away, but you have warmly welcomed the new child into our household tonight. You will want to know what to call him. The new baby will be named Pericles."

Pericles enjoyed the shared gasp—he'd heard that gasp in the Assembly when he'd announced that, if the Demos wouldn't pay, then he would himself pay for the ivory.

Steady as a helmsman, Aspasia held up the infant. "When good fortune favors him, the name will be his crown, and if she turns from him, it will be his shield."

It was no surprise to Pericles to see Aristocleia's crooked smile on Xanthippus' face. Xanthippus' first response to most things was bitterness veiled by irony—like his mother. In time, though, Xanthippus usually came around.

Palms hearthward, Pericles prayed to Hestia for the child's protection, the household's prosperity, and good health for everyone in it. Then he sent more wine sizzling on the flames. They all came up for a close look at the child, each adding a date, fig, or honeycomb wedge to the sweets piling at Aspasia's feet—Xanthippus tossed a raisin onto the lap of the little statue of the Mother Goddess. "It's all she can hold."

Pericles raised a toast, "To those who made Athens free."

Aspasia's face flushed. The toast should be to the baby. Xanthippus smirked. But if she made her own toast to the baby now, she'd be countering Pericles in front of his sons and all the rest of them. She and Pericles were allies, not these others. She let it pass. She'd won the prize, and it was no little raisin.

Birth drains strength from a woman, Pericles thought, but not his Aspasia. How rosy her cheeks looked, how bright her eyes. With one arm she supported the baby's back—days old and he looked as if he was sitting up by himself. Zoe called him a baby Heracles. He did look robust, able. And intelligent—you'd think he was watching everyone although, they say, babies that young can barely see. Or is it that they see and don't know how to make sense of it? Well, when it came to making sense of things, this baby had the right mother. Unlike the other boys—the young ones already back to startling Zoe's chickens and his older son— gone out already? Pericles reviewed the boys in the family . . . his sons Xanthippus and Paralus, his wards Alcibiades and Young Cleinias.

Now he had a Little Pericles.

How would this Little Pericles grow? What kind of man would he become?

One could even imagine . . . Aspasia had given him good counsel from the time he'd met her. She'd stood unwavering when he'd been voted out of office. With a mother who could do all of that for a man, this might be the son to take on the leadership of Athens. Although there was that problem of his citizenship.

She had the baby at her breast. Thinking of the Odyssey with large letters she'd made for her son before he was born, he smiled to himself. *She'll have him reading before he's weaned!*

The child would grow to read Homer and learn how Odysseus had found Nausicaa. He would learn how Odysseus had fooled the one-eyed Cyclops monster. He would learn how far and for how long Odysseus had been at sea before he found his way back home.

Aspasia smiled across to Pericles. He nodded back.

My Aspasia. With her, he'd discovered the sweetness in life.

Yes, that was true about the sweetness in life—and she might like to know that. He'd tell her sometime. But he knew he'd given this lovely woman what she'd wanted most, their son's name.

He leaned over to the child. "So, you're Little Pericles."

He'd always wanted a son who would bear his name into the future. In fact, he'd never realized it but perhaps that was what he'd wanted most.

That's how it seemed that evening.

CHAPTER 25

The Ostracism

"I told you never to listen to Alcibiades," Xanthippus said. "He lies."

"You mean the Athenians *won't* ostracize father?"

"I'd be glad if they sent him all the way to the Pillars of Heracles. But it won't happen."

Paralus rolled a pebble around under his sandal. "What makes you so sure?"

"Because father wouldn't have gotten them to hold the ostracism if he thought he'd lose it. Oh Paralus, don't get weepy on me now. I'm telling you it's all just to get Thucydides out of Athens so father can be elected General from all the Athenians."

Paralus licked away a tear. "But an ostracism is a vote, isn't it?"

Xanthippus thought for a moment. "It's a reverse vote since whoever gets the most votes loses and has to leave Athens for ten years."

"But father says you never know what will happen when men vote."

"He says that, but he's got them so excited about his new colony in Italy he knows he's safe."

"But if he has to leave Athens, Alcibiades says we'd have to live at Ariphron's."

"We'd live with our mother at Hipponicus' house. He's so rich we'd get anything we wanted, and we'd be rid of Alcibiades and Cleinias."

"Would Aspasia go back to being a hetaira?"

"That's all she is now."

"But where would she live?"

Xanthippus twirled his walking stick on a stone, making it stand up briefly on its own.

"Pericles would probably take her wherever he went."

"But would she go with him?"

"How do I know? I suppose so. You ask more questions than Socrates. Anyhow, none of this will happen, so stop listening to Alcibiades."

* * *

Pericles held the pottery cup—a kind no longer made—by the handles. The picture was so small he had to bring it close. Heracles was wrestling with the lion, pressing the animal to the ground with brute force. In a moment the lion would fall because with one hand Heracles held the lion's back leg, throwing him off balance. Pericles turned the cup to see the other side. Athena, wearing her Gorgon breastplate, was spearing a giant, who fell bleeding to the earth. The giant turned his face to look directly out at Pericles. He reached up to set the cup back on its high shelf but it fell and broke. His father would be angry. Maybe he could fix it. He picked up a large potsherd and saw letters scratched into the black glaze. He grew alarmed.

He cried out, "They spelled my name wrong!"

Aspasia was shaking him, which speeded the pounding of his heart like a spurred horse. In the balance, he was glad to be awake.

"What troubled you?" She wouldn't embarrass him with "frightened."

"Nothing—just a dream."

"Some dreams are dark—telling what happened in them can make the shadows disappear."

"No shadows, Aspasia. In fact, as I think back on it, there was nothing of concern."

"Breathe deeply."

He did, and on an outward breath he began recounting the dream.

Aspasia nodded her head. "I can tell you easily what that dream was about—the ostracism."

"How do you mean?"

"You saw your name on a potsherd—just as the day after tomorrow, people will cast their votes by scratching the name of the man they want ostracized on a sherd." He looked so troubled that she added, "And that man will be Thucydides."

"What about Heracles and the lion?"

"That shows it was a false dream."

"Why false?"

Dreams didn't predict anything, Aspasia thought, but bad dreams could be discouraging.

"Because *you* are the lion. You told me that your mother dreamed she would give birth to a lion. In the dream, the lion was losing to Heracles, but you know you won't lose the ostracism. Thucydides will. So the dream is false."

He did expect to win the ostracism, but—*beware of hubris.*

"What about Athena and the giant?"

"Probably because Phidias was talking the other day about painting the gods fighting the giants on the shield of the gold and ivory Athena."

"But why was the giant looking directly out at me?" For some reason, that made him most uneasy.

"It's odd," she said thoughtfully, "but it's not important. Now and then, somebody looks out in pictures."

"And what if my dream wasn't false?" Pericles smiled to dismiss the importance of what he was saying. "Maybe I'll lose the ostracism."

What if—What if would be no dream—it would be disaster. The second disaster of her life. Pericles would be forced—*forced*—to leave Athens for ten years. She had not asked where he would go—never allowed him a glimpse of uncertainty. And really, she *wasn't* uncertain. But where would he go? And would he take her and Little Pericles with him? Would her baby grow up in some new place she didn't know?

Her arm circled his shoulders. "The Athenians love your plans for the new colony in Italy. They're drunk on it."

"I don't want them drunk—I want them to understand."

Good, he was telling instead of asking—she'd brought him back again. Though that part about the lion had been tricky.

"The lofty thinkers see, as do you, something new and wonderful coming into the world, like Athena newborn from the head of Zeus—a perfect colony in Italy in which Greeks from many cities will live together in harmony."

"They'll share the same friends and the same enemies—it should be that way among the Greeks, always and everywhere."

"As for the other Athenians, they can't wait to step into the foothold for the Italian trade. And as you say, that's also a good reason."

"It's well timed."

"In more ways than one."

Pericles leaned back against the cushions.

"Ostracism isn't a punishment, but it might as well be. Do you know how I learned that my father was ostracized? My mother was wailing and I assumed he was dead. Then she said he'd been sent away for ten years. *Ten years*, Aspasia. Think of that."

She wished she could write Thucydides' name on a potsherd. She wished she could write it a hundred times. "But he wasn't away that long."

"They called him back to fight Persia. That's why ostracism is better than death. They call you back fast enough when they need you." He thumbed the edge of the cushion. "By my count, my father was away four years and one month."

"In Miletus, they say Athenians use ostracism to avoid civil strife."

"The Athenians established ostracism to prevent one-man rule. They'd had enough of tyranny. That was the idea anyhow. Do you remember Herodotus' story of the king who scythed down the tallest wheat in his own field to frighten his noblemen?"

"I've always thought it was a stupid waste of good wheat."

"Ostracism is like that. By the way, I've lined up Herodotus to sail with the colonists to the new colony."

"No—I want to hear the end of his history!"

"He likes to see new places. And he'll record what goes on there for me."

They settled down to sleep.

After a few moments, she said, "In the past they ostracized great men. Thucydides isn't worthy of it—though I'm glad you're getting him out of the way."

"It's better for Athens."

In the quiet, his thoughts circled back to his dream. Why had his name been misspelled on the potsherd? What would Aspasia have to say about that? But she was asleep. No matter, some questions remain unanswered.

* * *

Bronze clattered—a pot in the kitchen. Upstairs he could hear Paralus and Xanthippus rolling around the floor in their morning scuffle—Paralus' high, excited laugh meeting Xanthippus' new, deep, superior chuckle. Aspasia had moved his wards to the other side of the house to keep peace among the boys. Pericles, remembering his nighttime visions of combat and loss, saw they were irrelevant. He hadn't persuaded the Assembly to hold the ostracism in order to lose. They needed him to fulfill their plans.

The Athenians' plans were like children of different ages. Some were ready to be sent on their way and others still needed nurture. Still others lay like seeds. The Athenians might not know when they germinated, but he knew. And they trusted him to know. They turned against him from time to time, irritated with his success and tired of his knowing, but they wouldn't deprive themselves of him.

Not now when they were united in spirit about colonizing New Sybaris in Italy.

He wouldn't lose, but unless six thousand votes were cast, the ostracism wouldn't count. Thucydides the Sunspot would continue to float before his eyes. There was good reason for that high number—no one should have to leave his home for a trivial cause or someone's private revenge. But six thousand was almost three times the number of citizens who attended an ordinary Assembly.

So Pericles had ridden out to the demes urging everyone to come in to vote. He'd covered so much ground that he felt like Theseus unifying Attica. In each deme, each town, a friend with property

241

greeted him in the local Agora. Hearing that Pericles was coming, people gathered.

In Kerameis, a young man lofted a two-year-old high above his head.

"Pericles! Remember me?"

"Timaios! You helped us take Euboea!"

"Here's my son—born while we were fighting. What do you think of him?"

Since Timaios had asked, Pericles looked directly at the fat child. "What a strong boy! He'll make a fine Athenian, like his father."

An old man used his cane to push through the crowd.

"Pericles, how do you expect a poor farmer to lose a day's work coming into town for an ostracism?"

"Your hives are repaired?"

He nodded.

"Your figs are drying?"

"Already dry."

"You've pressed your olives?"

He nodded.

"Then mend your harnesses some other day and come into the city for the vote. You can sell some figs and oil in town."

He'd saved the day before the ostracism for Piraeus. Some farmers thought that with bees and figs, they could do without an empire, but not the sailors and traders. They were for him with one mind, as the sea is one. He rode down with Damon—Damon-the-democrat was almost as beloved in Piraeus as Pericles.

At Hestia's new shrine, Pericles inhaled deeply: freshly cut marble smelled like water at the source. The plane trees, grafts from Athens' Agora, were like the antlers of young deer with few points— another year and the sun wouldn't be in his eyes.

He stepped forward to acknowledge the decree passed in his honor.

"It's right that we spend funds on the design of Piraeus, on its civic, religious, and commercial buildings and on its docks and ship sheds. The funds of our league of allies come here first and are largely created by the activity of this great port. The produce . . . "

He raised his hand to quiet the applause.

"Without Piraeus, the produce of our lands and the articles we manufacture would be like words without deeds, for it's from here they're sent into the world."

Again, loud applause.

"In the past, people made just what their families used and men grew only what they needed for themselves. There was little movement of goods in or out of our territory. Back then, as Hesiod tells us, famine and injustice were men's constant companions. Now our shops are filled with our goods, and there's nothing grown or made in the world that can't be found in our markets. And if we run short, we have what it takes to purchase what we need—"

"And friends to give it to us!" someone shouted out.

"And why are they our friends? Why did the Egyptian Psammetichus send us the wheat last year?"

"Because we're rich and powerful!"

They clapped and laughed.

A beam hit a marble corner and cast a glint into Pericles' eye.

"In those early times, only men with substantial property could attend the Assembly but the poor man, or the sailor—and there were a few sailors then—had no say in government."

He gave them time to think about those days.

"Now all Athenians can vote." He spread his arms wide to embrace that vast idea.

They applauded.

"Now we have more sailors than any city in the world. And many of you are here today!"

They stamped their feet to show how many of them there were.

"Six thousand votes are needed to make tomorrow's ostracism valid. Your fathers' fathers could not vote. You can. Don't waste it. I want you to vote and I urge you to do so."

"Whose name should we write on our potsherds, Pericles?"

He smiled. "I won't tell another man how to vote but I'll tell you the name I'll write on my sherd—Thucydides, son of Melesias!"

"We will! We will!"

"Count on us!"

"We'll be there!"

Tomorrow he'd see.

Walking west toward the Great Harbor, Pericles and Damon slowed as they saw Hippodamus tripping over his cloak to catch up.

"I'm writing a book about the design of a city," Hippodamus said. "Just as we move in the course of the day from one activity to another, so in a city we should move—"

Up to now, Pericles had not been able to persuade Hippodamus to take on the job of laying out the new city for the Italian colony so he took the opportunity to push the point. "Why are you splashing ink on papyrus when you could be writing a new book on the surface of the earth, Hippodamus?"

"You mean New Sybaris in Italy."

Pericles nodded.

"I can't leave here with my work in Piraeus incomplete. We must build guesthouses for ship owners. The residential quarter is little more than a sketch in the sand. No, Pericles, I will not go to New Sybaris."

"You're not an architect who constructs buildings, you're a . . . " What was he, exactly? Since Hippodamus was the only man who did what he did, it wasn't clear what to call him. "You plan cities. If you go to New Sybaris, we'll complete your plan for Piraeus so you'll have planned two cities for one."

Hippodamus halted in the street—his own broad street—and Pericles and those around him stopped short.

"Things will go wrong without me here," Hippodamus said. "A slave will stretch a line *around* a rock—and you'll have a crooked street. Someone will refuse to move a broken stone because it's a hero's tomb and a house block will end up a house triangle."

"We'll follow your instructions to the line."

"The straight, the parallel, and the perpendicular." Hippodamus drew the forms in air. "It's so easy to construct perfection on a chalkboard and so difficult in the world of men."

A sudden swell of affection for Hippodamus filled Pericles' chest. Never mind the gaudy rings and trailing cloak—this man knew. As Phidias knew. As he himself knew. The chalkboard and the world of men. Did the philosophers know? Protagoras?—he was perhaps too much of the world of men. Anaxagoras—too much of the chalkboard?

"The most difficult route but the worthiest runs between great plans and the world of men. That's exactly why, my friend—" Pericles rested his hand on Hippodamus' shoulder, "—you must make the voyage to New Sybaris."

"Sorry my friend, but I've gone and bought a new house here."

"You've sold a house before—and at a good profit."

Picking up a boat, Pericles and Damon rounded the peninsula, crossing to the Zea military port, where the narrow keels of a hundred and forty warships sloped toward the bay like the hawsers of a hundred and forty anchors holding the land of Attica to the water. What an exhilarating sight! Soon many of these ships would set off for the Black Sea to convoy wheat back to Athens. Later that summer some would accompany settlers to Italy.

They rowed the length of the dock, hailing the work crews, praising their skills, and pulling in here and there along the way to exchange words with a foreman or a workman whom Pericles or Damon knew.

"Don't forget to vote in the ostracism!"

"We'll be there!"

Many of the men wouldn't give up the day's pay, nor could Pericles blame them.

"What do you need more, Pericles—warships or votes?"

"I need votes so we can pay for warships!"

As they sailed back to the western dock, it occurred to him—as it had other times when he'd needed a big vote—that it might be wise to propose a law that Athens pay its citizens to attend the voting Assembly.

When they passed the north boundary of the Agora, workmen were dragging wooden barriers into place for tomorrow's ostracism election.

Arriving home that evening, Pericles walked in on a scene he could never have imagined and would never forget. Aspasia, Silky and Zoe had set up a table in the middle of the courtyard and dragged in lanterns and—what *were* they doing?—the table was scattered with broken pottery. Aspasia ran to him. "Come and see."

Silky and Zoe rose politely and sat down again, back to work. They were scratching, Aspasia showed him, the name *Thucydides, son of Melesias* onto potsherds.

He thought of asking, *By Zeus, what are you going to do with those?* but there could be only one answer.

"I had the idea to have us all write Thucydides' name on the sherds so we'll have a big pile in the morning ready to give to voters for the ostracism." Aspasia spoke with pride.

He was silent.

Silky and Zoe's hands came to a stop and they looked up at him.

"I've told Philemon to hand them out on the streets leading to the Agora," Aspasia said.

"Where did you get all those potsherds?"

"Philemon dug them out of an old well he knew about, see—" She pointed to the bucket under the table. "We have plenty."

Pericles shook the front of his cloak as if ridding it of dirt. "That's the oligarchs' trick."

Aspasia frowned. She was doing this for him. "We're just making it easier for people to vote the way they should. It's not against the law. I checked."

Pericles drew her out of earshot of Zoe and Silky. "I can't quite say why, but there's something about it I don't like. It seems a less free way of voting."

"Nobody's forced to take our potsherds—we're just making them available. And you know perfectly well that Thucydides' men will be writing 'Pericles, son of Xanthippus' on plenty of sherds."

How did she know that?

"In fact, Dion told me that he saw your enemy with the peacocks, Pyrilampes, ordering twelve wreaths for a dinner."

"Twelve!"

"The way the three of us see it—" Aspasia raised her voice to include Silky and Zoe, "some Athenians can't spell 'Thucydides, son of Melesias' right without our help."

"Especially democrats," Silky offered.

Pericles walked over to where Silky had scratched into a chunk from an old amphora, "Thucydides, son of Me—" As he watched,

she bent her head and went back to work, carving out "—lesias."
Zoe, too, bent her head back to work.

His hand cupped his mouth to cover a smile. "You've said that
Silky knows how to write, Aspasia, but don't tell me Zoe can write."

"She can't exactly but you know how good she is at copying.
Remember the Gorgon monster she copied into the blanket she
embroidered. So—"

Zoe had a sample of what to write next to her, in Aspasia's
handwriting, as she scratched *Thucy* . . . into the broken bottom of
a cup.

"I've done it so many times now, I don't even have to look at
that old cup," Zoe said proudly.

Pericles was taking too long to like Aspasia's idea. "After all, it's
for the good of Athens," she said.

It was a fact that some Athenians might not vote against
Thucydides even if they wanted to because they couldn't write his
name, Pericles thought. Or they might spell it so badly that it was
illegible, or they'd leave off his father's name and the vote counters
wouldn't know which Thucydides they meant.

Finally he nodded. "You can do it because, in fact, it's for the
good of Athens, as Aspasia said." Heading toward the andron and
what he hoped would be dinner with Aspasia, he turned back. "Keep
your eye on that sample, Zoe—be sure to spell 'Thucydides, son of
Melesias' right."

And may they spell *his* name *wrong* at Pyrilampes' dinner.

* * *

Damon picked him up early to walk to the ostracism election,
but when they turned into the street leading to the Agora, Pericles
saw that Philemon had gotten there even earlier with his basket of
potsherds. "I had to fight him for this corner." Philemon pointed
to a servant from Pyrilampes' household across the street with *his*
basket of sherds. Damon picked up a sherd from Philemon's basket.
"Thucydides, son of Melesias," he read. "How'd you get these done?"

That a woman would have done this . . . it might reflect badly
on Aspasia, so he just said, "It's for the good of Athens."

In the center of the Agora was a huge wooden circle, like a wheel with ten spokes, forming ten wedge-shaped spaces for the tribes. Those who came early chatted and compared potsherds. Some went into the wine shops. Others sat on the steps of the courts. The public slaves pulled open the barriers for members of the Executive Council who had slept in their dormitory nearby.

"Step aside! Step aside!"

The herald opened the way for the Archon in charge of the archives and the Presiding Officer, followed by secretaries carrying copies of the laws regarding ostracism and, of course, the citizenship lists.

By sunrise, citizens were thick around the wheel, their conversations mixed with the rumbling of wagons, the braying of donkeys, the grating of barriers dragged across sand, and the squealing of sacrificial pigs.

"Sir, write 'Pericles, son of Xanthippus' on my sherd."

Spinning around, Simon the Bootmaker looked down at the short young man who had tapped him on the shoulder. "You're not old enough to vote. Run along."

"I'm twenty."

His cheeks had a peach's worth of fuzz. Simon raised his eyebrows toward Xenon in a question.

"It's not your business to decide, even if he does want to vote against Pericles."

Simon ran his hand several times across his forehead. "Why do you want me to write Pericles' name on your sherd?"

"I want him ostracized."

"Why?"

"So he doesn't become a tyrant."

"Pericles doesn't want to be a tyrant."

"How do you know?"

"Because I know Pericles and he told me."

The youth looked at Simon's broken fingernails, dark with leather grime. "You know Pericles?"

"I do. He often comes into my shop. He asks my opinion about politics, and I tell him."

"He never asks my opinion," the youth said.

"He doesn't get around to everybody. Now, let me write 'Thucydides' on that sherd of yours." He took a nail from his mouth and scratched "Thucydides, son of Melesias" onto the base broken off a wine cup.

A stir in the crowd made him look up. Thucydides had arrived, surrounded by his friends.

"*There's* the tyrant—parading with a bodyguard."

Xenon the Barber shook his head. "To you, Thucydides is wrong no matter what he does. It takes courage to show up when you're probably going to be voted out of the city. Friends make a hard thing easier."

"I never said that Thucydides lacked courage—he was a strong wrestler. And you're right, it does take courage for him to come here. If I were up for ostracism, I'd stay home."

"No one would ostracize you, Simon—or me. It's for the men at the top."

"There's Pericles now. Young man, you watch and see if he isn't my friend."

Simon, not usually a man to push through a crowd, made his way to Pericles.

"I won us another vote!" As Pericles brought his ear to Simon's mouth to hear the story of the changed vote, Simon caught the eye of a young man.

Every citizenship had to be verified and challenges raised resolved one way or another—lines for tortoises, not hares. It was mid-morning before all the sherds had been deposited, near the time of high market when every tribe had reported its tally, there was a wait while the figures were double-checked. The sun was two-third toward noon when the herald announced that six thousand, four hundred and thirty-eight Athenians had voted. The cheer that rose from men standing head-to-head was as deafening as a war cry.

Hands stretched over heads to pay for biscuits while the magistrates sorted the sherds by names. Vendors dropped fish onto grills. Pericles ate nothing, nor, he noticed, did Thucydides. The muscles of his rival's shoulder bulged toward his neck like piled stones around an uprooted tree. But nothing on his face showed that he saw exile ahead. Pericles admired that in the man. But Athens needed him out.

The herald brought order, and the presiding officer stepped onto the bema.

"In the Archonship of Lysanius, at the ostracism Assembly, held in the eighth Prytany, Satyrus is Presiding Officer, six thousand, four hundred and thirty-eight votes have been cast."

"We know that already!"

"Who goes?"

"Thucydides, son of Melesias . . . "

Interrupted by shouts and cheers, he waited until the herald quieted the crowd.

"Thucydides, son of Melesias, three thousand, six hundred and fourteen." The herald pounded his staff—unnecessary since fingers were at work, lips moving.

"Pericles, son of Xanthippus, two thousand, two hundred and ninety-three."

Cheers and hisses, like some broken musical instrument.

"Lacedaemonius, son of Cimon, sixty-four."

Loud whistles.

"Teisander, son of Epilycus, forty-eight."

Jokes and vendettas—a scattering of other names.

The laughter, the cheers, the whistles, the hisses stilled.

The Presiding Officer spoke. "According to the laws of Athens, Thucydides, son of Melesias, must depart beyond the boundaries of Athens and all Attica within ten days and must remain absent for a period of ten years."

Not a punishment, but it might as well be. It was a terrible fate. But Pericles had no choice, for the good of—

"Few voted against you," Damon said.

Ariphron pressed in, palming his temples. "'Son of Xanthippus' was scratched onto sherds two thousand, two hundred and ninety-three times today. That's not a few on my tablet."

Lacedaemonius swung by like a sailor aiming a looped rope toward shore. "Watch out, Pericles, son of ostracized Xanthippus."

"Not for as long as your father, Cimon, was ostracized!" Damon shouted after him. "Hubris," he said to Teisander.

Thucydides out of Athens for ten years. No more sunspot floating before his eyes. Grasping the helm of his own ship, Pericles rode the crest of the highest wave. Cubits beneath him, other waves rolling in appeared small . . .

But that's an illusion. Things in the distance only seem small. In fact, the crest of a wave itself is a seeming. Surging toward shore, it can shove boulders from one side of the beach to the other, knock over trees, knock men off their feet. But it's nothing but thin water through and through.

CHAPTER 26

Turning of the Sun

"You've never seen me wrestle, and I'm good."

Pericles smiled, though Xanthippus was blocking his light.

"You've said you've been winning. I'd like to see how you do it, sometime."

"How about this afternoon? You don't have much to do, you're not a general anymore."

Should he retort that at the next election he would be even more of a general than ever, General from all the Athenians? Or was that one more temptation to hubris? Pericles drew several papyri to the top of the tablets and scrolls spread over his writing table. "I'm organizing a new colony in Italy but I suppose you think that's not much to do."

"Only my pedagogue watches me—he's a slave, and everybody else has a father. Teisander comes to watch his son every afternoon. He'll be there today for our match."

Somebody was watering the garden. Pericles listened to the sounds of drops falling on leaves and pebbles turning underfoot. It was early in the morning and still cool, but it would be a hot, bright, long day—one of the longest when the sun pauses at the end of its journey north, appearing several mornings over the same peak of Mount Lykabettos. Soon it would turn back and take the old year with it. The pause may only be a seeming, but it is a truth that on those days the light floods the world, beating out the dark. People eat their dinners late, walk abroad in the evening, and sleep little. It was Pericles' favorite time of the year.

"If I win today, I might make the wrestling contest for youths at the Panathenaic Festival."

He looked at his son: handsome, though short.

Damon was coming later in the afternoon to continue their discussions about the governing of the new colony. "If I have no further interruptions and finish my work, I'll come to see your match." He would invite Damon to accompany him to watch the wrestling—Damon had no sons and would consider it an honor.

"Be sure to come."

"Be sure to win."

Pericles returned to listing Greek cities where he might recruit settlers for the colony, New Sybaris. The tip of the Italian peninsula was promising for trade and grain, reports said, but they'd need to find a new site because the old one lacked a good supply of fresh water. Either the citizens of a rival city had diverted the river, as the Sybarites there claimed, or the river had silted naturally and changed direction.

He pulled up a map. Demodicus, a captain on the first expedition to Sybaris, had cruised the loop of southern Italy and, at Pericles' request, drawn the shape of the land, writing in the names of the cities he had encountered. How narrow the land appeared at Sybaris, where the new settlement was planned. Had the captain drawn it right? He pulled over another map, from the captain's second trip there. The thin, black lines were rivers, the one drawn in and then crossed over would be the dry riverbed. Demodicus had indicated the hills behind the town with zigzag lines. The distance between the hills and the sea was the width of Pericles' thumb. That would be the fertile plain where they would establish New Sybaris. How large was it, really?

His hand on the map, Pericles closed his eyes, searching his mind for a picture of the broad land between the hills and the sea. He saw rock and stubble. Nothing was growing there now, he'd been told. But once the new settlement was established, the fields would be as yellow as the ears of grain, made in solid gold, that Greeks from southern Italy were rich enough to dedicate to Apollo at Delphi.

His thoughts turned to the images of the two cities engraved on the shield of the hero Achilles in Homer's poem about the Trojan War. In one city's Agora, men were buying and selling, and honest judges were making fair decisions, as if it were happening at this moment. Other citizens were celebrating festivals and weddings. There were meadows and watering places for the stock, the fields were fertile and well ploughed and . . .

> . . . a thriving vineyard loaded with clusters,
> bunches of lustrous grapes in gold, ripening deep purple
> and climbing vines shot up on silver vine-poles.

The labor of men and their celebrations in Homer's cities cast themselves like a veil over the abandoned plain of Sybaris.

The captain had said that nothing remained of Old Sybaris. A clean slate—Pericles had been trying to tempt Hippodamus with the allure of planning a city according to his vision, without being forced to compromise with the past.

"Nice rosebushes," Damon said. "I bet they take a lot of water."

"They do." Pericles masked the distance he'd traveled with Homer. "Athens must send out the call to Greeks from all the cities—let all those willing join us in settling New Sybaris."

"Sparta, too?"

"Sparta, the Peloponnese, Ionia—it will be Panhellenic. Greeks are brothers, we should come together. Anyhow, New Sybaris can't be all Athenian since we have to include the Old Sybarites."

Damon spat onto the pebbles. "Greeks will come together for one thing only—war."

"And the games. We share language, gods, many customs."

"But Pericles, we must control the place, and if New Sybaris is going to be founded with other Greeks, I don't see how we'll keep ourselves on top there—"

"The Athenians may not remain dominant in numbers, but our influence will prevail. The hearth of New Sybaris will take its fire from the hearth in our Agora."

"Have your brains gone soft to think cinders will ensure loyalty?"

Pericles plucked a lime. Rolling it between his fingers, he watched the juice form drops through the skin. The sharp scent refreshed him. In time he said calmly, "The government will be a democracy and democratic governments favor Athens."

"Will you sign a mutual defense treaty?"

Pericles glanced at the sundial; the afternoon had stretched to half its full length. It was time to set out to catch Xanthippus' match so he invited Damon to accompany him.

After the long walk beyond the city walls, entering the Academy was like entering the Elysian Fields. Scattered honeysuckle flowers lay everywhere. Pericles and Damon inhaled the sweet scent. Thirsty, they stopped at the spring beside the shrine of the hero Academus, who had given his name to the area. It was quiet—they heard the stream falling over the rocks behind the fountain house. In the distance men ran on the open track. Pericles dipped an edge of his cloak in the water that pooled at the base of the fountain and wiped his forehead. A nightingale took quick sips from a flowering quince.

On an impulse, Pericles pulled a few asphodels and, making a short prayer for Xanthippus' victory, laid them in front of the statue of Eros inside the shrine.

Damon looked astounded. "Have you abandoned philosophy for prayer?"

"One cannot do too much for one's son."

They stepped around the boys kneeling over knucklebones at the entrance of the palaestra. Inside, older boys clustered around Socrates.

"Isn't it clear," Socrates was asking, "that a youth who spends all his time practicing boxing will surpass in that sport another who not only boxes but also wrestles and runs?" With a nod, Socrates acknowledged Pericles and Damon.

"And throws the discus," one boy said.

"And the javelin," another said.

"And lifts weights."

"And races horses."

A youth, lit by a shaft of sun from the narrow window, was rubbing his back with a towel. His muscles seemed formed by a sculptor's caress. He spoke without turning. "One win in the pentathlon equals more than five wins in each single sport."

"Of course he says that because he thinks he's going win the pentathlon at Olympia," one of the boys told Socrates.

"I will, one day."

"Are you saying, my dear Hygiaenon, that you can surpass Lycaon here in the long jump—who beat you the other day?" Socrates asked. "Or that you can throw the javelin farther than Euergides, who holds the record for this palaestra?"

"But Lycaon's strength is in his legs," a boy said, "and Euergides' arm muscles are too big. Hygiaenon's muscles are developed evenly all over his body."

"Now, Pericles speaks more than any other man," Socrates said, "and so he excels all others in that skill."

"On those grounds, you're more expert than I am, Socrates."

"I could prove you're more expert, but by winning the argument, I'd lose it."

Euergides turned to face them. "How's that possible?"

Pericles took on the answer, his forefinger arching back and forth like an upside-down plumb bob. "If he wins, he proves he's the better speaker which means that I win, which means that he wins—"

"Which means that it takes a philosopher to prove that winning means losing," Damon said.

"You don't win by losing," Hygiaenon said.

"That's also true."

"Paradox, paradox," Damon said.

Pericles let it go at that—he was here to find Xanthippus. Except . . . instructing a young man can lead him to greater things. Pericles swung around.

"Hygiaenon, you can almost always turn a loss into a win—think of the great comeback of the pentathlon champion Lugadamis." He spoke of an athlete they'd all know but was thinking of himself— if he hadn't lost his tribal election for general, he wouldn't now be running for General from all the Athenians.

Xanthippus and Teisander's son, Epilycus, were lying on benches in the portico of the wrestling court, their trainers rubbing them with oil. Teisander stood nearby. Xanthippus' pedagogue dozed in a corner. A slave boy was pouring clean sand from a sack while another followed with the rake to break up clods and smooth the surface.

"We sanded for our own matches when I was a young man," Pericles said. He watched the trainer rubbing oil into his son's skin, already gleaming.

"Xanthippus usually does his own sanding," the trainer said, "but I want him rested for today's match."

"Looks like a rough match just finished." Damon pointed to the gouged sandy surface.

"Stephanus won," Teisander said. "He's sure to compete in the Panathenaic games this summer."

"Stephanus, son of Thucydides?" Pericles asked.

"Yes and his father trains him," Xanthippus said. "No wonder he always wins."

By the time the floor was smooth, many men and boys had gathered to watch the match. Socrates and those around him had come outside. Standing with their backs to one another, Xanthippus and Epilycus powdered themselves with fine dust. Then they stepped onto the sand and faced off.

Heads low, shoulders forward, knees flexed, they stood ready to spring, their hands darting out and withdrawing like small fish. Abruptly Xanthippus grabbed Epilycus' left wrist with his left hand while lunging forward to seize the forearm. Epilycus thrust his right leg between Xanthippus' thighs, checking the lunge with his knee against Xanthippus' groin. Xanthippus groaned, and with his right hand swinging under Epilycus' left arm instead of grabbing it, fell forward across his opponent's knee.

He's going to fall; Pericles set his face to mask his disappointment.

But the force of his own thrust set Epilycus back on the heel of one foot. To catch himself, Xanthippus twisted sideways and grabbed his opponent's left arm, causing Epilycus to slip backward so that his buttocks and then his shoulders hit the sand. Xanthippus nearly toppled crosswise over him, but by swinging his arms back, he stayed erect. Xanthippus had won the first throw. Two more would win the match.

"Xanthippus was trying for a hoist over his head," Damon said, "but didn't manage it."

"He's off to a good start," Pericles said.

Flushed and exuberant, Xanthippus circled the court on the balls of his feet. Epilycus brushed off sand, shaking his head as if to clear his thoughts.

They faced off again, coming close, touching heads, backing off. Xanthippus was still on the balls of his feet, his weight too far forward. Before Pericles could call out for him to pull back, Epilycus lunged forward and low and grabbed Xanthippus around the waist, hugging him like a bear, his fingers locked at the small of Xanthippus' back.

"Push back his head—*you've* got the free hands!" Pericles heard himself shout.

"Twist to the side!" the trainer yelled.

Xanthippus, pulling at Epilycus' forearms, pried them open just far enough so that he could twist his weight around over Epilycus' right shoulder.

"Trip him!" Pericles called out.

Xanthippus, maintaining pressure on Epilycus' arms, thrust his right foot from behind Epilycus' left thigh toward his right knee. Epilycus spread his stance to free his knee. They held there for a moment, Epilycus squeezing Xanthippus around the waist, Xanthippus gripping Epilycus' arms to pry them apart. Suddenly, Epilycus loosened his hold, and Xanthippus slipped down over his shoulder. Xanthippus squeezed his right arm around Epilycus' neck but before he could lock the grip, Epilycus stooped low, hoisted Xanthippus, and rolled him over his back to the sand.

Xanthippus lay there, catching the breath knocked out of him when his back hit the sand. Epilycus, leaning against a column of the portico, wiped the sweat from his forehead with the back of his wrist.

Epilycus' trainer bent over Xanthippus. "Will you forfeit the match?"

"Get up, Xanthippus," Pericles said.

"He just had the wind knocked out of him," Xanthippus' trainer said. "He'll be up."

Xanthippus rolled his head back into the sand so that his chin was high, his neck extended. He took shallow, controlled breaths.

"Ready?" his trainer asked.

Xanthippus pulled himself onto his right hip and sat leaning on his arm, his head hanging. The trainer extended his hand to pull him up, but Xanthippus did not take it.

Why didn't the boy stand? His oldest son.

With his hands under Xanthippus' armpits, the trainer attempted to pull him up.

Xanthippus clutched his side. "No, no! I can't!"

The trainer yanked him to a standing position. Xanthippus moaned.

"Hold your hands above your head." The trainer ran his hands over Xanthippus' chest, feeling for the ribs one by one.

Xanthippus howled.

"There it is—he broke a rib."

Everyone could see the bulge.

"It hurts so much," Xanthippus said.

"So far you're even with him," the trainer said.

Xanthippus looked at the sand.

In front of the portico, Epilycus took swings, shadowboxing.

Xanthippus' trainer said, "Try another round."

Pericles squeezed his fists as if ready to fight. Xanthippus *should* try—it would hurt like a burn later, whatever he did. But the ox of silence weighed on Pericles' tongue. His son might not try. The boy would feel less shame if his father remained silent.

Xanthippus shook his head.

Epilycus' trainer stepped up to Xanthippus. "Then you forfeit?"

"I've got a big horse race coming up." Xanthippus pressed the rib and coughed. "This has to heal."

"Epilycus claims the match," the trainer said.

The men and boys crowded around Epilycus.

Xanthippus sat on a bench in the shade while his trainer sponged the perspiration from his forehead.

Pericles was glad he'd kept quiet. "You're quick on your feet."

Xanthippus didn't look at him.

"You made a good start."

Xanthippus took the sponge and pressed it against his eyes. "The one time you come, I lose the match."

"It seemed to me that you lost the second round because you were overconfident at the face-off. In the future, you should avoid overconfidence."

"I don't need your advice—I win all the time."

"Nobody wins all the time."

"Even Pericles doesn't win all the time," Damon said.

"You never watched me before. I don't know why you did today. You brought bad luck."

"You asked me to come."

"Don't come anymore."

Pericles stiffly nodded. He walked over to Teisander.

"That was a fine strategy your son used—loosening his grip—and he acted at the right moment."

"Your son fought well also. He might have won if he hadn't been injured."

As Pericles and Damon walked back to the city, Damon said, "Young men now are more insolent to their elders than we were in our day."

"Xanthippus might have won if he hadn't forfeited the match."

At home, he found Aspasia under the olive tree, reading aloud from a scroll while Little Pericles drank from her breast.

He jiggled the bird bath's clay pipe to keep the water running freely and described Xanthippus' wrestling match.

"Clever tactic by that other boy. Sometimes it's best to loosen one's grip."

Her words struck him with a sense of apprehension. Was this about winning or losing?

"I'm surprised to hear you say that, for I think you've never done other than to hold tight."

"It's a matter of timing—one has to know when to hold tight and when to let loose."

He hastily sifted through his memory. There were times when he first knew her when her touch had seemed light, almost casual, and it had bound him to her even more.

"In any case, we should teach your child never to forfeit a match," he said.

That *your* he kept coming up with for *their* child—sticking her like a thistle in the garden.

* * *

On that night of the triumphant sun, it was so hot that, looking for a breeze, Pericles ushered his friends into the rose garden to discuss their assignments for the new colony. Paralus was there feeding his rabbit.

It occurred to Pericles that Xanthippus would benefit from listening to the discussion of civic matters so when Aspasia came out with the wine she'd chilled in the well, he asked, "How is Xanthippus feeling now?"

"He's sleeping off the pain from his broken rib."

The door fell shut on the rabbit's cage but Pericles caught Paralus' arm as he started off. "My son, I want you to listen since we'll be discussing matters of importance to the city."

The men were stretching their legs and dabbing the sweat dripping from their faces to the creases in their necks.

"The child's too young to be with men." The nose of Lampon the seer was so narrow that when he pulled in a disapproving breath, you could hear it.

"He's old enough to learn the challenges our city faces." Pericles passed a map to the ship captain. "Demodicus, please explain."

The captain spread the map and patted it flat. "There's your Italy."

Damon leaned across for a better look. "Drawn out like that, Italy looks like a boot."

Paralus, drawing animals on a waxed tablet, looked up. "Where?"

"Right there, young man." Lampon chuckled. "Poseidon the sea god passed by and left his footprint in the water."

How typical of a seer to see a god where there is none, Aspasia thought. Such fancies among men annoyed her—and the worst was to mislead a child. But she didn't correct Lampon because Pericles wanted something from him.

The captain pointed out the narrow stretch of land. "The location's ideal for an Athenian settlement. If the weather's rough for sailing, we can drag the ships across."

Paralus, sketching Italy, punched a dot into the wax, saying softly, "The arch of the foot."

"That's a long haul across for dragging ships," Damon said.

"Maps don't tell you what's long and what's short, just what's longer and what's shorter." Aspasia hadn't meant to blurt it out, but she *knew* about sailors' maps from her brutal voyage to Athens. She looked past Damon, glaring at her.

Demodicus' forefinger traced a valley between the coastal hills. "Our manufactured goods will flow north and their timber and skins south."

Directing his sarcasm to Damon, Lampon bore down heavily on his "*alpha:* we shouldn't expend our resources and, *beta*, take the risks to, *gamma*, play an unfortunately small part in a big city."

"It's not unfortunate, it's an opportunity," Pericles said. "We Greeks share the same language, the same customs—"

"The same athletic festivals," Paralus said.

No—not to interrupt his father—Aspasia's hand went to her lips. *Pericles should have sent the boy into the house.*

But Pericles nodded. "New Sybaris should be as Panhellenic as the Olympics."

"I came here from another city, so did my friend Protagoras here—" Hippodamus reached over to pat Protagoras' arm. "There are many of us, so looked at that way Athens is already Panhellenic."

"You are not a citizen," Lampon sniffed.

"All you Athenians care about is who's a citizen. I've done more for Athens than you ever did, you liver-sniffing buddy of the gods!" The faceted stone in Hippodamus' ring pricked with light like a cat ready to scratch, but he smiled the way he did when he made a nasty joke.

Pericles tapped the arm of his chair. "Each of you has a key role to play in New Sybaris and arguing among yourselves has no place in the formation of a new colony."

All you Athenians care about is who's a citizen. True. Aspasia's thoughts had turned to Little Pericles in his crib upstairs, an infant who could not know, yet, that he would never be a citizen. Unless . . .

"Now," Pericles cleared his throat, "Protagoras, beyond all other men, you know best matters of law in a democracy. Therefore, I intend for you to take on the task of writing the laws of the new colony, modeled on those of Athens."

Aspasia smiled to herself—Protagoras, who was usually impatient to push forward his ideas over those of others, was silent in the attempt to contain his excitement.

Pericles turned to Lampon. "An Athenian must be the city founder and you, Lampon, know beyond all other men the ways of Apollo in founding of cities. I want you to be the official Founder of New Sybaris in accordance with Apollo's laws."

"Hmm." Lampon was working hard not to smile too broadly. "It would mean living there for awhile. Of course I need a little time to . . . "

He had his Law Maker and his Founder—he could move on to city planning.

"Now, Hippodamus, beyond all men you—"

"No." At the mention of his name, Hippodamus was already shaking his head.

Pericles continued. "I want you to design New Sybaris the way you designed our Port of Piraeus, with reason and number, so even though people from many cities will form the colony, they will learn to think like Athenians."

"Hippodamus made Piraeus a geometry lesson but in Athens the streets curve and diverge for no apparent reason and then end abruptly." Protagoras raised his teaching finger. "This proves that designing a city with reason and number is not what makes people think like Athenians. It's the laws, I tell you, it's the laws that teach men."

"I agree with you about the importance of the laws, Protagoras, but clarity and reason in the surroundings will influence the citizens of New Sybaris to think with Athenian clarity and reasonableness."

Demodicus looked up from the puzzle. "I can just see those smelly barbarians coming into town now, dragging their rawhides and shaggy logs. Oh look, a straight street—I think I'll study philosophy. Right son?"

"Right," Paralus said.

"What's your opinion, Hippodamus?" Pericles asked. "Do well-ordered cities educate people?"

Hippodamus looked toward the stars. "You may remember that I'm writing a book on the very topic which you can read when it's complete."

"We're waiting for the book, but we can't wait for your pledge to participate in New Sybaris."

Hippodamus spun his ring on his finger as if where it landed would decide.

"You said we all had a role to play," Damon said. "What's mine?"

"To make sure that everything we do is sufficiently democratic."

When they'd left, Aspasia said to Pericles. "It's not like you to speak untruthfully."

"What did I say that wasn't true?"

"You said that Protagoras and Hippodamus know more about cities than anyone else. But they know parts. You know all of it."

Pericles thought of the boy training for the pentathlon that afternoon. "We'll have to see whether I was successful tonight in one of the most important city skills."

"What—? Oh, of course."

In the light of the small lamp, Pericles traced his finger over the drawn lines. "It's odd. Each time I pass my hand over this map, a picture of a whole city springs into my head."

"Like Hippodamus, you're a designer of cities."

"It reminds me of when Ictinus scratches the outline of a temple into the stone base and then erects the temple—only it happens immediately in the mind."

"That's what I mean—you're an architect."

"You think I can do everything, but I couldn't make a building, nor, I think, could I lay out a city."

"You make buildings and cities happen . . . and everything in them."

"You say more than is true." *What would she answer?*

"Here's the proof: would the Parthenon come into being without you? Or the Music Hall? Or the Hall of Mysteries at Eleusis?"

"Or the Long Walls," he added. "Or the new Piraeus."

"None of that would happen if you hadn't thought to do it."

"This new settlement will be good for Athens and good for Greece." He had risen from his seat as if to get a better look at it.

"And it will be good for Pericles." She too had risen and was looking directly at him, her eyes like sparkling waters of a river. "It will unify the Athenians and excite them—like war, but not war." It would also ensure his election as General from all the Athenians, she thought, but to avoid tempting the Fates, left it at, "You're a clever man, Pericles."

"And you, Aspasia, are as clever a woman as ever set her pretty foot on this earth."

He slipped his arm around her as he had before the baby was born. Feeling the curve of her waist beneath his palm, he had the sense of returning to a familiar shore—yet what shore was it? He closed his eyes, blocking out the lamp and the stars, and breathed in the scent of wine. He remembered Odysseus in Homer's wine dark sea, swimming against the waves, and reaching the shore of Nausicaa's island.

"My Nausicaa," he said softly.

"My Odysseus."

For cooler air, they went to the roof to spend the short night left to them. Zoe was there, bent over Little Pericles who slept in a basket as she fanned him with slow sweeps of a smoothed acanthus leaf. Pericles looked for his older sons—he saw their two naked bodies sprawled out on their backs. Others of his household on the roof—and on all the roofs of Athens—slept, turned on their mats, coughed and sighed as when men are bivouacked in war. There were occasional whispers.

Pericles thought he hadn't slept when he became aware of dawn's abrupt warmth. Aspasia was already awake and had the baby with her on the mat, supporting him under his elbows so he was almost standing and finding out what his legs could do.

"That baby is a young Heracles," Pericles said, making the sign of the horns to avoid the evil eye—not that he really believed that praise put a child in danger.

He walked to the edge of the roof. Looking toward Mount Lykabettos, he watched with pleasure the sun emerge from the same peak as yesterday. Heraclitus taught that we can't step twice into the same river. True, change is everywhere. But the great sun takes its pause, bringing days in which, after warming and illuminating the earth with exceptional ardor, it seems reluctant to leave.

He felt the full heat of the sun on his face like the joy in his heart. Why should there not be a time of constancy? Long days of a shining sun?

CHAPTER 27

The Golden Age

Pericles had been a general almost all the time she'd known him and now he'd been elected General from all the Athenians which put him above all the other generals. People were saying that Pericles was so powerful in Athens, he could do anything. Some thought he'd become too powerful. With all that power, the least he could do was pass a special law for the son who bore his name.

But he refuses, Aspasia mouthed under her breath.

She looked down, surprised to see her right hand formed into a fist, which gave her the idea of shaking it as men do. She came up with an emphatic punch for each of her words, "Pericles won't do it." Just then, Little Pericles came in with Zoe. Embarrassed and wanting no questions from her son about what Pericles wouldn't do, Aspasia quickly turned their attention to the honey cake the child had dropped. "No," she said quickly when Zoe reached for it. "He must learn to pick it up himself."

Just as he must earn his citizenship for himself—or so Pericles said. *Earn his citizenship*—the child was barely five years old.

"I don't want it." Still he scooped up the pieces and dropped them into Zoe's cupped hands.

Aspasia opened her arms and he climbed onto her lap. She opened the scroll so he could see the words, too. "Shall we read about the first people?"

He nodded, running his finger over the papyrus.

Zoe pulled up a stool.

"Long ago, the gods made men out of gold, the best material. It was a Golden Age. The cities were at peace." She raised her eyes as if to a distance so he would try to see it with her. "The people were like beautiful gods. They grew their food easily and no one had to work hard."

"Were there slaves then?" Zoe asked.

Aspasia looked over the scroll. "Hesiod doesn't say anything about them here." She resumed her storytelling voice. "No one felt sorrow."

"What's sorrow?" Little Pericles asked.

"When Papa sailed away to Euboea to inspect our new Athenian colony, you cried—do you remember?" He nodded. "That was sorrow."

Aspasia glanced at the scroll to see what she'd left out about the Golden Age. "No one ever looked old, and there were many festivals. After that, the gods created people who were made of the second-best material, silver. This was the Silver Age. These people were nothing like the first ones. They fought all the time and didn't honor the gods."

"Did they have festivals?"

"Rarely. Then the gods made a third group of men—and these were the worst yet."

He yawned. "Did they have festivals?"

"No. They fought one another with their bronze weapons. It was a Bronze Age."

"What's bronze?"

"Papa's helmet is made of bronze."

"And his shield?"

"The outside is bronze. Next the gods—"

"And his breastplate!"

"The next men were somewhat better than that."

"Shin guards!"

"The new men were very brave. They were heroes."

"What about his sword?"

"That's iron. Think how sharp it is."

The boy nodded.

"But after that, Hesiod says, came the worst time: now."

"*Now* is the worst time?"

"Hesiod lived a while ago so now . . . "

Philemon signaled to Aspasia from the door.

"Now's the best time because Pericles is here." Little Pericles slid off her lap.

Pericles paused to look at her before kissing her, his gaze as precious to her at the kiss itself. It was so *personal*. But this evening, she noticed that the groove between his brows had deepened since his kiss this morning when he'd left the house. The latest rebellion among the allies must be weighing heavily on him.

Little Pericles jumped up. "Let me wear your helmet!"

Pericles lifted him into his arms. "It's still too heavy for you."

The boy ran his hand over the smooth metal. "It's bronze."

"Very good, so it is."

"We're reading Hesiod," Aspasia said.

"Good, I'll listen—as long as it's not the part I hate about how the world is getting worse and worse."

She hesitated. "We were reading about the Golden Age."

"Oh. That's the part—but perhaps there's some good in it."

He was being kind but Aspasia rolled up the scroll. "We'll read something else tomorrow."

"Don't worry, Papa—that worst time was a while ago," Little Pericles said.

Pericles smiled, roughed up the boy's hair with his fingers, and said, "You're very smart." And *that* was a picture Aspasia liked.

Later that night, Pericles said, "I'd prefer you found something more inspiring to read to the child."

There had been other indications that Pericles took an interest in their son's education but she was always hungry for them. Her fingertips stroking his forehead gave over to her insistent thumb flattening the worried groove. "They'll be learning Hesiod when he starts school so by reading to him now, Little Pericles will be ahead of the other children. But what offends you about it?"

"That idea that man's life on earth began well and has only gotten worse when it's really the other way around. The first men were ignorant. Do you realize, Aspasia, they didn't know how to use fire? They were uncivilized. That was no golden age. There was nothing godlike about them."

"'They lived the random planless years.'" To soften the moment, Aspasia quoted one of Pericles' favorite playwrights, Aeschylus.

"Random and planless—exactly. Don't teach the child these untruths. If there's any golden age, it's now."

It was a golden age for Athenian citizens. But what about their son? "Pericles—" But the groove between his brows cut deep again as he sensed a request he might not want to fulfill. So she put her arm around his shoulders and smoothed her cheek against his. He breathed in her oiled scent and after a while said, "I hear that my closest friend, Sophocles, is writing a play that puts me in a bad light."

So that's what was worrying him.

But he'd gotten it wrong. Playwrights didn't write about real people. Anyhow, she knew all about Sophocles' new play from Dion; the pale bookseller had captivated Sophocles. "It's nothing about you—it's the story of Antigone, that crazy girl King Creon forbade to bury her brother but she went ahead and did it anyhow."

"In the myth she's Antigone but I can see right through that. It's really about a tyrant, *me* in the guise of King Creon, who prevents a woman from performing the rites of burial for her brother."

Preventing the rites of burial . . . She started to say, "You didn't—" but stopped.

"Surely, Aspasia, you remember that when Deinomache was desperate to have her husband General Cleinias buried privately on our family property. I insisted that he have the honor of a state burial."

She remembered watching that state burial from a distant hill, the only vantage point available to her, back when she was new in Athens, a foreigner, a non-citizen, a girl weightless as a ghost in the city.

"You were right to do it. Deinomache's husband died fighting for Athens. He deserved the state burial. You forced her to accept what was right."

Zoe looked in with a pitcher of wine. Aspasia told her to bring Pericles' favorite cup.

"Certainly I was right, but the point is there's a parallel between the myth and myself. Seen simply, the city's ruler prevents the family rites of burial desired by a woman." Pericles' fist came down on the serving table with deliberate strength. "I'm telling you, Aspasia—Sophocles, my oldest friend, is using this play to criticize my power."

"No no no." She rushed to spare him pain that would lurk with the thought of betrayal. "Cleinias was a *patriot* and Antigone's brother was a *traitor* and deserved what he got—his body left to the vultures. No state burial for a rebel! The stories aren't similar—they're exact *opposites!*"

Closing his eyes and rubbing them to suggest ordinary fatigue—a way he had of playing for time—Pericles looked back in memory. He had been angry at Deinomache for demanding a family burial for her husband but had insisted, properly, on the official burial. Pericles could still hear her voice, squeaky as a bat: "I won't have my husband crowded in with all those other men." She made the city's fine burial trench sound like a common bathhouse. But communal burial for all the war dead—under a single, magnificent monument—was the new law of the land. *His* law, in fact.

He was circling his thumbs and repeating, "Antigone . . . Deinomache . . . "

She filled his wine cup.

He wrote an equation with his finger in the air. "King Creon to Antigone equals Pericles to Deinomache."

Watching him sip his wine, Aspasia thought of the contrasts Pericles' equation left out. Silently she ticked them off. Deinomache wanted to bury her husband, not her brother. And obviously Pericles didn't expose General Cleinias' body to the birds like King Creon did with Antigone's brother. But were those essential or details? Did it matter that Antigone lived in Thebes, not in Athens? Was there some truth in Pericles' severe ratio?

He took another sip. "I say that Sophocles is accusing me of being a tyrant through this play about Creon and Antigone. Playwrights hide behind their masks like actors."

She sipped her wine. "I've never liked Sophocles, mainly because I feel he disapproves of me. But I don't believe he'd turn against you."

271

"The comic playwrights have been ridiculing me for years. It was only a matter of time for the tragic writers to jump into the game." He swilled his wine, watching the circles form on the dark surface. "I will admit, though, that it makes me sick to think that my oldest friend would turn his talent against me."

"King Creon will be one matter and Pericles quite another. The person's character makes the difference. Anyhow, you're not a king."

"But I am General from all the Athenians. You know what I heard today about the ram?"

Oh no, not the one-horned ram again.

"Surely you remember that ram born with a single horn. Everyone believed the philosopher Anaxagoras when he showed that the single horn was simply a phenomenon of nature."

"Not everyone."

"But now, since we changed the laws so that I could be elected General from all the Athenians, people are claiming the one-horned ram was a prophesy. They say it foretold that I would take over one-man rule." Some wine splashed from his cup. She reached for a cloth Zoe had left and wiped it up.

"You changed the laws about generals legally through the Assembly. They voted on it. This is a democracy and you're not a tyrant."

"Nevertheless, some are accusing me of governing as a tyrant—or like a tyrant."

As a tyrant, like a tyrant—there was a difference, but not to the point.

"It's always that way for a leader."

When he lay back against the cushions, she put her face close to his and whispered. "You're a great leader and they're fortunate to have you. And all that story about Antigone against the tyrant Creon took place in Thebes, not Athens—ah look, we can start to see the girl swimming in your cup."

He drank again, bringing the naked girl drawn on the bottom of the cup into view. He swilled his wine to make her seem to swim. It was a clever device. Aspasia had the cup made to delight him years ago. The rumor was that Aspasia herself had gotten to Athens by escaping from a pirate ship anchored far offshore and swimming to

272

shore . . . it was hard to believe and she refused to speak about it. Would he ever know the truth?

Aspasia had soothed him for the evening but she was uneasy. Sophocles had great prestige and not only through his plays. He headed up the all-important board that collected tribute from Athens' allies. Pericles had nominated him. Was it possible that Sophocles, his age-mate and friend, would attack Pericles' leadership through his play? In front of seventeen thousand Athenians in the theater?

Pericles' political rivals had been hurling slurs and insults in his direction for years. But that was in the democratic Assembly. Nobody had ever presented a tragedy attacking Pericles, although comic playwrights had found ways to attack his power in the city by ridiculing his over-large head. Sometimes they sniffed around his love for Aspasia, all to give a good laugh to thousands of Athenians.

Politicians, comic playwrights—Pericles had stood fast against the insults wherever they arose. Aspasia's eyes filled with tears as she roved over the past in which, against slanderous challenges to his reputation, he had held to their love like Odysseus holding to the mast. It was a moment when she wanted to express her gratitude. Wanting to tell him she loved him she turned but saw that, head back on a cushion, he was breathing easily, asleep.

He had taken her into his home. In front of those seventeen thousand Athenians and more. In front of all the Greeks, in front of the world.

He had given his name to their child.

CHAPTER 28

For All Time

After years of getting used to prosperity, the Athenians were feeling poor. So much for having voted for Thucydides for General, a land-rich aristocrat averse to mercantile wealth and the democratic aspirations that followed it. In the one year that Thucydides had grabbed power from Pericles, he had thwarted Pericles' plans for an Athenian colony in Italy and had reduced Athens' income by lowering the tribute Athenian allies paid in return for military protection. And the arrow that plunged deepest into Pericles' heart—Thucydides had cut funding for the Parthenon and for the gold and ivory goddess who would live within it. Given enough time, Thucydides would annul the popular democracy itself and Athens would revert to the old governance of tyrants and aristocrats.

But now Thucydides was out and Pericles was in.

Pericles' first task, upon which all else rested, was to rebuild the treasury.

But how to do it? Raising the tribute assessments abruptly would tend to spark rebellions among the allied cities, all the more because under Thucydides' leadership, the tribute had just been lowered. How could Athens replenish its treasury *and* make the alliance firmer than ever?

Damon, Pericles' political advisor, said, "If we send out more soldiers to collect the tribute, we'll pull in more money." Logical but it would set up that loud "no" men hear between their ears when they're not doing things freely.

In fact, it set up that unpleasantly loud "no" in his own ears. His way was to point out the best path and to persuade others of its rightness through reason.

With money, Pericles decided, better meant fairer.

In proposing to the Assembly that Athens reassess the tribute a year ahead of schedule to catch up on recent losses, he stressed fairness. The Athenians would investigate the resources of each city and facts would replace the estimates that had been in use. Since the right to appeal was a popular feature in treaties, he proposed they let all their allies have the right to appeal their tribute assessments. With a goal of fairness and justice, even military enforcement would be acceptable because people would understand that the Athenian soldiers collecting tribute from recalcitrant cities were only ensuring that no ally benefited unfairly at the expense of others. Athens would be praised for being just instead of criticized for being arbitrary. The Athenians, exuberant in their anticipation of the money that would be flowing to Athens from the enhanced tribute, voted also for his proposal to restore full funding for the Parthenon temple on the Acropolis and the gold and ivory statue of Athena.

Stepping out of the barbershop, Pericles ran his hand over the smooth curls of his beard—Xenon had the trim the way he liked. He opened his chest to a deep breath of satisfaction. Plans for the new colony in Italy as well as for improving the collection of the tribute were underway. Shading his eyes, he looked up against the bright sun toward the Acropolis. Heavy-wagon men were hauling goods up the steep path. What was in the wagon? He narrowed his eyes for a sharp view. A load of marble—he could see the flat top of a large stone above the sides of the wagon. The sight of the marble flooded his chest with something stronger than relief at the sign of progress—it was longing to see the work moving forward on the project closest to his heart: the construction of the Parthenon temple and its image of Athena.

He invited Xanthippus to accompany him to the Acropolis, thinking it was time that he took interest in his city's accomplishments—past time. But Xanthippus was training for a horse race, so Pericles made the climb to the Acropolis with Phidias.

After the recent rains, the ruts up to the Acropolis were soaked with marble dust—anywhere else it would look like spilled milk. Near the top, they heard shouts and ran the rest of the way. Two men were fighting, their raised hands locked together, now one pushing forward, now the other.

With long strides Phidias crossed the hilltop and struck each of them on the wrist with the side of his hand.

What if the sculptor injured his hand?

The men dropped apart. One rubbed his wrist. Then they were grappling again.

"Stop!" Phidias raised his hand. Some of the men—maybe also concerned about Phidias' hands—ran over, looped their arms under the fighters' shoulders and pried them apart. The fighters stumbled back, trying to free themselves.

"Gut worm!"

"Persian!"

They stood, sweating, arms pinned behind their backs. Pericles recognized the young apprentice with the wiry build, Agoracritus, a smart one.

Phidias let them breathe heavily for a moment before asking how it started.

Agoracritus made a high chin. The fat one spat.

"You're too old to fight boys, Menon," Phidias said.

Menon was rubbing is wrist. "He disrespects his elders."

"I respect elders who know their craft."

Menon lunged but was caught up short. He lowered his arms, then shrugged off the man who held him.

Phidias turned to Menon. "You worked at the temple of Zeus at Olympia years back, didn't you?"

"No one can equal that."

"That temple you're always talking about has twelve carved metopes," Agoracritus said, referring to the series of rectangular relief carvings under the roof. "Ours has ninety-two!"

Phidias smiled but said to Menon. "You know how to cut stone."

"But not like we do it now. This old guy's ruining the Parthenon. Look!" Agoracritus pointed.

Two rectangles of marble, wrested from the quarries of Mount Pentelicus, leaned side by side against a wheelbarrow. On each was a carving of a mythic encounter: a centaur with the upper body of a man and the lower body of a horse struggled with a fully human hero. As Pericles turned his eyes from one stone to the other, he saw what was worrying Agoracritus. Uneasy, he raised his hand to stroke his beard. Yes, the subjects were the same but the ways the sculptors had carved the two stones were so different, they looked like they were sculpted for different buildings at different times. Placed together on his temple, they would break the harmony he and Phidias had so often talked about, so often planned for the Parthenon.

"See how the shadows around my centaur's eyes seem to flicker—he looks like he's thinking." Agoracritus thrust a thumb toward Menon's metope. "*His* centaur's face is stiff as a mask."

"Centaurs are supposed to look masked—that's how the painters do it." Menon brushed himself off.

"The *old* painters," Agoracritus said. "Phidias, why do you keep this old guy on?"

Pericles was wondering that also.

"Have you seen a centaur, Agoracritus?" Phidias asked.

"*Nobody* sees centaurs but everybody *knows* their upper parts are like a man. Therefore I gave mine a man's face."

They waited hushed as Phidias studied Agoracritus' slab. "So you did."

Agoracritus ran with his advantage. "His hero's so stiff he couldn't tie on a sandal. But look how mine twists from his chest through his waist to his toes. My hero is *really* fighting for his life!"

"To show the body twisting is extremely difficult. It took me years." Phidias squatted before Agoracritus' carving. "But you grew tired at the legs."

"How can you—?"

"Your hero's leg looks flat where it's folded under him as he falls back." Phidias looked over at Menon's stone. "Menon has shown the swelling muscles of the thigh pinched in at the knee, more as in nature."

Agoracritus looked at his stone. "I'm not finished."

Menon smirked.

"Then finish—at your own workplace. Men, help him with that stone. And watch the edges."

"I brought it over to teach Menon how—"

"I do the teaching here." Phidias turned to Menon. "It's a good knee but if you want to keep your job, chisel down that exaggerated bulge so the muscle of the thigh flows smoothly into the calf muscle, as in nature. Back to work, men."

"I was relieved to hear you instruct Menon since I'd been wondering if you're giving your sculptors sufficient direction."

"You were wondering if *I*—" In his most dismissive gesture, Phidias flicked his thumb nail under his front teeth.

Pericles didn't want to anger Phidias. No one could replace him in his art or in his ability to organize this large project. And after years of working toward a common goal—their common goal— he loved the man. Still, the contrast between Menon's carving and Agoracritus' carving—that was stark. "Agoracritus carves in the new way—to see that beauty crushed together with Menon's old ways . . ." Pericles shook his head. "We won't have harmony—we'll have dissonance."

"There are always compromises, as you know better than most, Pericles."

He did know. The chalkboard and the world of men. But the thought of anything less than perfection for the Parthenon pained him. He must beware—worship of perfection was a kind of hubris.

Phidias gestured toward the fifty or so sculptors chiseling, drilling, hammering, sanding, a few in the upper reaches of the Parthenon's scaffold polishing the capitals of the columns that were carved like huge, loosely coiled scrolls. "I can't get fifty like Agoracritus. And don't forget we're making ninety-two of those carved metopes."

"I'm not likely to forget since I argued for every drachma, just as I fought hard for the other *extra* as my opponents call it—even though a carved marble frieze of Athenians honoring our goddess is worth any price!" Again, Pericles sensed hubris. "That is, *almost* any price."

"Speaking of the frieze . . ." Phidias steered Pericles toward the west end of the temple. "I have a surprise for you."

Surprise—like lavish peacocks his political enemies claimed he'd used as bribes, like the one-horned ram they said marked him for a tyrant. Political insults had come to Pericles by way of grotesque surprises. His heart thumped unpleasantly at the notion of another. It wasn't enough to put a friend in charge here on the Acropolis—he had to keep his eyes on everything.

Phidias continued walking. "I've carved your portrait."

Had Phidias gone over to his enemies? By Hades, why would the sculptor kick over his own trough? Pericles reached for a lightly disbelieving tone. "My portrait? You must want me exiled from Athens."

"And worse—this section of the frieze sits right above the door on the west where everyone will see it!"

So that's why Phidias had steered him toward the west.

He'd best speak with particular clarity in case it had to be remembered afterwards. "Thucydides claimed that including real men on the temple would be an impiety. I assured the Assembly that there would be no specific man on the frieze—certainly not me—but that the figures in the frieze would represent all Athenians of all time bringing a gift to Athena." *Best to repeat it.* "No specific men, no specific time, Phidias. All Athenians, for all time."

He quickened his pace to keep up with Phidias who didn't seem to be listening.

"Thucydides is gone for now," Pericles continued, "but others are coming over the hill ready to attack me and undermine my policy—more than ever since I've been elected General from all the Athenians."

The stone could be re-carved—smashed if necessary.

Phidias stopped short, as did Pericles.

The carved slab, the span of a man's arms, sat in golden late afternoon sun on the far side of Phidias' workshop. It showed a cavalry commander with his horse. Pericles peered at it, then stepped back to view the whole, stroked his beard, and moved forward for a closer look. The procession of Athenians planned for the frieze—the Athenians for all time—would just be getting underway in this part of the frieze, so why had Phidias chiseled the exceptionally spirited horse already breaking into a gallop, checked by the commander's hold on the reins.

Where was the portrait?

The commander was around his own age and wore his beard short, but outside of that he saw no resemblance to himself. He looked again. No likeness whatsoever—the commander's low, sloping forehead was the very opposite of the over-high dome of his own head. Nor were the thin lips like his, nor the bent nose—his thumb checked his own long straight nose.

Since Phidias was waiting for a comment, Pericles said, "He's certainly working that horse."

It simply was not him. Thanks to Zeus! Firm ground after a fast tide.

How disappointing!

That he was disappointed it *wasn't* his portrait—Aspasia would be amused.

He wouldn't tell Phidias, though, because the sculptor might bite on the idea.

Still, Phidias must have something in mind. Stepping back, Pericles kept his eyes on the stone so as not to reveal his lack of understanding.

He should have been angry at his sculptor for the scare, but the carving was extraordinarily fine. On this carving, the horse was beautiful, as was the commander for an older man, but what made them both so exceptional wasn't their beauty of form—Polyclitus, the sculptor whom the southern Greeks were so proud of created equally beautiful forms—it was their vigor. Their lives pressed out from the stone. The horse straining against the bit practically leaped ahead. The commander exerted control with one hand forward on the bridle under the horse's chin while the other held the reins high and behind the horse's head—that way, although the horse was brought up short, he wouldn't stumble. This was a man skilled in the art of training the most difficult horses. The animal had great physical strength, but the man had intelligence, skill, and patience—and plenty of strength of his own in those sinewed arms and legs. Pericles looked at the face. He was godlike in remaining calm while exerting great force. One had confidence that the spirited horse would hold to its rightful place in the procession to Athena on the frieze if this man held the reins.

But what did this trainer of unruly horses have to do with him?

He felt excitedly warm.

It wasn't the first time he'd found that by using the right words to ask himself a question, he had the answer.

"You've made me the trainer of the Athenians."

"Otherwise they'd run wild," Phidias said.

"Giving them rein while providing constraint."

"A firm, constant pressure."

That's what he did. Every day. Pericles sighed deeply in relief, as when Aspasia caught on to his tactics.

"Phidias, it's as much your portrait as mine."

"How can you say that when clearly the man's not bald."

Pericles brushed aside what now seemed incidental.

"It's everything we do that's most difficult."

"I hadn't thought of it that way." Phidias viewed his sculpture with his fingers to his lips. "But perhaps."

"Did you have me in mind from the first? You showed me the sketches, but I don't remember this cavalry commander."

"At first, I was only going to direct the carving of this frieze. I have too much work to do here as it is—recording accounts, keeping the others moving, constructing the gold and ivory goddess for the interior of the temple." Phidias gestured to the workshop in which the new Athena was under construction. "When the marble for this section of the frieze arrived, I inspected the slabs. Were they in good condition? Had they measured them right at the quarry? Had they left us good margins? How was the color? Were there iron streaks that would cause breaks? Which was the central slab? This one."

Puffing his cheeks like a pipe player, Phidias blew away marble dust that had lodged in the grooves of the horse's mane.

"I decided to carve one piece—teach the others how to do it. Since the overhang will shadow the frieze, its light will come from below, so I had the idea of carving deeper at the top than at the bottom for clarity. I wanted the other carvers to translate these calculations properly onto their stones. Anyhow—" Phidias gave the horse a firm pat on the rump. "I like to carve. I give it a little each day. Not finished yet, I have to drill out these folds more deeply."

"But that doesn't bring you to me."

"I wanted a group above the door that's both in motion and still. I told you that—remember? Doors are important—stop and go, stop and go."

"I remember saying it was like catching the critical moment."

"The more I carved, the more spirited the horse became and the more I came to admire the trainer's skill. That's when I started thinking about you and Athens—you were working on the new colony then."

Pericles turned from the carving to look around. Chipped stone littered the ground. Planks lay crosswise on planks. Powdery marble clouded the air.

"How messy this all is." He took a deep breath against fatigue.

"Building isn't tidy."

"It's taking too long."

"No one has built works this large and intricate this fast."

Pericles looked to the roofless top of the temple and to the standing columns, many without their capitals. "How much will be complete by the time of the Greater Panathenaic Festival for Athena?"

"The columns will be in place. The stones will be in place to the level of the cornice. We'll have carved many cubits of the frieze."

"No politician's holding up the money—for the moment. I want to know what will be *finished*."

"The metopes will be carved and installed."

"On all four sides?"

"Easily."

"What irony," Pericles said. "Thucydides liked to complain that the construction moved slowly."

"Thanks to his interference."

"We're rid of him. So when the procession arrives—"He looked again at Phidias' carved horse trainer—"I mean the procession of the *living* Athenians—I want something complete to show them. By that time my new Music Hall will be built. The music contests will be magnificent there."

"Unquestionably."

Phidias picked up a pouch from the ground, emptied fine sand into his palm, sprinkled some on a piece of soft leather, and rubbed it into the bulging shoulder of the spirited horse. He stood to one side and inspected the shoulder in the slanting light, then returned to polishing the stone.

Pericles, too, noted the sun's position in the sky. "I don't want carving this frieze to slow your completion of the gold and ivory Athena."

"I'm in a hurry, too." Phidias was now rubbing in a circular motion. "But I don't see that a month this way or that will make a difference—"

Pericles raised his hand to object but Phidias continued, "—because when you argued for funds, you promised the Assembly that these sculptures will be for all time."

CHAPTER 29

Antigone

Aspasia, wrapped in a cloak against the cool winds, looked up from her book to check the rose buds. They looked tight and she saw no sign of worms, and she thought they would grow to be healthy roses. This had once been Aristocleia's rose garden but since the divorce, this precious, rare, private rose garden, was hers—well, it belonged to Pericles but it was hers. As she reached to pluck off a caterpillar, Dion came in holding a theater mask in front of his face.

When she had first come to Athens, she and Dion had run around town like children no one cared about. Now, living with Pericles and as the mother of his child, she was careful of her dignity and spent more time at home. Dion always knew what was happening around town and Aspasia loved to be in on the latest news.

"Why the mask?" she asked.

"Sophocles has started rehearsals for his new play about Antigone."

Aspasia's hand went to her chin. "That must be the one you told me about where Antigone defies the king." Pericles thought Sophocles might be criticizing his new, powerful position as General from all the Athenians in that play.

"And listen to this: he's chosen me to act in it!"

"An actor!" She saw that Sophocles was smart to choose him— the audience would hear every one of Sophocles' words because Dion's voice resonated like a drum.

Aspasia reached for the mask and thoughtfully turned it on all sides. The hollow mask with its big open mouth would send Dion's voice to the top seats. Luckily his mask and costume would cover that over-white skin he was born with—most people don't want to see the gods' mistakes. That's why Pericles never went among men without wearing his helmet—for him that was a kind of mask. And he was right to do it. Pericles couldn't be a great leader if people turned away at the sight of him.

"This one's my girl mask," Dion said. "I play three parts—Antigone's sister, a guard, and Antigone's betrothed, Prince Haemon."

Aspasia thought back to the story. "Doesn't Prince Haemon defy the king too?"

"By the end, just about everybody defies the king. Here's a riddle for you, Aspasia. Who in Athens can be both a non-citizen and a prince?"

"That's easy—Dion the actor."

Dion's lips thinned. "Be sure to tell that one to Pericles."

Since Dion was not an Athenian citizen and he was playing the prince, the riddle made sense but she heard the nasty note in his voice. He still blamed Pericles for refusing to help him get back on the citizenship lists some years ago when he was eliminated because his mother was a foreigner. Dion thought Pericles could do anything as most people did, but Aspasia knew it wasn't true. Pericles couldn't even pass a law to make their own son an Athenian citizen. Although in time . . .

"I don't think Pericles would like that riddle." Becoming Sophocles' lover had made Dion bold.

Dion struck his chest with exaggerated regret. "Too bad, but maybe he'll like this one. Who stays with a man like a wife but isn't his wife?"

A foreign woman in Athens. *Herself.* Dion was being mean.

"You were so quick on the first riddle, Aspasia. What's taking you so long on this one?"

She was readying her comeback—"An actor loving a playwright"—but he was out the door.

* * *

"Pericles, the Festival of Dionysos is next week."

Why would Aspasia say anything so obvious? Ah, he guessed what was coming and a formidable "No" immediately arose in his mind.

"Pericles, I'd be pleased if you'd buy me a token for the theater."

"You know that's impossible."

"I don't know why it's impossible."

"It's not what women do." That did not usually deter Aspasia. She'd been reading plays since she first came to Athens and no other woman did that. He caught her hand stroking his forehead and brought it to his lips. "I know that you are very brave and will do things other women never dare and I'm proud of you for that. But this is impossible."

It was not like him to repeat himself—he was tired, she should leave the subject. But—"My friend Dion is in a play."

He shook his head. "Aspasia, if you did go to the theater, which is impossible, you'd soon be sorry, one woman among thousands of men."

"Are there no women there at all?"

"An occasional prostitute . . . a few women selling cakes . . . But you'd be different because of your association with me. It's one thing that you live in my home—the Athenians are tolerant of what men do in their private lives. But in the theater, you'd be a target of seventeen thousand Athenians, Aspasia. Every eye would be on you. As I think of it, the police would force you to leave."

"Do they force out the other women?"

Inwardly intent, he didn't hear her. "And then, once they'd gotten rid of you, every eye would be on me." He imagined them laughing at him, pointing, kicking their heels into the stands. Throwing things. Aiming at him. None of this, he thought, was exaggeration. In fact, he might be prosecuted. Or impeached—an earthquake that would topple him to the bottom of a crumbling mountain and smother him under the rubble. He put aside the ugly drama that had played in his mind. He just said, "It would be the end of my career."

His worst fear. And her worst fear was to be the cause of it.

* * *

Two hundred and forty bulls were sacrificed for the festival of Dionysos and at night the smoke from the grilling meat blocked out the stars. Mortals and gods smelled the same good fat. Seals were broken on wine skins.

In the morning, Pericles ate a larger than usual breakfast of boiled barley to see him through the long day at the theater.

"I made something special for you, General Pericles," Zoe said.

"You can sit on it while you're watching the plays!" Little Pericles said.

"Don't bother Pericles with that now, Zoe. He has to leave soon." Aspasia poured warm goat's milk into Pericles' bowl and Little Pericles' cup.

Pericles sipped the milk. "I hope you haven't stitched a gorgon monster on that cushion to protect me—like the one you stitched into Little Pericles' blanket."

Little Pericles jumped from his seat. "Show him what you made, Zoe, show him!"

Zoe held up the cushion—two embroidered roosters, hackles raised, wings fanned, claws spread. "I copied the picture from a cup." She winked at Little Pericles.

"A gorgon is right for a new baby." Little Pericles raised his pointer finger like a teacher. "*This* is right for the theater because the playwrights fight like cocks to win first prize."

Sitting on a stone seat all day—that cushion would be a comfort. Pericles reached for it to examine closely the tiny, even stitches and tilted it to catch the light. The colors were brilliant as jewels. "Are these threads silk?" Zoe smiled. This wasn't the sculpture of the Parthenon and Zoe said she'd copied it—Phidias made his own designs. Still, even though Zoe was a slave, he felt he had to say it. "This is fine work, Zoe. You'd win if we had a contest for cushions."

Zoe flashed her "I told you so smile" to Little Pericles.

The cushion tempted him, but Pericles was concerned that the Athenian citizens filling the theater might that day hear Sophocles attacking him for the immense power he held in his rank of General from all the Athenians, even though they'd voted him into that position. So he refused the cushion.

His defeat in running for general the year before had sent him into what felt like exile—the upper seats at the theater. Now that he'd turned that vote around, he'd be back in front with the ten other generals. He didn't need a cushion.

* * *

As Pericles made a ceremonial libation in the center of the Theater of Dionysos, the applause was intoxicating, as if he'd drunk the wine instead of pouring it into the earth. The clapping and shouting rose again when Sophocles—Treasurer of the Athenian League as well as a playwright—marched at the head of the wagons of gleaming silver ingots paid to the Athenians as tribute by their allies. The applause crested for the eighteen-year-old sons of men who had died fighting for Athens; they wheeled about in their new armor, the city's gift, throwing the light from two hundred undented shields across the faces of the spectators. By the time Sophocles had readied his actors and chorus to present his plays, the sun had risen three fingers above the hills.

Was Sophocles remembering that Pericles had given him the high post of League Treasurer? A shadowed thought at a brilliant moment and Pericles pushed it aside. Instead, he held himself erect in his marble throne of honor, but he leaned forward in his mind. He had risen above opposition to his policies, criticism of his methods, betrayal by friends, ridicule of his huge head and now of his love for Aspasia. He had arrived at a new height of power. Was he about to discern criticism of his power from Sophocles—masked or unmasked? Betrayal of their friendship?

But Pericles put those thoughts aside as the early sun, crossing the theater, warmed the spectators and lit the stage. The play, *Antigone*, began.

Antigone

In front of the palace of Thebes. Antigone and her sister Ismene emerge from the great central door.

They are alone—out of the hearing of others, and soon they are arguing.

"So do as you like," Antigone tells Ismene. "I will bury him myself. And even if I die in the act, that death will be a glory."

Antigone's brother had gone to war against his own city and in retaliation, King Creon had determined to deny him the sacred rites of burial. But for Antigone, her family ties superseded any edict of a king, and she was determined to fulfill her sacred duty. She was ready to bury her brother with her own hands.

Though Pericles was focused on clues to criticism of his own leadership, he was amused to hear a familiar voice, pinched high, coming from behind a girl's mask—as Aspasia had said, Dion was playing Antigone's sensible sister, trying to temper Antigone's audacity. But Antigone was beyond compromise. Defiant and claiming she was happy to die to fulfill her duty, Antigone skipped the middle and hit the extremes. Pericles suppressed a frown and firmed his mask of absorbed interest, knowing heads would turn to gauge his reaction, some to follow his lead, others to seek his Achilles heel.

Although warned by her sister that her plan to bury her brother was hopeless, Antigone refused to hear reason. "—leave me to my own absurdity, leave me to suffer this—dreadful thing."

Pericles heard in that a bit of sophistry: Sophocles had slid from *hopeless* to *absurdity*. But hopeless does not equal absurdity. Why had the playwright manipulated his meaning? Had he emphasized Antigone's absurdity to link it to Deinomache's well-known insanity in order to bring Pericles to the minds of the audience? The equation he had sketched for Aspasia passed across his mind like a banner: "King Creon's opposition to Antigone's desire for a proper burial for her brother *equals* Pericles' opposition to Deinomache's desire for a proper burial for her husband."

No, Pericles! He chastened himself. *You're spinning too intricate a web.*

Creon appeared onstage, introducing himself to the populace as having recently inherited his kingship. Pericles' election as General from all the Athenians was recent. Ah, but consider the difference, Pericles thought. Creon inherited his kingship. I achieved my position through a democratic vote. Athens abolished inherited kingships Olympiads ago, thanks to the gods and to men who love liberty!

Creon was describing an ideal ruler—one of Pericles' favorite topics. A king should listen to the opinions of others and seek advice, Creon stated. Pericles nodded in agreement; he habitually sought the views of others. If that linked him with Creon, fine! Creon insisted that he put the interests of his city first. There again, Pericles' love of Athens was beyond doubt.

When Creon proclaimed that a leader must advise the right action, even at the risk of antagonizing the populace, Pericles felt a joyous sense of kinship. To win an election, some politicians will say whatever voters want to hear. Pericles unfailingly laid out for the Athenians what he knew was their best path, even if that meant disappointing or angering them. He thought of the concessions the Athenians had hated to make, but that he had insisted on in order to achieve the Thirty Years Peace Treaty with Sparta.

Creon turned to his plans for Antigone's two brothers who had died in the war. The one who had fallen nobly defending his city would be honored with a fine burial. Men shifted uneasily in their seats because they knew what was coming.

The other brother was a rebel and a traitor. In vengeance for being exiled from the city, Thebes, he had gathered an army and mounted an attack, intending to seize the kingship. Pounding his staff, Creon described how the rebel had "returned from exile, home to his father-city and the gods of his race, consumed with one desire—to burn them roof to roots—who thirsted to drink his kinsmen's blood . . . "

. . . *drink his kinsmen's blood* . . . That wasn't in the story. Creon was as overwrought as Antigone.

The enraged King Creon issued his public decree: ". . . he must be left unburied, his corpse carrion for the birds and dogs to tear, an obscenity for the citizens to behold!"

Without burial, the spirit of the dead man would find no find peace. Realizing he was frowning and stroking his beard, Pericles crossed his hands on his lap and regained his attentive mask.

As Creon's language turned bloodthirsty and his vengeance extreme, the credit he had built with the audience through his wise words dissipated.

Antigone, stubborn as Creon, faced him down. Claiming that eternal laws justified her decision to bury her brother, she won the audience to her side. "Nor did I think your edict had such force that you, a mere mortal, could override the gods . . . "

The audience began to cheer

". . . the great unwritten, unshakable traditions. They are alive, not just today or yesterday . . . "

You could hardly hear Antigone say, "They live forever."

Pericles felt the vibrations of heels kicking the stands in his teeth. He found himself loving the defiant Antigone, while thinking that no leader could enjoy applause for defiance. Unless, that is, he was leading a rebellion.

If the Athenians in the law courts applauded the actions of unruly citizens, the laws would wither. If the Assembly cheered for rebellions against Athens, those silver ingots of tribute the Athenians exacted from their allies would go uncollected.

Yet how thrilling to watch a mere girl argue passionately against a king.

For moments, Pericles melded with the audience in admiration for Antigone, almost against his will because, he reminded himself, she made no effort to find common ground. Nor did Creon look for common ground. Pericles' hand was back to stroking his beard. Between these two, was common ground possible? He tried it out for Creon. Then Antigone.

Sometimes compromise is impossible. Not a thought Pericles liked to contemplate.

Because those are hard times in a city.

As the king held to his decision to punish this girl who would die rather than obey him, applause swelled for obdurate Antigone. When the guards led her away to her punishment, slow death in a rock tomb, Pericles' eyes and those of many of the seventeen thousand Athenians in the theater grew moist. Judging from his well-practiced sense of the noise of crowds, Antigone had won the day by a sizeable majority.

291

If women were mannishly brave like Antigone, households would crumble and when households crumble, cities crumble—the cities that protect us all. Then why did the audience of men who hated disobedience in their wives love Antigone?

Dion came on as Creon's son, Prince Haemon—what a surprise to see that weepy boy as a bold antagonist of the King. Although he had said the opposite in public, Creon now told his son that he intended to rule *not* on behalf of the city but for his own benefit. Finding his father's autocratic egoism unbearable, Haemon answered by lunging at him with a sword. Dion the unpainted was born with his costume—as he raised his sword arm, his cloak fell away to reveal his totally white body. That odd pallor Dion carried from birth, which Pericles had always found repellent, now made him seem divinely illuminated, at least for a moment in the theater.

"It's no city at all, owned by one man alone." Dion's voice so resonated with the love of freedom that Creon had to wait for the cheers to die down to speak his next line—which was another abomination.

But . . . Not his worst enemies—not even Thucydides—had ever accused Pericles of ruling Athens to profit himself.

But . . . If he hadn't been elected to the highest of all positions in Athens that he had himself invented, General from all the Athenians, Sophocles would not have produced this play ringing with a challenge to autocracy.

He was accustomed to Thucydides and his crowd labeling him an autocrat. But for Sophocles, his oldest friend, to turn to the side of his enemies, for Sophocles to criticize him to the Athenians through his playwright's mask, to subvert the theater in order to accuse him of being a tyrant. For a moment, Pericles felt angry and fearful so that the cheers and jeers around him seemed to come from underwater. He shook his head to clear his ears.

Then, with a deep breath, he looked directly at that dreaded word, *accuse*. Accusations were made in the Assembly and in the courts. If Sophocles wanted to accuse Pericles before the Athenians, he knew how to do it.

Or . . . Was Sophocles speaking to him?

Was Sophocles warning him? Of what? That he was treading a dangerous path? That he might be accused?

Was it a warning that he was straying from his democratic ideals?

To whom was Sophocles speaking? And what was the message?

Sophocles' mask was more subtle than the painted linen that covered an actor's face—a king mask, a queen mask, a girl mask, a prince mask . . .

Sophocles wore the mask of ambiguity.

It was a useful mask, for Sophocles. And for Pericles. Practical. And ironic.

Sophocles would retain any critical thoughts he might have about Pericles' power behind the mask.

Pericles knew the colors of the magic veil that, like the veil that protected Odysseus against high ocean waves, would protect him. He would listen to the opinions of others, speak the truth to the populace, and use his leadership to further the best interests of his city. As always.

* * *

Cheers from the audience floated over the walls surrounding the rose garden.

Mother and son looked up toward the square of sky.

"What happened right then?"

"Those sounded like happy cheers," Aspasia replied. "I think that's where the prince defies the king."

"I think so too!" Little Pericles said.

She was right not to break off entirely with Dion after his argument with Pericles. Knowing she'd want to read the play, Dion had given her his rehearsal copy of *Antigone*.

Aspasia tapped the scroll. "We're up to where the chorus sings, 'Numberless wonders, terrible wonders walk the earth but none the match for man—the greatest wonder—'"

"I'm going to be a man," Little Pericles said.

"You're already a great wonder." Aspasia smoothed her cheek against his.

"What about you, Mother—are you a great wonder, too?"

Aspasia checked to see how Sophocles had written "man." The playwright could have used a word that meant "men only" so she felt relieved that he had chosen the word that included women. She liked him better for it.

An explosive burst of applause from the theater came over the wall.

"Maybe *that* was when the prince—"

"That's the trouble with not being there, we don't know. But let's find out how we're wonderful." Her oval fingernail found the place—"The song tells us about man 'crossing the heaving gray sea, driven on by blasts of winter on through the breakers crashing . . .' See, we're wonderful for being able to sail in boats."

"You're calling it a song but you're only saying it." Little Pericles was working a splinter on the weathered bench.

"I'm doing my best. When you're not there you can't hear the music. Now see here where Sophocles wrote that man 'wears away the earth, the immortal the inexhaustible—as his plows go back and forth, year in, year out—'"

"What's good about that? Slaves and poor people walk behind ploughs."

"That's how we get our food. You wouldn't want to go hungry, would you? Now look here—the song is about hunting and I know you'll want to do that when you're older . . . 'And the blithe, lighthearted race of birds he snares, the tribes of savage beasts, the life that swarms the depth—'"

"Father says my brother Xanthippus spends too much time hunting and not enough at civic responsibilities."

Pericles criticizing his oldest son. She couldn't help but feel pleased. Pericles' disappointments grieved her—she always rushed to soothe them. But if he had to be disappointed about something, she didn't mind that it was about his self-centered son.

She squeezed Little Pericles' shoulders. "I know that *you're* not going to spend too much time hunting."

"It's about proportion—this is to this as that is to that." Little Pericles' forefinger traced his ratio in the air.

"You're right!" Oh how smart he was, and how much he took after his father. She wished Pericles had heard him.

"What else did we men invent?"

Sophocles was harder to read than Homer but he was old enough to try. "Read right here."

"Sophocles made a mistake."

Aspasia leaned in for a close look. "Where? I don't see a mistake."

"He says that men tame wild animals like horses and bulls but horses and bulls aren't wild. We have them on the estate."

"That's what Sophocles means. They *used* to be only wild but men tame them now and they're useful."

"When were they only wild?"

"A long time ago. Now look," she hurried on to move past the uncertain *when*, "here's my favorite invention—language!"

"Language invented? That doesn't make sense." Little Pericles yanked the splinter free. "We couldn't talk without language." He shook his head. "Impossible."

"That just shows what a wonder man is to invent it. And here Sophocles says that our thoughts are quick as the wind." *Quick as the wind? Faster than a bird could fly*—she saw in her mind thousands of Athenians in the theater, Pericles on a throne at the front, outsiders high up on the grass outside the theater. She rested her chin on the curved back of her hand. Birds in flight, a slung stone moves fast but thoughts move faster. She wouldn't have realized it if she hadn't read it.

"Sophocles should have included *reading* on this list of man's inventions," she said.

"We'll tell him the next time we see him," Little Pericles replied. "He could fit it in up there with language."

"Good idea." She nodded. "And see here—we invented laws so we could live together in cities." *It was all the opposite of Hesiod who thought the golden age was gone forever—Sophocles agreed with Pericles, thanks to Zeus!* "It's just as your father always says—man's life has gotten better. The golden age is now!" *That is, if there ever was one.*

Later that night, Pericles, back home, picked up the scroll. "Now what have you been reading to Little Pericles—oh—" How like her.

"So, Aspasia, since you've read *Antigone*, do you think Sophocles means the autocratic Creon to be me?"

"You can squeeze out of it some things you often say but also things you'd never say. For instance, Creon says that money ruins a city—you think the opposite."

"That's how I understand the play—" Pericles passed the scroll across his lips—"more or less."

"What do the Athenians think about the play. What's the talk?"

"That young man Socrates said that it's a contest between laws of the state and laws of religion and people kept repeating it as if he were a philosopher. Frankly, Aspasia, that kind of careless use of words annoys me, because, *alpha*, there are several kinds of states and, *beta*, a kingship is not a democracy."

"Creon and Antigone are so extreme that you can't draw general conclusions from them anyway."

Pericles stroked his beard. "Still, the audience admired Antigone for defying Creon and following the higher law."

"Really! I'm surprised. Are you sure?"

"By the end, the majority felt that she was right. At least, that's how it seemed when they applauded."

"Antigone caused her own problems," Aspasia said. "I would not have applauded."

"Then you'd have been in the minority."

She shook her head *yes*, then *no*, then shrugged her shoulders. "I'm the wrong person to decide whether Antigone was right or wrong."

"Why on earth?"

"Because to me, Antigone is a truly fortunate woman. She's going to marry a prince. He loves her—he's willing to die for her. If I were in Antigone's place, I'd stay alive and marry the prince. He'd become a king someday, and we'd have a son who'd be a prince. As for the gods, they can take care of themselves."

He contemplated her pretty face, her long, slim arms, her finely curved nails. She never let him forget her desire to be his wife and for her son to be a citizen. He couldn't give her what she wanted, but he felt impelled to say something to give her equal comfort. "You're no less loved than Antigone."

It had not occurred to him until he spoke those words that he would be willing to die for Aspasia—not that he wanted to, but a man doesn't want to die for his city either.

CHAPTER 30

An Easy Victory

General Glaucon entered the Music Hall, sword rattling. Why did Glaucon, that restless young commander, come late, cause a stir and startle the cithara contestant? Pericles turned his mind back to the music. But a thought intruded: Glaucon had little interest in music. The citharist swung the plectrum from below his breastbone the full distance upward, like the long sail from Athens to the Hellespont, his hand coming to rest on Byzantium. Pericles waited until the strings were silent. Then he swung round to beckon Glaucon who moved quickly to his side and knelt to whisper in his ear. The state ship *Paralus* had docked in Piraeus with bad news from East Greece. The island of Samos was in full rebellion against Athens. The oligarchic rulers had refused Athenian arbitration to settle their conflict with Miletus over a mainland town.

The Athenians could not let one of the largest and richest members of their alliance stray from the fold. It was equally essential that they defend Miletus, also an important Athenian ally, against Samian aggression. The Athenians would have to sail to Samos to vanquish the rebellion. Pericles hoped that the next contestant would regain the attention of the other judges after the abrupt departure of two generals.

Three days later, and one day after the close of that year's Panathenaic Festival, Pericles, in supreme command, sailed for Samos with forty ships, along with Generals Glaucon, Andocides, and Sophocles. In assigning Glaucon to the Samos campaign, Pericles had in mind the election for general he'd once lost to this young tribesman. Since then, he had overcome the competitive situation in his tribe by persuading the Athenians to create the position of General from all the Athenians so that one tribe could have two generals—and had won the election for the new position. But the fact remained that they were two big men from the same tribe, and Glaucon continued to treat him like a rival. He seemed to have forgotten that Pericles had promoted Glaucon's importance among the Athenians, taking him on as an aide in the crucial mission that saved Athens from a Spartan invasion. In this campaign to Samos, he might pull Glaucon closer to his circle, or at least offset his hostility. Meanwhile, by being an elected General, Glaucon had gotten what he wanted which made him as trustworthy as any man—until he wanted something else. General Andocides was brave, experienced and a friend; he had proposed on Pericles' behalf the new Athenian law that allowed for the election of a General from all the Athenians. Sophocles was not elected General for his military skills—he was loved for his plays. He was a peacetime luxury and the Athenians were still at peace because, as Pericles reminded the Athenians in the Assembly, the Peace Treaty with Sparta allowed each of the two great powers of Greece to discipline its own allies. Punishing Samos did not break the Peace Treaty.

* * *

For the Athenian fleet, embarking for Samos was like leaping onto the back of a running horse. The crews, impatient at crisscrossing their own wakes in training, were eager to cross the Aegean Sea. Each of the forty ships carried a crew of one hundred and seventy crewmen, twenty hoplite ground soldiers, ten archers and several officers. They sailed in four squadrons, each headed by a general. The helmsmen set a pace that would excite the men without tiring them. The squadrons bedded down on Chios the first night, Tenos the second and Icaria the third, and set out for the small island of Corsiae, near Samos, on the fourth day. Later that morning the four generals met on the beach across from Samos to review their battle plan.

"Did I hear something about *you don't agree?*" Pericles looked over at Glaucon—the young man's thick hair was wind-blown. The surf crashing on the rocks thinned out voices.

"We should fight them in their bay—not in open water." Glaucon's finger chased the Bay of Samos on Pericles' map that was flapping in the wind.

A gust smacked the map against Pericles' chest. He unpeeled it so they could continue their review and looked to Andocides to answer this pointless interruption.

"When we worked out our plan, we all had a chance to say what we thought." Andocides hurled a stone which skipped toward Samos in the blithe way flat stones have, even in a rough surf.

"These winds are stronger than I knew when we were back in Athens." Glaucon brushed the hair out of his eyes.

"Here the winds are always strong," Andocides said. "I guess you're too young to have ever made it across the Aegean Sea."

"We've won battles everywhere in tight waters, ever since we destroyed the Persians in Salamis Bay," Glaucon said.

"As a boy, I led the song to celebrate that victory." Sophocles looked to the sky, remembering.

"At Salamis, our ships were agile, our rowers fast, we crowded them in the bay and smashed them to bits." Glaucon spoke like a proud schoolboy.

Andocides was following the bounces of his skipping stones as they disappeared into sea glare so Pericles said, "Not this time, Glaucon."

"We worked out our—" Andocides looked around to make sure they were alone on the beach, "—diversionary attack. When they meet us in open water, they'll have already fought one battle *and* have to rush back at a fast row while we sail in rested."

The four generals peered north toward where on the next day the Athenian and Samian fleets would clash. "You're a good student of history, Glaucon." Pericles said. "Here's a question for you. How many ships did we lose in the Battle of Salamis?"

"We sank three hundred Persian ships!"

Eyes half-closed, Sophocles hummed. Andocides skipped a stone. Pericles waited.

Glaucon brushed his thick hair back. "But we lost forty ships."

"Forty ships." Andocides, his cheeks wet from the surf, patted them dry with the edge of his cloak and then blew his nose loudly. "Fighting in a tight space even when you win . . . " Andocides shook his head.

After a good night's rest and a breakfast of barley meal mixed with olive oil and an extra ration of wine, the united fleet set off for Samos at medium speed and soon reached the southern, populous shore of that big island.

Rowing in close along Samos Bay so they'd be seen, the Athenian ships approached the western end of the city harbor but did not enter it, instead drawing abreast in the open sea, holding their line against a brisk wind, and waiting. The sun was halfway to noon.

Soon the Samian ships, alerted to the arrival of the Athenian fleet, rounded the cape at full speed from the skirmish with Milesians and their allies that Pericles had arranged. Without breaking rhythm, the Samian line turned north and tried to lure the Athenians into the harbor but the Athenians held back from chasing the Samians into the bay. The practiced skill of the Athenian rowers was set to maintaining their line of forty ships in the strong wind and currents.

Four Samian ships entered their own bay but the Athenians, instead of following them, moved to cut them off from the rest of their fleet; this forced the main Samian line to engage the Athenians on the sea side of the breakwater. While the Athenian left wing, commanded by Pericles, skirmished with the Samians right, an Athenian ship near the center, under Glaucon, was blown forward by the wind. The rowers tried to regain the line but the wayward Athenian ship swung starboard, whereupon a Samian ship rushed in and rammed it. Seeing it founder and spill Athenians into the water, Glaucon sent four ships of his remaining nine to the rescue. He had to save the men but the action split the Athenian line into two sections. The Samian center and right rushed through the gap while the Samian commanders held back their left, setting the Samians up to encircle the remainder of Glaucon's ships. But before they could close the trap, the split sections of Athenian ships reformed into two facing lines. To do it they executed a maneuver they'd often practiced—and no less astounding for that—each section pivoting ninety degrees with the ships near the ends traversing vast stretches of water at top speed, and so they closed in on the Samian ships. Pericles' squadron, having disarmed two Samian vessels near the harbor mouth, sped past the rear of the Samian center, engaged the Samian left and prevented the entrapment of Glaucon's squadron. The Samian vessels, their rowers arm-weary, were rammed as they sought to speed away between Glaucon's vessels.

Some Samians died in the water—drowned, shot with arrows, speared, or crushed between ships or wreckage—but the Athenians took as many alive as they could. With the Samians in disarray, the Athenians broke line to chase those fleeing through the bay toward the city, capturing several, although many Samians reached the shore and escaped through the marshes. Some Samian ships fled across to the mainland where many of their aristocrats, who hated Athens and its democracy, owned land.

With the damaged vessels in tow, the Athenians sailed into port. The Samian democrats and those Athenians who had been settled on Samos to keep an eye on the oligarchic government came out to meet them, cheering wildly. Pericles and Glaucon led the armed Athenian hoplite foot soldiers into the city, leaving Andocides and Sophocles to guard the ships. The Samian garrisons had fled their posts. By noon, the Athenians had taken over the Samian Acropolis and garrisoned the towers of the city walls, built by the tyrant Polycrates before the Persian Wars.

Pericles' first goal was to capture hostages from the oligarch families. The Athenians acted quickly before the boys had fled— they could choose the men later from among those taken in battle. Pericles sent Glaucon out with his men who, guided by Samian democrats, rounded up fifty boys from the larger farms—none remained in Samos City—and brought them into the palace built by Polycrates. The hostages were locked in the fortress under heavy guard, as were the captives from battle.

Meanwhile, Pericles met one by one with the Athenians living on Samos as well as with the island's democratic leaders, gathering information on the family connections and political alignments of the islanders, learning who were friends of Sparta, and at the same time judging the character of those he interviewed and their probable loyalty toward Athens. The sun had sunk to two fingers above the peaks of Mount Karvounis when he learned from Glaucon that the hostages were secured. Pericles then sent out runners to bid the Samians assemble in the theater; he chose a trustworthy Samian democrat, Antipatrus the potter—the oligarchic leaders of Samos had murdered his father for setting up his own trade contacts in Egypt—to organize the Assembly.

By the time the Samians had been searched for weapons and were gathered in the theater, the sun's rays were golden—an ordinary Assembly would be ending. Pericles watched the rows fill, some men frantic with worry for captured relatives, some excited, all hurried and hot. Like sculptures on a temple roof, an Athenian guard of archers ringed the top of the theater. A strong breeze blew in from the bay, carrying the first cooling air of night. The Samian herald called for order. A priest sprinkled pig's blood on the dancing ground. A woman's cry from outside penetrated the silence. The crowd stirred uneasily. The archers drew their bows.

Pericles mounted the bema set up that afternoon on the dancing ground, made his silent prayer, and addressed the gathering.

"When the Persians set out to conquer all of Greece, a Samian bridged the Great River for the Persian king to make it easier for his army.

"When Ionians revolted against Persian domination, Samian ships deserted the common cause"—Pericles clenched his fist—"and the Ionians were enslaved."

"The Milesians were enslaved," someone called out. "Samians were never slaves!"

Two hoplites standing guard near the man moved to seize him, but Pericles gestured for them to desist.

"When Persia mounted the largest army ever assembled to move against Greece, and Greece resolved to resist, the Samians fought for Persia." Pericles looked toward the man who'd made the disturbance. "You say you weren't enslaved? No Greeks—unless they are slaves— would fight against Greeks on behalf of Persia."

He let his words weigh like a goad against the neck of an ox.

"We sent five hundred Athenian prisoners back to you!" called out a man who looked old enough to remember those days.

"Now free our prisoners!" someone shouted.

"Free our prisoners!"

The cry rippled throughout the theater, but soon trailed off.

"Yes, the Samians sent five hundred Athenian captives home—but not until we Athenians vanquished the Persians in our Bay of Salamis and you and all of Greece saw the Persian King scramble like a rabbit back to the safety of his palace in Persia.

"Now I hear some reminding me of what Samos did for the Greek cause. Why would I need a reminder that, after our victory at Salamis, it was *my father*, General Xanthippus, who liberated Ionia. Even though that was the first time you'd ever fought on the Greek side, my father generously praised the bravery of the Samians who fought with him at the Battle of Mycale."

Pericles looked east to Mycale, within view. They followed his line of sight, and back.

"And my father praised the bravery and seamanship of the Samians who went on with him to liberate the Hellespont."

Pericles paused as if turning in his mind thoughts of his father's battles. And for a moment he did hear his father's voice speaking about his victories liberating Ionian Greeks from Persia.

It occurred to him that he, like his father, was here to liberate Ionians.

True, his father had liberated them from Persian domination. But Athens had invented a new kind of liberation. To bring democracy to a Greek city as he was doing now, to rid Samos of its oligarchs, was also liberation.

Surely his father would see it that way.

"Nor have we Athenians forgotten that, since then, you've been our loyal allies, seeking to wash away your earlier sins as, they say, some rivers in southern Italy can turn black hair to white. You've sent your ships and men to fight with us at the Hellespont, in Egypt, at Eion, at Scyros . . . " Some Samians applauded. "At Eurymydon . . . " The applause grew louder. "At Memphis, where your Captain—" Pericles raised his voice above the cheers and applause. "—captured fifteen Persian ships! Athens and Samos have been friends."

The applause continued, then faltered.

"But, Samians, in the matter of Miletus, your city refused Athenian arbitration. While we tried to help you arrive at a reasonable settlement, you continued to wage war on the Milesians. And Miletus is also our friend.

"Your island of Samos contributes fighting ships to our defensive league but the contribution of Miletus is also impressive—five talents each year."

"That's nothing compared to what we pay in ships," someone called out.

Athenian soldiers advanced toward the man but Pericles signaled them to stop. "We assess the cities of our defensive alliance fairly so that each pays what is just."

"Your league pays to build your temples," someone shouted. "Where's the justice in that!"

"You're decking out your city like a whore at our expense!"

Those words bounced toward him like an unwanted, inescapable echo. They were the words his rival, Thucydides, had used to argue against the funds for the Parthenon temple.

He glanced up at the archers—their bows were taut.

"We're not here to argue with you about the wisdom of our alliance that has kept the Persians at bay for forty years. An argument requires a measure of equality between those in the dispute and Samos is not the equal of Athens. Not when we've destroyed your ships, captured others, occupied your citadel, and hold your men and boys captive."

The word struck him—"captive"—yes, to guarantee the peace.

"We're here to end the war between Samos and Miletus. Since Samos refused to arbitrate, we've done it by force of arms. Now we will take the actions necessary to ensure that Samos will maintain the peace that we establish.

"Some of you are spreading fear that we'll deprive you of your ships and arms. Others say we'll punish you through ruinous fines. That's not in our interest any more than it's in yours. A strong and prosperous Samos has been our powerful ally. Why would we wish you otherwise?

"And we don't blame all Samians for pursuing war and refusing arbitration. These were the acts of a few, self-interested oligarchs. We do not punish the many for the acts of a powerful few.

"Hostages will be held from among the oligarchs of your island who have fomented discontent against our league and pursued acts of war against our allies. Your treasury will be charged for the costs to Athens of this campaign. Your government will be arranged so that the many will rule, not just a few. No one will be barred from political activity because of poverty, and every man will be equal before the law.

"In this way you'll discover the benefits of democracy. Once you've tasted the fruits of free public life, you'll never willingly surrender your freedom to a handful of oligarchs who place their private interests above public concerns."

That night, in the palace of Polycrates, who ruled Samos as a tyrant many years before, the Athenian generals ate supper on ebony couches, the silver legs turned at the feet into lions' heads. The old steward supervising their meal told them that the King of Egypt had sent them as a gift to Polycrates' wife while the two rulers were still allies. Not long after, realizing the tyrant's power was about to crumble, the Egyptian king withdrew his support.

"Then the Persians lured Polycrates to Cape Mycale with a promise of gold, and when he got there, they nailed his body to a cross in view of the Samians. He hung there alive for ten days." The steward's voice trembled with awe, even though he must have told the story a thousand times. He was probably the one who'd told it to the historian Herodotus, Pericles thought.

The steward shook his head. "Polycrates should never have left the island—everyone warned him."

"He needed the gold," Andocides said. "He'd exiled the Samian aristocrats because he thought they'd grab his power, and then he learned the hard way that without them, he lacked the funds to defend Samos against her enemies."

"Just like King Creon in Antigone." Glaucon glanced at Sophocles, then at Pericles. "Tyrants hate opposition."

That was sheer hubris on Glaucon's part—even more in that his actions that caused the breach in the Athenian line of ships that morning that could have cost them a victory. And, though Glaucon was proud—and Pericles had hoped to strengthen his ties with Glaucon on this expedition—men must learn. It was essential to discuss Glaucon's error.

Andocides, looking to cast off the melancholy, raised his cup for the first toast.

"To Sophocles, the first to win the wreath of poet *and* general." They all raised their cups but Sophocles handed on the toast. "And to Glaucon, who won the day!"

Pericles set his cup down.

Surely that was one of Sophocles' ironies—he wasn't *that* useless a general—but the egoistic Glaucon might believe him.

To Pericles' displeasure, instead of setting down his cup, Andocides raised it even higher. "Under Glaucon's leadership, victory came with only one damaged ship."

Andocides was not without his own ironies.

Glaucon, his face grim, slammed down his cup. "That rammed ship was under my command."

"You saved all the survivors and the ship can be repaired," Sophocles said. "Drink up!"

"Tell me, because I was on the right," Andocides said, "did it really require four ships to pick up the survivors?"

"No one died."

"That was too many ships to pull from the line," Andocides said. "Do you agree, Pericles?"

"I agree."

Glaucon rose and, in the way he had, went for the dagger he didn't carry to dinner. "The ship was rammed full on the side in a rough surf. My men were scattered into the sea."

"When you sent four ships, did you know the Samians would try to break through the breach?" Pericles asked.

"I was certain that if they did, we could reform and surround them." Glaucon tossed the swath of hair from his forehead.

"You could be certain we could reform, but you could *not* be certain we could surround them," Pericles said. "Not in the midst of battle."

"And in those waves." Andocides said.

"With a narrower breach, the Samians wouldn't have attempted to break through," Sophocles said.

No irony there.

In the silence, Glaucon raised his cup. They listened to him swallow several times.

"If I hadn't saved the men, the Athenians would have prosecuted me."

"They would have prosecuted you if we'd been surrounded because you sent too many ships," Andocides said.

"Pericles' quick order turned your error into our victory." Andocides raised his cup. "To Pericles!"

"We owe our victory to the skill of our rowers," Pericles said.

"Man rides the waves and takes his way through the deeps," Sophocles sang. "Raise our cups to our rowers!"

Glaucon drained his cup. Looping the handle around his little finger, he spun the cup so that the dregs flew out, hitting the bronze lamp stand with a solid, resonant ping.

"There's a victory for Glaucon!" Sophocles said.

"It's easy to win when you're the only one in the game!" Amused by his own joke, Andocides laughed but Pericles winced. Glaucon had been more thoroughly beaten than was useful and if Glaucon took Andocides' laughter as ridicule, he would become dangerously enraged. But Glaucon, on his couch, turned his head back and forth like a bull sensing an interloper he might have to chase from his pasture. This proud young man wasn't done.

"It's too bad you two weren't in the theater to hear Pericles eloquently praise his own father for liberating the Greeks of Ionia from Persian domination," Glaucon said.

"And now we're here liberating Ionians," Andocides said.

"To liberation." Sophocles raised his cup.

"But not everyone calls what we're doing 'liberating.'"

The three generals swung around toward Glaucon, shocked as if his hair had caught on fire. Sophocles' cup stopped mid-air. Pericles watched as, eyes half-closed, Glaucon lay back on a cushion, slowly passing his wine cup back and forth across his lower lip. Glaucon enjoyed shocking the older generals, Pericles thought. Youthful pride and rivalry in the tribe they shared—Pericles had confidence he could work that out. Although if Glaucon was truly in Thucydides' camp, anything called "friendship" would be more elusive.

"If you're thinking of Thucydides," Andocides said, "we exiled him by a democratic vote of ostracism."

"I doubt our allies feel liberated when time comes to pay us their tribute."

Excited and angry, Andocides rose from his chair. "That's their contribution to our common defense! How else are we going to defend them! We're here defending our allies. The Samian oligarchs attacked Miletus—by the rules of our defensive league, by the rules of the Peace Treaty with Sparta—" Andocides was waving his cup in circles—"by all the rules there are we had the right to defend—"

"The duty," Pericles put in.

"—the right and the duty to defend Miletus."

"And to install a democratic government favorable to ourselves."

"Right—so we don't have to come here again."

Recalling the thought that came to him when he was speaking earlier in the theater, Pericles said, "Athens has invented a new kind of liberation. We've brought democracy to Samos."

Shaking his head, Glaucon stared at the floor as if he were reading something bad in the dark joins between the stones. "The Samian aristocrats we locked up don't feel 'liberated.'"

Despite his combative demeanor, Glaucon had learned a lesson that day that would make him a better strategist for the future. Pericles wanted to salvage a friendship with this young general from his own tribe and so he allowed Glaucon to have the last word.

Before leaving Samos, the generals visited Hera's large but incomplete temple which they'd sailed past on the day they captured the city. Although they set out early, the sun burned on the marsh as if to boil the mud. The Samians pointed out a grassy knoll near the river where Zeus and Hera, who were brother and sister, first lay together, hiding from their parents and enjoying love's pleasures before they were married. The river was narrow and covered with slime—only the gnats moved quickly. But when the rains began again, it would become a torrent, the Samians assured them, and beside the riverbank, Zeus would again make love to Hera, who became a new virgin each time.

Pericles heard this divine gossip with impatience. It demeaned the gods to speak of them this way. True, he was thinking out a prayer in his mind to thank their hosts where he would speak of Hera as "she who sleeps in the arms of Zeus," but in general terms, doing no more than referring to divine power in words listeners would understand. When making a prayer, one can't talk like the philosopher Anaxagoras.

The holy precinct had been strewn with willow branches, and couches had been brought in. Good, they'd eat now and leave soon after. The temple to Hera was overlarge and too lavish—it would suck in the resources of the Samians like footsteps in mud, and even then they'd probably never complete it. He'd be glad to leave this place with its gnats and flies, its tangled willow branches and ancient rumors of divine incest. The gods should be worshipped in high places and in a clear light. Seeing this temple made him more in a hurry to return to Athens and complete his Parthenon the right way.

The Athenians left Samos garrisoned and the democratic Samians in control. To keep it that way, one contingent stopped at the island of Athens' loyal ally, Lesbos, and installed the oligarchic Samian hostages there. The other—Pericles sailed with this one—went directly home.

CHAPTER 31

Mind

"'All other things have a portion of everything, but Mind is infinite and self-ruled, and is mixed with nothing but is all alone by itself . . .'"

Anaxagoras had always spoken his teachings. Now, approaching the shadows of old age, he was trying out writing them on wax. Pericles had summoned Phidias the sculptor and Ictinus the architect of the Parthenon temple to hear Anaxagoras for the good of the Parthenon temple, because philosophy helped men do their best. As for Sophocles—when ideas went askew, the playwright brought balance.

Anaxagoras read with stylus in hand. "'. . For if it was not by itself but was mixed with anything else, it would have a share of all things if it were mixed with any . . .'"

How lovely Aspasia looked with Little Pericles on her lap, her cheek pressed against his, the child playing with her earring, Pericles thought. Abruptly she raised her chin. "I don't see why if Mind, which I've heard you explain is the force of intellect, were mixed with *one* other thing, it would have a share of *all* things."

Xanthippus sighed with the impatience of a young man who considers himself an expert because he hangs around the philosophers in the Agora. "He just said that all other things have a portion of everything, so Mind, at the center of the cosmos, would pick up a bit of everything, no matter what you mixed it with."

"I couldn't hear well because of the child." Aspasia disentangled Little Pericles' hand from her hair and sat him on the couch next to her. The men would be more inclined to listen to what she said if she didn't have a child on her lap.

Anaxagoras murmured over the tablet, "'. . . for in everything there is a portion of everything . . .'" He pressed his stylus to his lips. "I'll add 'as I said earlier.'" He tucked in the words. "Now it's, 'For in everything there is a portion of everything, as I said earlier.'"

"Now Athpathia can catch on," Alcibiades whispered loudly to Xanthippus.

What a disrespectful boy, she thought. The fact was, she did not feel sorry for Alcibiades even though his father had died in war—he was too much a troublemaker. But Pericles and his brother Ariphron were his guardians and, though Alcibiades was staying at Ariphron's (thank the gods she'd managed to arrange that!), Pericles felt it would be educational for him to hear Anaxagoras that night.

"Women don't understand philosophy." Xanthippus palm-slicked his hair.

Flushed with anger, Aspasia looked directly at Pericles. Briskly he tapped his walking stick on the floor. He didn't send Xanthippus and Alcibiades out of the room though, as she'd hoped, because he was pleased they seemed interested in Anaxagoras' philosophy. It had made him a better man, and he expected it to do the same for them.

"I understand perfectly," Aspasia said.

"'Mind controls all things, both the greater and the smaller, that have life,'" Anaxagoras continued, reading from his scroll.

"Mind thounds like Pericles," Alcibiades whispered. Xanthippus grinned. Aspasia glanced at Pericles who seemed not to have heard. Or more likely, she thought, had held back to encourage the flow of ideas.

Anaxagoras tapped his foot. "'. . . Mind controlled also the whole rotation, so that it began to rotate in the beginning. And it began to rotate first from a small area . . .'" Phidias was spinning a drawing stick between his thumb and forefinger. "'. . . but it now rotates over a wider and will rotate over a wider—'"

Phidias jumped up. "I see it!"

"The rotation?" Pericles asked.

Phidias spun the charcoal he always had at hand.

When Phidias worked his charcoal, it meant pictures were springing to his mind so Pericles raised his hand to maintain the silence. Phidias, he knew, saw figures in a piece of coal. Just as when he, himself, looked at a sketched map and saw a whole city spread before him. That's the Mind in things.

Phidias looked toward the ceiling, then back to his charcoal. He breathed deeply. They looked away when they saw the tears in his eyes. He started to speak, then stopped, smudging his forehead with charcoal.

"Finally I can see the position of the god Zeus in the East Pediment of the Parthenon."

They all gazed at Phidias like respectful initiates celebrating the Mysteries, hopeful for the revelation.

But Ictinus, architect and practical man that he was, cracked the silence. "Zeus sits on his throne in the center and you can't change that—not after the labor you pushed on us to insert the iron supports into the stone under him to hold the weight."

"Of course he sits in the center. The question is, should he turn toward the right—" Phidias spun his wrist in each direction—"or toward the left?"

"Obviously Zeus should face directly forward." *Obviously . . .* Pericles was surprised to hear the word come from his own mouth.

"Apollo turns his head to his right in the temple at Olympia," Ictinus said.

"Olympia, Olympia," Phidias murmured.

"Apollo isn't king of gods and men," Sophocles said. "I'm with Pericles on this."

"Apollo's *only* on the *wetht* pediment at Olympia because he's less important than Theus. They put *Theus* on the eatht like we do because—" Alcibiades raised his forefinger like a teacher—"where the thun comes up counts motht."

How did that boy know so much about the temple at Olympia? Aspasia wondered. He was too young to have been to the Olympic games—anyhow, because he was Pericles' ward, she knew what he'd done and hadn't done. But Alcibiades was one of those boys who grew up knowing everything. She patted Little Pericles' knee. Soon her son would know everything, too. She was right to have him here—the child would catch on that discussion was important, even though he couldn't follow the philosophy. Not like Paralus, upstairs and in bed early, claiming he had a cold.

"You're on the east end of the Parthenon, standing at the base." Hands on his hips, Phidias took the broad stance needed to look high. "Your eyes follow the columns upward like tracking a bird." Phidias' long arm traced an arc from the mosaic floor of Pericles' andron to the top of the bronze lamp. "Way above, you see Zeus." Phidias' head was bent back on his neck. He squinted, as if for a sharp look at that height. "If Zeus sits squarely to the front, you can't see past his knees." Along with Phidias, they all craned their necks upward. There, it seemed, were Zeus' majestic knees blocking his chest and face.

"Then let him stand up." Xanthippus shrugged, as if how one saw Zeus didn't much matter one way or the other.

"Homer says Zeus rules from his throne," Sophocles said.

"The iron support bars are installed, we keep the throne," Ictinus said.

Silky, Ictinus' lover whom he'd brought along to share his couch, had so far been silent, but now she whispered something to Aspasia, who told her to speak up for herself.

"Zeus wouldn't want to stand up right after giving birth." Aspasia was the only one who knew that Silky had some years ago given birth—since the child was defective, Silky had left him on the far side of the river, giving him up to chance and the elements.

Silky looked down shyly as the others smiled, but Phidias nodded. "I've thought of that. Anaxagoras—say again how the rotation starts up."

Anaxagoras shook off his annoyance at the long interruption. "'. . . at first it rotated from a small area . . .'" Phidias was spinning a drawing stick between his thumb and forefinger. "'. . . but now it rotates over a wider area and in time it will rotate over a wider—'"

"Here's what we do." Phidias twisted an invisible coil of clay between his flat palms. "Zeus turns to look at Athena who he just gave birth to from his head. Even he can be surprised—"

"Born from Theus's head mutht be why Athena's thmart as Aspasia."

"Athena's wisdom itself," Phidias said, "so his loins, which took no part in her birth, turn the other way. See—he twists in two directions and starts off the great rotation!"

Sophocles raised an eyebrow. "That's awkward for a god."

"Pericles, sit straight." Pericles drew back as the sculptor put his hands to his face.

"Here! I'll be Theus." Alcibiades grabbed Xanthippus' walking stick and brandished it like a thunderbolt.

"Dion can be Zeus." Sophocles pushed forward his lover who'd come to share his couch. "He's the actor."

"Dion, sit with your head this way and swing your knees that way and . . . yes." Phidias pushed Dion's legs opposite. "By Zeus, relax your back!" The sculptor viewed the pose. "Now, lower your knees. Stretch them out."

"Like this?"

"Yes!" Ictinus called from the farthest corner of the room, where he lay with his cheek pressed to the floor. "That gets the knees out of the way. Somewhat."

"You have to consider where people will be looking from—I learned that the hard way when I built the statue of—"

"We've strayed from our topic," Anaxagoras said.

"You can't mean that just by twisting his torso, Zeus becomes that cosmic vortex you're always talking about," Xanthippus said.

"That's exactly what I mean. He sets the rotation into motion." Phidias glanced at Anaxagoras. "From the center."

"But how will they know it's my cosmic rotation?" Anaxagoras eyed the words on his tablet. "People may think that he's just shifting his legs to get comfortable."

"We already decided that the sun's chariot will be rising from the sea on the south and the moon's chariot will descend on the other end. That's cosmic enough for anybody."

"Then it must be dawn," Dion said.

"Athena's birth starts a new day," Aspasia said.

"And another rotation." Alcibiades bent at the waist from one side to the other, his arms curled over his head like a dancer—or a lamp stand—to imitate the rising sun and setting moon.

"You're all assuming that Zeus is Mind as if it's the only way to think of him," Sophocles said.

Anaxagoras circled his forefinger. "He *is* Mind, the very force of intellect."

"That's what we believe," Pericles said.

"Nothing else makes sense," Aspasia said.

"The Athenians won't look up at the pediment of their temple expecting to see Mind," Sophocles said. "They'll be looking for Zeus. Look at this coin I picked up at Olympia." Light fell across the outspread eagle's wings on the brilliant gold disk Sophocles held between his thumb and forefinger. "Carve him the way we know him, Phidias, with his eagle and thunderbolt, and so on."

"Theus of the thunderbolt!" Alcibiades waved the walking stick.

"Zeus will look exactly as the Greeks expect," Phidias said.

"With his thunderbolt?" Alcibiades feigned suspicion.

"Yes, thunderbolt . . . staff . . . eagle . . . "

"And the throne," Ictinus said.

Xanthippus' hands flew apart. "That misses the point. What about Mind? What about rotation?"

Pericles was pleased—his son seemed even more seriously engaged in philosophy than he had thought.

"*You're* missing the point," Dion said. "Zeus will be ordinary Zeus for ordinary people, and he'll be Mind for those of us with true understanding."

Dion never had much to say for himself, Aspasia thought, but was good at explaining the ideas of others—not that she needed his help with philosophy. But from the time she'd come to Athens, he taught her that the plays, too, were philosophy. Was he now saying the same about sculpture?

Alcibiades gave his thunderbolt a shake. "And for those without underthtanding—"

"That's almost everybody," Xanthippus said.

"Like Thophocles—he'll be thtill be Papa Theus."

Aspasia looked to Pericles to send the rude child away, but he said, "You must remember, Alcibiades, that there are many ways of understanding Zeus."

"What does a philothopher think?" Nothing stopped him. "Anaxagoras, do you believe Phidias' Theus, Hera's husband and everybody's lover, who will just happen to be thitting under the roof of our temple with his thtaff and thunderbolt—"

"And eagle," Silky said.

"will be Mind? The finetht of all things?"

Phidias leaned forward for the answer.

"What *is* your opinion, Anaxagoras?" Pericles asked.

"Phidias' Zeus could *also* be Mind, for those with understanding."

Phidias took a deep breath.

"First you said that Mind is unmixed and now you say it's mixed with Zeus." Xanthippus looked bitter.

"You contradicted yourthelf!"

Anaxagoras shook his head. "Mind *is* unmixed and pure but the sculpture of Zeus can represent Mind in a way our senses can grasp. If you want to be a philosopher, young man, don't forget the most important lesson of philosophy."

"Which is?"

"Appearances are a glimpse of the obscure."

Pericles had always taken "appearances" to mean the world of natural phenomena. Could that apply also to works of art? Did they help men glimpse the obscure? Was that part of their beauty?

Alcibiades laughed. "What's *that* thupposed to mean?"

Xanthippus threw up his hands as if he'd already decided it meant nothing.

Maintaining his pose as Zeus, Dion moved only his lips. "In a play, you see beyond the actor, you see beyond me to Prince Haemon . . ."

"You can move now." Phidias, who had been sketching, held up his tablet. "Here's Zeus on his throne—he's partly turned to look at Athena—the twist in his torso comes right through here." He retraced a line noisily, as if carving his correction. "There's our rotation—that twist is always hard to draw. This is just the idea." He brushed away charcoal crumbs.

Anaxagoras snapped open and closed the lid on his tablet. "Shall I read on, or . . . "

"Continue," Pericles said.

"Where was I? 'For it is the finest of all . . .' No. Hmm . . . ah, here, '. . . it rotated from a small area but now it rotates over a wider area and in time it will rotate over a wider—'"

"I can carve that," Phidias said.

A lyre, slanted at an angle, hung on the wall behind Phidias' head. Nearby, two gold cups sat on a shelf, and next to these was a colorful wine pitcher Pericles' father had brought back from a trip to Corinth. The gold wreath that Hipponicus had given Pericles hung on the other side of the shelf. A lamp stand stood on the floor.

Facing the wall, Phidias wiped all that away with a gesture. "Here's Mount Olympus. Zeus is at the center sitting both ways and looking at Athena, who has just sprung from his head. Over here are her spear and shield, and here's her helmet." Phidias outlined the dimensions of the large goddess.

"You're making her too big," Silky said. "She can't have grown up that fast."

"She's a goddess. Now, as she springs away from Zeus' throne here—on the other side Hephaistos, the metalworker among the gods who opened Zeus' head with his axe, runs the other way, looking back at Zeus and Athena—"

"Hephaistos must be amazed at what came out," Silky said.

"All the gods must be amazed," Sophocles said.

"Not yet. But they'll sure be amazed when they find out what happened! Those who are on the spot know and they're spreading the news. See?"

Pericles, always reluctant to disappoint Phidias, searched for what the sculptor might mean. "Is it—we glimpse the obscure through appearances so it's best to see things with one's own eyes?"

Aspasia smiled: what a clever answer.

Phidias' chin shot up. "This isn't a riddle. Here, in the center, the birth of Athena. The gods nearby know right away, Hera, here, and Hephaistos—" Phidias was drawing in the air again. "The gods farther from the center don't know yet, but they're learning from the ones who know." Phidias moved along the wall to make his point.

"For instance, Artemis, goddess of the hunt, running here looks back over her shoulder toward the center while reaching out to the goddess of the earth, Demeter, seated here. Demeter swings around toward Artemis, she raises her arms—see? She's asking, what happened? And Artemis is about to tell her."

"Kore the Maiden sits next to her mother Demeter on the big casket," Ictinus said. "The support bars are in place."

"But I'll turn Kore more away from the center to show that she knows less than her mother."

Alcibiades twirled his pointer finger toward Anaxagoras. "Another rotathion."

Silky was wide-eyed. "As soon as Demeter hears the news, she'll pass the word to Kore because mothers and daughters tell each other everything."

"That's right," Phidias said. Silky blushed.

Pericles rose and looking at the wall tried to piece together what Phidias had described. "I understand—the nearer you are to the center, the more you know, but the news is spreading outward."

Phidias raised a triumphal fist.

Pericles stroked his beard. "The sculpture tells the story of the spread of knowledge. Aspasia, what do you think?"

"If, *alpha*, Zeus is Mind . . . "

"Zeus *is* Mind," Xanthippus said.

"And, *beta*, he gives birth to wise Athena from his head, and the news, *gamma*, spreads from god to god, yes, it's what Anaxagoras teaches." She looked at the wall where she saw the cups and other objects of their lives. "My father would be surprised to learn that marble carvings can be about philosophy."

"Philosophers learn new things," Anaxagoras said.

"Then you agree with Phidias?" Pericles asked.

Anaxagoras tapped his stylus against his tablet. "My words are sufficient."

"But you don't object?" Pericles asked.

"What I object to are interruptions, because my ideas are connected and each one carries the thought farther."

"Like Phidias' gods." Dion raised his hand as he did when he won the prize for acting.

"Pericles, don't you find this plan to carve ideas instead of gods rather—ambitious?" Sophocles set off "ambitious" with a cocked brow, as one might "impossible" or "foolish."

"Not instead of!" Phidias' fists were now at his sides. "I said nothing about instead of. I love the gods. Haven't I been making their images all my life? And the Athenians are paying to see them up there. I'll carve them to express what we know now about Mind and nature—*and* the old way."

Sophocles cleared his throat. "What I say won't be welcome here."

"All ideas are welcome here," Pericles said.

"You can't have it both ways. We *are* talking about instead of, because Zeus and Mind cannot hold dominion in the cosmos together."

"Why not? Thparta has two kings."

"That's clever, child—but the cosmos ruled by Mind would not be the cosmos ruled by Zeus."

"On that one point," Anaxagoras said, "I agree with Sophocles."

"And I have no desire to live in the cosmos of Mind," the playwright said. "It's a cold, hard place."

Anaxagoras frowned. "Mind arranges all things including the rotation of the stars, the sun and moon—"

"And in the corners of the pediment, the chariot of the sun will rise from the sea, here, on the south." Phidias pointed toward the entrance to the andron. "While at the same time, the chariot of the moon will descend below the earth on the other"—he gestured toward the lamp stand—"there's your great cosmic rotation." His long arms traced the arching voyages of sun and moon, like the arms of a balance scale given the rare freedom to swing to their full potential of one hundred and eighty degrees

"The chariots of the sun and moon were journeying across the sky and under the earth long before Anaxagoras came up with his notions," Sophocles said.

Since childhood, Pericles had rarely seen Sophocles angry. He reached to touch his friend's shoulder.

Aspasia caught Pericles' eye and said, "Don't forget Xenophanes—'No man knows, or ever will know, the truth about the gods and about—'"

"Anaxagoras' Mind isn't just another god," Sophocles said. "If he's correct, there are no gods at all."

They were silent.

Xanthippus shrugged. "Then there are no gods at all."

How varied, how complicated, how unpredictable was a city such as Athens—and how interesting, Pericles thought. Sophocles, Anaxagoras, Phidias, Aspasia, Ictinus, Dion, Silky, all lived here. His own sons. Cleinias' children. Others. Damon, Andocides, Hipponicus, and Aristocleia. Crazy Deinomache. Simon the Bootmaker, Xenon the Barber, Socrates the Stonecutter. Old Thucydides was out of the way for a while, but his sons lived here. Men and women. Citizens and foreigners. Craftsmen, storekeepers, farmers. He'd better return to the conversation—but how much more varied, complicated, and unpredictable must the cosmos be?

"We don't need to sharpen the blade so thin that it will break," he said of Xanthippus' remark. "Phidias will make sure the gods are recognized."

"I want to know what you thought of the Samians' temple to Hera," Ictinus said.

"Very fine, but the sanctuary is in a swamp," Pericles said.

"It's an old and holy place." Sophocles explained the location of the sanctuary as if defending the goddess Hera.

"It's huge," Pericles said, "larger than the temple the Ephesians built for Artemis."

"It's intricately carved," Sophocles said.

"How far along are they?" Ictinus asked.

"They don't have a roof," Pericles said.

"I know—but exactly how much have they done?"

"The foundation is complete but there are no steps except on the front and no columns on the sides," Pericles said. "The ones on the front are there to make a good impression and these aren't complete either because you can see they're planning twenty-four columns in front—"

"Twenty-four." Phidias shook his head.

"—of which twenty are erected, but the channels of the shafts are only cut in sixteen. Nevertheless, the columns that stand are of immense height and great beauty."

"Marble bases, I believe," Ictinus said.

"Marble bases and capitals, yes, but the shafts are only limestone. In some places you can pull shells right out of the stone."

"Ours is all marble," Ictinus said.

Sophocles looked bemused. "Pericles, I never noticed you counting the columns and pulling shells out of the stones."

"I thought Ictinus would want to know."

"Next time you go to Samos, I'll come and draw it," Ictinus said.

"We have subdued rebellion in Samos and brought them back into our league as tribute paying allies." Pericles' fist came down firmly on his knee. "There will not be a next time for Samos."

"The democrats control Samos and we control the democrats," Sophocles said. "That's how we left it."

"The way we control the colony of New Sybaris in Italy." By saying "we" for Athens whenever she could, Aspasia felt she was assuring others of her loyalty.

"From east to west," Phidias said, "like my pediment."

"Then Pericles must be in the thenter of the pediment inthtead of Theus."

"Pericles *is* Zeus," Xanthippus said.

"Shh—that's absurd!" Pericles made the sign of the horns.

"Since you became General from all the Athenians, people call you 'Zeus' all the time," his son retorted.

"Only the comic poets," Aspasia said.

The boys never missed a chance to link him to Zeus—and it did him no good, although he saw their point. The best way to get them off that game would be to supplant it with a new idea, a fresh field for their youthful intelligences to rove.

"Since we're talking about the spread of knowledge, I'll tell you what should hold the center—Athens. All the Greeks learn from us. They copy our currency, our law courts, our Assembly—they even copy the way we make pottery for the dinner table! They write plays everywhere in Greece and call them 'Athenian tragedies,' and just look at the education we gave the Samians in democracy."

"How do you know they wanted to learn democrathy?" Alcibiades asked.

"Maybe the Samians didn't want to go to school," Xanthippus said.

"Now—you can see how the gods respond one after the next to the birth of Athena." Phidias showed them his tablet. "Knowledge travels like a wave through the sea. That's us here—but the news is spreading to the ends of the earth." Phidias pointed to a goddess who exclaimed with wonder and joy at Athena's birth.

Alcibiades nudged Xanthippus. "Maybe the Samians don't want to pay the thchoolmathter."

CHAPTER 32

The Big Fellow

A boy must know his father's land if he's to feel that he's his father's son. For some time, Aspasia had been wanting to go to the family estate at Cholargos with Little Pericles, but Pericles put her off because of the press of responsibilities in the city.

"I want our child to see Cholargos."

"He'll find his way there often enough when he's older, as Xanthippus and Paralus do. They love it out there, more than is best for them."

"There's so much for boys to do in the country."

"There's plenty of work but they just ride and hunt. They do nothing for my estate."

"They assume your steward Euangelus will look after everything."

"I'd like them to take more responsibility—and to learn more from Euangelus. Someday it will be their estate."

What would he settle on Little Pericles?

Then, in the coldest time of winter, Pericles decided that they would all go to Cholargos.

"We'll celebrate the country festival of Dionysos. Take your warmest cloak."

"Wonderful! Though I didn't know those rural festivals interested you."

"An election's coming up, it'll be good for the men of my local deme to see me. Glaucon seems to think buying a piece of land out there entitles him to act like it's his deme. Anyhow, there's no foreign news in this weather."

"I don't understand why you're pleased," Silky said when Aspasia told her. "The city's more comfortable this time of year—and here everyone knows you're Pericles' wife—almost—but out there . . . " Silky sped up on the bobbin so the shortened thread drew her closer to Aspasia. "His sister's used to being the only woman of that house," she whispered. "And the servants won't listen to what you say."

"It takes them a day or two, but they listen."

Bundled under sheepskins in the jolting wagons, they arrived at Cholargos when the shadows were long. A new storage tower stood taller than the cypress trees. Aspasia straightened her back in the wagon, letting her sheepskin fall from her shoulders. Pericles, his cheek level with Little Pericles', pointed out the house, midway up the hill opposite. A dog barked.

"There's Argos." Pericles touched his lip to the boy's soft cheek. More barking—other dogs. A bell clanged. "And that's Euangelus letting everyone know we're here."

"He said he'd show me the beehives!"

The wheels were still turning when Xanthippus jumped down and ran behind the house to the fenced hounds. Paralus started toward the stables but a cold gust from around the hill sent him into the house with the others.

In front of the fire, Pericles' sister, Calliope, greeted them without wiping the flour from her hands and returned to kneading dough. Little Pericles stared at the armor hung above the hearth. "That's different from what's at home."

"It's older." Pericles had a houseman lift it down so Little Pericles could see it better. The women, stirring and frying near the fire, stepped aside to make room for the ladder.

Calliope scowled. "Don't burn my sauce."

"I can't move the cheek piece," Little Pericles called from inside the helmet. "Help! I can't breathe!"

"Those pieces didn't move then." Pericles lifted the helmet from his son's head and held it so it caught the firelight. "See the name scratched here—this helmet belonged to Alcmaeon, the first general in my family."

Impulsively, Pericles lifted the helmet onto his own head, recalling the many times he'd done so as a boy. He angled himself so that he could see his reflection in a shield leaning against the wall. He glanced toward Aspasia, who smiled admiringly. "The trouble with this old armor"—he took off the helmet—"is that it's too heavy. It protects a man but makes it harder to fight."

Aspasia, near the fire, felt chilled. Her head hurt and she might have caught a cold. The man carrying her box to the second floor bumped it on each step. Abruptly, she arose. Let the children sleep up there. She never liked being upstairs in the women's quarters. Wasn't there a large room down here that backed up to the hearth?

She stepped onto the porch and found the room she remembered, empty of furniture, except for a loom next to the window. The band of weaving was no broader than the last time she saw it. How neglectful of Calliope. Maybe she'd finish it herself. She ran her fingertips over the threads. The wool was lustrous and well dyed but didn't spring back like Milesian wool. In the slanting light, she could see gold threads twisted into the woven border of lotus flowers. Even if she completed the piece in her own way, it would look old-fashioned— nobody wove those flowers now. Below the border were the tops of heads just begun to be filled in, the beginning of a story. Which one? In the center, a man's head and a woman's head inclined toward one another. The woman wore a crown of flowers and the man wore a helmet. That would be the departure of a hero to war. She didn't like to see all those tiny stitches wasted—perhaps she *would* take it up herself.

The only other object in the room was an amphora, set in a niche, with the picture of Odysseus after his shipwreck when he swam to the island and found Nausicaa playing ball.

There was plenty of room here for their sleeping couches. She put her palm to the wall and felt the heat of the hearth. Shivering, she pressed her face to the wall. The white plaster was smooth and powdery, like a woman's cheek.

Calliope's voice came through the wall. "When a household is preparing food for a festival, it's hard to feed visitors."

Aspasia held her breath to catch Pericles' answer.

"Are we expecting visitors?" He sounded surprised.

She heard no reply from Calliope.

Was he speaking seriously? Or teasing his sister? If she could see his face she'd know. But it made no difference—either way he'd made her smile.

She returned to the hearth. "We'll stay in the room on the corner."

"That's too large to heat," Calliope said.

"The sleeping couches can go against the hearth wall. We'll be comfortable."

"Pericles hates to waste charcoal."

"If Aspasia thinks it's best, we can bring in an extra brazier," Pericles said.

That night, in the large room in the country house, with the kitchen clatter and smells of several kinds of cakes baked at once coming from the other side of the wall, Aspasia felt like a girl. She wasn't surprised when Pericles told her his parents had used the room in winter.

"I was probably born in this room."

She pictured the day of his birth, and his mother, Agariste, fighting to keep him alive.

General Xanthippus (he might even have been wearing that impressive old helmet)—*Look at his ugly head—it's huge. Agariste, you've given birth to a deformed child. He is not meant to live.*

"I told you, Xanthippus, just a few days ago I dreamed I would give birth to a lion. That's why he has a large head. My dream knew. This child will be my lion."

"We already have one son. A normal son, thanks to Zeus. I order you to put him out beyond the river . . . "

Ariphron, a small boy, waiting outside the door. "I want to see my new brother."

Agariste—"In a moment, dear . . . "

They arose at sunrise—the boys had left earlier to go after hare—and went to the burial ground of Pericles' family, where they poured wine for the dead and tied ribbons around their tombs.

"I am Megacles," "I am Cleisthenes," the tombs proclaimed. "I am Agariste."

As they stood before Agariste's tomb, Aspasia felt the weight of Pericles' arm fall on her shoulders.

"I'll never lie here."

Fear of death landed the ox of silence on her tongue.

"I'll be buried in the state cemetery," Pericles said.

The sound of pipes reached them, a thin whistle through the cold air.

"Or perhaps I'll fall out of favor when it's too late to recover, and end up like an old warship, no longer of use, wrecked and abandoned on the beach."

Partly sunk in the sand. She had passed an abandoned ship on her way to Athens.

"That's how General Themistocles' father warned his son that people are ungrateful to their leaders." Pericles' finger followed the grooved letters of his mother's name, gently brushing off dust in the corners with the edge of his cloak, like cleaning the sand crusted eyes of a baby. "And that's exactly how Themistocles finished his life."

She loosened her throat to release her words. "The people are changeable, but you so often show them their best course, they'll never put you aside or forget you."

"You may be right." He seemed serious, then smiled. "My place in the state cemetery is probably assured."

"There's the Big Fellow!" Little Pericles jumped up and down. "Xanthippus said I'd see it today!" Zoe gripped his hand to keep him from running.

Calliope shook her head. "That is the god Phales."

"It's as big as Xanthippus said!"

With the wood penis—or god, however one saw it—bobbing at the front as its bearers struggled to keep it steady on a thin pole, the procession filed through a field of grapevines, cut and tied for winter. The pipes grew shriller. Shouts and laughter mixed with the music.

Little Pericles pulled Zoe's arm. "Let's go closer!"

Those of the deme of Cholargos who weren't escorting the Big Fellow to the old shrine were there waiting for it. Pericles moved among the crowd, greeting his friends. Aspasia watched at a distance from the wagon so as not to annoy those celebrating the festival. She did him no good among the townspeople. She knew—not only assumed but *knew*—that in their whispers, she was his "foreign whore." But Pericles would not make this family visit without her. She loved him for that. Even those of the town who didn't turn their heads gave way as he passed among them, like soldiers when a commander passes through camp, catching any words they can, as if only he possesses knowledge on which their fate rests.

"Let everyone keep holy silence!" said the priest, Pericles' cousin, but the wind carried off his voice.

"They're coming!"

Older children ran across the square toward the procession. Zoe kept a tight hold on Little Pericles. Near the front was Glaucon carrying a small girl on his shoulders.

"Holy silence!" From the steps of the shrine, the priest raised his hands toward the advancing god, pressing his elbows to his sides to anchor his cloak in the wind.

Pericles looked around. Where were his sons? He'd told them to return for the sacrifice. Xanthippus was a man now and should have taken charge.

The Big Fellow dipped forward, caught in a crosswind. The bearers struggled to raise it like sailors at a sail.

"Get it up!" someone shouted. The crowd roared with laughter.

"Looks like it's too heavy for you, Achilles!"

"Grab it from behind!" called out one man, adding, when everyone laughed, "That always works!"

"He got it up! Now, keep it up!"

"Keep it up! Keep it up! Keep it up!"

"Keep holy silence!" The priest funneled his voice through his hands, his cloak blowing open.

The deme should hire a herald for this festival, Pericles thought. But if he suggested that, they'd expect him to pay for it. It was enough to send the ox from his farm. On the other hand—he'd talk with his cousin later.

Xanthippus rode into the square at a gallop, Paralus clutching his back. As the boys slid down and Xanthippus tied the sweating horse, the crowd applauded—Glaucon did so softly, but then his arms were tight against his ribs securing his daughter by her ankles. Pericles felt delighted by the applause, even though his sons were late and Xanthippus had run the horse into a sweat in winter.

"I see your sons made it in time for the distribution of the meat," Glaucon said.

"Good, since I paid for it. The gods have blessed you with a fine child, too."

Glaucon's arms tightened around his daughter's legs but, in making the compliment, Pericles, following custom, avoided looking directly at the child, turning not just his eyes but, for emphasis, his head away. That would be enough, he thought, to remind Glaucon not to tempt fate.

They were born into the same tribe, but this deme belonged to Pericles.

Led in behind the Big Fellow, the ox was tied at the altar, his front feet on the low step, his head hanging, a mist rising from his nostrils to his ears with each panting breath.

"He breathes warm air." Paralus' hand was at the ox's muzzle.

Only a few years earlier Paralus had wept at the sacrifice of an odd, one-horned ram. Thanks to Zeus he was older now and wouldn't humiliate him with tears in front of his deme and Glaucon. Xanthippus manfully helped the priest with the ritual instruments.

"No need to hobble him," Xanthippus said, and the priest nodded agreement.

They didn't do it that way in the city, but—

Having recovered its wind, the ox bucked its head. Xanthippus grabbed the horns from behind and leaned back, tucking his legs under him off the ground long enough for the priest, with a blow of the axe, to cut the thick, exposed throat. Xanthippus leapt aside. The ox's knees buckled. After a pause—always suspenseful despite the sure outcome—the animal fell to the ground, raising dust.

It was well done. Xanthippus, although short, was known here to be quick and strong, and the priest was skilled.

As the animal was skinned and butchered, Pericles listened to the favorable comments made about the fat ox and Xanthippus' deft courage.

The priest clapped him on the shoulder. "Your son was a young Theseus with that ox."

Pericles looked toward the wagon. Aspasia smiled and waved. Too bad she couldn't hear what they were saying, but she'd seen it and would know the sense of pride he was enjoying.

Averting his face from the blaze, the priest threw the thick white fat from under the ribs and the tail onto the flames, sending out sparks and a juicy, searing odor. The burning tail jumped skyward, assuring everyone that the god had accepted the sacrifice. People pushed in for their allotment of cake and held out jugs for Calliope's sauce, some eating on the spot but most bringing it home. Xanthippus distributed the meat, setting aside for the priest one choice section of thigh and for Pericles another, and saving for himself a fine cut off the loin.

Back at the house, they feasted on the meat, the hares Xanthippus had caught, and Calliope's cake with sweet sauce poured from a metal pitcher that took the heat directly from the grill. Pericles had never eaten so fully.

That night, he held Aspasia close. "Did you see how they applauded Xanthippus when he rode up?" Her head lay against his chest. "They like him here. The priest said he was as heroic as Theseus conquering the Bull of Marathon."

Grabbing the horns of a haltered ox from behind was not equal to confronting a wild bull. "Xanthippus is very quick," she said.

"People sometimes say *I* am another Theseus—unifying the Athenians."

"You've done everything for Athens they say Theseus did, and much more."

Raising applause with a stunt at a country festival, with one's famous father looking on, was a far cry from leading Athens. If any of Pericles' boys would be another Theseus—or another Pericles—it was her son.

CHAPTER 33

The Siege of Samos

Coming home from a meeting of the Executive Council, Pericles took a long time petting Argos. Finally he said, "There's bad news, Aspasia."

"I did hear there's some trouble in the Italian colony." She rested her hand on his shoulder. "I've prepared your favorite iced—"

"Samos, Aspasia, Samos." He forced himself to look into her eyes so she wouldn't guess that, along with disappointment and alarm, he was embarrassed.

"Not Samos—again?"

"The Samians are in rebellion. They've abolished the democracy we set up for them, overcome our garrison and blockaded our guard ships in their harbor." He drove each of these points hard at her, as if hearing the word Samos should have been enough to for her to know the whole of it.

She heard Alcibiades' lisp in her mind: *Maybe the Samians don't want to pay the thchoolmathter.* "That's extremely ungrateful after you arranged that wonderful democracy for them. You even gave them favored treatment in our law courts."

"Of course it's not the Samian democrats—it's their oligarchs. They've murdered our democratic friend Antipatrus. Where's that drink you made for me?"

She handed him the cooled mixture. *How would this new Samian rebellion effect Miletus?* Since his enemies claimed that her influence had led him to favor Miletus over Samos, she didn't want to ask. "You had high hopes for that democracy."

"It may be the end of democracy elsewhere on the coast. From their mainland base, the Samian oligarchs may be thrusting south toward Phoenicia—by Hades it's hard to get news in winter."

The mainland coast—that meant Miletus. "How do you know all this?"

"One of our ships made it out of Samos. We'd better look to our ally Byzantium in the north. That whole coast could fall away from our alliance like a cliff into water."

The whole coast? "How did the oligarchs get so far so fast?"

"Support from Persia—I don't know it for a fact but that must be it." He wouldn't tell even her about the hostages until he was certain. He had just undergone a fire and tongs attack in the Council about what his enemies insisted he'd done wrong in Samos the first time he went there to subdue rebellion—no reason to seem more wrong than necessary.

But he hadn't been wrong. Men take setbacks as failures and a leader must remind them otherwise. Had Athens failed when the Persians invaded their city? Burned their temples? Forced the citizens to flee? No. His city had risen from the ashes of invasion like an Egyptian phoenix—correct that: the Egyptians put too much faith in magic. The fact was the Athenians had climbed hand over hand from the bottom of a well. They'd battled their way from invasion to victory. They'd bought and sold their way to prosperity. They'd— what? Talked their way to a full democracy. He had, like Theseus, led his Athenians through the maze of obstacles and digressions, out of the dark toward wealth and freedom. The lesson of persistence was there for all to learn.

Still, it was a lesson he'd learned better than any man alive, except for Olympic champions. Unless, as he truly felt, he had been born with the knowledge. Phidias said that's why he had so large a head and maybe he was right.

By the time the Assembly was set to debate his proposal to recapture Samos, Pericles had overcome the difficulties of gaining news in winter.

At the debate over his plan to send the sixty ships, Glaucon spoke out. "I told Pericles after our victory at Samos we should tear down their walls and seize their ships. 'Let's not just take hostages,' I said, 'let's get rid of these oligarchs once and for all and sell them into slavery' but instead he exiled them—to the mainland." He shook the hair from his forehead. "Now *they* hold our entire garrison hostage and we don't even know where. If Pericles had been severe the first time, we wouldn't have another revolt there now."

Lacedaemonius, never Pericles' friend, echoed Thucydides' old gambit. "Not long ago, Samos had no quarrel with Athens and we should never have quarreled with her. Samos' fight was with Miletus. But Pericles, out of his great *passion* for Miletus . . . "—he gave them time to think of Aspasia—"married Miletus' cause to Athens. And then, after giving his beloved Miletus a gift, control over the city of Priene—"

The Assembly knew this was untrue and booed.

"Well, then, having broken Samos' hold over Priene, Pericles decided to give the Samians something he thinks is best for men—democracy.

"But the Samians don't love democracy and they've thrown it out. Should we therefore attack Samos? Though we—and Pericles—prefer this form of government, should we push it on the rest of the world? No. To force democracy on others in the name of freedom is tyranny. The Samians have chosen their government. It's not our business to change it. Our only business is to bring back our men they hold hostage and rescue our ships—at great cost to our treasury."

Pericles rose.

"The previous speakers have violated the Assembly's rules because they've talked about the past and ignored the agenda item, our course of action regarding the rebellion in Samos. They offer no plan in the face of an attack by what is, in fact, our relentless enemy—Persia.

"Who paid bribes to release the Samian hostages so that the oligarchs could attack without fear for their relatives? Persia. Who is paying the oligarchs' mercenary army of seven hundred men? Persia. And where—if any doubt remains—are the captured Athenians of our garrison now imprisoned?"

He let them say it. And say it they did. Loud. PERSIA!

"And who will bear the cost of returning our garrison?" Hearing confused responses, he answered his own question: "The Samians!"

"Yes, Lacedaemonius, we prefer democracy, but that's not why we sailed to Samos and deposed the oligarchs. We did it because in initiating hostilities against our unarmed ally, Miletus, and then in refusing our arbitration, the Samian oligarchs defied us and acted against our alliance.

"As for those severe means you spoke of, Glaucon, selling Greeks into slavery is beyond my way of thinking and in any case not in our best interests. Samos was an easy takeover and we returned to Athens with no Athenian lives lost, despite Glaucon's unnecessary maneuver from which, I'm sure, he has learned but that at the time risked the loss of lives and ships. In dealing with Samos, we acted in our best interest, because to destroy the richest city of our league and a powerful war ally would weaken us. Therefore we sought to obtain our means by other ends. This Samian rebellion is cause for concern but not for surprise and whatever the costs may be, the Samians will pay them into our treasury. Challenges like these will arise if we are to maintain our imperial alliance—"

"Call it what it is—*our empire*," Lacedaemonius shouted.

"—and we are well prepared. We have the comfort of knowing that sixty ships is only a part of our navy while they'll have to muster their entire force against us and risk total destruction. I ask for fast action."

The Assembly voted to send Pericles to Samos with sixty ships under his command. The generals' terms for the year had not yet expired and so, among his commanders, he took two from the first Samos campaign, Sophocles and Glaucon. He left his trustworthy friend Andocides with chief command in Athens—the best man for dealing with any slackened commitment to the war. With the Persians feeding this rebellion, Samos might take a while.

"I know you're taking Sophocles because the allies love his plays," Aspasia said later. "But Glaucon?" She covered her anger with a show of amazement. "How can you reward him for speaking against you?"

"I'm waging a war with peacetime generals. That will change when the next board of generals takes over but until then, Glaucon is the best naval commander I have available, outside of myself."

"Are sixty warships sufficient?"

"I don't need you to doubt my military judgment, Aspasia." He took a breath, knowing she meant well. "Sixty ships are sufficient because the Spartans honor our Peace Treaty and have refused the Samian requests for aid, even though Corinth is trying to pull them in against us. Right there you see my Peace Treaty with Sparta protecting us."

She touched his chin. "I'm concerned for your safety."

"I'll be fine."

That's what men going to war always say, Aspasia thought. But the two generals who'd led the Athenian military force to suppress a rebellion in Boeotia weren't fine—they were killed, and one of them was Pericles' kinsman, Cleinias. That's when grief turned Cleinias' wife into *Crazy* Deinomache, and Pericles and his brother Ariphron became guardians of Cleinias' two sons, lisping Alcibiades and his feeble-minded brother. But if Pericles died in this war with Samos, there would be no wealthy kinsmen to take on the upbringing of *her* son.

She wanted to say, "Your son needs his father more than other sons," but he wasn't going to change his course for that or any other reason. Her hand still to his chin, she locked her gaze with his, committing to memory the almond shape of his eyes and the keen character of the intelligence with which he looked at her. So she said, "I will count the days until you return."

Every woman says that when her lover goes to war (not that he'd ever heard those words from his former wife). But the ordinariness of the words from this original woman made him feel part of an eternal pattern, like the image of the departure to war of a hero Aspasia was stitching into her tapestry. He put his hand to his heart to express his gratitude and love.

The next morning, after Pericles had joined the other commanders and Little Pericles was weeping because his father had gone to war, Aspasia showed him a polished black bowl and told him that each day they would put a stone in it until Pericles returned.

She thought it would be good practice in counting before he started school since her boy needed to be better at numbers, and at everything else, than the other boys. Athens paid for the upbringing of dead Cleinias' sons and the other boys whose fathers died in battle—at eighteen, they even gave them a full set of armor! But Athens would pay nothing for the upbringing of her son if *his* father died in battle because his mother came from somewhere else and Little Pericles was not a citizen.

* * *

Pericles set out with sixty ships to Samos, with forty more soon to follow. While his force encamped on a remote island in the middle of the Aegean, awaiting the reinforcements, he sent four ships under General Sophocles, beloved throughout the Greek world for his plays, to Lesbos and Chios to requisition additional reinforcements from those loyal allies. Then, when word came of a rebellion in Phoenicia, Pericles sent General Glaucon out with twelve ships to proceed south and prevent the passage of any Phoenician ships he encountered or, if they were too numerous, to send him word. But, seeing a way to take advantage of the reduced numbers of his fleet, Pericles directed Glaucon to first head to the mainland and row within sight of the main body of the Samian fleet who were harassing Miletus. When they counted Glaucon's ships, the Samians would understand that Pericles' fleet was short by considerable number. They would be in a hurry to wipe out the Athenian fleet before reinforcements arrived.

Thus, Pericles lured seventy Samian ships, fifty warships and twenty transports, to engage with the forty-four Athenian ships off the island of Tragia. The Athenians intercepted the Samians before they reached where they expected the Athenians and, catching the Samians by surprise, the Athenians routed them, sinking many Samainas, as Samians called their ships, with minor damage to their own.

Reinforced by forty additional ships from Athens, plus twenty-five from Chios and Lesbos, the combined fleet sailed to Samos, now empty of its fleet. The Athenians did not know the whereabouts of those Samian ships that had survived and fled after the battle off

Tragia but did not try to track them down: they were fully engaged with blockading Samos and building a siege wall around the city.

A fast ship from Athens brought the generals at Samos a pouch of correspondence including reports and instructions from the Chief Archon and the Executive Council. That night in his tent, Pericles placed on his table a letter addressed to him alone. None from his oldest son—well, Xanthippus was probably too busy, on duty with his age-mates guarding the perimeter of Attica.

The letter from Aspasia was tied with a yellow ribbon. He brought it to his face and, overcome by the scent, brushed it across his cheek, his eyes, and his nose where, after hesitating, he inhaled it fully and touched it to his lips. He observed the wax seal with the tiny image of Odysseus, impressed straight from the engraved pendant he'd given her that always lay between her breasts. In their most tender moments, she called him "my Odysseus."

He broke the seal with the image of Odysseus longing for home.

> **Aspasia to Pericles, greetings.** *As the ship that took you from me disappeared into the fog, I asked myself what shall I do until my Odysseus returns? Here is my answer. I started a class for women because these Athenian women can't read their way through more than a laundry list, and now we are reading Sophocles' play about Antigone . . .*

Pericles tapped a writing brush against his lips. Aspasia teaching women . . . the Athenians would not approve . . . it would reflect badly on her . . . and on him . . .

> *Just think of it—Sappho only taught girls, but I teach married women!*

And yet, how like Aspasia who always found something large to do when he was away. He smiled remembering that while he was capturing Euboea, she bought a house! This class of hers was almost predictable.

I visited Glaucon's wife because she's only nineteen and I thought she'd be sick with longing for her husband. She was but after that there was nothing to talk about. Athenian women could be Scythians for all they know of poetry or philosophy. One thing led to another, when Anticles' wife came, she brought Sophocles' wife with her. I didn't invite Silky because she wouldn't fit in with the wives of important men. None of the women will take a man's part in the play so I must do all the men. I told them that men take women's parts in the theater so we can play men in our class but they don't see my logic.

Be proud of Little Pericles. He counts from one to a hundred and has learned the letters from alpha to omega so, as you wished, I'm rewarding him with a little wagon with bronze wheels.

Now, I have a riddle for you, Pericles: what man is on everyone's lips but not on mine? (Hint: his mother and father gave him a name that foretold his fame.)

That last was not correct. His mother had given him the name, not his father who, seeing the infant's bulbous head, wanted him dead. In time, though, Xanthippus had come to love his intelligent son. And, by the gods, Pericles had become as famous and illustrious as his name predicted, known beyond Athens, even beyond Greece. Ask the king of Persia, "Who is Pericles?" and you'd get the right answer. Because the child was defective, his mother gave him that name as extra protection. With a start of recognition, Pericles realized that Aspasia had held out for the name *Pericles* for their son in the same way—he, too, needed extra protection. He must do something wonderful for Aspasia, he thought, and something for the boy. There was much merit in women.

Bringing Aspasia's letter to his lips, Pericles kissed it once for his mother and again for Aspasia and drew out a papyrus to write to her. His letter was interrupted by an urgent message from General Glaucon, brought to the Athenians by a Milesian merchant. The

Phoenicians were in rebellion from the Athenian alliance and were about to launch a major military effort to support the Samian cause. They had readied their warships and were mustering transport vessels to carry Egyptian archers and horses to aid Samos' fight against Athens.

It was not the worst military message Pericles had ever received but it was among them. Samos and Phoenicia joining forces—horse-carrying transport vessels. Pericles cracked his knuckles. Only one course of action was possible. He must prevent the Phoenicians from sailing to Samos, though it would take a large force away from the effort at Samos to do it. He would have to draw ships from the Athenian blockade and thin the Athenian fighting force but he had no choice. Thanks to Zeus, Athenian reinforcements were arriving soon at Samos. After verifying the merchant's trustworthiness in all ways, Pericles sailed out from the Bay of Samos south to Phoenicia with sixty ships.

As they neared the Phoenician port of Sidon, Pericles smelled the exotic scents, recalled from his youth. Gulls screeched over scraps of jellylike fish Greek gulls didn't know. But as he cruised closer in, he saw only fishermen casting their nets from small boats a hundred cubits from the sandy beach. There was not a Phoenician warship in sight.

Realizing he'd been tricked into weakening the Athenian force at Samos, he spun back north, fearful that the Samians may have broken through the Athenian blockade. On the run back to Samos, the Athenians overcame and captured a Samian merchant vessel. The captain, his neck throttled with an oar, squeezed out that once Pericles and his force had sailed off, the Samian democrats and aristocrats had rallied to their ships, broken through the Athenian blockade and now held the Athenian ships trapped in the harbor. Pericles did not know if the captain was lying but he did know that he had twice misjudged Samos. The Athenians would accuse him of taking bribes to withdraw sixty ships from the Athenian blockade for this fruitless trip south. Samian bribes. Persian bribes.

That night, which was not one for sleeping, Pericles anchored his ships off the cape in full view of the Samian fleet that held the Athenian ships locked in the harbor. His presence would give heart to the trapped Athenians and he hoped that it would frighten the Samians in their livers. In the light of a thin moon, Pericles watched the Samian fleet abandon the blockade and turn about, taking their time, knowing the Athenians wouldn't chase them at night. In saving their ships, the Samians were probably planning another attack, but with reinforcements on the way, the Athenians would be stronger than ever. As the first sun turned the dark ships gold, Pericles rowed across the strait and reunited his fleet.

Glaucon, of course, had never sent the message that lured Pericles on the wasteful and dangerous run to Phoenicia. Returning to Samos and learning that his name had been used by the Samian rebels in their deceptive maneuver, Glaucon proposed an immediate, massive charge of the citadel to punish the Samians. Pericles overruled him. If the main body of Athenian forces left the sea for the land, the Samians with their ships—wherever they lurked—would grab the chance to capture the unprotected Athenian ships. Nor, with a hostile populace at their backs, could the Athenians risk sailing far from the harbor to chase enemy ships. They must maintain the blockade, wait for reinforcements and squeeze the Samians on supplies.

Athenian scouts reported that goods were being carted overland to the walled citadel so Pericles sent out teams to discourage smugglers. Since Glaucon was eager for military action, Pericles permitted him to launch an attack on Samian stoneworkers fortifying the city wall across a valley south of the theater, but the armed workers, instead of retreating within the walls, stood and fought, killing four Athenians.

At one point, the Samian ships appeared as if courting battle. The Athenians quickly rowed out to open water where their superior numbers gave them an edge, but fearful of straying far from the city, they didn't chase the Samainas and most fled safely away. Pericles was pleased with the results of the skirmish: the Samians had five fewer ships, and the Athenians had the harbor in which to make some needed repairs.

With the threat from enemy ships reduced and the Samians' industry about their walls and citadel becoming ever more obvious, Pericles intensified the forays inland to harass their supply routes. On a hot day in early August, forty new ships arrived from Athens. With them came the newly elected and experienced generals, his good friends Hagnon and Anticles, along with Phormio, who was developing a reputation as an excellent naval commander. Pericles' heart skipped a happy beat at the sight of Squirrel from the Parthenon work crew because, watching the skinny young man swing down a ship's ladder, he knew that the ridge beam of the Parthenon must be in place—otherwise, war or not, Phidias would have kept his highest of the high climbers on the Acropolis.

Sophocles and Callistratus were replaced by generals who'd been elected for war. It was time for Glaucon to go home, too—the first Samos campaign had given him a reputation for impulsiveness, and the harsh attack of so young a man against Pericles in the Assembly confirmed him as a hothead and lost him the election. The Athenians had gauged rightly—Glaucon hadn't yet found the narrow strait of good judgment between Scylla's deadly rock and the whirlpool of Charybdis. Still, Pericles was not pleased to see him leave because in Samos, Pericles could keep an eye on him but as soon as he got back to Athens, Glaucon would start running for next year's election: he'd be talking up that phantom diversion that had sent Pericles to Phoenicia and spreading his poison, reminding everyone that, under Pericles, the Athenians had been forced *to return* to Samos to suppress rebellion—two tries and it wasn't over yet.

The only antidote was *win the war*.

Samos City was encircled by the thickest and tallest walls in Greece and, it was said, a hidden tunnel ran from outside the walls with a pipe that carried water into the city from a source in the hills to the north or west. Standing before the walls, briefing his men on the strengths and difficulties of their position, Pericles felt like King Agamemnon, the leader of the Greeks at Troy. He would outdo Agamemnon, though, because he wouldn't waste ten years at war. He'd already been away from Athens for too long. His oldest son, he learned from Damon and Aspasia, had taken a first in a horse race at the Panathenaic Festival that summer, and he hadn't been there to see it. Not a word about his middle son—Paralus was probably doing something important like feeding his rabbit. Little Pericles was playing songs on the small lyre. Phidias wrote that they needed Pericles in Athens because the priests of Artemis were opposing a new entryway to the Acropolis that would crowd their precinct. The ridge beam was now in place and Ictinus was roofing the Parthenon—Pericles longed to set his eyes on that. Nor did he want to—he *would not*—spend ten years away from Aspasia, like an Agamemnon at Troy. He had fewer years ahead of him than he had behind him which meant too many years without her.

He thought of bribery to rid himself and Athens of this Samos war. When the Spartan army had nearly invaded Athens a few years ago, he had rushed back from a northern campaign and induced the Spartan king to retreat by a bribe. What a wonderfully quick and bloodless way to end a war! But the circumstances in Samos and the personalities he had to deal with were stubbornly different. For the young Spartan king, the silver Pericles thrust at him was a way out of the imposed equality of the Spartan way of life—and those dreary communal messes. In contrast, the philosopher Melissus who led Samos was a rich and independent aristocrat of a prosperous island fortress. No one told him where to eat, how much money to spend, or when to sleep with his wife. Being rich didn't make a man immune to corruption but it raised his price. Moreover, Melissus was a proven patriot while the Spartan king had been an untried youth. Then, too, the Spartans had been on Athenian territory, far from home while Melissus had at his back the men of Samos defending their territory, their goods, and their families. Any bribe sizable enough to tempt Melissus would far exceed the "necessary expenditures," as Pericles had cautiously listed the money on his account sheet, that had satisfied the Spartan king. And bribery brought its own dangers because one's enemies could twist the meaning of any secret exchange of money. In a word, bribery was out. So Pericles rode the circuit of Samos with his generals to assess the possibilities of locking the city into a siege.

The walls of Samos bristled with armaments as if immense thistles had taken hold on their heights. The Samian ships hadn't dared to show again but they could hold out as long as the Persians continued to pay them. The Athenians suspected, however, that some of the crews had hidden their ships and filtered back to defend their city. Since Athenian sailors were ardent democrats and his loyal supporters, Pericles was disappointed that not one Samian sailor had come over to their side, but the unify-a-city potion was at work—sprinkle Persian gold over men's natural patriotism and stir well.

The Athenian allies Lesbos and Chios sent fifteen ships. Sophocles, that canny diplomat, having seen to their outfitting and despatch, returned to Athens.

Nothing entered Samos through the Athenian blockade of the Great Harbor but it was clear that supplies were flowing from the highlands like water after heavy rain, finding a way to the city, nudging stones. Small boats dropped cargo at night in the sliver-like coves along the precipitous north coast. The Athenian navy could not monitor the entire perimeter of the island without running the double risk of being picked off in isolated patrols and thinning the blockade. With their huge force, however, the Athenians could effectively man a wall. Thus, Pericles met with his generals to discuss strengthening and extending their siege wall to sever the population from the countryside and supplies.

"We must do it," General Hagnon said. "We must cut them off from their ships—"

"Wherever they're hiding," General Phormio said.

Hagnon nodded. "And their crews and any Persian gold that comes with them."

General Anticles shook his head. "Burn the fields and starve them out."

"They have enough grain for two winters in that fortress," Phormio said.

"We don't know that," Pericles said.

"They're bringing it in by the medimnos."

"That's a guess," Pericles said. "But we know that when we occupied the city last time, there was no stockpile and no warehouse."

"They may have prepared themselves since then by accumulating grain."

"And they have water from their secret tunnel," Hagnon said.

"Then we must find this tunnel and destroy it," Anticles said.

"It's like looking for a gem in the sea," Pericles said. "We must keep searching for it and build a siege wall at the same time."

"The seas will be closed first and we'll have to spend winter here," Anticles said.

Pericles regarded this young man whom he had mentored and aided in his climb to the rank of General. He'd certainly become independent minded. "That's why we mustn't burn the fields."

Anticles' eyes scanned the city walls. "Maybe we'll find the tunnel when we dig trenches for the siege wall."

"They'll run out of grain before they run out of water," Hagnon said.

Phormio pressed one big fist against a thumb-and-finger circle. "They can't bring water for an entire city through their tunnel."

"They have enough of both unless we find otherwise," Pericles said.

Rain hadn't fallen in Samos since spring. It passed among the Athenians that if a Samian tried to escape on a moonless night, he'd be found by the "Samos smell" of sweat, dried fish, and human dung overlaid with sweet Persian perfumes—they still had plenty of those.

The Athenians surmised that even if there was a hidden water supply, it wouldn't be abundant for dousing fires and so they erected a scaffold with the idea of slinging buckets of flaming pitch over the walls. They'd attempted this maneuver in sea battles, but there it was extremely dangerous because the positions of the vessels changed quickly and sudden shifts of wind could throw flaming pitch at their own ships. Squirrel, who'd proposed the plan, argued that it was easier to wrestle with unexpected contingencies on land, so he was placed in charge of the structure which he set about building near the main gate on the west side: westerly winds could help carry the flames into the city.

Though it would have saved time, the Athenians didn't drag in fallen logs but cut fresh, moist wood from the lowlands near Hera's temple and planed off the bark. Athenian spirits rose with the network of beams they constructed five cubits from the stone walls. They sang as they worked, and again at night as they drank the wine of the countryside and feasted on sheep.

Hygiaenon, one of the most beautiful young men among the Athenians at Samos and ambitious for the pentathlon, borrowed a cithara from the bard, and composed a song at a drinking party:

> I will answer your question frankly. My lover is Athens,
> Tall, white-armed, untamed by the foreigner's spear,
> She asked me to plant her barley before the winter.

He paused, threw back his head, and drained his cup before singing the last line:

> Dionysos of Freedom will meet me in Piraeus.

Castor, who longed to share Hygiaenon's blanket, immediately arose, grabbed a lyre, and sang out,

> We celebrate a state, yet call a whore
> A wench who loves all men, both rich and poor.
> More to the point, she's far and I am here,
> Choose Castor and . . .

Castor hesitated, looking to finish as well as he'd begun.

> "He will be your dear," someone sang.
> "You'll have a lover near."

"Never mind," one man said, "we know what will happen if he chooses Castor!" Everyone laughed. But it was Hygiaenon's song the men picked up. Pericles heard it often as he passed among them, reviewing their work on the siege wall. "Dionysos of Freedom will meet me in Piraeus."

Two swordsmen and two archers flanked each carpenter, three thousand hoplites stood in battle array, and a thousand archers, half of them mounted, trained their arrows upward until the scaffold reached within three courses of the top of the wall.

Despite the ample reward Pericles offered, there were no chinks in the wall of Samian unity and he could not recruit spies. Without knowing the number of fighting men within the walls, nor the location of the Samian ships that had fled, nor who might have joined them, he could not be sure what form the defense might take nor from what direction it might come. And what about Phoenicia which had been quiet earlier? What was the situation there now? Like Pylades protecting his friend Orestes from all hazards, Pericles had to be watchful in every direction. Ignorance was a kind of siege.

It seemed unbelievable that the morning on which the scaffold was nearly complete, the Samian side of the wall remained quiet. Were they going to allow the Athenians to reach the top unchallenged? Surely they'd seize the advantage of superior height. It was a relief when, midway to noon, about twenty-five Samians appeared suddenly on their wall. The Athenian archers immediately attacked, sending the Samians ducking out of sight.

This small success, after so much waiting, heightened the Athenians' vigor so that the last cubits of the scaffold rose quickly, like a plant watered by gods. At the top, the Athenians could not see across the wall into the city because the Samians had hoisted a long curtain of bulls' hides stretched on poles opposite the Athenian scaffold. The sail-like structure wobbled as the autumn gusts whistled across the top of the wall—the heavy buckets of pitch would topple it easily. Whatever the Samians were planning for their defense, falling hides would trap any of their men near in a flaming web of their own making.

The Athenians strung a pulley of their heaviest rope, soaked in seawater to resist fire from a spark. As the first bucket of molten pitch was hauled up in its leather sling, its chain coiled around it like a resting snake, the men cheered. The bucket swung slightly as it traveled upward.

Squirrel, having seen to the launching of the first bucket, rushed over to Pericles. "As easy as setting the roof beam on the Parthenon."

"Easy or difficult doesn't matter—only that it works." Fingers curved against his lips, Pericles' eyes followed the path of the bucket. Why did lifted things swing side to side instead of following a straight path? He would ask Anaxagoras, or take it up with that philosopher Democritus—a young man with new ideas.

If Squirrel's plan with the pitch buckets failed, the Athenians would be forced to complete their wall around Samos and starve the Samians out—at great expense. If it succeeded, they could leave before the sea closed for the winter. Pericles allowed himself a moment to think of home. He saw himself, as in a painting on a wine cup, reclining after dinner, Aspasia pouring his wine the way Athena pours for Heracles at the end of his labors. Little Pericles shows him something—a wagon. Pericles sent his thoughts back to the wall.

Four buckets rested on sledges at the top of the scaffold, their long chains fastened to beams overhead. Squirrel's plan—igniting the buckets, gripping the attached leather straps and swinging the buckets back, running forward with them, guiding them on their chains across the top of the scaffold, and shoving them over the wall required many men. Veterans had shaken their heads but younger men had vied for the honor of sending the buckets over the wall. Success would bring glory to Athens and send everyone home with extra pay. Now, led by Squirrel, the volunteers—all the more vigorously because Pericles' eyes were on them—clambered up the scaffold, shouting their war cry as if crossing a field into battle.

The acrid smell and a few sparks from the fired pitch reached earth. Smoke blacker than any sacrifice wound upward from the top of the wall. The team of men laid hold of the leather straps and pulled together, leaning in with their bodies, setting the first heavy bucket into motion backward. Moving deftly, given the weight of their burden, they drew the smoking pot across the open woodwork. It was risky, but the men were brave and able. It was exhilarating to witness. Squirrel laid the torch to the second bucket.

Suddenly Pericles heard a roar and a crack—he looked to the sky for a sudden storm. The top of the scaffold tilted downward toward the stone wall. By the gods, was Apollo fighting for Samos as he had for Troy? But Pericles felt no tremors in the earth. The roar grew loud as a tidal wave. Everyone on the ground ran as the structure shook and beams facing the stone wall cracked and split, sending heavy, ragged planks shooting outward. The flaming buckets careened down on the Athenians and men fell through the crumbling wooden network. The scaffold stumbled front first, a wooden horse with broken legs.

"Zeus, let it not catch fire, and I'll complete your temple in Athens," Pericles prayed. In giving great honor to Athena, had he neglected her father?

He heard the cries of men fallen from a height or trapped between the planks. How many were silenced?

Hoplites ran up from shore. Athenians and their allies crowded around the disaster. Pericles grabbed the reins of two mounted bowmen and sent them with word to Anticles and Phormio to maintain the Athenian deployment around the wall, in the ports and beaches and in the surrounding waters to keep Samians from escaping in the confusion.

As he ran to attend the dead and wounded, he saw the earth fall in beneath one of the tall legs on which the scaffold still rested, further tilting the structure. Had they built their scaffold over an underground stream? Perhaps they'd found the hidden water supply!

Quickly, as the dust settled, the Athenians saw that the earth had fallen in elsewhere under the structure. Digging to the cave-ins, they discovered collapsed tunnels leading to the main supports. While they'd been erecting the scaffold, the Samians, with astonishing speed, had dug underneath it. They'd waited for the right moment— clearly hoping to set the whole thing burning—then yanked the ropes attached to the wooden supports by which they'd kept the earth and stones at bay as they dug, causing the structure above to fall. Rightly the Samians were famous as engineers.

Some Athenians were climbing down from the scaffold, others clung to its broken beams, and others lay on the ground below. It took a while to reach all the wounded and place the bodies of the dead side by side in the field. Hygiaenon was dead from burns. Castor pleaded to lead into the walled city of Samos a squad of those who'd lost brothers or lovers, insisting they could dig their way through the soft earth and broken stone of the collapsed tunnels and capture the city by surprise. Others were clamoring to go with him, but Pericles refused to allow it, for if they didn't die underground, they'd be picked off as soon as they saw light on the other side of the wall.

Squirrel had leaped outward from the top of the scaffold, "feeling the wind on my palms," he said later. The surgeon bound his broken legs with willow splints. Pericles found him sitting on the ground, his short legs extended, his cloak covering his face, grieving over the failure of his plan like Castor for Hygiaenon. It would be his last climb.

Thus, in the Fall, while Demeter's Mysteries were celebrated in Athens, the Athenians completed encircling Samos by linking their siege wall to their chained line of ships across the harbor. Then, resigning themselves to a winter siege, they set about plowing and planting so they wouldn't go hungry if the grain ships were delayed in the spring. Pericles wrote to Andocides in Athens instructing him to prohibit the comic poets from writing about the war. Since Athenian poets felt free to write whatever they wished in their plays, Pericles knew that some would be quick to call his ruling undemocratic, but with Athenians wounded and dying here, there was nothing about Samos to laugh at.

It took ten years for the Greeks to capture Troy and the Trojans were mere barbarians. In the end, necessity conquers. It isn't absolutely necessary to run in a procession wearing a wreath, but men must eat wholesome food, drink clean water, find shelter, and rid themselves of filth. One can't feed a city by farming within the walls—although, when the Athenians finally entered the town, they found cabbage and onion growing in the sacred precincts.

The Samians held out during the winter. They probably could have held out another summer if siege sickness didn't strike them and, for all one could know, another winter as well. That water pipe that eluded the Athenians gave the Samians strength. But no matter how long the Samians might resist, the Athenians, with plenty of money and the world to draw on for supplies, could outlast them.

Every day brought a bloody encounter. The Athenians moved always in groups and maintained constant watch, but they'd been attacked chopping down trees, gathering fuel, hoeing fields, and seeking food, drink, and women in the countryside. Men in outposts had been ambushed at their campfires and killed in their sleeping rolls. The Athenians had been surprised at first to learn that being democrats was no defense against attack. They also learned that many Samians were willing to face certain death for the chance to kill an Athenian.

Pericles found no Antipatrus this time, no democrat among the Samians who would help the Athenians, either for money or the promise of power, whether by opening the gates of the city or by exerting his influence to welcome them.

The longer he had so many men and ships at Samos, the more likely it was that other cities of the Athenian alliance would rebel. The allies were required to bring their tribute to Athens in the spring, at the time of the Festival of Dionysos. To ward off potential rebellion, the Athenians should be out of Samos before then.

The idea of bribing Melissus was even less attractive than it had been in the summer because, since then, the siege had cost so much money. Samos had been costly enough back when Squirrel had proposed the scaffold, but those were summer expenses, and the Athenian navy mobilized every summer, war or not, to maintain its skills. In forcing the Athenians to build more ships, necessity had acted on the side of good fortune because, after more than five years of the Peace Treaty, they were needed. But a winter siege was another matter. It costs much more to keep a man fed, dry and warm in winter. Cold and rain are thieves, robbing men of their health and good spirits; they sneak in through every chink of make-do temporary quarters. In winter, the besiegers are as trapped as the besieged. The only antidote to the poison of a winter siege is money—for food, drink, games, prizes. Cold and rain are blackmailers.

Nor could Athens raise the tribute assessments. Sophocles had argued convincingly that an increase would cause revolt among the allies—though Pericles disagreed with those who wanted to reduce it. A strong Athens was the best defense for all the Greeks. But there was no question that Athens besieging another Greek city brought the word "tyranny" to the lips of oligarchs and democrats alike. Though it might be reasonable, it was impractical to require that the allies pay more for the order and safety Athens brought to the Aegean and the Greek world. The impasse, and the large daily expenditures, made him angry. No, he would not pay Melissus nor any Samian to end this war. Samos had cost too much.

And in that thought, he found his solution.

With the worst of the winter storms past, and reports of starvation in Samos, he had Phormio conduct daily naval maneuvers in view of the city. Tied securely to his litter, Squirrel directed the raising of four iron battering rams. Pericles sent a herald to the Samian Council to invite Melissus and three men of his choice to meet with him and the other generals to discuss surrender. The herald returned with the word that the leaders of Samos refused any accommodation with the tyrants.

Good: he preferred to meet the enemy in private.

He invited Melissus to his quarters on the next moonless night with pledges of safe passage. Such talks are secret only as in a play, where actors assigned major roles can speak to one another while everyone else on the stage seems deaf. Nevertheless, "secret" talks have the advantage that one negotiates with one party at a time— the other side. One doesn't have to persuade one's own side—that task, sometimes the more difficult and rancorous, comes after. Was that Melissus' reason for preferring secrecy? Secrecy had provided the young king of Sparta with the freedom to be corrupted. That was another advantage.

Melissus came to the villa Pericles had sequestered on a rise east of the city from where he could watch the harbor and straits between Samos and Miletus, though on that damp, moonless night he couldn't see where land met water. While he knew that his own word was trusted throughout Greece—those who hated him granted that he was honest—he admired Melissus' courage in coming to the armed camp of the besieging enemy. The Samians weren't thirsty, but they were hungry. Unlike Priam at Troy, Melissus would have to take back to his people something more than the dead body of his son. His own sons coming to mind, Pericles shook his head to cast away the thought.

"Greetings, Melissus, son of a son of the goddess."

"Greetings, Pericles, spoken of everywhere."

It was a way to think of the meaning of his name, but by dropping his voice at the end, Melissus implied that Pericles' fame didn't spread outward, like ripples from a stone, but downward, as into a sump. It was a tactic of those who believed they had gods in their lineage. Pericles smiled as if complimented.

"We know who we are but must discover what we want." He extended a bowl of figs stewed in honey toward his guest.

"I want what all Greeks want—freedom." Melissus ignored the figs but stretched his fingers over the glowing coals in the brazier. Samos must be low on charcoal.

"By speaking as if I need instruction in what Greeks desire, you insult me."

"I'm not insulting you. I'm being clear."

Pericles chewed a fig. "But you weren't clear because what's meant by freedom differs from man to man. I would think that as a philosopher, you'd have noticed that." Pericles turned away as if bored by imprecision.

"Samos is surrounded by Athenians on land and sea. Only an Athenian would call that freedom."

"That is a matter of war. If it's the freedom of your city that concerns you, let's discuss that."

"We would have won our war with Miletus if you'd stayed out of it. Your Assembly's decision interfered with our protecting our interests. That's not freedom."

It was freedom for Athens but there was no point in inflaming Melissus' anger by saying so. "It's more freedom than Samos would enjoy if Persia enslaved Greece."

"Athens, not Persia, holds our city under siege and blockade."

"The Samians brought the siege and blockade on themselves by threatening the security of our alliance."

"Our argument was with Miletus, not Athens."

"Miletus is in our alliance, and by bringing war against her, you forced our hand. Melissus, surely you can understand that our allies must benefit from our alliance. Miletus prefers contributing money rather than ships and men to our common cause. Since we accept her tribute, we have to defend her when she's attacked."

"Benefit." Melissus nodded his head toward his imprisoned city. "Samos can't be said to benefit from Athens."

"Not now because you broke with us. But when you were a friendly member of our alliance, you roamed with no constraints from us across seas that we'd cleared of pirates, you set up your markets where you would, enjoyed access to our ports, and above all, were secure in the knowledge that the Persians wouldn't encroach on our seas nor so much as threaten you East Greeks. All this we do for Greece. Considering what we provide, we ask very little."

"You ask a great deal—including that we become democrats."

"We consider that the best government for men."

353

"We don't and requiring the cities to follow your form of government is tyranny."

"We do not require the cities to follow our ways. For many years, Samos was an oligarchy and one of our most favored allies, and one of the few still contributing ships and men."

"You poured democracy on our heads."

"Only after you violated our interests, and those of our alliance, by attacking Miletus."

"So you believe that democracy is a punishment—not, as you said, the best government for men."

"Since Athens is a democracy, we believe that democrats in the cities will be loyal to us." It was usually so. Samos was exceptional, being the wealthiest.

"Because they can't maintain power without you."

"A good reason."

The Samian was silent a moment. "You arrange everything among the cities to serve the interests of your city. That's tyranny."

"Do you love your city any less, Melissus?"

"I've proved my love for Samos by fighting for her."

"Now you must prove your love by bringing the fighting to an end."

"I will die rather than surrender. The Samians are of one mind."

"Ah, yes, the fight to the death—the one choice that carries certain success."

"And glory in the memories of men."

"But if you love your city as you say, and I believe you do, then you must end the war in the way that best serves her interests and not your glory."

"That *I* think best serves her interests? Or that *you* think best serves them?"

Although Melissus had taken care to control his voice as if stating a fact, Pericles noted it was his first question.

"As rational men, we can agree on what best serves the interests of Samos, under the circumstances."

"The circumstances being . . . "

"Siege and blockade." Pericles pulled a slate near as if consulting a list. "One hundred and sixty ships . . . eighteen thousand men . . . when the seas open . . . "

"That's a lot of men to feed and pay."

"That's why I'm giving you a choice besides fighting to the death."

"We can hold out."

"When the seas open, another forty ships."

"The longer you keep a large force here, the more likely rebellion will erupt elsewhere in your empire."

"That's the last hope of those with no other recourse— Prometheus railing against Zeus."

"It's as they say—you think you're Zeus himself."

"No, and Athens isn't Olympus. But in exaggerating our dangers, you're underestimating our strength."

"What do you intend for my city?"

The second question. "A fair settlement." Pericles studied his slate, stalling for more questions.

"What does the Athenian consider a fair settlement?"

A lamp sputtered. Pericles scanned the slate, his head held tilted back to make out the thin letters.

"First, the Samians shall demolish their stone walls."

"These walls have protected our city since the time of our grandfathers' fathers."

"They were built to maintain the power of a tyrant who cared nothing for your city. Second . . . " Pericles consulted his slate. "Samos shall no longer maintain a navy, but accompanied by the Athenian navy, the Samians shall locate their remaining ships and these shall be turned over to Athens."

"So we'll be like the other 'independent cities'—dependent on you for our own defense."

"Third, Samos shall pay the full cost of the illegal rebellion raised against the Athenian people." Pericles thumbed through a nearby scroll. "That would be, if hostilities were to cease today, one thousand two hundred talents, plus additional costs for constructing the siege wall—"

"You're exaggerating. Over a period of nine months, a warship would cost, let's say, a talent a month—"

"We came here twice. Nor is there any uncertainty about the amounts expended. Our treasurers paid out one hundred and twenty-eight talents the first time we occupied your city—"

"You'd charge us for both campaigns? You count drachmas like a Phoenician. That's what happens when an aristocrat mixes with the Demos."

"It's fair—in fact, generous—and if you love the Samians as you say, you will help them understand that."

"I said I love Samos—not the Samians." When Pericles looked startled, Melissus said, "You're not the only one who notices when another man's words miss the mark."

Samos and Samians. Athens and Athenians. Pericles tried it out in his mind—*I love Athens but not the Athenians.* It made no sense for, as he always said, a city and its citizens are one. When the Persians invaded, the Athenians were no less Athenians for taking refuge on the island of Salamis. If they'd relocated entirely, it would still be Athens. Yet, it caused one to wonder, how much of the city was the place? The Agora with its Hill of Ares, and not some other. The streets leading toward it. Those twisting streets around Hippodamus' house where Aspasia had lived that had drawn him night after night. The path he and Sophocles used as boys to reach the Acropolis—his Parthenon wasn't there back then. How could one leave all that? True, he didn't love everybody in his city—Thucydides was gone for a time but he could do quite well without Lacedaemonius or Pyrilampes, or that new loudmouth, Cleon, but . . .

That must be how the Athenian oligarchs talked privately at their dinners, he thought. "We love Athens, we just don't love the Athenians." It sounded like squaring the circle. He would give it more thought. For now, it would be no use for discrediting Melissus, who would deny having said it.

Melissus broke the silence. "One thousand talents."

It hadn't hurt to slow down.

"One thousand and two hundred talents with the additions of—"

"Such a sum will ruin us."

"You should have considered the consequences before you attempted your revolt."

"You might as well push us into exile. We can't pay that much—we've had our own war costs, too."

"The ruin of Samos is not in Athens' interest."

"You might as well murder our men and enslave our women." Melissus started to tear at his hair.

"If you don't listen to my words, you can't help your city. If we wanted to ruin Samos, we'd carry the siege to its end, which we're well able to do. Our best interest is a prosperous ally."

"You sailed here twice to reduce Samos as if you were the Great King of Persia and we your vassals—and you speak of a prosperous ally? Even if you mean now what you say, you'd feel hatred toward us, and we could never trust you."

"We don't need the Samians to teach us what's in our interest. We know the sum isn't beyond your means and I'm careful about sums. At our last assessment, among the Greek cities, only Athens surpassed Samos in wealth."

"Before the war, yes, but now Lesbos and Chios are far wealthier than we—"

"There you see the benefit that accrues to our allies. And Samos can be among them again if she agrees to our terms." Pericles took another fig and extended the bowl. "Samos was once our ally and comrade-in-arms. In the light of these past services to our alliance, we may consider extending the payments over a period of some years. We'd do this to ease your burden."

Pericles wrote something on the edge of the slate.

Melissus swallowed a fig before replying.

"According to your terms, we must demolish our walls and surrender our ships. Then, when we're helpless—"

"No more helpless than Miletus."

"—we must pay a ruinous fine, though not all at once."

"There will be a fourth condition. Samos shall be governed as a democracy established under the—"

"No."

"—supervision of the Athenians. And there will be the usual requirements of swearing loyalty to Athens, of hostages, of setting up stones with the terms inscribed—"

"Samos will not be a democracy."

"Otherwise we will continue the war, the city will be destroyed—that's ruin, Melissus—the men executed and women sold."

"Democracy puts the reins of government into the hands of men who've done nothing more than walk behind a mule. Democracy ruins the best men and elevates the worst."

Was Melissus as maddened as Ajax, forgetting whom he was talking to? He smiled so that Melissus would be forced to recognize the absurdity of his charge.

"It hasn't worked out that way in Athens. But I'm not here to argue the merits of these forms of government. I would have been willing to do so once, but war puts an end to arguments."

"The oligarchs made Samos prosperous. The gods want oligarchy in Samos—your democracy collapsed here once already."

"We shall be more careful this time but that's not your concern. What you must do is convey our terms to your people and persuade them they're reasonable, under the circumstances."

"We will not live under democracy."

"Then you'll be defeated by an Athens that will have no cause for gratitude."

After Melissus had been escorted from his quarters, Pericles paced his room, stimulated and wide awake. Ah—*there, Melissus, you see the benefit that accrues to our allies!* Nearness to the goal brought new strength. Pheidippides must have felt this way when, having run the distance from Marathon to alert the southerners to the Persian invasion, he spotted the hills of Sparta.

Since he couldn't sleep, he'd write down the main terms of the treaty as he wanted them cut into stone, matching his slate to a fresh scroll. There would be other opinions, consultations, perhaps some changes, but he'd be ready.

Then his forehead fell hard on his hand.

It had been extremely difficult to return to the same ground. Samos and Samos. Euergides. Hygiaenon. So many young men had died here, it was as if the year had lost its spring. The same, he thought, could be said of him. Youth was far behind him. The wet winter made his bones ache. Never had he felt so weary.

But he must hide his fatigue. It was the only way to keep his enemies at a distance and his friends near. He had fresh horsehair inserted in his helmet crest. For sailing home, he chose a cloak of Milesian wool, readily available again—Aspasia would like to see it. Then he settled himself in his workplace in the forward part of the ship.

CHAPTER 34

Pericles and Phidias

Sailing past Cape Sunium, the headland of Attica, toward the city was a strong tonic. Pericles rose from his seat as if swooped up by a breeze. The shore, lined with excited Athenians, rippled like the edge of a dancer's gown. "Welcome home, Agamemnon," they called out! Not *all* heroes are from the past. Excitement shoved fatigue overboard. And he'd captured *his* walled city in nine months—not ten years. He checked the quay for his enemy Old Thucydides—a habit. No Sun Spot! Pyrilampes and Lacedaemonius were head-to-head with Cleon, but the mutterings of opposition were drowned out by the multitudes calling him "The Victor of Samos!" "The New Agamemnon!" Their shouts carried the joy of music and he raised his hand in gratitude toward those pressing in to see him, to touch him, and to acclaim his victory.

At home, Aspasia also greeted him with "My brave Agamemnon!"
Her pendant bounced as she ran toward him across the andron and they embraced tight as a grapevine and an olive tree.
They heard the scuffle at the door, and Aspasia drew back in that way she had of being able to pull away—from the first that had drawn him to her all the more.
"Little Pericles has something to show you." She clapped her hands and his two younger sons came in, Little Pericles off balance because of the weight of the bowl he cupped in his arms, while his older brother Paralus was tugging at it.

No sign of his oldest son—perhaps with so many fathers coming home, Xanthippus couldn't get off border patrol duty to welcome him home after his absence of nine months and winning the war.

"It's too heavy for you," Paralus was saying.

"Look inside the bowl, father!" Little Pericles tugged the bowl from Paralus' grip and held steady. "I put in one stone for each day you were away."

Pericles examined the pile of stones, all smooth, white and of the same size. The effort that had gone into selecting the perfect stones was touching, and he put his hand on Little Pericles' head, noting how the boy had grown.

"I showed him where to find them," Paralus said.

Pericles put his arm around Paralus' shoulders. "I'm proud of you for helping your younger brother. Now, my Little Pericles, can you count how many there are in there?"

"I know already—two hundred and seventy-three!"

"That's a very high number," Pericles said.

"I can count to any number—all the way to the top!"

"All the way to the top—excellent!"

Pericles studied the little boy, his face flushed with excitement and his chest puffed out with pride. Was it possible that of his three sons, *this* was the one who would follow him all the way to the top? He glanced at Aspasia. Her smile and a nod told him that she knew what he was thinking.

That night when they were alone, Aspasia opened her arms to him. "My brave Odysseus!"

"It was you who taught me bravery, Aspasia." The words floated out of him the way some say the soul leaves the body.

She laughed at the absurdity. "You were bravest of all Athenians before you knew me." He remained silent. "You were a great man before we met. Were my letters enjoyable? Did they help make you brave? I don't remember writing 'fight bravely for our city,' although I tried not to let you know how much I missed you."

She waited.

"It's true that before meeting you, I thought I was brave. But now I understand that no matter what exploits a man pulls off, unless he also knows what is sweet in life, he isn't truly brave. You see my logic, don't you? You are what is sweet in my life so it follows that . . ."

He tasted her tears.

"Back then I just took risks," he whispered into the pale coil of her ear.

Agamemnon returned to a wife who murdered him. Ajax killed himself in a mad frenzy before ever reaching home. Odysseus finally reached home to find rebellion in his city. Here, too, he surpassed the heroes.

Not everyone, however, thought he was a hero. After he concluded his official speech honoring the war dead and pretty girls were bringing him flowers, an old woman with a perfume that overwhelmed the scent of the flowers pushed a bouquet at his face. *Who let her so close?* The murder of his democratic comrade, Ephialtes, sprang to mind. "You led the Athenians into battle against Greeks instead of *enemies* of the Greeks as General Cimon did." He felt her hot breath in his ear. By the hounds of Hades, it was Cimon's sister. He hadn't seen her since the night before he'd brought Cimon to trial. She'd come to his house late and scented like a whore and pleaded with him not to prosecute her brother. She was still bold. Who else had heard her?

"Old women shouldn't seek to be perfumed." He brushed past her and her bouquet.

Aspasia did not treat the matter with irony. "She should be punished."

"We Athenians don't punish people for speaking their minds."

The Athenian "we": he spoke from pride but, leaving her out, it hit her as a warning to veer off.

She separated the shells on the tray from the nuts. "Anyhow, I don't see what that old poem about perfume had to do with her rudeness."

"Her perfume brought that line to mind, and I figured it might stop her tongue. She was vain as a young woman and she's probably vain as an old one."

"It did make her seem ridiculous."

"As for who sent her, I know where my opposition lies." He observed closely the grooves on a walnut shell, like rivers cutting through the earth. "In a way—not to take anything away from their achievements—the heroes of the Persian wars had an easier time than we do."

"Weapons are much more complicated now—look at the helmets they wore then, and—"

"Our armor is actually lighter in weight. What I mean is that it's easier to know your enemies when they speak a different language."

That heavy sigh. She took his hand. "Someone out to harm you is an enemy—in any language."

"But when you're fighting someone who speaks your language, it takes more words to explain the reasons to others."

* * *

"I don't care if it's the King of Persia, no one enters—Phidias' orders."

Nine months away and he was unrecognized on the Acropolis.

"Sorry Pericles—that guy's new here." Phidias' apprentice Agoracritus ran up to open the gate for Pericles. "We've been transporting the gold for Athena's statue section by section from the workshop to the temple. They'll take anything that's not guarded. Last week we lost three rasps and a hammer and the week before two drills and—"

"—the week before four files and a running drill." As Phidias ran toward him, his wide arm span blocked the early sun. "Agoracritus is right—someone's setting up shop. But come this way, Pericles. She's waiting for you."

Squinting against the sun, they passed the line of dedications presented by Pericles' family—he'd give them time on the way back. At the temple's entrance, Phidias took a spear-thrower's wide stance and pointed inside, his arm the weapon.

The drilling, rasping, scraping, pushing, pouring, squeezing, and hammering ceased, leaving dust particles drifting in the light from the door.

The gold and ivory Athena was as tall as the walls of Samos.

There she was, born from measurements listed in black ink on papyrus.

The expanse of gold was astonishing.

"I told you there'd be enough light," Phidias said. "And we haven't even filled the pool."

Winged Victory, lightly balancing on Athena's open palm, was taller than a man.

"I remember when you first invented this Victory," Pericles said. "Athens' victory over Persia. Athena's gift."

"Revised. Now it's Pericles' Victory—"

Pericles pressed his finger to his lips, a warning. Of course people would link it to his victory at Samos—the timing was perfect! But it shouldn't come from his own circle.

"That Peloponnesian sculptor Polyclitus never did anything as fine," Phidias said.

It's hard to praise a man who praises himself but, in fact, the work called for it. "It has the value of something only one man can do."

"But that doesn't stop the treasurers from watching me like a slave." Phidias clicked his thumbnail against his teeth.

Behind the statue, the aisle was so narrow Pericles had to lean against the wall to get a full view to the top of the sculpture.

Phidias followed him. "They try to catch me stealing so they can be heroes."

"They're just protecting themselves for the accounting."

What does Athena really look like? Once that question had worried Aspasia. He'd been amused, thinking that it was a young person's question. Yet Phidias, a mature man at the height of his powers had also asked it. At any rate, here was the answer.

"You win the wreath, Phidias."

"And you haven't even seen the shield!" Phidias, in his informal way, nudged Pericles around to the side for a view of the ancient myth of the Amazon invasion of Athens he had created, in gold, on the outside of Athena's shield.

It was as if, on the round, gold face of the shield, a troupe of Amazons were in full battle, storming the Athenian Acropolis the way the Persians had during the war of Pericles' youth. But what a difference! The Persians had defeated the Athenians and burned the Acropolis but—the big "but"—the Athenians had been victorious against the Amazons. If a picture could redeem a loss, Pericles thought, this one did. Amazons battled their way uphill, facing an onslaught of Athenian swords, spears, and arrows. The picture on the round shield was filled with scenes of the war as if Phidias had lived back in the time of the heroes and seen it with his own eyes. Pericles stroked his beard, examining the details. One Amazon, hit by an arrow, plummeted head first from the height of the Acropolis, her hair streaming beneath her.

"If Squirrel had taken that fall at Samos, he wouldn't have survived," Pericles said.

Phidias wiped his arm across his forehead.

"But I wish I could see the order of battle."

Phidias laughed loudly—was he tense? "You know they didn't fight in phalanxes back then."

On the shield, Greeks and Amazons were engaged in hand-to-hand combat as if war was fought in the palaestra. War rarely came to that now—although it might happen in rocky terrain. But Phidias was correct: Homer said that the heroes fought one-on-one.

A few Athenians had fallen. One strained to get a grip on an arrow wedged between his shoulder blades. Comrades dragged another from the battlefield, his right hand limp across his knee—probably dead, judging by the heedlessly acute bend of his wrist.

The Acropolis was steep and rocky but flat at the top—as it is in truth. On the plateau, which rightly was at the top of the shield, two Athenians, fighting back-to-back in defense of the Acropolis, warded off the Amazon invaders. Pericles stepped back to get a better look. Those two Athenians had the situation well in hand, yet—it was Pericles' turn to point—upward.

"Phidias, there's a mistake. At the top, you've got that tall Athenian hurling a huge stone."

They looked up three times their height, Pericles supporting his neck with his hand to study the scene. It angered him that Phidias smiled over an error. And in gold!

"That's no mistake."

"Barbarians and giants fight with stones, not us. Not only that, but instead of armor, he's wearing a workman's tunic—and by Zeus he's bald!" Backing up, Pericles bumped into a column. "Phidias, that looks like *you* up there!"

"Of course—the one with the stone."

"I've never known you as a man to hurl stones, Phidias—when we fought at Achaea you used a sword like the rest of us."

"I *work* with stone." Phidias threw his arms wide as if to embrace the new temple and the entire plateau. He dropped his arms and said quietly, intimately, "It came to me while I was showing Agoracritus how to rough-chisel a new piece of marble. The stone was under my fingers. It was cool. I smacked it with the flat of my hand. I'm a man who works with stone, I thought, and then the idea came to show that warrior fighting for Athens with a stone."

"You should have consulted me about including yourself on the shield."

"You were away."

"You contacted me about other matters."

"I thought it might be considered of little importance."

"The Athenians will see it for what it is—hubris."

"Painters of wine vessels put themselves into their pictures all the time."

"Don't compare a joke on a wine jug with Athena's shield. And the city isn't paying for the jug. Change it."

The sculptor crossed his arms.

Pericles peered closely at the workmanship. "You can just hammer out the gold so that he wears armor. No soldier confronts the enemy wearing a workman's tunic."

"That philosopher Socrates does."

"He's eccentric. You'll also have to change the features of the face, or—" Pericles regarded the details. "You could have his arm cross his face like that general."

"You mean the man next to him," Phidias said.

"From the way they're fighting back-to-back, you'd think they were a two-man team, defending the Acropolis by themselves."

"Comrades-in-arms."

"Or his helmet could drop low over his face like the general's—I see you gave him a tall helmet like the one I always . . . " Had Phidias crossed over to his enemies? "That general next to you is me, isn't it?"

"Comrades-in-arms—defending the Acropolis."

Pericles' mind spun to the horse trainer on the temple's sculptured frieze that Phidias had carved earlier. Phidias was having his fun again—but the trainer only resembled him as an idea. This could cause real trouble.

So that was why Phidias had him come alone.

"Have you considered that I could be exiled from Athens for this likeness—or worse?"

"Likeness, hah! If I made your likeness, it would so match you that no one could tell which was art and which was Pericles."

If Phidias was betraying him, he'd betrayed himself more openly. The stone thrower had the very look of Phidias, whereas one could not be sure that the general was Pericles.

But the Athenians ostracized generals, not artisans.

"They'll guess your intent."

"I covered the general's face with his arm to spare you from any guesses."

Pericles regarded the general. If an enemy looked closely—a Dracontides who as Chief Priest of the Old Athena temple hated this new Athena—he might guess that it was Pericles. But he could not prove it in court.

"Only we will know." Phidias' voice startled Pericles as if his own thought had taken audible form.

"It will stir gossip."

"I've never known you to fear gossip."

"Everyone will figure that since that's you, the general defending the Acropolis with him must be me—that and the helmet will leave little doubt."

"Two heroes," Phidias said.

Comrades-in-arms. Defending the Acropolis. That *was* a subject for a temple.

"If not for me, aren't you afraid for yourself?"

Hands on hips, Phidias leaned back as if shouting. "I want future generations to know who made these works."

Pericles recognized a new fear. Future generations might *not* recognize him as the general who fought beside Phidias for the Acropolis.

It wouldn't be just. He'd done as much as Phidias, as Aspasia said.

In Persia, Egypt—everywhere, in fact—kings and emperors placed their likenesses on the temples they built, and their names, to seal their own posterity.

Could his likeness be made clearer?

Kings. Emperors. Persia. Egypt. His hand touched his forehead to stop the spinning that can overcome a man on the topmast. It would be hubris. He'd have to live—and die—with the uncertainty. And as for future generations, they'd have to be uncertain, too—if they even thought about it. Unlike those kings and emperors who put their names and portraits on every monument, he led free men, a higher honor.

"Must I remove the two comrades-in-arms?" Phidias asked. "I can if you want me to. Easily."

The man had the timing of an actor.

CHAPTER 35

Athenian Mathematics

He had ensured thirty years of peace with Sparta, sent a colony to Italy, and won the war against Samos. He has seen to the construction of two hundred warships and to the training of their crews, and he would soon take fifty of them on Athenian business to the Black Sea. The grand expedition to the Black Sea filled his mind: he would firm up Athenian ties with Byzantium—how impressed the Byzantines would be with his new ships, armed and in perfect formation, sailing through their Hellespont strait! And equally essential, he would establish a stable supply of northern wheat for Athens—no more depending on erratic gifts from volatile Egyptians. The gods must be pleased, but whether they were or not, he was pleased.

Not the comic poets, though.

Damon asked Cratinus, "Why does everything Pericles does displease you comic poets?"

"And what's his answer?" Pericles asked.

"'On the contrary, everything Pericles does pleases us *enormously*.'"

Hearing that, Pericles nodded, shook his head, and nodded again.

The bit tugged the corners of Damon's mouth. "It's in men's nature to find fault with good men."

"It's a strange mathematics that makes everything large small and everything small large," the philosopher Anaxagoras commented.

Aspasia raised a sarcastic eyebrow. "Athenian mathematics—you have to be born here to understand it." Instantly she regretted her words. Pericles didn't like even the scent of criticism of Athens—especially by non-Athenians.

"Our poets are free to write as they wish," he said. "Since that's not true elsewhere, maybe it *does* take an Athenian to understand it."

There were moments, however, when Pericles wished he could limit the comic poets' unrelenting personal attacks on individual citizens such as himself. Anaxagoras had endured jokes about his philosophy, or what the comic poets took to be his philosophy. But Anaxagoras—or anyone else swiped for a laugh—couldn't gauge the strain of remaining calm when a poet turned the theater into a honeycomb of stings aimed not just at his policies but at his person and his family. And the worst of it for Pericles was that he didn't get his turn. All points of view were heard in the Assembly and two points of view in the law courts, but in the theater, they heard only the poets—and more Athenians were at the theater than the Assembly or the courts. Since at the theater, the only voting was for the best poets and performers, he had reconciled himself to the annoyance.

But not when the most private part of his life was dragged onstage.

Back after attending a dramatic festival in northeast Attica, Pericles swept past Zoe at the door. The farmers in that rural region opposed his plan to further enlarge the fleet in peacetime so he had decided it would be politic to make an appearance at their dramatic festival.

"It never happened and not that way!"

Aspasia saw he wanted to tell her what was angering him but was holding back. "Was it that joke about Zeus whose head swelled up like a pregnant woman's belly because Athena was gestating inside of it?" She chose that one because Zeus' head enlarged from carrying Athena before she was born made everyone think of Pericles and his large head. And Aspasia was in no hurry to reach a worse conclusion.

"You're close but no." He set his helmet onto its peg. "Let's just say I wish it *had* been about my head."

She poured a drink—he liked his pomegranate juice mixed with honey. "Hmm . . . but something about you being Zeus?" The jokes comparing him to the autocratic king of the gods worried Pericles because they suggested that he was seeking one-man rule in Athens. On the other hand, since Zeus gave birth to Athena, the goddess of wisdom and military might, she suspected he felt flattered. At any rate, she doubted that another *Pericles is Zeus* joke would make him so angry as to ignore a servant at the door.

"Enter the chorus. They sing that Zeus, who comes on wearing a helmet—as if Zeus ever needed a helmet!—lusts for mortal women and so he pays sums of gold to a sculptor named—guess what—Phidias—to provide him with prostitutes."

Aspasia took comfort in the plural. Some saw her as a common prostitute, not the fine hetaira she was, because many overlooked the distinction. But the fact was that Pericles was faithful to her alone. There were no others.

Pericles' voice sounded deeper the more slowly he spoke. "They named Phidias—they're fortunate they didn't name me."

As if there were anything he could do if they *had* used his name—but no need to remind him. She searched for a hopeful suggestion. "Maybe they mentioned Phidias by name and not you because they're not attacking you—they're after Phidias."

"Why would anyone attack him?"

"Because of the money he spends on the buildings."

"He doesn't argue for the money to build—I do."

No point to evade the truth and seem stupid. "I suppose they may be pecking at you roundabout through him, but it's important they didn't use your name."

"By the next scene no one could miss that Zeus was—" His thumb slammed hard into his breastbone.

"How can you be sure if they didn't use your name?"

Politics was not fought on an open field. Pericles thought back to the time that his arch political enemy, Thucydides, had brought Pericles' intimate love for Aspasia into the Assembly's view. And why? To make a political point. Against spending money on the Parthenon. "We Athenians are like bewitched lovers," Thucydides had said, and the entire Assembly had turned their necks like a flock of geese to look at the man whom Athenian gossip had decided was a bewitched lover—Pericles. And Thucydides did not stop with that. With his customarily vulgar figures of speech, Thucydides had degraded not only Athens, and Pericles, but his elegant, educated Milesian girl, his precious love, Aspasia.

At that early moment in their love, he had decided not to tell Aspasia of these events in the Assembly that touched on her but one kiss and he had told her all of it. That's how it had always been with Aspasia: he did not hold back. She was sure to find out about the play anyhow.

"One of Phidias' girls claims she's a Milesian fugitive from the war with Samos."

The old fear grabbed her: that his love for her would be too heavy a political liability, leading him to ease her out of his life. But the fact was that he'd remained steadfast. He hadn't left her at the beginning when that obscene Thucydides had besmirched her in the Assembly. Instead he told her about it. Since then, time had woven them more tightly together. And they had a son. She did not think he would leave her now. Still, she would know best how to handle whatever came up if she knew all. She held to a serene expression so he would continue.

"'Poor unlucky girl,' says Zeus, caressing her. Some laugh. And I have to sit there."

He looked to her for a response, but she only nodded.

"Don't you understand, Aspasia—it was as if I was caressing you in front of all those—" He gestured as if discarding a bilious liver.

She nodded and frowned.

"Then, when she has him under her spell, she tells Zeus that she'll only surrender to his lust if he comes to the aid of Miletus in the war against Samos."

Aspasia looked down. That was a hard one. Causing a war.

"As if Zeus would go to war for love," he said. "As if any man would."

Homer flashed through her mind—but Aspasia doubted the that the Trojan War was really fought over Helen. "You had excellent Athenian reasons to attack Samos," she said quickly.

He sipped the juice. "If I had a rebellious Samos in front of me again, I'd act the same."

"That's what matters."

"How things appear matters. You're Milesian, and I led the Athenians against Samos on behalf of Miletus."

"You led them on behalf of Athens—that's the truth."

"Protagoras says men make their own truths out of appearances."

"Anaxagoras says truth exists behind the mere appearances of things."

Whatever the nature of truth, insult grows heavier the longer it's borne. Aspasia brushed her palms as if she'd just put floury bread in the oven. "Propose a law banning slander in the theater like you did during the Samian War."

"That would be tyrannical in a time of peace."

"I don't understand why you can't arrange these matters more to your liking." To heighten her plausibility so that he might consider her statement, she shook her head as if bewildered.

But he didn't need time to think. "It's the puzzle of leading free men."

His acceptance of the paradox thrilled her. It made her own coquettish bewilderment seem small—or, worthwhile in that it brought into high relief his dedication to freedom. How stunning to care about the fate of so many. Not that she wished anyone ill but, like most, her concern extended to herself and those at her hearth, well, her hearth had a few she could do without but, at any rate, it was an inverse ratio—the farther from the hearth, the thinner the warmth. But for Pericles, the hearth was city size. And sometimes she suspected he planned to warm the world with it.

Now, that was a play in which she had a *real* role—not some comic absurdity.

You taught me bravery, Aspasia.

She made life dear to him.

For me, you are what is sweet in life.

He was a liberator among the Greeks, but she helped.

Pericles stretched. "We could call this insult a compliment."

"A compliment!" She was accustomed to his quick changes of course but he would enjoy her surprise.

"To say one's under a woman's influence is the insult leveled at the greatest men."

"That's true. They say Cyrus the Great was influenced by his mother—"

"Never mind the Persians, think what they say about Themistocles."

"I've heard that—"

"When a man makes no errors, no miscalculations—when there's nothing else to level against him, they say that he's influenced by a woman."

He *did* have a way of finding the silver in the darkest clouds. "Who wrote this play?"

"That's another reason to know it was aimed at me."

"Your so-called friend Pyrilampes?"

"Not a friend of mine—a friend of yours."

Her friend, that was unfortunate. "Was it Euripides?"

Pericles shook his head. "Someone who's never produced a play before."

"Socrates?"

"Dion."

She winced. Dion had tried to remain her friend by dropping off rehearsal copies of plays he acted in—hard to turn down since those plays were useful for teaching her class. "Oh, Dion's still angry because you didn't help him become a citizen. But he won't be bothering us long—he's leaving Athens." She took his hand in hers. "You know, Pericles, you are such a great man that people think you can do everything."

He stroked his beard. "Aspasia, I must keep these restless Athenians busy. As the pressure of a war lightens, they forget how much they need me and turn to mischief, like Dion's play." He nodded as if to the truth of his own thoughts. "I've seen this before when we signed the Peace Treaty with Sparta."

"Dion's silly play, Cimon's silly sister, those are nothing—"

"Men need large tasks."

What about women—did they need large tasks? She certainly had large tasks. She wanted to think more about that but—

"Aspasia, here's a riddle for you—what's gold in color but more valuable to Athens than the Golden Fleece?"

Her hand went to her chin. "Gold . . . Golden Fleece . . . more valuable . . . That expedition to the Black Sea for wheat you've been talking about?" She brushed her hand across her forehead so he wouldn't see her frown. She had become used to the pleasure of having him home.

"Remember the year when we had to depend on a gift from that Egyptian for enough wheat to bake our loaves. That must never happen again. I must secure a stable supply of northern wheat, all the more since that barbarian Spartacus and his brothers have seized control over much of the north shore of the Black Sea. Aspasia, wheat grows there in fields the size of all Attica—think of that!"

He was thrilled by what he saw before him. She nodded vigorously to match his excitement.

"And just as important, I will secure our alliance with Byzantium. I can't let a major ally slip away, not after what it took to subdue Samos."

CHAPTER 36

The Golden Fleece

The new riddle around town: *What has the Athenians as inspired and unified as war but Ares has no part of it?*
Pericles' expedition to the Black Sea to secure our wheat supply.

Back in the time of myths and heroes, Jason and his companions, the Argonauts, sailed far east on the Black Sea to bring back to Greece the gold fleece of a sacred ram. Now, in the excitement about Pericles' Black Sea expedition, bards sang tales of Jason's adventures, newborn boys were named "Jason," and potters stocked their shelves with wine cups painted with the exploits of Jason and the Argonauts. Down the street from The Three Jugs bar in Piraeus, some speculator opened The Golden Fleece bar (but the sign nailed above the door depicting a ram's fleece couldn't compete with the three round breasts painted on the sign of The Three Jugs).

* * *

Pericles encircled Aspasia's shoulders with his arm so they could both read the letter that Aristocleia had sent over. Aspasia settled in close, as if a sealed scroll delivered by a servant of his former wife's household was an ordinary event and caused her no unease, though neither was true. He slipped his knife under the seal. He read aloud the few words: "Take our son Xanthippus with you to the Black Sea and give him opportunities to lead men. If our son is to amount to anything in the city, he must distinguish himself in a campaign."

Every day, it seemed to Aspasia, there was some new reminder of the unfairness Young Pericles faced. Xanthippus could choose whether to distinguish himself or not—he was a citizen just by being born. While her Young Pericles would have to achieve some outstanding exploit just to reach that starting line.

"Or at least take part in one," she said of Xanthippus.

Sensing sarcasm, he reached for a firm retort. "That's one thing Aristocleia and I agree about."

"I thought Aristocleia didn't admire men who try to distinguish themselves."

"She's as ambitious as anyone. She just found my dedication to the city excessive—and she may be right."

Now he was agreeing with his former wife. Her hatred of Aristocleia was a stab to her breastbone. But he was reading the letter with her, not with Aristocleia—*that* was what mattered. So, feeling the warmth of his arm on her back, she followed his tack. "In fairness to Xanthippus, since he came of age Athens has been at peace—but that's all to the good."

"Exactly—young men must have opportunities to make a name for themselves in peace, not just in war. That's one reason I'm going to the Black Sea."

A reason she hadn't heard before.

"You're providing other opportunities—Hagnon's expedition to establish a new Athenian colony in Thrace is leaving soon." She smoothed her cheek to his hand holding the letter. "Didn't you tell me that Hagnon will be taking cavalry?"

"My son should go with me. He can see how I manage the men, make decisions and solve problems. He can learn how to lead."

She knew as well as he did that Xanthippus had made no effort at leadership in Athens. She was always ready to promote the virtues of her own son, but it pained her to see Pericles sad—even if it was about those other boys.

She smiled and stroked his hand. "And they say that men are foolish about women."

"What's that to do with it?"

"Men and their sons. They see them as better than they are or worse than they are—never as they are."

Pericles nodded, shook his head, and nodded. "I suppose I complain too much about him."

"Well . . ." she spoke slowly as if reluctantly, ". . . you have said that he has no interest in bettering the city."

"All he does is run his horses and follow the philosophers around." Pericles unrolled Aristocleia's letter for another look.

"You aren't against philosophy."

"I was pleased when he took up philosophy. But he should attend the Assembly."

"His study of philosophy may benefit the city—as Protagoras says."

"So you think I see Xanthippus as worse than he is?"

"If that were true, he wouldn't disappoint you so often."

"I'd like to be proud of him."

She decided to take the leap. "Have you considered that he may do well following Hagnon who'll look out for him like a father without being his father."

Pericles tapped Aristocleia's crisp papyrus against his lips several times. "I have given it some thought. Since Hagnon is taking cavalry, Xanthippus can ride if he follows him. Xanthippus is more a man of the land than the sea. There, too, he's different from me."

She hated to see Pericles unhappy but she never liked his spending time with anyone in his first family when she wasn't present. "He may surprise you. He may so distinguish himself in the cavalry that he'll run for military office when he returns."

The image of his son came to him—Xanthippus letting his cloak fall open and the young man's chest beneath, each muscle lined as if by an engraver. It pleased him to think of having the boy with him. He allowed the warm, tan image to fade.

"He may prefer to ride. I'll ask him."

The fact was he did not really want Xanthippus along to oppose him at every turn in front of his officers—with that boldness his sons allotted to themselves. He smiled thinking Aspasia, as so often, must have known how he truly felt. That must be why she had pushed for Xanthippus to go with Hagnon. He'd miss her more than he would Hagnon.

"How will you spend your time while I'm in the north?"

"I'll hold my classes—the women are more likely to attend with the husbands away."

"Whose plays will you read?"

"Euripides'. He writes about what interests them, more than Sophocles."

"His plays don't match Sophocles', but he's original."

"And I might even write a play myself."

"You?"

"I have one in mind."

Wasn't it enough that he lived with her openly? Next she'd want him to produce her play in the theater of Dionysos. Wouldn't that give the Athenians something to talk about—and not for his good. Or hers, for that matter. But the Priest of Dionysos would never permit it, that was lucky. Some women did write poetry—Ionian women, and she was Ionian. But none wrote plays—none that he'd ever heard about.

"Whatever would your play be about?"

"Zeus and Io," she said with pride.

At least it would be about love like Sappho's poems. A fair subject for a woman.

"Io will have to choose between two lovers, a dependable mortal and divine Zeus, whom she truly loves."

"That'll interest your women."

"It will, because all women make choices like that."

How could that be since their fathers choose for them? He didn't want to hear any more. "All that should keep you occupied for a summer's expedition."

"And I'll be busy teaching our Little Pericles that, as the poets say, he must 'win his own renown.'"

"I'm sure you will," Pericles said. Winning renown was Young Pericles' only chance for citizenship. "And I hope I'll be there to see it."

* * *

General Pericles to Damon in Athens, from Byzantium. Greetings. *The Bosporus strait leading toward the Black Sea is so narrow it's easy to see how the Persians bridged it with boats when they tried to capture Greece. Turning my head, I can easily see both coasts. The Byzantines love us even more when we come with fifty ships. Men streamed to the coast to greet us. Since the harbor is crowded, I had the channel cleared of ships for ours to enter in formation. Here's what you are to do: see to it that the Assembly votes 500 drachmas to repay the Byzantines for the customs duties they lost in accommodating our entry. It's a small amount, but since it's unexpected it will seem large. And they know the Spartans would never do it. Tell the Athenians the Byzantines have learned the lesson of Samos.*

General Hagnon to General Pericles in Byzantium, from Amphipolis in Thrace. Greetings. *I plan to found our new Athenian colony upriver from the bridge connecting Macedonia with Thrace. With a river on three sides, only an island could be stronger to defend and no island has trees as thick as five men around. From the hill, we control the path from the north to the sea. We could erect a Hecate with nine faces, so many roads cross here. There's gold—Thracians who come looking to trade for our oil, wool, drinking cups, or anything Athenian ride with gold circles sewn onto their shirts and gold ornaments strung on their horses' tails. So we can get all the timber we need, no matter what the Macedonian kings feel about us from one day to the next, and plenty of gold no matter who rules Egypt. Your son Xanthippus is prospecting for gold in the north.*

Stay clear of the crashing rocks. May the gods guide you on your journey. Make sure we have plenty of wheat, no matter who rules Egypt.

Protagoras in Thurii, Italy, to General Hagnon in Thrace. *Thank you for asking my advice—more city founders should do that. Here are my rules for the new city which we began by calling New Sybaris but now call Thurii. Let all who accompany you act in a way important to the city's health and in line with their strongest skills. Much needs to be done fast and the man working only for himself is working against the rest. Do this also because in old cities, men are accustomed to their importance or lack of it in comparison with their neighbors while in new ones the memory of recent hazards and shared hardships makes them think they share worth as well. This can lead to political faction, which is more deadly in new cities than in old ones because it's like a disease from which an adult may recover but which kills a child. Now, it's evident that some men have many skills, some a few, some only one by which they gain their living. Don't undervalue the man with only one skill but take care that he uses it for the common benefit. Even slaves will work in harmony with their masters if entrusted with important tasks.*

After seeing to fortifications, develop all precincts at the same pace. If you build only one section at a time, the Council chamber or the city hearth will spring up like a banyan tree to suck water and shade the growth of everything near. Let men build their dwellings and sow seed while they build the temple. In allowing them to establish their households, you give them reason to defend the city, for men won't easily leave a place once it's theirs. A well-founded household is a bulwark against attacks by barbarians or jealous Greeks.

As you requested, I'm sending Hippodamus' plan of the precincts he laid out here. It served us well so you're smart to want it for the new city you're establishing in Thrace.

General Pericles to General Hagnon in Thrace, from Heraclea on the south coast of the Black Sea. Greetings. *This south coast is belted with mountains. At Heraclea, we beached the ships since the harbor is little more than a cove. Scores waded out to pull us in. The market is not large enough to supply us but the people bring what we need. I received word from our friendly democrats in Sinope, farther east, that their oppressive tyrant, Timesilaus, is only pretending to prepare a force against us while he's plotting to escape. He has learned the lesson of Samos.*

I'm not pleased that Xanthippus is prospecting for gold. He's spent enough time in the hinterlands of Athens patrolling our boundaries. Also it's risky because he knows less than he thinks about the ways of the Thracian riders. A few encounters with Boeotian Greeks on our border don't teach a man about barbarians. I prefer he remain with you where he can take part in founding and defending the new city and learn the skills of leadership from a good man.

Aspasia to Hippodamus in ~~New Sybaris~~ Thurii in Italy, from Athens. *Be calm, my friend. I doubt on two counts that Pericles wrote Hagnon to follow the Thracian way of laying out his new city. First, the Thracians don't live in cities but in small towns and those are half-underground. I checked in Herodotus' book before writing you. Ask him yourself since he's there with you in Thurii (We know New Sybaris is now called Thurii because you threw out the Sybarites). Second, Pericles wouldn't find a barbarian way as excellent as that of a Greek.*

I say finish your scroll about the details of your plan and— this is most important—include your reasons. Then no one would confuse your plan with anyone else's and your fame would be assured for all time. A sculptor from southern Greece, Polyclitus, has written a book in which he claims to have found the right system for making a sculpture of a man, and now Athenians are saying he's a better sculptor than Phidias who's never written anything. If philosophers and sculptors gain renown from putting their ideas into scrolls, why not Hippodamus?

Simon the Bootmaker in Athens to General Pericles at Sinope on the south coast of the Black Sea. *I did what you asked, though not because I knew why it was the best plan. I urged the Council to place the item about sending seventeen more ships to that Black Sea town of Sinope on the Assembly's agenda. By the time you receive this letter, the Assembly will have met. Be confident of the outcome. I told Anticles to stand ready to make the motion to send the ships to Sinope. He was surprised to have a visit from the bootmaker, I can tell you. But I asked myself, shouldn't Pericles remain in Sinope after he overthrows their tyrant to ensure a strong democracy? Consider how the aristocrats expelled the democrats the first time you left Samos. Then I asked myself, doesn't Pericles always have a reason for what he wants? He simply didn't write it down for reasons of state.*

Since the lots had just been drawn, I was surprised you learned so quickly—and you so far away—that I'm on the Executive Council.

Sophocles in Athens to Pericles at Sinope on the southern coast of the Black Sea. Greetings. *You flatter me that I'm an expert on coinage because I served one term as Treasurer of our empire. And I only did that because you flattered me—not into believing that you needed me for the task, but into believing that you believed I was. At any rate, here's my opinion. Once you throw out the tyrant, don't force the new democracy you're setting up in Sinope to adopt our Athenian coinage. Yes, they must rid themselves of their old eagle's-head coins when the tyrant's gone but let them decide for themselves what they want in its place—something about* *the country. Athens has profited from the uniform coinage in our empire, but the Sinopians have had their own coinage for too long to force a change. Let the men of Sinope choose freely.*

Socrates in Athens to Xanthippus in Thrace. *Do I think the daughter of Teisander is beautiful? Xanthippus will be glad if I write yes because he'll have agreement with his own opinion which men enjoy, and it pleases me to gladden the heart of a friend. As well, a short, stocky, barefooted, bald man with rough features and hands might find almost any woman beautiful.*

Yet I will not say it for coming from an honest man, the word would pass for truth, but a word is not truth, and since truth is a great and lasting good and gladness a passing and lesser one, I would have injured a friend which I wouldn't willingly do. Were you here, Xanthippus, I'd speak my answer and as when we've talked, my answer would be like an anxious lover intently awaiting your answer which again would be anxiously awaiting mine and mine yours and thus we'd progress, each of our answers a step on the path to truth we'd walk together as we have in the past, passionate lovers of truth that we are. But it's the nature of words that, once written, appear final and are easily mistaken for the end of the path to truth when they are mere steps along the way.

As for whether you should marry Teisander's daughter when you return even though your father has said you must wait until you're thirty, I won't answer that question for the same reason. I will say that to refrain from marrying her out of fear of your father is poor judgment. How often have we said, Xanthippus, that Eros is a powerful god? Your father is only a powerful man.

King Philip of Macedonia to the Tyrant of Sinope. *You claim, Timesilaus, that if I give you refuge in Macedonia that you'll bring information about the Greek cities, yet you* *seem unaware that Athens controls the sea. If Macedonia and Athens were not friends, we would need mountains on our seaside like those that protect us on the north. Write to me again when friendship with Timesilaus would be as useful.*

General Pericles to the so-called Tyrant of Sinope, Timesilaus. *Leave Sinope now and leave with your life. Do not think you can resist us. Your citizens thronged to welcome us at the port. For us, Sinope is a city without walls. We have come with fifty ships to your eighteen and are ready to bring ten times that number against you. No one can think Athens boasts of its numbers. Recall the lesson of Samos.*

Artaxerxes of Persia, Great King, King of Kings, King of countries containing all kinds of men, king in this great earth far and wide to Timesilaus, Tyrant of Sinope. *You Greeks are liars. You said that you would ensure that we Persians alone could buy cinnabar, and that you'd keep the Athenians out of the Black Sea. In return we promised to send you money each year, and to guard your mountain passes. Black Sea towns are now mining cinnabar and selling it to our enemies. We ceased sending you money, but we continued to guard your passes. Now Athenians are cutting through the Black Sea like a scythe through grass. Why, then, should we give you refuge? You who failed in all you promised as a tyrant have little to offer as a poor Greek.*

Aspasia at your estate at Cholargos to Pericles at Sinope on the south coast of the Black Sea. *This is a strange summer. Not because you are away, that, alas, is not strange. But nothing has gone as I expected. I am at Cholargos with Young Pericles and Paralus who came after his tour of military training. It was so hot in Athens that it seemed best. Your sister isn't pleased, but I came anyhow because it's healthier for the boys. I have hired a trainer in the pentathlon for Young Pericles—I chose that because it includes five sports. Thus Young Pericles is being trained not*

*in one excellence but in five. Paralus hunts hare or quail
with other young men of the neighborhood. You'll be pleased
to know that our son has taken an interest in farming your
estate. He often rides out with Euangelus to check on the
tenants tending your fields.*

*And what is Aspasia doing in the country with no one to talk
with? I'm not bored because I am writing my play. Now I
understand why Euripides spends his summers alone in that
cave on Salamis just to write. My play fills my thoughts, except
of course for the thoughts that carry me in my imagination to
you or bring you home to me.*

*The wife of Sadocus the Thracian was wearing a bracelet
with two facing lion heads that is so fine it almost looks
Greek and yet I haven't seen anything quite like it among
the Greeks, nor is it quite like the Persian. If you should
bring me such a bracelet, I would wear it with pleasure
with the gold earrings you gave me on my name day. Also,
I understand that Thracian women have beautiful mirrors,
though whether they're as good as the Greek I can't say, and
I only want you to bring me one if they are.*

*I long for your return and urge you to take no risks. I hold
to my opinion that you are even more necessary to Athens as
a city leader than as a commander in the field, and Young
Pericles and I could not exist without you.*

General Pericles in Sinope to Timesilaus. *Be out of
Sinope with your four hundred followers by sunset. Use the
southern path, each man taking no more than what two
mules can pull in one wagon. Settle in no Greek land nor
land controlled by Greeks, nor anywhere in Sicily, Italy,
Macedonia, Thrace or Scythia. If, as you say, the Emperor of
Persia will settle four hundred Greeks who'll fight for him,
it's because Greeks are great fighters. Four hundred will do
him little good against us.*

Dion to Aspasia from Syracuse in Sicily. *I'll bet you never thought you'd hear from me again. I can imagine you and Pericles saying to each other, "We're glad he's gone." Well, I'm in a better city. People have more taste here in Sicily than in Athens—they prefer Euripides to Sophocles. There I was of no account because I wasn't a citizen, but here I head an acting company. I've already produced six of Euripides' plays and acted in four of them myself.*

Now, I could tour the cities of Sicily but instead, I want to take my company on to Italy where Protagoras is heading up that new Athenian colony, Thurii. You're friendly with Protagoras (so is Pericles, but he'd never do anything for me). Please write to Protagoras at Thurii and recommend me and my company. Tell him that we produce the Athenian plays exactly as in Athens. We supply the masks, costumes and actors and will train the local chorus and supervise the building of the backdrop in the Athenian manner. We'll divide the receipts but don't go into that, I'll handle the financial arrangements. I just need an introduction so he knows he'll be getting real Athenian theater. You know how well I know all the plays and what a great actor I am—tell him that. Remember that I helped you when you first came to Athens. Remember that we were friends and write this to Protagoras.

General Pericles to Timesilaus. *Waste no time with questions or we'll attack at first light. Whether your wagons carry goods and chattel or children and wives is of no concern to us so long as you take no more than two mules can pull. What we do with the remainder is not your concern.*

Tleson on the Black Sea's south coast to his father Tleson the jailer in Athens. *You can't imagine how much there is here of everything—tuna, sturgeon, herring, and so much wheat that the land looks like a yellow sea when the wind is blowing. Don't turn your new field over to wheat* *even if it will grow there. Everyone says that the price will go down.*

I have learned the helm from Pericles' helmsman and will aid him in guiding the ship when we sail across the Black Sea to the north coast.

Herodotus at Thurii in Italy to Pericles at Sinope on the Black Sea's south coast. *Yes, I'd follow in the wake of Jason who sailed the Black Sea all the way east to Colchis in his quest for the Golden Fleece—if I were young again and traveling the world. But if I were a General with business with that new tyrant, Spartacus in Panticapaeum, I'd turn north immediately. You must avoid the storms that swoop like eagles upon the Black Sea in late summer.*

Rowing day and night you can make the run from the south to north in two days, bringing the boats in south of Panticapaeum—but you don't need me to tell you this. Surely, Pericles, you didn't write me for knowledge you have from your helmsmen but because you're longing to go to Colchis as Jason and his Argonauts did. Because you've reached Sinope, now you want to go farther—it's how men are. Here's what I learned in my travels: it is given to the gods—maybe birds, also—but not to men to see beyond the horizon. I say that having traveled farther than any Greek. I went to Thebes in Egypt, but not to Ethiopia. I'll probably die in Thurii and doubt that I'll see the Pillars of Heracles, although if I found a trustworthy Phoenician captain, I might make the attempt.

Anyhow, Colchis is only a small trading town now and the Golden Fleece isn't there anymore. If you've time on the way home, see the Palace of Scyles in Olbia, surrounded by marble griffins and sphinxes, and try not to miss the statue of Apollo by our Greek sculptor Calamis in Apollonia. It's thirty cubits high!

Captain Demodicus from The Three Jugs in Piraeus to General Pericles at Sinope on the south coast of the Black Sea. *You flatter an old man, you with Antigonus, the best helmsmen, to guide you, but I know those coasts from sailing with a load—that's how to learn. Don't try to make Colchis unless you want to winter there—it's too late in a short season. If you get there without hitting a storm, you'll curse your luck because you'll certainly hit a worse one on the run back. I'd head for Byzantium now, but I'm not Pericles and we need the wheat. Here's how to cross the Black Sea north to Panticapaeum. Four parasangs past Market Harbor at Sinope are the three pointer rocks, two on the beach, one in the water, in a straight line north. That's where the current turns, and the Sinopians will tell you to pick it up there. Don't do it. It's fine for a merchant like me, or a small force, but the current takes a powerful turn, there are shoals, and you'll want to pull the fleet around in deeper water. Row until you see sheer rock cliffs all the way to the shore with caves above. Turn there. Row straight north for as long as it takes to sing "Siren's Song," "Calypso," and "Home, Again." Make a slow turn back west, singing "Medea the Witch," and you'll see the current. Catching the current and rowing day and night you'll reach the north shore in two days. Watch for the white bird rocks and bring the ships in from the east. From there you can make Panticapaeum whenever you want— that is, if that new tyrant Spartacus is as pleased to see you as you think he'll be. If not, you know those northerners, they'll sacrifice you to Artemis. Don't delay, Pericles. Secure the grain coming out of Panticapaeum for us—that's worth more than the Golden Fleece.*

Spartacus, Tyrant of Panticapaeum, on the Black Sea's north coast to Leucon in Nymphaeum. *I embrace you, my brother. No one grieves for us now that they know the Athenians themselves are coming to pay us court. Even the Scythians are quiet.*

Yet I think the Athenians treat us lightly. We're masters in Panticapaeum and they arrive expecting to have their way in all things. I had sewn onto my sleeve in Thracian, "They can't get enough wheat anywhere else." Come in three days to the banquet I'm preparing for these Athenians on Mount Mithradates. I want them to know we have Greeks in our family. My armed guard will flank the road. After, they may have their wheat—at my price.

Fifty warships are in my bay. I must close now and meet the famous democrat.

General Pericles from Panticapaeum on the Black Sea's north coast to Anticles in Athens. *Tell Damon this: we're not settling Athenians to live here under the thumb of the tyrant Spartacus—we're buying wheat and fish. If we obtain wheat and fish, what does it matter that Spartacus is a tyrant? We might as well refuse to buy from him because he's Thracian. Tell Damon to think instead of what we've achieved in Sinope, our new ram in the democratic fold. The Athenians we're settling there will secure the democracy. That will make him happy. In any case, he must not oppose us in the Assembly.*

Tleson from Panticapaeum to Tleson the jailer in Athens. *Father, we've taken to calling this the Friendly Sea. When we sail into port, crowds wave from the shore as if we were returning home. What we need is in the markets they set up for us. Athenians are like kings here. General Pericles is fond of saying, "They have learned the lesson of Samos." People are mixed, although they follow many Greek ways. Here on the north coast Spartacus, who rules Panticapaeum and along with his brother most of this region, invited our entire army to dinner last night. When he learned that Pericles would assign a large number to remain guarding the ships, Spartacus arranged a feast for them tomorrow. Though a barbarian, he's a Greek in hospitality. This is what I mean* *when I say they are much like us. I heard that when an important Thracian dies, they kill his horses and women to keep him company, but I've seen no sign of that. Nor do I believe anyone would kill a good horse.*

We ate on the sacred mountain in tents hung with cloth that was so soft it must be what they mean by "silk." They butchered a hundred oxen, a hundred pigs, and a hundred sheep, all sacrificed with proper prayers, and there was every kind of fish, both fresh and salt. I ate the fresh, since here one can always get the salt. Black roe and wheat bread. They said the wine was from Thasos. I'm not sure about that, but it was good. What we couldn't eat we took back to camp.

I changed my plans about being a helmsman. When we leave here, I'll settle in Sinope on the south coast. Pericles says they'll soon parcel out to Athenians the lands of the tyrant we chased out of there along with his friends, and I'm taking a land allotment. If the gods fished and farmed, that's how much there is here of everything. A poor man can get rich here. Tell mother not to be sad, tell her I'll be a landowner.

Pericles to Aspasia at Cholargos from Panticapaeum on the Black Sea's north shore. *I haven't seen all I wished but I've accomplished all I intended. All shipments of grain and fish from the north coast ports will be directed to our own Piraeus and from there we'll control distribution to our empire, collecting our port taxes. No Athenian will ever go hungry. Nor will Spartacus lack ready access to our markets. We swore to aid him against the Scythians and garrison the Hypanis and Bug Rivers. On the south shore, we have expelled the Tyrant of Sinope. We've consolidated our trade connections and are increasing the number and strength of our garrisons to protect the cities of the south shore against Persian inroads. Athenian settlers are on their way to Sinope. There are so many volunteers, we're planning another colony that we're going to call Piraeus. Athenian cities lining the* shores—that's as it should be. The waters of the Black Sea flow into our Aegean. I plan to put in at Apollonia to see Calamis' statue of Apollo, and to stop at Troy if the winds hold off. Will I ever see Colchis? No matter. It's for that we have painters and poets. And sons.

CHAPTER 37

Home

Pericles met the fingertips of his friends with his own, among them Andocides, Teisander (surprisingly close), Lysicles (a new friend), Pyrilampes (a friend again?), and Anticles (always a friend). The King Archon of Athens had come to Piraeus to greet him. General Phormio had been fighting in the west that summer—he must be here somewhere. General Hagnon, behind the Archon, caught his eye and smiled—the man was like a son to him. And at Hagnon's shoulder, Xanthippus. He felt a surge of affection and pride—Hagnon must have found him useful or the boy wouldn't be near him.

He was in a hurry to talk to Xanthippus. Crossing from the Black Sea, he had decided to take up problems of state with his son as he did with Damon, Hagnon, and Aspasia. Hagnon had written that Xanthippus fought bravely against barbarians. True, he hadn't stayed on hand to establish the new colony but he had ridden north with a small squadron, harassing the natives and enlarging the perimeter of safety—and that too was an essential task.

He embraced Hagnon and, turning to his son, gripped his shoulders and looked him in the eyes. It was like looking at Aristocleia. She claimed that he didn't pay enough attention to his son. He would now—Xanthippus had earned it. He would explain the arguments for and against proposals before the Demos. Xanthippus would understand how he arrived at decisions and how he governed the city. The boy would admire him.

In the midst of his thoughts, he noticed General Phormio approaching.

Nor would he forget to ask Xanthippus his opinions because men love to be asked their views. In return, Xanthippus could keep him in touch with what people were talking about in the palaestra since he spent so much time there.

"Pericles." Why was Xanthippus accosting him at this moment?

Pericles disguised his annoyance with a tight smile. "We have much to discuss—later."

"It's important—"

"See me at home tonight."

"I want to talk about—"

Embarrassed by his son's persistence, Pericles turned aside but Phormio had moved away.

If it weren't for that squall, they'd have reached Athens before noon. Now the sun was halfway to horizon and it would be twilight before he reached the Acropolis.

Teisander tugged his cloak. "We need to speak."

He managed to find another smile at the end of a deep breath since in a few years Xanthippus would marry Teisander's daughter.

"Don't tug Pericles' cloak," Anticles said. "He doesn't like it."

"Come to me tomorrow morning," Pericles told Teisander.

Xanthippus stood before him again. "Why didn't you talk with Teisander?"

"I've only just arrived. Whatever it is must wait."

"Everything you want is done right away and everything I want has to wait."

His son, Teisander . . . Hades!

Xanthippus put Pericles' fear into words. "I'm marrying Eucleia next month."

"Marry!" He hoped his astonishment would shame Xanthippus into dropping the subject.

"Teisander agrees . . . or will if you agree . . . "

"You haven't built your reputation."

"I protected the new colony at Amphipolis."

Pericles caught Andocides' eye and forced a smile.

"Hagnon protected the colony, not Xanthippus."

"I enriched the goddess."

"She won't notice a few pieces of silver."

"Gold!"

The animals that would be sacrificed to honor his homecoming had not yet reached the precinct.

"You're too young to marry."

"Glaucon married young."

"At twenty-six. You are twenty-two."

"He was twenty-five."

"Shh!" Pericles looked around. "A man marries at thirty. I did."

"It's different now."

"It's no different. Our cousin Euryptolemus was thirty-one. Lacedaemonius was thirty-two."

"That doesn't concern me."

That was the trouble with Xanthippus—others did not concern him.

"You're arguing with me—"

"You're trying to stop me from doing what I want."

The King Archon was approaching.

"And in public."

Pericles embraced his son—people understand that—but turned from him unsmiling. Xanthippus would see him march into the precinct ahead of everyone except the King Archon and the Priest. It was he—not the Archon nor the Priest, and certainly not Xanthippus—who had secured the Black Sea grain supply.

It was hot before the altar after being on the sea.

"What's keeping us waiting?" Pericles asked.

A messenger informed him that the pig had bitten the ram and they were bringing in an unblemished ram for the sacrifice.

Why was no second animal on hand?

Pericles shaded his eyes and looked toward the Acropolis, his thoughts arching like an arrow to the gold and ivory Athena dwelling, now, in his temple. He told them he would forego the welcoming sacrifice.

With a loud crack, a wheel broke on the ride up from Piraeus, sliding him forward and knocking his arm against the side of the cart. Pain shot from his elbow to his shoulder. Carts should carry extra wheels like military wagons. He lacked the patience to wait for a wheel from Athens. "Take one from a supply cart." They could do without a perfect match.

Waiting beside the cart as the wheel was replaced, he rubbed his elbow. In the distance, two men sauntered down the side path of the Acropolis where, as boys, he and Sophocles had raced to the top. There were no shortcuts through time. First he must report to the Executive Council.

They stood and applauded as he entered. He lingered before speaking, feeling like the King of Persia. Hadn't he earned the right to test the pleasure of having all of them on his side for once? At least no one dared act otherwise. That's how it would feel if, just once, every vote went his way. "For Pericles' motion, five thousand votes. For Thucydides', none." It's with good reason that Greeks don't drink unwatered wine.

To work, Pericles.

"In obedience to the Council and Assembly, I led fifty triremes and ten cargo ships manned by eleven thousand crew, with one thousand hoplites and officers, eighty spearmen, seventy archers and sixty officials to the Black Sea.

"We return with new guarantees of friendship between Byzantium and Athens. To those who had doubts after Samos about the loyalty of Byzantium, I can say that rebellion is dead there. To prove it, the Byzantines have made a gift of one thousand bushels of wheat to the people of Athens, in my name.

"Heraclea, a small Greek city on the south shore, agreed to the sole rights for shipping their fir in our ships, with first option on the logs to Athens—we get a sure supply of highest quality for shipbuilding. They have no fleet and had been paying high shipping charges and we'll charge only a commission after sale, so the agreement benefits Heraclea as well as Athens.

"At Sinope—they call it the Jewel of the Southern Shore, but in fact it's the only city of any size or wealth on the southern shore— we liberated the people from the tyrant Timesilaus. Democracy now reigns there. We've heard that Timesilaus made his way to Persia where tyranny is at home. With Timesilaus out, the Sinopians chose to establish a democracy that adopts our institutions, so favorably do they view our ways. In fact, they've requested a copy of our written laws to use as a guide. The first act of their new Assembly was to vote one hundred talents to erect a monument to the Athenians for liberating their city. Let those who claim we enslave others witness the gratitude of the Greeks of Sinope to Athens the Liberator.

"At a small depot for spices and wood from the Asian interior, a few miles farther along the shore, we established a democracy and already have increased the population and supported their strength by recruiting volunteer colonists from Athens and our allies. So much do they love Athens—let those who claim we enslave cities bear it in mind—that the people renamed their city Piraeus with the hope their city will become as great a port on the Black Sea as Piraeus is on the Aegean.

"Now, on the north shore, Panticapaeum—which I know everyone likes to hear about—is the finest and richest city of the Black Sea and controls vast territory along the coast and well inland. It's less Greek than Sinope yet it tames the violence of the northern barbarians while securing the rivers, so that the raw materials of the barbarians are sent down through the rivers of Panticapaeum to the Black Sea and on to our own cities, and they receive our goods by the same route. Even the barbarians up there have a keen desire for works of Athenian manufacture."

Those gold pyramids . . .

"Wheat is so abundant that the warehouses overflow and they pile it outside on the quays in great pyramids. The ruler, Spartacus, entertained our whole army in tents decorated with rich woven hangings, like those from Persia but with different designs. We signed an agreement with Spartacus that all wheat he sends to Greece will move through our harbors at a regulated price. We get a sure supply of wheat at a fair price. We relieve Spartacus of shipping and distributing his grain, and they have ready access to the markets of our empire, that is, the cities of our alliance.

"Fifty triremes under oar in perfect order—most people there had never seen anything like it and won't forget it. Indeed, no one in the world has seen the like. I've heard about some losses Corinth suffered this summer. Wouldn't they like to have done half as well through war as we did peacefully. Yet I'm told that, for all their boasting, they limped home after losing many ships in fighting against General Phormio, and that two hundred of their men are prisoners in Corcyra.

"In contrast, the expedition to the Black Sea has been as useful for Athens as any military action since we fought Persia—and no Athenian lost his life."

He saved that for the end so they'd leave talking about it, spreading it around and stirring good feelings. With so many men expected in the full Assembly tomorrow, he could not anticipate the total approval he enjoyed from the Executive Council on the day of his return.

Since it was late, he and the other generals had to stay to dine with the Executive Council instead of just sharing the usual cakes.

By the time he reached his house, he was angry.

"Why didn't you write about this marriage?"

Everything had been done for his comfort. Aspasia had whitened her face, tweezed her brows and put on the yellow gown she saved for his homecomings. Her heart thumped with anger and disappointment. She'd seen him come home from victory sad but never angry, certainly not at her, never at her.

She pressed her wrist against the pitcher to test the coolness. "Whether they're Odysseus or Agamemnon, returning is hard for men."

"I expect you to keep me informed of everything important."

"I tell you all I know. If there's something I don't know—"

"I thought Aspasia knows everything."

"Generally I do."

He didn't let her see his smile.

"Everyone is saying your Black Sea trip was a great victory but you are angry as Ajax." She handed him a brimming cup. "*Who* wants to marry?"

"Xanthippus."

"I knew it."

"Then why didn't you tell me?"

"*Now* I knew it was Xanthippus. He's the only person who troubles you so." She didn't dare say "disappoints."

"He's my oldest son."

Aspasia shook her head slowly, exaggerating how sad she felt. "He's very young to marry."

"Young!" Pericles struck his palm on the couch. "He's barely past being an ephebe."

"How did you learn of this?"

"He insisted on telling me when I was greeting the officials."

"How embarrassing."

"Fortunately they looked away."

"I don't think it's widely known or I'd have heard."

"He must have spoken to Teisander since he claims he's agreed to it—if I'm willing."

"You can say you're not willing."

"I know what I can say."

"I was just remarking—"

"I know it amazes you, Aspasia, that even when you are not with me I manage to know what to say."

"Of course you—"

Not even Damon could wedge between them this way. She felt as angry at Xanthippus as Pericles did, for her own reasons. Her anger so distracted her that she started at the scratching on the door.

"May I enter, Father?"

They exchanged a look of surprise. Xanthippus had called his father Pericles from the time he was a boy. She could read in Pericles' face how amused and touched he was to hear "Father" spoken in his son's voice.

She moved to the door before he nodded for her to leave.

Xanthippus had dressed as if for a lover. That fine scent hadn't clung to him that afternoon. Pericles inhaled it—the scent of the oil was familiar, but he didn't recognize the ebony walking stick Xanthippus rested against the low table.

"Your campaign in the north did you no harm," Pericles said. "You look well. Being a soldier suits you." Pericles placed a cup of wine before him and took one for himself. "You're a credit to the grandfather whose name you carry."

Xanthippus shrugged.

"You have nothing to say? You had plenty to say in front of all the officials this morning."

Xanthippus ran his palms over his temples. The oil's scent—Ariphron's, Pericles palaestra-loving older brother.

"You don't want to hear what I have to say."

"I'm displeased that you want to marry so young."

"When I tell you how I know I must marry, you'll think differently."

"No, I won't."

How widely could you circle a cup without spilling the wine? Every day men spoke absurdities to him, and he listened patiently to please them. Reason enough to expect no such nonsense in his own home.

"Listen to me, Father."

Or was it the other way around—if he could be patient with others, why shouldn't he hear out his own son? Perhaps for once his son would be pleased.

"You fought well against the barbarians, Hagnon assures me. I put it in my mind that we should speak together more when I returned. I was thinking about matters of state."

"I saw her for the first time when we were escorting the holy objects from the Hall of Mysteries at Eleusis to Athens. I was so surprised."

"However—Where did you see her?"

"She's as beautiful as a painting—so is her mother. She was in Aphrodite's temple where we stopped, she and her mother were sacrificing. Other girls were there, but I could look only at her. That's how I know I must marry now." Xanthippus drained his cup.

"*Why* must you marry now?"

"I just *told* you." The dregs of Xanthippus' cup hit the lamp with a good ping. "I could look only at her."

Pericles brushed his cloak as though shaking off dust. "You think that because you looked only at Teisander's daughter is a reason to marry at twenty-two years?" He *was* hearing nonsense.

"I was compelled to look at her—I had no choice. That shows it's the gods' will—" Xanthippus caught his walking stick as it slid from the table. "Probably Aphrodite's since it was in her temple."

"I thought you and your friends don't believe that the gods drive us to action."

"Sometimes they do. But whether they do or not, why shouldn't I marry when I want? No law forbids it. I checked—I did, don't look so surprised. I went to the archives in the Royal Stoa and read the laws. They say nothing about when to marry."

"It's custom and that, too, has weight. However, I don't oppose your marriage simply because of custom but because it's custom backed by reason."

"Don't tell me it's because people will cast dark looks in my direction—not after the way you live openly with . . ." He gestured broadly toward the rest of the house.

"I thought Socrates and the other philosophers taught you to keep to a point, but you stray like a mule."

"So now I'm a—"

"As I was saying, custom with reason is doubly strong, like an army fighting a war on its own territory."

Pericles waited for his son to ask what reason there was for a man to marry at thirty, but Xanthippus was silent.

"A man has to build his reputation and his wealth," Pericles said. "The foundations are the hardest part, and they take all his force and thought, but a wife and children are demanding of a man's force and thought. You don't think it will be so, but it is. An older man is stronger than a younger one in this regard. He's had time to develop his manly habits. He's learned the custom of achievement. I've noticed that where the men marry young, people do little more than scratch a living from the soil, whereas we who marry late achieve greatly and bend others to our force and daring. So, my son, lay your trenches deep, set your foundation stones straight, let us see the courses of your temple rise. Then you can marry."

"I don't care about my reputation and I have your wealth."

"If you weren't my son, I'd end this conversation but since you are, I'll remind you that a man's reputation is never his to abandon. You owe it to the family that raised you and to the city that nurtured you. A man who pays no heed to his reputation doesn't live in freedom as some claim but in debt."

"You sound like Solon the Lawgiver."

"Thank you. As for my wealth, you live on my estates. When you've increased their worth, then you can bring your wife. Only in this way will none in our household have less."

"There'd be plenty for all of us if you didn't sell the crops to the tenants ahead of time and then send Euangelus out to buy what we need at Agora prices. You can only lose doing it that way."

"I do it to serve the city. What's your reason for letting it continue that way?"

"You could be rich as Hipponicus but you throw it all away. All you do is 'serve the city.'"

"I've always done my duty for my household. But a man must act in the way that seems best to him."

"That's all I want."

Pericles rubbed his beard. He considered telling Xanthippus he admired his determination—it was the truth. He would tell his son that determination is a virtue when it is directed toward a manly goal.

But Xanthippus would push the argument, forcing Pericles to state that to possess a desirable woman wasn't a manly goal. Inevitably that would lead to Aspasia and his own determination to live with her openly—Xanthippus wouldn't miss it.

So he withheld praising his son's determination.

"I'm not a stubborn man. Still, I can't allow you to act wrong-headedly. Wait a year or—"

"I don't want—"

"Hear me out. You fought well this summer at Amphipolis. You demonstrated yourself as a soldier. Now show me you can maintain the estates. Show me you can do better than Euangelus. Go with him for the fall sowing and negotiate the rents." Pericles bit into a plum and, raising his brows at its sweetness, extended the open fruit toward his son. Xanthippus turned away.

"Here's what I'll do," Pericles said. "I won't rent out the south orchard this year but let you oversee your own crew. You can take charge of the pruning next month, bed the roots—hope that it's not a cold winter—dig in the dung, smoke out the bugs, and see if you can grow plums sweeter than these."

"I'd rather work with the horses."

"You can do that, too. I'll put the stables in your charge, for now. But if you want me to reconsider this matter of your marriage in a year or two, you must get beyond the stables out onto the farms."

"Teisander is willing for the marriage now."

"Teisander is too eager for marriage with Pericles' family—his daughter is only fourteen. If you're to be her husband, you should think of what's best for her. That's too young for a girl."

"Teisander—"

"should be thinking of what's best for his own daughter."

Xanthippus squeezed a lump of wax from the wine seal. "While I'm in charge of the stables, can I purchase a chariot team to train for the Olympic games?"

"Out of the question."

"Why not? Uncle Megacles won the chariot race!"

"Megacles had a large fortune. If you want to race chariots, you'll have to make your own fortune."

"But that will take time."

"Get to it."

"I can't make a fortune in a year and then have to build a team for a chariot win—that takes too much time!"

"You don't have to win a chariot race to marry. I just want you to wait awhile, show me you can act like a man and run the estates."

Xanthippus held up the wax in his palm to see if it was round. "If I take charge of the stables, can I buy a new filly?"

"Star-nose is very fast."

"Not as fast as she was three years ago."

"You placed in that race."

"I took a third."

Xanthippus was a little old to race, but he was small and light. If he trained, he might yet take a first or second at the next Panathenaic Festival. And if Xanthippus did nothing with her, Paralus or Young Pericles could use the horse.

"We can buy a filly."

"Hippocleides has a group of Macedonian two-year-olds. I have my eye on a bay."

"Take your cousin Euryptolemus with you and follow his advice—that family knows horses."

"And in a year—"

"In a year I'll reconsider the matter."

"You'll talk with Teisander?"

"In a year. Examine the feet," he called after his son. "After you race her, you can use her in battle."

"I thought we were at peace," Xanthippus said from the corridor.

"We're never quite at peace."

He doubted Xanthippus heard him.

CHAPTER 38

The Dedication of the Gold and Ivory Athena

It seemed the whole of Attica—animals and men—gathered at the Dipylon Gate, so intense was the sweet, foul smell of creatures whose young drink milk. Pericles found things orderly as he walked along the line of the Panathenaic Procession, although a visitor might not have seen it that way. Nursemaids held umbrellas above the heads of young girls. Boys spun-dug amphoras into the sand, each contesting to be first to make his round-based jug stand on its own. The most handsome and distinguished older men—Sophocles among them—brushed away flies with green branches. Rich resident foreigners lined up behind the citizens, the lavish folds of their linen cloaks proof of the Athenian prosperity that held them here far from their own cities. Their sons wore gold in their hair, around their necks, and on their arms, and held trays of honeycomb and sesame cakes for the goddess. On the far side of the great gate, hoplites stood armed, visors raised until the last moment. Beyond them were sailors, beyond them archers, and after them those who, on the next day, would ride in the chariot games. Athletes in short chitons followed, their hair curled and their bodies oiled although their contests wouldn't take place until the next day or the one after.

The cavalry formed an honor guard for the sacred ship which was provided with wheels for moving on land. Pericles found his oldest son among the riders and patted his horse's flank; Xanthippus quickly brought the sidestepping animal back into line. The horse's tail was braided in five strands but the mane was loose and combed so fine that it looked like a girl's hair after she's washed it and dried it in the sun. Xanthippus loved to ride fast and believed that the fastest horses had the loosest manes.

Holding pens were opened; the bleating of sheep and lowing of cows grew louder as the animals pushed through the gates as if in a hurry. A horse whinnied at the cows and sheep.

How various it was compared with an army muster. Pericles rejoined the generals, all present in this summer of peace—all, that is, except Hagnon who was settling the new colony at Amphipolis in the north.

As the trumpets blared, Pericles turned his gaze to his goal. High and distant, the Parthenon shone with the whiteness of cut marble—only sun on water is brighter. Picturing the broad interior, he saw the gleaming gold and ivory Athena. He would like to dip his fingers in the pool in front of the Parthenon that Phidias had concocted to brighten the interior—not this day, when others would imitate him and turn the temple into a bathhouse, but someday.

Visors snapped shut. The whistle of the pipes rose above the clank and rattle of armor, the snorts of animals, the rasp of feet moving through sand and the commands of the marshals. The long column started forward. The slope that ran from the Dipylon Gate to the Agora was gentle, like an orator's first mention of things to come.

Some of the young men, Xanthippus among them, had trained their horses to mark the rhythm of the music with a slow trot. They rode directly behind the sacred ship. In front of them Athena's new peplos, the city's birthday gift to their goddess, billowed from the mast like a sail as if it were the wind and not the wheels and ropes of the Athenians that moved the ship along. Ahead, the police cleared out the entertainers who'd been amusing the crowd. The acrobats somersaulted away.

Entering the Agora today was like passing through a defile in the mountains, so tall were the stands, so loud the echoing of applause. *Where was Aspasia?* The parade slowed, a welcome pace in this month when the sun was hot as soon as it arose.

There she was at the top of the stands! Pericles' ward, Alcibiades, was in the center—that boy always knew how to grab whatever people considered best. Paralus held Aspasia's umbrella tilted against the sun. A kind boy, but soft. Alcibiades, though the same age as Paralus, would never hold a woman's umbrella.

At that moment, Aspasia raised her arm—she'd spotted him among the generals and was pointing him out for Little Pericles who stood next to her on the bench. The child jumped up and down with excitement. Pericles suppressed a smile at the sight of his small son wearing the small helmet they gave him on his name day.

Starting up the incline toward the Acropolis hill, the procession slowed again and halted when the front reached Demeter's temple. Each marshal relayed the signal to stop to the head of the next group in line the way, the poets say, the news of Agamemnon's victory had traveled from Troy to Greece.

Athena's peplos fluttered as libations were poured. Then boys clambered up the ship's mast and, as at sea when a ship shifts to oars for speed and precision, they drew in the peplos. The priests folded it on the deck, their garlands slipping forward on their damp foreheads. The precious cargo was handed down and placed in a fine cart with spoked wheels, the kind that carries a bride to her husband's house if there's any money in the family.

With the sailors hauling at the ropes, the ship executed its awkward turn, boys and men steadying it on its wheels. Cheers arose as, scraping the earth, it started up again, heading toward its home port, the sacred mooring near the hill of Ares. The cavalry escorted the ship while the rest of the procession continued up the Acropolis. The division of the procession at this point always seemed an imperfection to Pericles, but a ship, even a sacred ship, can't climb a hill.

Experiencing the incline as a weight on his thighs, Pericles threw back his shoulders and looked toward the top. Where the area had been cleared for the new entrance building, the blue sky touched the ground. To Pericles, who longed to see the entrance building completed, the empty space was like a missing tooth. Beyond, the Parthenon was hidden by the looming rock. Children ran beside the procession, veering off like dolphins swimming with the fleet. When they were boys, he and Sophocles had broken away and raced one another up the Acropolis hill.

After making the middle turn, the front of the procession paused to give those leading the animals time to catch up. The peak of the Parthenon pediment surfaced like a mast followed by the full hull emerging from the horizon. Anaxagoras the Philosopher said that this proved that the earth was thick like a large rock, not flat like a discus. The sun was a rock also, he said, and there were many rocky suns flung across the heavens. He'd seen pieces of these rocks that had fallen from the aether into a barley field. Judging by appearances, Pericles thought, it was hard to believe that the earth was not like a discus, but philosophers, while disagreeing about everything else, were of one mind that truth was not found in appearances. Like that young Philosopher Democritus who claimed that solid things were really void dotted with small pieces of matter . . .

The marshal raised a hand to catch the signal from the back and, spiraling in the toss, sent it forward. The animals had made the turn quickly. Past the debris pushed aside to make way for the new entrance building, the Parthenon came fully into sight—afloat though it was made of stone. Hera's temple at Samos, mired in a swamp, came to Pericles' mind. Temples should be built in high places.

Now came the second awkward split in the procession but—two temples, two Athenas—it was the best Pericles could arrange. Part of the line passed around toward the front of the Parthenon while Pericles led others toward the old temple. First the ancient Athena of the City would receive her gift. Pericles had decided it was not unreasonable—Dracontides' Athena *needed* a new peplos while *his* Athena was clothed in materials that would never fray, soil, or in any way show the rough fist of time.

Judging from his friendly greeting, Dracontides had also decided the plan to make an initial sacrifice at his temple was reasonable. The end of the procession circled behind the altar of the old Athena Temple like a gown trailing a dancer. The lyre took over from the pipe. Sunlight sharpened every fissure and broken edge of the building. In time, Pericles thought, he would rebuild this temple, too.

The cart with Athena's new peplos reached the steps and the gown was lifted onto the arms of the King Archon and the Priestess who followed Dracontides inside, a temple boy helping support the heavy wool. The girls also needed help bringing in the golden stools. The officials and after them everyone who could manage—those not carrying a large sacred object or a heavy jug—pressed through the narrow door. It became disorderly, even dangerous. He'd have it better ordered next time.

The image of Athena that Phidias and Aspasia disliked faced him. They were right that it was graceless—straight where a human being curves. And worse, he detected no sign of thought behind the eyes with their grape-round centers. How could a goddess see with those chipped pupils? But the Athenians loved her. It would take time for them to worship his new Athena with the same devotion. First they would revere her and when their pride in her had become one with their pride in the city—as it always had been for him— they'd turn their minds from this old goddess. Love doesn't always come quick as an arrow.

The Priestesses dressed the old statue in the new gown. Seeing the girls laying flowers on the statue's lap, Pericles glanced around for Cimon's elderly and over-perfumed sister—nowhere in sight, thanks to Zeus. The gates locked in the smoke from the lanterns, the incense, and the breath of many people. It was a relief when the King Archon turned from the statue and they followed him out, everyone rushing to regain the order of the procession as best they could while a few women stayed to arrange the peplos into even folds.

Dracontides had seemed pleased by the compromise of presiding as Honorary Priest at the sacrifices for Athena of the Parthenon in exchange for sacrificing the first cow at the old temple. Nevertheless, as Pericles watched a single animal being prepared at the vast altar, it looked like a bad ratio for Dracontides who was probably thinking the same thing.

The hair of the girl carrying the barley was so thick it rounded out behind her neck and billowed over her shoulders. *She must be Teisander's oldest daughter since she has the honor of carrying the basket.* Pericles hadn't expected the girl promised to Xanthippus to look so near to fully grown. She *was* a beauty, his son was right about that.

When she raised her arms to steady the basket, her breasts, already larger than Aspasia's, rose. He wished he could see her arms but her long sleeves were tight at the wrists. Still, he saw what his son had seen of her in Aphrodite's temple, and understood why a young man might be in a hurry to marry.

Dracontides' son lifted the basket from the girl's head—like Aspasia lifting away the weight of his helmet when he came home—and set the basket at the altar. Then he sprinkled barley over the cow; some nestled between the ears and some bouncing on the stone like sudden hail. Out of the animal's view, Dracontides lifted the knife from the basket, holding his hand between the knife and the sun so that no startling beam would leap from the blade to the animal's eyes. Deftly he slit the throat. The blood spurted so vigorously that it streaked the animal's white face and flanks, a good sign. But Pericles, who had often attended this sacrifice, suspected that it might have been too brief a ceremony to satisfy Dracontides. He'd better think of a way to even the ratio on Dracontides' behalf before the man thought of one himself.

Pericles had chosen to speak about the new Athena from the top step of the Parthenon so people wouldn't tire facing the sun. The sun would fall on him. Now he surveyed the crowd assembling around Phidias' long, reflecting pool. Those in attendance would tell others what he had said—from the Acropolis to the Music Hall, to the stadium, to the course for chariots and horses outside the Long Walls, to the harbors and beyond to open waters. Along with Athenian goods and stories of their adventures, travelers would carry his words home like pollen-loaded bees. But where was Dracontides? Evidently the priest felt he could do without listening to Pericles—no surprise there—and would arrive later to preside over the sacrifices of the rest of the cows.

The girls who'd woven the sacred peplos leaned in over the fence. Xanthippus should have been here—his son would have benefited from hearing his speech. But by now Xanthippus and his friends were racing their horses in the hills. Too bad, his son could have had another look at Teisander's beautiful daughter.

It was time to pour a libation and speak to the Athenians.

"We are standing where the invading Persians set their fires when they sacked our Acropolis to ruins. As a boy, I saw the flares color the sky as if we had two dawns in one day. And it *was* the beginning of a new day because we drove out the invader and established our freedom. Not content with securing our own freedom, we liberated our fellow Greeks in Ionia and vowed to maintain the freedom of all Greece against the Persians. Have we fulfilled that vow, Athenians?"

"We have fulfilled that vow!"

"We won through the help of the gods and the valor of men once young who are now the oldest among us. But the gods' temples remained in ruins, and the gods were deprived of their treasures stolen and carried off to Persia."

With a sweep of his arm—he'd borrowed the gesture from Phidias—Pericles created a whole for them out of all the work currently underway on the Acropolis.

"Today, in dedicating the gold and ivory Athena, we are repaying the gods."

He saw tears in the eyes of one of the girls near the gate. *Good— the young should know and weep.* He mastered the tightness of tears in his own throat with a careful breath. Still he paused, feeling joy surge within him.

"More people are attending this year's Panathenaic Festival than ever before. Every man's home is filled with family and guest-friends from abroad, our inns are full and tents have been set up beside the Long Walls. Athens has become like Olympia!"

Pericles heard pride mixed with amusement in their laughter. His own house was so filled with guest-friends that his steward Euangelus had brought in four servants from the country; the expense of feeding his visitors was considerable.

"Our Greater Panathenaic Festival now rivals the festivals of Olympia, Nemea, Delphi, and Isthmia in numbers and range of events!"

It occurred to him that just as Greeks held a sacred truce for the Olympics and the other festivals, they should do the same for the Athenian Greater Panathenaea. He would give it further thought.

"This is the greatest Panathenaic Festival because Phidias has completed the statue of Athena of the Parthenon. It contains more gold and ivory than any other statue in Greece, but its beauty goes beyond that of the costly materials. Athenians, this statue has the breath of divine likeness. When Heracles became a god"—Pericles beheld the wide blue sky—"and saw Athena waiting for him at the summit of Mount Olympus, this is how she appeared to him."

What was that savory odor?

"Like all virgins, Athena comes to us with something precious— Victory! Enter the temple, look upward and you will see Athena extending her gift of Victory toward us on her open palm, winged Victory, all in gold."

Something was cooking. What was it?

"This is also the greatest Panathenaea because our population is larger than ever before. Thirty thousand male citizens live in Attica, along with their wives, children and households. Add to that many resident foreigners whom we've welcomed here, and their families and households."

Fat searing—some animal.

"'Pericles,' you'll say, 'we all know that now Athens is by far the greatest city in all of Greece. But how do you know about the greatness of Athens or the numbers of our citizens in the past?'"

Beef.

"Homer tells us that the King of Athens led fifty ships to Troy but Agamemnon of Mycenae had one hundred ships. This proves that in the distant past, Mycenae, not Athens, was the greatest city in power and numbers—in power because Agamemnon compelled the other Greeks to sail with him, and in numbers because he had the largest force."

Beef roasting. Men were turning their heads to trace the smell.

"But we sailed against Samos with one hundred and sixty ships! All our own! And each ship carried more men than those that sailed to Troy for it's in men's nature to make ships larger over time. In the past, a large ship had fifty rowers but now our triremes have one hundred and seventy rowers and carry many armed men besides. Athens is the largest city in Greece, and only a Spartan would argue that we're not the most powerful."

People sniffing the aroma were catching one another's eyes.

"In the variety of events also this is the greatest Panathenaic Festival, as well as in their refinement. In the past, after the ceremonies for the goddess, the festival was over except for feasting. Now we have days ahead for men to prove their worth against others, providing refreshment for the spirit of citizens and visitors."

Someone called out, "Dracontides is preparing some refreshments, Pericles!"

"Once the chariot race, horse race, boxing, wrestling, discus, javelin throw, jumping, and running had no place in the Panathenaea but, over one hundred years ago, my kinsman added these and paid for the prizes. Later, we included contests for boys, so the young could look ahead to their full strength.

"'Pericles,' our visitors may say to me, 'you're fond of claiming that the other cities learn from yours, but all of these things were done first at Olympia, Delphi, Isthmia, and Nemea. How then can you call your city an education for the Greeks?'"

Teisander's daughter made a pad with her hands and pressed her cheek against it, looking toward the old temple.

"We initiated the contests for reciting Homer's poems, and for speed and precision in maneuvering ships—these Greece learned from us. Furthermore, we alone hold contests for dancing in full armor, and for manly excellence that celebrates the union of strength and beauty."

Gesturing toward the tent-like roof of the new Music Hall, he saw the smoke. By Hades! Dracontides was roasting the cow's thigh ahead of time.

"You would have to go separately to Delphi, to Delos, to Nemea, to Sicyon, to Corinth, and to Sparta to hear music such as you'll hear at our Panathenaea."

So much scent from a single roasting bovine thigh. Dracontides was evening the ratio alright—by distracting the crowd.

"Philosophers from many cities read their scrolls aloud at our Panathenaic Festival and sharpen their wits against the edge of argument in a contest of ideas."

They'd all risen before dawn and done plenty of walking, waiting, and climbing. Their hunger was high—and now came this hot, penetrating odor. He should round off his thoughts.

Light from the reflecting pool leaped upward. Joy kept him talking.

"I've heard artists say that to make an image of Aphrodite, they imitate the large eyes of one woman, the full lips of another, the fine shoulders of still another, and so on, creating the most beautiful goddess from many beautiful parts. In the same way, things of great worth for which men search the world—finding this here, that there—can all be found in our city."

A gust, a flare-up, and heads swiveled north. He had time—the beef would still be raw inside.

"On this day on which we dedicate the gold and ivory Athena, we can be proud that our new Athena doesn't wield her spear, but she does keep it near at hand. In this, we're like her for—"

His words sought to feed their minds and heighten their expectation—but he'd better finish fast.

"Now, Phidias is waiting to guide those of you who wish to see the statue as close as if you were the sculptor himself. Climbing the stairs so you will observe the gold Victory on Athena's palm, as well as the ivory Gorgon and Golden Fleece on her breast. Mounting another story, you'll reach Athena's helmet to see the griffins and the sphinx."

As the still temporary doors of the temple opened, the glints from the gold and the glare from the pool joined and flashed across Pericles' face like sunrise but, unblinking, he held his gaze to the brightest of all, the golden goddess. She stood tall as the walls of Samos, clothed in gold, her face and arms crafted in ivory so finely cut that Phidias alone knew how to do it. Pericles had seen the goddess several times, but his heart was pumping as fast as Pheidippides at the end of his long run across Greece. He felt that it was at this moment when the Athenians first filed past her, gazing upward with awe and love, that Athena's divinity finally suffused the Parthenon. She was an image born, he felt, from his own mind and heart, and created by Phidias, but the Athenians brought her to life. She seemed to have been waiting for them—not the way Aspasia waited at home for him alone, but for all of them. The thought brought him a joy, and the hard pumping of his heart subsided. He had completed a run he was born to race.

Although . . . about completing those sculptures for the temple's pediment . . .

He moved past the throng and stepped outside. Above the tall entry, the pediment of the Parthenon that would be populated by the Olympian gods was still empty—a desolate colony.

But the marble Panathenaic Frieze that showed the Athenians bringing gifts to their goddess as on this very day was fully populated. The carved priestess in the center, standing with her elbow tucked to her waist, reminded him of Aspasia—in the next moment she'd rest her chin on her hand. Alarmed, he looked to see if Phidias had intended a likeness. Did the ruling magistrate standing next to the priestess resemble himself? Hard to say. The two of them stood amid gods and heroes, their backs to one another but alert to each other's presence, like a husband and wife busy with the same sacrifice. The young attendants near them, of different ages, made it seem that he was looking up at his own family on Athena's temple. It would be hubris to say that aloud but fortunately the gods didn't look into a man's thoughts.

CHAPTER 39

An Injury to the Gods

"Phidias is in prison!"

The sculptor Alcamanes leaned against the column of the Council Hall, sucking in air.

"For what?" Pericles asked. Thoughts and fears—with rage at the top. "In prison for *what?*"

A withered drunk sitting on the steps looked around.

"Theft from the statue."

"Theft of what?"

"I don't know . . . must be gold."

"Who accused him?"

"Menon—that old guy."

Passersby were stopping to listen.

Death was the punishment for theft from the gods.

"You should have stayed with the statue."

"Agoracritus is there and the Acropolis guards."

Pericles sent Alcamanes to notify General Glaucon to bring in his ephebes-in-training to bolster the Acropolis guards and ran to the prison.

They were waiting for him.

"Here comes the thief!" Cleon, eyebrows straight and dark as a furrow, with a gang worthy of Thucydides behind him.

The Agora was well policed, and Pericles had nearly reached the prison gate. "False speech against a citizen is slander," he said.

Cleon stepped in front of him. "We'll see if they're false words!"

416

"You're acting against the law."

"Don't listen to him, Cleon," one of the gang called out. "There's no law against standing in a man's way."

"As long as you don't hit him," another said.

Cleon took a broad step toward Pericles. "There's no law against blocking the way."

"Our laws forbid hubris." Pericles stepped around Cleon who shook his fist but dropped back.

The corridor was stifling. Phidias was in the one cell that had two windows, a good sign. But Pericles' relief vanished when he saw Phidias' wrists were chained so tight that his gnarled knuckles were buried in swollen flesh. He feared for the hands that created the gold and ivory Athena.

"They want me to say I stole from the gods," Phidias said.

"Did you tell them that you didn't steal anything."

"They didn't listen—just dragged me here. Pericles, these chains are too tight."

"I will prove in court that you stole nothing." He beckoned the jailer, leaning against the door jamb. "Remove these chains."

"Prisoners must be chained." The jailer showed his open palms. "I'm sorry, General, but they'll prosecute me if I don't follow the law."

"Look at my hands, Tleson—they're purple," Phidias said.

Tleson—Pericles knew that name—but from where? "I'll have to prosecute you, Tleson, if Phidias can't fulfill his contract because he's injured here. What's owed the gods is theirs. An injury to Phidias is an injury to Athena. Remove the chains."

"But if Phidias stole from the gods . . . "

Ah yes, Tleson, who had served on his ship to the Black Sea. This must be his father. Pericles had set that boy up on a fine piece of land on the south shore. "How is your son doing on his farm at New Piraeus?"

"You remember my son!"

Pericles nodded. "Muscular but agile, fair hair, straight nose. He could have been a helmsman but preferred farming."

"My son's a rich man, General Pericles—rich in land, not in money but he says that will come."

"He'll be able to take care of his father and mother in their old age. You tell him Pericles wishes him good fortune the next time you send him news of home."

Phidias raised his bound hands toward the jailer.

Pericles nodded. "Now, Tleson, loosen those chains. Then you'll be on the right side of both the law and the gods."

Tleson looked at the chains, glanced at Pericles, pulled out his key, released some slack, tested that he could squeeze only one finger between Phidias' wrists and the chains and, with his eyes on Pericles, demonstrated it again.

Pericles nodded. "You're following the law, Tleson."

The relieved jailor turned host.

"General Pericles, can I bring you dates? cakes?"

"Bring Phidias water." When Tleson jumped to get it, Pericles turned to Phidias. "Stir the blood—move your hands."

With a quick turn of his head, Phidias signaled for silence—the cistern was across the corridor.

The jailer returned with a full ladle which he brought to Phidias' mouth. The sculptor kept his lips shut.

"He won't drink because the chains are causing pain," Pericles said.

The jailer inspected Phidias' hands and released two fingers worth of slack.

"Now, Tleson, we'd like to be alone."

"That's not against the law."

When Tleson left, Phidias breathed like a bellows, stretched like a ferret, and rotated his hands and feet like a dancer.

"Get me to Elis," Phidias said.

Phidias let his hands go limp: the chains were as slack as the spent strings of an old cithara. Pericles heard Phidias' silent message but chose another option.

"I'll have you back on the Acropolis in a day."

"My life's at risk."

"There's no risk—we'll weigh the gold."

"The ivory can't be weighed." Phidias worked to smooth a broken thumbnail with a fingernail. "Slivers are lost working it."

Pericles felt a stab of fear. "If the gold weighs forty-four talents, they'll be satisfied."

"Python of Elis has been here urging me to build their gold and ivory Zeus at Olympia." Phidias rotated his hands, fixing his eyes on them as if examining something new. When he had Pericles' gaze where he wanted it, he slipped the chain over the protuberant bone of his sweaty wrists, then back again. "Python stays in Piraeus at Mycerinus' Palace."

"If you flee, everyone will be certain you're guilty."

"Don't try to remove the ivory from the statue," Phidias said. "It will split and fray."

What a terrible turn of events—for the completed gold and ivory Athena, for the incomplete pediment sculptures of the Parthenon, for Phidias, for himself, for Athens.

"You vowed my pediment sculptures would be in place for the next Panathenaic festival."

"Alcamenes and Agoracritus can complete them with my drawings and measurements."

Pericles frowned. Phidias surpassed all sculptors in his ability to take an ingot of bronze, a bar of gold or even a hunk of stone dug out of a mountain and turn it into something that seemed alive—his gift was near to godly.

"They do finer work when you supervise."

"The figures will truly be my creations because I thought about them first. My *mind* gave birth to them." The strong, long, sculptor's fingers gripped Pericles' shoulders, demonstrating the tight hold Pericles should maintain on what he had said. "If you believe Anaxagoras that Mind is the force of intellect that sets the cosmos in motion, believe me about this."

Like Pericles himself, Phidias always had an answer.

"Fleeing will look like a confession. You'll never be able to return."

"Visit me at Elis—you can come for the Olympic games."

"You'll be deprived of your citizenship." Pericles grasped Phidias' forearms to keep his attention, to keep him in place. "People everywhere want most of all to be a citizen of Athens—they connive for it, they try bribery—and the only way is to be born to it." Well, that was basically true. Mostly true. Aspasia's desire for him to make their son a citizen came to mind. "Phidias, Citizen of Athens—you can't abandon that."

Phidias shrugged his way out of Pericles grip. "Think about Hippodamus—he was born Milesian, he stayed in Athens for years, now he's Thuriian. I spent eight years at Delphi—why? because I was working on a sculptural project. That's artists for you."

Pericles paced the four walls of the small cell. "You'll never set eyes on the gold and ivory Athena again."

Phidias' eyes closed. Was he restraining tears? Or seeing the goddess?

"My gold and ivory Zeus at Olympia will be the envy of all Greece."

Hades!

"I want the best sculptor for the Parthenon's pediments."

"Athenians turn against the best. Aspasia calls it Athenian mathematics."

"That's not true, Phidias. In your case—"

"They ostracized your own father."

"Nor for long—"

"Look what they did to Themistocles."

"Themistocles brought it on himself."

"They killed Ephialtes who, you like to say, taught you democracy."

"True."

"I hope I never hear at Elis that they've killed Pericles."

"Your mind is dark because of the events of one day."

"There's always a Menon to accuse a man."

"Menon won't weigh the gold."

"This matter won't be settled by the scale."

"But that's how we planned . . . *Why* won't it be settled by the scale?"

"Because it's you they're after. If Phidias went astray, it's easy for people to believe the same is true of Pericles."

"But we'll prove in court that neither of us went astray."

"If the gold weighs forty-four talents, they'll complain about the ivory—or someone will notice our likenesses on Athena's shield—and we'll never have any rest from it."

"There's a tactic for each battle."

"Look at the company he keeps, they'll say of you, whores, philosophers and sculptors."

"They've said it for years."

"Not thieves."

"Phidias." Pericles rested his hands on the sculptor's shoulders. "The gold will weigh forty-four talents, is that correct?"

"The gold will weigh the full forty-four talents we put into it—unless Anaxagoras has invented a way to make matter turn into aether."

"I don't want any of your jokes."

"It will weigh forty-four talents—unless they've shaved the coin this afternoon."

"I've made sure they can't. So then?"

"The gold will weigh forty-four talents."

They were both under attack, true. But it's one thing to be in chains and another to walk freely out of a jail. Phidias had the opportunity to create the gold and ivory Zeus awaiting him in Elis. Was it wrong to hold him here to finish the pediments, work in mere marble? Was it an injury to Zeus? If the gods commissioned their own sculptors, Olympian Zeus would undoubtedly choose Phidias.

Soon the jailer would be in with a lamp. Phidias would have dinner. In the bright light of afternoon, in the suddenness of events, it had seemed possible to have Phidias back on the Acropolis as if nothing had happened—a sponged error. But once night had marked off another stroke of time, would Phidias ever return to the Acropolis? In the dim cell, it had become impossible to picture a new day.

If he was going to contact Python of Elis, he'd better act fast. It's easier to get an accused man out of prison than a condemned one—not that Phidias would be condemned of course, but certainty is hubris.

Whatever Phidias had or hadn't done, *he* was their real target. It was unthinkable to let Phidias risk the hemlock on his account.

But could he, himself, break the law?

Pericles looked at Phidias long enough to hold his face in memory if that should be necessary.

Phidias held his gaze. "Everyone says that a good beginning is half of a good outcome." But then Phidias turned away. "And we're way past the beginning."

Why had Phidias diverted his gaze? To avoid accusation? Or to avoid an untidy release of aspirations, plans, memories, emotions, and knowledge of deep places in each other's mind that flowed between them, worse than useless in this place.

Pericles tried to press three drachmas into the jailer's palm for Phidias' extra ration of food and a good wine but, fist closed, the jailer refused his money.

Pericles felt uneasy that there was some way he hadn't thought of to protect Phidias so he patted the jailer's fist. "Keep in mind, Tleson, that any injury to Phidias is an injury to the gods."

The jailer looked at his hand, pressed the back of his fist to his lips and pressed that hand to his heart. "I will write my son in New Piraeus that General Pericles remembers Tleson, son of Tleson the jailer in Athens.

CHAPTER 40

Democracy

"We don't know for a fact that Phidias is guilty," Simon said to his friend Xenon.

"Obviously he's guilty—he fled," the barber retorted.

They were climbing the Assembly Hill for the emergency meeting the Executive Council had called to act on the accusation, lodged by the sculptor Menon, that Phidias had stolen from the gods.

Simon tongued his cobbler's nail to the other side of his mouth. "I'm waiting to hear what Pericles has to say."

"You're not going to hear from your beloved Pericles today."

"Why not? He and Phidias are close friends."

"That's why he won't speak. Anything he says about Phidias not being guilty will make everyone sure he's guilty himself."

"Just because they're friends doesn't mean—"

Xenon shook his head. "There's no way Pericles can speak, not here, not today. He's too implicated."

"General Pericles is not accused of anything."

Pushing past, always in a hurry, Cleon knocked Simon's shoulder. "Stretch them both on the rack—then we'll get the truth."

The cobbler's nail dropped from Simon's mouth.

"The rack for General Pericles—that's outrageous." Xenon put his hands over his ears.

Simon retrieved the nail. "Torturing a citizen is against the law, Cleon. You should be charged for suggesting it and I have a mind to—"

But Cleon was way ahead of them.

Pericles heard the Athenians shifting in their seats, coughing and rearranging their parcels—the familiar buzz reached his ears today like gnats searching out skin. There was no comfort for him today in the rituals that ushered in an Assembly because, by Zeus—his right hand gripped his thigh to contain the frustration—on this crucial day he was powerless to control the debate. Phidias was accused but he was the magistrate responsible for the gold and ivory Athena. The shadow of guilt fell on him, darkening how people would understand anything he would do or say. His enemies hadn't dared to accuse him—he was too loved. So they were trying to drag him down with a fabricated accusation against an easier target—Phidias.

He was bound by suspicion as Phidias, the day before, had been bound by chains.

Bound by suspicion but not constrained to silence—not officially. This Assembly would test his ingenuity. Where would he find his opening? As the Presiding Officer began to speak, Pericles's left hand clamped his right hand to his thigh, clamping in his mind the need for constraint.

Douris of the deme of Alopeke was President that day—that was to the good. He lived in town, going out to work his farm beyond the walls, and Pericles gave special trust to men who liked the city. Douris had no experience in government—good again, he'd made no alliances, perhaps. He spoke slowly for an Athenian which may have been why he'd never spoken in the Assembly until this day when the hand of democratic equality—the chance of the lottery— made him the Presiding Officer.

"Menon son of Lycaon of the tribe of Pandion and the deme of Acharnae, recently a stonecutter on the Temple of Athena Parthenos, known as the Parthenon, on the Acropolis, in the fourth day of November—" Douris looked up from his papyrus. "That is, yesterday."

Laughter. Shuffling of feet.

"Menon went to the offices of the King Archon and brought to his attention that Phidias, son of Charmides, had committed actions harmful to the gods—"

"Harmful to the gods!" Douris' next words were lost.

"—evidence to prove his charges, the King Archon authorized Menon to arrest Phidias, taking with him ten police, but stating he feared for his life, Menon—"

"Hurry up!"

"What's the charge?"

"What's the evidence?"

"What did Phidias *do?*"

"That's coming because Menon wants to speak for himself. But first I am to tell you—"

"Never mind you—let's hear Menon!"

"Let him speak!"

The herald pounded his staff.

"Menon!"

As Douris and the secretary of the Executive Council conferred, everyone got in on the chant: "We want Menon! We want Menon!" Pericles' right hand balled into a fist—how could he interrupt the rising clamor? They were confusing their enthusiasm to hear Menon speak with approval of the man himself.

And then—what an astonishing relief—Douris looked at Pericles with his eyebrows raised. In front of all of them, heedless of the hovering suspicion, Douris had sought his guidance. Immediately Pericles mouthed "Menon."

"I call on Menon," Douris said.

A burst of cheers—you'd think Menon was a favorite athlete.

General Hagnon leaned in toward Pericles to whisper, "What's Menon's great exploit?"

Menon also seemed to have visions of Olympic glory for he bowed low as if donning not a speaker's wreath passed from head to head but a wreath of victory.

He hoisted his shoulder to make the steps because of the shortness of his legs and the roundness of his belly—no athlete here. Phidias maintained Menon quit work on the Acropolis because he was too lazy to make the climb. That explained why he didn't arrest Phidias himself—he let others do his climbing.

With a glance at a patch of papyrus spit-glued to his palm, Menon began to speak.

"The King Archon prevailed upon me to bring a charge against Phidias and to tell you about his wrongdoing and ask the Assembly for an investigation. I didn't want to because I worked for Phidias many years."

Professing reluctance to accuse—an orator's trick. *Who's been coaching Menon?* Pericles asked himself, surmising the answer.

"Finally, though, I decided to say what I know, placing the good of my city first. Nor do I speak for personal gain, but I weep for the injuries Phidias caused the gods." Menon pressed his cloak to his eyes.

"What did he *do*?" someone called out.

"What's it all about?"

"Let Menon calm himself," someone else said.

Menon took a long breath. "The Athenians gave—" He glanced at his papyrus, and started over. "General Pericles gave to one man, his friend Phidias, the job of planning the construction of all the works on the Acropolis and keeping the records. Phidias has the custom of working at night to complete the work in a timely way, or so he says. Because he calls the Athenians impatient and inconstant, and told me he feared that if the work wasn't done quickly, you'd give the job to someone else or drop it entirely."

Stir up indignation. *Another orator's trick.*

"He worked on the records at night, for we sculptors don't trust lamplight for making images but it's good enough for keeping accounts."

"Pericles keeps his accounts in the dark!" Cleon shouted.

"No wonder he makes mistakes!" Some crony making sure no one missed Cleon's point.

Pericles was enraged—he'd never made an accounting error. But he was practiced at riding out taunts.

"Silence!" The herald pounded his staff.

"What were those so-called *necessary expenditures* you never told us about, Pericles!" Cleon brayed.

Douris signaled to Menon to continue.

"Now my house is on the road to Acharnae—past the cemetery, on your right hand heading north—where I have my shop and can provide you with an image of any of the gods, of horses or other animals, whatever temple gifts you may require. Also I make hands, ears, feet, legs, wombs, breasts, eyes, and so on for dedications to the healing gods and—"

Laughter.

"What did Phidias do wrong, Menon?"

Menon nodded. "Then, however, I was working on the gold and ivory statue of Athena and I had to live near because Phidias kept us working from sunrise to sunset. On this night, my wife's sister had come from Acharnae to sell charcoal and, since it was a warm day, she set out with only a light cloak, but it turned cold and, with my wife complaining that we didn't have enough warm cloaks in the house, I recalled the wool cloak I'd left on the Acropolis. After hearing awhile from both on the subject of warm cloaks, I went up to the Acropolis to get it. The guards recognized me, of course, and I went on to the workshop. Lamplight was coming from under the door so I assumed Phidias was inside.

"I scratched on the door and—no answer—scratched again. I thought maybe he left the lamps to burn out, and when I kicked open the heavy door, there was a loud noise. I was startled! On the hill at night, with the lamp lit but nobody there, I thought of ghosts. But then I saw the wind that came in with me had blown over the scale along with a piece of dried fish that must have been in the scale pan—that's what made the noise."

Chasing the pace of events, Menon speeded up.

"I ran over to pick up the scale and set the balance, and while I was trying to make the fish look alright, I noticed my slate on the table. That day a piece of ivory tusk had arrived he planned to use for Athena's face."

The ivory tusk . . . Pericles thought back to the day he and Phidias had rowed out to the Syrian merchant who'd sold the ivory to Athens . . . they'd met him on his boat in Piraeus Bay . . . they'd climbed down to the hold, seen the tusk . . . Phidias had fallen on his knees as if he worshipped . . .

". . . and set it on the balance and I wrote down the weight. My number was there but lined out—yes, lined out! And another number written beside it. I was more startled than when the scale fell. Wherever he is, I thought, he'll be right back and he'll kill me!

427

"When I picked up the scale—my hands were shaking—I saw on the table the leather sack that held the ivory tusk and next to it a pile of ivory coils, like lemon peels only thinner. No one can slice ivory as thin as Phidias—he invented how. I wanted to make sure that the wind hadn't scattered any or he'd suspect someone had been there, but I was scared and ran out. And I still didn't have my wool cloak. Even on the run I knew what I'd seen and that Phidias was guilty."

Ivory . . .

Not a word about gold, Pericles thought. The gold that honored and beautified Athena was part of an emergency war fund and for that reason, Pericles had instructed Phidias to design the statue so that the gold could be removed and weighed. When the war was over, the money could be recouped and the gold restored to the statue. But not the ivory. Phidias had formed the face and hands of Athena of ivory, pale, fine and as a natural woman's skin. It could not be removed, weighed like gold and set back in place—not without destroying the statue. Surely the Athenians wouldn't destroy the gold and ivory Athena that was already drawing many visitors who came just to set eyes on her. Athena was paying the Athenians back for every drachma they'd spent on her.

"After that, Phidias stopped checking the materials off with me when they arrived Instead, he waited until night to weigh and list them himself."

Douris leaned forward. "Why didn't you reveal this wrongdoing as soon as you learned of it? Your delay has increased the cost to the Demos."

Someone shouted, "He already said he didn't want to accuse a friend!"

Whose voice? Pericles held back from turning and revealing his concern.

"Everyone knows people fault a man who reports a friend's wrongdoings even if that friend injures the city. So I kept my knowledge to myself, like the Spartan boy who held the fox under his cloak, even though it chewed away painfully at his chest."

The Spartan boy and the fox story—some Athenian Spartan-lover had been coaching Menon. It could have been Lacedaemonius, son of the general whom Pericles had prosecuted for bribery. Or Melesias, son of his nemesis Old Thucydides. Or both. In league. These sons of his enemies—he'd never be done with them. It was like a play by Aeschylus where sons avenge fathers to the ends of generations.

"Finally, though, I decided I must speak out for the good of our city because I remembered the words of Solon our Lawgiver." Menon glanced at the papyrus in his palm. "'The best city is one in which those who are not wronged are as zealous in prosecuting and punishing wrongdoers as those who are wronged.'"

But for describing events in the studio, Menon had not needed to refer to his papyrus. Pericles felt a stab above the liver.

The herald pounded his staff. Douris studied his papers and, buoyed by his presidency, steered the Assembly back to the alleged theft. "Menon has accused Phidias of stealing ivory intended for the goddess and proposes that the Assembly hold a full investigation into events surrounding this theft and the flight of Phidias and, if warranted, to try Phidias."

"It's warranted!" Menon called out.

"Don't forget the gold!" Cleon yelled out. "It's not only ivory—it's gold!"

Pericles flushed, thrilled. The gold could be weighed. Numbers are proof. He had considered signaling Hagnon to speak about the gold—how much better that Cleon had done it.

The secretary pointed to Menon's original accusation. Douris examined it. "Menon's accusation is that Phidias has stolen ivory. There's nothing here about gold."

"But he said gold," Cleon shouted. "Gold's worth more."

"Ivory's worth more!" someone called out.

"It's all worth a lot," Douris said.

"We must investigate the theft of gold!" Not to be missed, Cleon waved his arms above his head and turned full circle. Inwardly, Pericles cheered him on like a runner at the games.

"Will you include in your accusation that Phidias stole gold, and to include that in the investigation?" Douris asked.

Menon bit a fingernail. "Well, he stole more ivory than gold."

In the silence, someone called out, "Menon, maybe he just stole that dried fish!"

There was some laughter.

"He's afraid to be fined for falsely accusing a citizen," Hagnon whispered to Pericles.

"He'll figure the Spartan-lovers who put him up to this will pay his fine."

"Menon, will you add gold to your charge?" Douris asked. *Zeus, put "yes" into Menon's mouth.* Pericles' silent prayer.

"Yes, Phidias stole ivory and gold."

I'll remember, Zeus.

Dracontides sought urgently to speak next. As priest of the ancient Athena of the City whose temple was across the way from the Parthenon, he had fought the creation of the gold and ivory Athena as if he owned the Acropolis. Douris recognized Dracontides.

"I favor Menon's proposal to investigate the theft of gold and ivory. But this man Phidias is only a mere artisan following orders. You assign magistrates to oversee costly works, including the magistrate responsible for the construction of the gold and ivory Athena."

Dracontides gave them time to follow his gaze to Pericles. Every man there knew that Pericles was the magistrate—they'd elected him to it.

The gold will weigh the full forty-four talents we put into it. Pericles carefully traced Phidias' words in his mind as if they had been cut into stone.

"Therefore, we must be prepared to hold those in charge complicit, whatever their high rank, whether for failing to oversee Phidias' actions or for themselves profiting from thievery.

"As our General from all the Athenians—" again Dracontides looked directly at Pericles who returned an unblinking stare. "—as Pericles himself takes every opportunity to insist, in our Democracy, no man is above the law, no matter what high positions he holds.

"Now, Athenians, this is not ordinary theft. For example, if a man makes off with a sausage when the seller's eyes are turned the other away—that's ordinary theft."

"What about when the tanner charges you for kidskin and gives you a goat's udder like Cleon did to me?" someone called out. "Is that ordinary theft?"

Pericles learned there that Cleon, his newest enemy, was a tanner.

"What about when Laches steals my grapes for his wine—is that ordinary theft?" someone said.

The herald pounded his staff.

"Or when Hermippus steals my jokes for his plays?" the comic poet Cratinus called out.

"Or when Hipponicus steals Pericles' wife?" was Hermippus' retort.

Hagnon kneeled beside Pericles to give him the steadiness of a triangle. It was unnecessary of course, though well meant.

Dracontides ignored the laughter. "When men steal from the gods, that's an extraordinary matter. And that is what we face—theft from the gods. To steal from Athena—" His voice broke.

The Assembly was attentive.

"Therefore, prosecution for this extraordinary crime calls for extraordinary measures. For this matter goes way beyond goat udders."

No one laughed at the mention of udders.

"Thus, the magistrate responsible for the gold and ivory Athena must turn over to the Council all accounts of expenditures in material and labor for the Goddess. Add this to Menon's call for investigation."

Dracontides had turned the searching lantern of investigation on Pericles. The words had a vindictive cast, although Pericles knew that it was ordinary and lawful for a magistrate to turn over his accounts for investigation. He had himself undergone examination of his accounts as General and for his several magistrate positions. And he was confident that, because of his diligence, his accounts were accurate and correct. Sometimes his sons teased him about the time he spent with his head bent over his accounts, checking and cross-checking. He had done it for occasions such as he now faced. He must tell them so.

But Dracontides was not finished. "Furthermore, it would be unworthy for trials involving this unholy theft to be carried in our ordinary law courts in the Agora. Add this: the juries for trials shall be specially selected and the trials shall be held on our holy Acropolis, with the jury casting its ballots at the altar of my temple of Athena of the City, and with ballots sanctified in my temple of Athena of the City."

Pericles' hand gripped his thigh. Dracontides' unprecedented departures from the law were wreathed in piety—the hardest rock for an orator who bases his arguments on reason.

Excited and impressed, the citizens were murmuring among themselves. "special jury . . . altar of Athena . . . sanctified ballots . . . Athena of the City . . . "

Douris put his hand to his ear and leaned forward. "Did you really say that trials that arise from this investigation should be held on the Acropolis?"

"Yes, with ballots sanctified by Athena of the City and—be sure to get this in—we'll count the ballots at my temple of Athena of the City, not at that new Parthenon."

I must explain to them the dangers of violating their own procedures. But no matter what Pericles said, he would seem to be defending himself. Which would make his guilt seem more probable. Though he had been accused of nothing. He felt like one of those Babylonian slaves with his tongue cut out.

With his arms spread wide so that his cloak fell like sheets of water, Dracontides turned the full arc of the Assembly—you'd think he was Zeus welcoming Heracles to Mount Olympus. "Oh Athenians, let us climb her sacred hill and in the presence of my Athena of the City—the true Athena—try these cases of theft of her holy things. Thus we can punish the perpetrators of this sacrilege."

"Do you have all that?" Douris asked the secretary who, scribbling fast, nodded.

Special ballots and a change of venue would instill fear and self-importance in the jurors, a powerful and unpredictable combination.

Preparing for the vote, Douris was conferring with the secretary.

How much they needed his guidance to stay on the path of reason!

The herald pounded his staff although all was quiet.

Pericles drew his right hand free from under the left.

He must speak. There was no one else to do it. He could not brief Hagnon in front of the others—and Hagnon would not know how counter Dracontides' religious fervor. Anyhow, among all the Athenians, he best understood the law.

Pericles raised his hand. "I wish to speak concerning the investigation."

In the stunned silence, Simon's words rang loud. "I told you he'd speak up, Xenon!"

Pericles took his place on the bema.

"Though I have been accused of nothing and have done no wrong, some may think I've risen on my own behalf. But I am not here to defend myself. I am here to defend the law.

"I believe an investigation is called for because I welcome truth, and for that reason I propose that for any trials arising from this investigation, we must maintain our customary legal procedures with the firmness of Odysseus at the mast, avoiding the Sirens' call of diversions.

"Therefore, here is what the decree we pass today should state— and may the secretary please note this: 'The Assembly requires an investigation into the accusations made by Menon, and that for the investigation—'" he took a moment to clear his throat, he simply had to—"'the magistrate responsible for the gold and ivory Athena shall turn over his accounts'"—Pericles continued over the gasps of surprise and hoots of derision—"'and that if trials arise out of the investigation, they shall be held in our true courts of law in the Agora, with ballots and ballot counters approved by the state.'

"Now some may ask, 'What's wrong with trying cases on the Acropolis?' 'What's the harm in special ballots?' 'Who cares where we count them?' I even heard, 'What difference does it make?' But it *does* make a difference, and it is wrong.

"If I asked Dracontides what advantage he sees in trying cases on the Acropolis, I believe he would say that the jurors, impressed by the sacred site, would hear the arguments with heightened attention and arrive at their judgment with an exceptionally diligent weighing of evidence." Noting that Dracontides was in heads down, ear-to-mouth conversation with his brother, he added, "Isn't that what you would say, Dracontides?"

Dracontides didn't hear he was addressed until, at a nudge from his brother, he looked up and nodded vigorously, though by then Pericles had moved on.

"If we adopt this novel procedure, it will cast into doubt all past judgments arrived at in our courts. In addition, it will make suspect all future judgments reached according to our legal system, in our new and costly courts in the Agora.

"Consider this, Athenians—if we need special ballots sanctified in Dracontides' temple for this case of theft, why is anything less called for in, let's say, a trial of adultery, since a man can be executed for adultery?"

"Do you think they can execute Phidias for this theft?" Simon asked Xenon.

"Not if they can't get their hands on him."

"Pericles says adultery is as bad as theft of holy things," Dracontides called out. "He should be tried for sacrilege!"

The herald pounded his staff.

"After he's tried for theft of holy things!" Cleon shouted.

"We all know the sculpture in our Agora of the man whose arm demonstrates the standard length of a cubit." Pericles extended his right arm and touched the center of his chest with his left to represent that exact cubit measurement. "Weavers test their lengths of cloth against our canon of measurement to show customers they're getting what they're paying for. Architects ensure the accuracy of their measuring rods by testing them against our true cubit.

"Athenians, the law is our measuring canon. It protects men because it does not change. We must hold the rod to the measure. This is the way of reason."

"I object," Dracontides called out. "I'm not changing the law, just modifying the procedure for a sacrilegious—"

The herald pounded his staff.

Some would follow his argument about the canon of law, Pericles knew, but he had to take on his opponent directly.

"Now, Athenians, as a military commander, when I receive a message in the field, I always consider not just the message but the messenger, and so I ask who is Dracontides who seeks special juries for trials with his special ballots to take place in his Temple of Athena of the City instead of in our courts, and those other unprecedented procedures he's advocating? You may say, we all know Dracontides as a distinguished Athenian citizen who as a young man fought valiantly in the cavalry.

"And, like his father and his father's father, Dracontides is the Chief Priest of Athena of the City whose cult is practiced in the old Athena temple—the place he specified for trying these cases—a remarkable coincidence! For it's at the altar of this temple, which he often calls his temple, where the special ballots are to be both sanctified and then cast by his special juries, an altar sacred to the Athenian people that he evidently believes is *his* altar. And another remarkable coincidence—that Dracontides is priest of the temple where he plans to count the special ballots!

"You may ask whether I am suggesting that an upstanding citizen like Dracontides would produce false ballots or subvert a vote? Keep in mind, Athenians, that many distinguished citizens have endured accusations of dishonesty and worse—fairly or unfairly—because, as I have reminded you often, in our democracy the laws are the same for all men.

"But I am not accusing Dracontides of harboring such dishonest purposes as to falsify the vote for personal reasons—perhaps to punish those who have built the new Parthenon and the image of Athena, in gold and ivory, that dwells there. Nor am I suggesting that others who derive their livelihood from Dracontides' temple— the caretakers and temple boys and the women who instruct the young girls who weave the cloak—would aid him in such a purpose.

"I do not fear that such things *will* happen but that they *could* happen. For this reason, I urge that any trials arising from the investigation shall be held in our lawcourts in the Agora according to our usual procedures.

"Anything else, Athenians, would be illegal."

"Who wishes to speak?" Douris looked directly at Dracontides who, having made the amendment to the decree Pericles wished to reverse, had the right to speak.

But Dracontides was slicing the air vigorously with his right hand while his brother, lips compressed, his face turned from Dracontides, emphatically shook his head. When Dracontides started to rise from his seat, his brother grabbed his arm. Amidst laughter over the public argument, Dracontides stood again and approached the bema, adjusting with one hand the cloak slipping from his shoulder and waving his walking stick with the other.

"Those who are free of guilt have nothing to fear from Athena's scrutiny. It's she, not I, who'll keep watch over the trials carried out as I've proposed. As for those who find something illegal in ballots sanctified by the Goddess, I can only say—" He breathed deeply as if requiring extra strength from the life-giving air. "This is what comes from allowing men who call themselves philosophers to stroll the Agora speaking at will, proclaiming false doctrines that the Earth is a stone and that Zeus is a vortex and so on and on to the point where one might live as well without the gods as with them. If this is what reason teaches, then I say let reason reside in Hades and leave the Athenians to return to the piety of our fathers and our fathers' fathers that has guided us to victories over our enemies and a position of preeminence in the world."

Dracontides moved forward as if ready to step down from the bema but then changed his mind.

"And these men who are forever posing questions about the gods and formulating absurd answers, these and their followers are the same men who dare to question the integrity of those who serve the cults of the gods, men such as myself, and who accuse honest priests of trying to use their position for self-serving ends."

"No one accused you of anything," Damon called out.

"My proposal takes these trials out of the control of those who forever scurry between the Executive Council, the courts, and the city offices—Agora rats, I call them—paying others to tend their farms while they make the city's business their own private business. Well, that's something of another matter and I'm only concerned with what's best and those who accuse me—"

"You haven't been accused," Damon shouted.

"I *have* been accused—Pericles said I wanted the ballots sanctified by Athena of the City because I am her priest and accuses me of forging ballots or hiding them or—"

"He said a person *might* do that," someone called out.

"You should listen to what's going on, Dracontides!" Damon shouted

The herald pounded his staff.

"Everyone knows I'm Priest of Athena of the City so by saying—"

Again the herald's staff.

"We cannot have arguments between the speaker and the Demos," Douris said. "The herald will eject the next citizen who speaks out of turn. Now finish up."

"When an honest man can't talk before the Demos without having his reputation . . . " Dracontides was shaking. "They, not I, have committed theft and yet I'm accused—"

"You aren't accused," someone called out.

Some turned to see who'd spoken but he'd disappeared into the crowd.

"You see! you see! That's why I want these trials on the Acropolis! The Demos is a child who needs the rod!" He stepped down from the bema. "You're fickle as the wind!"

Here's to a quick vote! Pericles took a deep breath from below the ribs so no one would notice how little air he'd drawn during Dracontides' speech. With a long gaze he answered "no" to a question he saw in Damon's eyes. No more speeches.

"Whoever wishes to speak to this issue must do so now, so we can complete our agenda." Douris gave little time for a response and—ignoring Cleon's hand—called for the vote.

"Raise a hand, all who favor an investigation into the accusations of theft of gold and ivory made by Menon, and that the magistrate responsible for the gold and ivory Athena shall turn over his accounts, adding in Dracontides' provision that if trials arise out of the investigation, they will be held on the Acropolis with a special jury who will cast ballots sanctified by Athena of the City's priest at the altar of Athena of the City with the ballots counted at the temple of Athena of the City."

The hands went up fast. "Cleon—You can't raise two hands!" Damon called.

The vote counters met and conferred and reported to the secretary who handed the report to Douris who nodded and gave it to the herald.

The herald faced the Assembly. "In favor of the proposal with Dracontides' provision, two thousand, four hundred and thirty-eight."

"Continue the vote," Douris told the herald. "And speak that last part very loud to make sure they see the difference."

"Raise a hand, all in favor of an investigation into the accusations of theft of gold and ivory made by Menon, and that the magistrate responsible for the gold and ivory Athena shall turn over his accounts, adding in Pericles' provision that *if trials arise out of the investigation, we shall hold them according to our customary procedures in our true courts of law in the Agora, with ballots and ballot counters approved by the state.*"

There he was, sitting through another long, painfully suspenseful vote count. For the moment, he wished that there was a canon of measurement for the noise made by an Assembly vote. He could just deposit the loudness of two votes in the balance and know the result immediately instead of this interminable wait for counting, checking and conferring. But the senses can't be measured like a piece of cloth. Hearing, vision, smell—they can all delude a man. And touch. That first summer of his love for Aspasia, while he was away with the army, Damon had placed a cup of wine in his hand and suddenly he had felt Aspasia's breast resting on his palm, flooding his body with searing desire. The weight of that breast—remembering that passionate longing, it seemed to him that his desire to win this vote weighed equal in the balance. He found a smile for the thought.

Douris was handing the report to the herald.

Pericles' heartbeat doubled.

"In favor of the motion with Pericles' proposal, two thousand, five hundred and fifty-nine."

Hagnon rose from his seat, excited. "You won!"

Pericles calculated he'd won by one hundred and twenty-one votes. *Only* one hundred and twenty-one.

General Phormio, nearby, asked, "Was that five hundred or nine hundred?"

"Five hundred," Hagnon answered.

Phormio shrugged. "Close vote."

"We got enough votes to win," Hagnon replied. "That's democracy."

Hagnon's right, but with reason on my side and a foolish adversary, I should have had a bigger win, Pericles thought. Men had heard his words but failed to follow his logic. Was that why he felt disappointed? Or was it because he had expected more loyalty from the Athenians? More love?

What nonsense, Pericles. He shook off those dispiriting thoughts. The investigation would be held without whipped-up piety or self-serving sanctifications. Objective measurement of the weight of the gold would reveal the truth.

CHAPTER 41

Shooting from a Kneeling Position

He sipped the iced wine Aspasia gave him in his favorite cup, pushing aside thoughts of the cost of ice. But he wondered if Phidias had time to drink the expensive wine he'd arranged for him in jail before fleeing.

"What a battle you've won today!" Aspasia exclaimed. "How did you do it!"

"It wasn't only what I said, but what I didn't say."

"That's the way with a good speech."

"And even better—what I said I didn't say."

"What you said you didn't . . . ?" She was frowning, puzzled. He was pleased since it was not easy to puzzle Aspasia.

"I mean that I didn't accuse Dracontides directly. The man has too much credit with the Demos. So I merely suggested the possibility of a dishonest outcome and it worked."

"Pericles, it must be hard to always have to speak so carefully."

"To speak so carefully . . . " His unspent anger rose to the surface, followed by the fatigue of restraint. He closed his eyes.

When tired now, he looked old. It was too soon, their son was still a child. She reached to stroke his forehead but her hand stopped mid-air when he abruptly opened his eyes. "Sometimes before speaking, Aspasia, I pray to Zeus that no matter what occurs, I remember what I want most. Like Perseus' cap, it protects you from all dangers."

"I feel the same way."

"Protected from all dangers?"

"Yes—as long as I keep in mind what I want most."

He smiled and drank deeply into his cup until the picture painted on the bottom of a girl swimming came into view. He swilled the wine, setting the swimmer in motion, then took another sip to get down to where he could get a clear look at the naked girl, her body gliding in a long stroke.

"Some philosophers say you're safest if you don't want anything," he said.

"That's not my way of thinking!"

"Nor mine!"

They laughed about the ways they were alike.

Still smiling, Pericles rested his head back against the cushion. Could he have imagined laughing with a woman—not merely at something amusing, as one might with a hetaira, but with shared understanding? What a remarkable turn Aspasia brought to his life. Hastily brushing past the memory of his former wife's steady hostility, he recalled his early fascination for the princess Nausicaa in Homer's *Odyssey*. As a boy, gazing at her picture on his parents' painted amphora, he had loved her, but she was just a girl in a story.

They had been talking about wanting things. He reached for Aspasia's hand.

"So, my Aspasia, what do you want most?"

"I want these threats against you to vanish—as if by Perseus' cap."

"That's what you want for me. What do want most for yourself?"

How many men would ask?

She wanted two things. One was that he love her forever, but it's not wise to constrain a man with words; she could speak carefully, too. Besides, she'd come to think his love would last, and didn't want to waste a wish.

"I want our son to be an Athenian citizen."

"He'll have to merit it."

"He's intelligent and spirited and tends to his lessons—he has your ability with numbers. He bears your name. He's sure to merit citizenship."

Pericles had turned his head aside. With all he'd been through, she hesitated to burden him more, but he'd asked. "Can you help him?"

His answer came with a puff of impatience. "When he distinguishes himself on behalf of the city, I'll do what I can."

But to distinguish himself, Little Pericles would have to grow up. Was there time?

"Aspasia . . . " Pericles thumbed the small gold image of the goddess hanging across his chest. "When you asked Phidias to make this seal of Athena for me some years ago, did you pay him for the gold?"

"I did."

That did not ease the question in his mind because she'd had her own way of getting what she wanted from men in those early days. "But did you pay him with *money*?"

"I didn't have much then."

"Then you paid him, for example, the way you used to pay Dion for books?"

She nodded.

"That leaves open how *Phidias* paid for the gold."

"It's a small amount of gold. He could have paid for it himself."

They exchanged a look.

"He could have," Pericles said.

* * *

He had succeeded in ensuring that the investigation and any trials would be held on level ground. Nevertheless, when Pericles tried to sleep that night, questions crowded his mind. Had Phidias betrayed him? That's how Aspasia would put it. He pushed his thoughts to his own, specific way of thinking. Had Phidias stolen ivory? The embattled soldiers Phidias had designed on Athena's gold shield in the Parthenon came to mind. Had Phidias stolen gold? It was difficult to believe he had because . . . why exactly? Because of the risk of exile or death. But if he believed he wouldn't be found out—or at least not until he made it to Elis and his work at Olympia—it might have been enough for him.

Would Phidias have put a friend at great risk? A comrade-in-arms? Himself?

Phidias was a workman. Were they comrades?

His head turned one way and then the other.

While he lay sleepless, Phidias was feasting in Elis. When any case against Phidias would be tried in Athens, the sculptor would be constructing a gold and ivory Zeus for the temple at Olympia equal to Athena in the Parthenon. By Hades, it might surpass Athena if Phidias was angry enough. And he could match Achilles for anger. Phidias clamping his lips on the jailer's ladle . . .

He was struck by a pain he took as fear before recognizing fear's younger brother, jealousy.

Safe in Elis, no verdict of death would reach Phidias. A verdict of exile would have no practical effect. Like the cutter of small stones whose jasper hung around Aspasia's neck, artists follow opportunity—always on to the next commission, the next creation.

For himself, exile was the equivalent of death. He had no other work. Athens was his creation.

But Phidias was born Athenian. They'd fought like brothers for Athens. They stood together on Athena's shield in the Parthenon, defending the Acropolis. That was Phidias' idea, not his, and now—

He looked at Aspasia sleeping. "To betray you—after all you did for him!" she'd say.

He'd argued for Phidias' funds. He'd diverted the proceeds of the empire to the building program. He'd sustained vile slurs. He'd risked ostracism.

But he hadn't done it for Phidias.

Athens had the finest temple in Greece. Wasn't that fair value for the money? The goddess nearly reached to the ceiling—and if any gold was missing, it was hard to see where. It was certainly the brightest statue anyone had ever seen.

"What does Athena really look like?" Aspasia's question of years ago had been answered for the whole world and for all time: like Phidias' gold and ivory Athena on the Athenian Acropolis.

Did the sculptor owe something more?

Let him fare as well with his Zeus at Olympia—if he can.

But in the end, Phidias did owe him something—though it wasn't a debt.

Aspasia would enjoy that one.

What isn't a debt yet is owed? *Loyalty to a friend.*

How would he know if Phidias betrayed him? If the gold weighed wrong, he'd have an answer. But if it came to the right weight, there then was the question of the ivory. What if—

Pericles! Rejoice if the gold weighs forty-four talents.

He must remember to teach Little Pericles that betrayal is a risk of leadership.

His other sons showed no signs of leadership. His nemesis, Thucydides, though in exile, was nonetheless a fortunate man: he had his son, Lacedaemonius, carrying on for him in Athens, though they were both on the wrong side. His own son Xanthippus looked handsome on a horse but had yet to receive a promotion in his military group. Nor did he attend the Assembly or care anything for the affairs of the city. If Xanthippus had been at the Assembly today, would he have voted with his father? Anger churned as if Xanthippus had raised his hand against him.

Did that humiliation lie ahead? Pericles' son votes against his father? Pericles closed his eyes against the thought.

As for Paralus, he'd probably never see that boy in the Assembly either. He was always on the farm, which would be useful if he'd learn to manage the estate, but all he did was curry the horses and run the dogs.

What a yield he'd derive if he attended to his farm himself! If he gave to his estates a fraction of the attention he gave to Athens, he'd increase the family fortune tenfold—as he had the city's. That's what his sister wanted him to do—so during their marriage had Aristocleia. But his path didn't run between the vines and barley, but from the Agora to the Assembly Hill.

For how long could he keep selling the yield of his fields to his tenant farmers at below market value so they could make some profit, while buying his own foodstuffs at the Agora? Without Euangelus to manage his property, he couldn't do it at all.

Pericles shifted to his side, careful not to wake Aspasia. He wanted to be alone with his thoughts.

Now General Cleinias' son Alcibiades—all the boys follow him, even though he lisps. His tongue was probably that way from birth—like my own head, Pericles thought; these things can't be changed. Alcibiades has spirit. He's amusing, charming. He's handsome. He's fearless. But he does make trouble—led a group of boys to Silky's and refused to pay after. Pericles shook his head. And the boy's too young to be going to Silky's. He might drown in the whirlpool. Cleinias' other boy hasn't learned to read or count though he's past the age for it, let alone play music. And his widow, crazy Deinomache haunts the women's quarters like a ghost. Cleinias is fortunate in what he doesn't know.

How had he come to envy others? First he'd envied exiled Thucydides, now he was envying Cleinias, a dead man. Achilles had reported from Hades: "Better to be a slave to the lowest man on earth than king of all the ghosts."

Someday he'd be a ghost and find out for himself.

Which was why a man had sons—to carry on.

Had he a son who'd carry on?

As for Young Pericles—how could he leave his estate to an illegitimate non-citizen? Impossible. Nor could a man who was barred from attending the Assembly lead the city. The pain of it hit him in the chest, as much for Aspasia as for himself.

In the years before his citizenship law, several foreign princesses had married into General Cimon's family but, because of his own law and position in the city, he felt he could not marry Aspasia; nor was she a princess, far from it although . . . He shifted to his other side. Enough of envying Cimon.

Aspasia turned over. He lay still, not wanting to talk lest he weep from the anger and sadness mixing in his soul.

She stirred again, and he held himself rigid.

He felt cold as a dead man.

Carefully he turned his head to see whether any light was showing at the window, but it was dark as an owl's wing.

Who else might betray him? Damon? Hagnon? Teisander? Anticles? Lysicles?

Safety lay in shared advantage, and certainly it was to all their advantage for the city to prosper. "A man does well whose city flourishes," Solon said. But obviously shared advantage wasn't the whole of it, for though his proposals were always to the city's best advantage he never won all the votes.

Perhaps it was wrong to try to keep Phidias in Athens for the marble pediment of the Parthenon once Elis had presented its offer to him for their gold and ivory Zeus at Olympia. It *was* wrong, because he should have known it was impossible. "My work here is complete," Phidias had said after the dedication of the statue of Athena.

Hagnon, who stood by him, should be next to him on the shield, not Phidias. And put Damon and the others in there somewhere.

In the darkness of his vision, he saw Athena's golden shield as if his eyes, instead of his memory, roamed over the battle it depicted between Athenians and the Amazons. More kinds of weapons were shown than were used in battle—swords, daggers, spears, a battle ax, yes, but also bows and arrows, even though in war archers don't fight beside the hoplites. And Phidias' stone. Artists don't show things exactly as they are.

On the shield, some fighters struggled to reach the top of the hill while the wounded toppled down its cliffs to be trapped in gullies. As Pericles stared at it, the shield turned, the fighters near the center moving slowly while those on the outside spun faster, as Odysseus must have seen the whirlpool. The fighters sank and bobbed. Like dolls with movable arms and legs, they brandished their weapons, advanced against their enemies, and fled from their pursuers. Just below the rock from which Pericles himself fought, a Greek drawing his bow faced an Amazon whose raised spear was aimed directly at his chest. A bow cannot match a spear. Still holding the bow drawn and ready, the man retreated, ducking suddenly to take cover behind a rise in the rock. But the Amazon gave chase. Though mightily tired, the man rose again and fled, but she pursued him, repeatedly taking new aim as he dodged and sprinted. Terrified, he broke into a run with bow in one hand and arrow in the other, but he stumbled over an exposed root, his weapons flying from his grasp. With his leg painfully bent under him, he twisted around toward his pursuer. Still running, the Amazon hoisted her spear behind her head and took aim. He had no time to stand and flee. He reached into the sand, pulled his weapons toward him, and in a single motion set the arrow, drew his bow, and shot at her from a kneeling position. The arrow plunged between her ribs. She staggered back, her eyes showing white, and fell headfirst from a rocky ridge. He heard the scream.

His heart was rocking in his chest—no, something else.

Aspasia was shaking him. "Are you alright?"

He nodded and lay there a moment with his eyes closed—it was pleasant to feel his heart cease its rabbit leaps.

There was no reason for his heart to be pounding. He had no cause to feel fear—it was that other man on the shield who had narrowly escaped death.

CHAPTER 42

━━━━━━━━━━━━━━━━━━━━━━━━

Coming Out Even

10. . . 10. . . 2. . . 2. . . 18. . . 18. . .

It was the morning of the weighing of the gold and Pericles knew all those numbers by heart. Still, feeling restless, while waiting for Hagnon and having numbers on his mind, he decided to review his accounts for the multiple payments and disbursements for the less precious materials.

14. . . 14. . . 20. . . 20. . . 20. . .

His neck was tired spinning from one column of numbers to the other.

20. . . 12. . .

A scroll rolled shut. Hades! He weighted the edge with a stone.

12. . . where was I? 3!

He pressed his hand to his forehead and closed his eyes. The scroll snapped shut.

"By Hecate!" Who startled him?

"I'm thorry that your father can't balance his accounts."

Was his hearing growing dull? When had Alcibiades come in? And his son Paralus, shuffling behind him.

Pericles turned toward the young men. He would have liked to hit Alcibiades, but instead spoke slowly and clearly.

"I can balance my accounts. I can do this because I take care to check my quantities and costs." He didn't need Alcibiades reporting all over Athens that Pericles couldn't balance his accounts. "Bring me some clean, heavy stones."

Alcibiades had seen him resting his head on his hands. It was best to show he wasn't afraid to give a command.

The boys left—Pericles didn't expect to see them back with stones.

Nor, in fact, was he afraid. Had he not submitted to countless investigations?

No. "Countless" was a lazy man's answer. How many soldiers did Cyrus lead against Greece? More than anyone could count. How many Persians died in the battle at Marathon? Countless. Not true. Six thousand, four hundred Persians died at Marathon. Not exact, but they'd counted them as best they could. And how many Greeks had fallen? One hundred and ninety-two. And that *was* exact.

His heart thrilled, as always, to remember that victory against the odds.

How many ships did Samos man against Athens? Countless. He laughed to himself. It was ninety.

The philosopher Anaximenes had taught that air was infinite. Some of the young philosophers claimed there were countless worlds. Well, counting may be difficult when thoughts turn to the cosmos, but in the affairs of men nothing was beyond count.

If a war with Sparta should break out, how many talents of gold would it take to ensure Athenian victory? "Countless," Lacedaemonius told the Assembly, as if large numbers bored him. Large numbers didn't bore *him*: he was amassing six thousand gold talents in the treasury in case it was needed for war with Sparta. Today they would remove forty-four of those gold talents from the gold and ivory Athena for the investigation and—Hagnon was waiting for him at the door to accompany him to the weighing of the gold.

Everything on the Acropolis looked as clear that morning as if outlined by a painter's brush, including the ten ugly, wood tables intruding on the marble inner chamber of the Parthenon. At each sat an auditor and a speaker, their heads close together, studying his accounts.

Simon! The bootmaker's bald head shone, bent over the scroll. Now that's a true friend: one who manages to be assigned to his friend's investigation.

But that tuft of hair springing from a round forehead—Hades! Pyrilampes was at the end of the row. He'd been in Persia buying peacocks—and returned too quickly.

Pyrilampes had the hubris to look directly at Pericles and, catching his eye, the boldness to smile. Pericles thrust his jaw forward, grim-faced, but then—one never knows the mind of a man—smiled slightly.

Not that it mattered which auditors had been assigned—the accounting would run smoothly if they made no errors, and if they made errors, he would correct them. Some liked to say "everyone makes mistakes"—the same people who said that Chance, not Zeus, ruled the cosmos. He never left things to Chance. He checked his numbers.

That was something Alcibiades and Paralus didn't seem to understand—but they were still young.

The accusers and their assistants sat on benches across from the auditors. He didn't look their way; he knew who they were.

Phidias' men stood chatting near the statue—they would always be Phidias' men though Phidias would never again set foot in Athens. What they knew about designing figures, chiseling and drilling stones, cutting and polishing ivory, setting jewels, making molds, casting bronze, working gold, erecting scaffolds—whatever knowledge they would put to use in finishing their labor on the temple they'd learned from him. Had he taught them enough?

Alcamenes leaned against the center post of the scale. Agoracritus bounced forward and back on his foot levered against the base of the statue—it took a sculptor to be sufficiently at ease with the goddess to risk familiarity.

The hooks attached to the ropes encircling Athena's breastplate, high above, dangled like the claws of Heracles' lion's skin. Each hook was sheathed in leather.

While the sacrifices were poured, Alcamenes began his haul to the top of the scaffold. He was not a boy to be clambering up the cage, but Alcamenes and Agoracritus had thrown knucklebones for the honor of overseeing the weighing of the gold from the highest position, and Alcamenes had won.

"Here's how to set the hooks," Alcamenes called out. Everyone looked up—not just the workmen—as if one of Euripides' gods had appeared above the stage, hoisted by that machine he'd invented. Pericles, too, strained to see as if he wanted a lesson in lifting heavy loads. Alcamenes was old for climbing but his strong voice was suited to directing men.

"If you don't push the hooks all the way in, they'll shift with the weight and bruise the gold. You have to press hard because the leather is thick, but be gentle. Think of a bridegroom clasping his bride's wrist." Alcamenes curved the fingers of his left hand around his right wrist. "That's how you must take the gold with a hook."

Alcamenes' wordy explanations, Pericles thought. Phidias just showed how.

"Check the hooks," Alcamenes called out.

Many cubits below, Agoracritus examined each hook to ensure it was set vertically so no uneven pressure would pucker the molded surfaces. He lay his cheek against the hooks, looking for light—there must be no slippage.

Though he knew the weight, Pericles checked his scroll again: six talents.

Antigonus began to turn the wheel, lowering the breastplate. After bringing warships about, this must have seemed light to the helmsman. The wheel turned as slowly as the sun in midsummer. Still, when the metal breastplate touched the pan, the scale shuddered.

Squirrel, confined to a cart since his fall at Samos had ruined his legs, kept his bright eyes on the scale. The men stood waiting while the pans settled.

Squirrel raised a hand. Then he nodded. "Now."

Antigonus held the gold in place as bronze counterweights were placed in the pan opposite to build to six talents. The men steadied the pans with their fingers on the rims, shifting their eyes like cats to keep Squirrel in sight.

Squirrel nodded again. "Now."

Another fifty-weight weight.

"Now."

Another.

"You can put in a hundred, we all know what it weighs," someone said. He must be a friend, Pericles thought—but to speak aloud at such a moment . . .

"Silence," the herald said but didn't pound his staff.

"Fifty," Squirrel said, and when the scale was still again, "Fifty."

Squirrel nodded. "Twenty-five."

Pericles watched the scale settle.

"Twenty-five."

His heart besieged the inner wall of his chest.

"Ten," Squirrel said, eyes on the scale. "Ready, Antigonus?"

Pericles looked up to Antigonus. Beyond him he saw the toothed and grooved wheels in the dimness of the temple heights.

"Ready."

"Ten." And when the scale was still, "Five."

It was like the low water in the speaker's clock.

Squirrel cocked his chin. "Five."

If, by chance, the breastplate turned out to balance at anything less than six hundred, the weight would be made up on another piece . . .

"Now five."

He'd ordered Phidias to keep to even numbers for each piece. Had he done it?

"Five."

People no longer watched the scales but had fixed their eyes on him.

"Five."

Five more should do it.

"Now, add five one-weights," Squirrel said.

"Just add a five." It was the person who'd spoken before, though the words seemed to be his own thoughts spoken aloud.

"We need ones in the pan in case adjustments are needed," someone else said.

"We can always take out a weight and—"

"Silence!" the herald said.

Was there nothing Athenians wouldn't argue about?

With a nod from Squirrel for each, the five ones were placed in the pans.

They waited until the pans stilled.

"Now." Squirrel addressed the citharist—he'd won a second in the music contests at the Panathenaic festival. "Watch my hand as you pluck your string."

Squirrel took a slow breath and raised his hand from his waist upward. The citharist launched the low note. The crowd stirred, the sound was lost.

Squirrel frowned. "Again."

They all attended the note on its long voyage to silence.

"Did you hear the steps by which the sound changed from loud to soft?" he asked.

The boys steadying the pans knew it was theirs to answer. "No, Squirrel."

"Yet, it changed, didn't it?"

"Yes, Squirrel."

"That's how you're to raise your fingers from the pans, breathing in, as we practiced it. Now watch for my signal."

The boys lifted their hands from the pans, everyone breathed with them, a sighing filled the chamber. Pericles tried to breathe in with the rest, but his chest felt pinched. He was dizzy. Squinting, as if they were distant, he watched the pans.

For all the care taken, the pans swung up and down.

"Yet they're balanced," Hagnon whispered.

"They're still moving."

"The same amount each side."

They watched the swings of the pans diminish at the same rate, like one of Pythagoras' equations.

There could be no doubt. The pans would settle even.

People bent their knees or tilted their heads, or hunched forward at the shoulders as Pericles did, to bring their eyes to the height of the pans.

The rims were level as a calm sea.

Hagnon gripped Pericles' arm. Throughout the Parthenon, people cheered.

"I want to see the weights," Menon called from the bench.

Would the sudden noise cause the scale to vibrate? Pericles kept his eyes on them, but the pans did not move.

"The scale balances at six talents," Squirrel said.

"Six talents is the weight of the breastplate," the secretary reported to the magistrate.

Pericles kept a steady eye on the pans. Balance was beautiful.

"Record six talents for the breastplate," the magistrate told the auditors.

Menon pushed forward. "I demand to examine the weights!"

"He has the right to examine the weights," Lacedaemonius told the magistrate.

"Does Menon have reason to doubt that they're official Athenian weights?" the magistrate asked.

"With the law, particular care must be taken to assure fairness when powerful men are involved." Menon cocked his chin toward Pericles

"I wish to examine the weights also," Pericles said.

"Why, by Zeus?" Hagnon whispered.

The magistrate scratched his chin. "Pericles, what objection do you have since the weight of the breastplate agrees with your accounts?"

"Special care must be taken to assure fairness, whoever's involved."

He had not expected applause.

"You may each examine the weights," the magistrate said.

With the same care with which it had been weighed, the breastplate was lifted from the scale and set aside on a wooden frame, like a shield resting on a stand. Then, surrounded by the police, Pericles with Hagnon, and Menon with Lacedaemonius, accompanied by the magistrate and secretary and followed by the auditors and speakers, examined the weights arranged by size on the temple's marble floor.

When Menon bent to pick up a five, his belly squeezed like a wine skin.

"Are these official weights of the Athenians or are they not official weights, Menon?" the magistrate asked.

Menon turned the weight in his palm. He traced the raised letters with his finger.

Light from the temple's entrance raked across the weights on the floor, illuminating the words "Property of the Athenian Demos."

Menon took the wide edge of the weight between his teeth as if it were a thin coin. Lacedaemonius browsed, as if in Dion's bookshop, along the row of weights.

"Do you acknowledge that these are official weights, Menon?" the magistrate asked.

Menon looked at Lacedaemonius, who shrugged his shoulders. "I am satisfied."

"Pericles, do you wish to test the weights further?"

Pericles shook his head.

"Then we can get on with weighing the gold."

Antigonus hauled the sling upward and brought it to rest opposite the bloused waist of Athena's gown gathered at her belt. Hooks were set in place. The workmen guided the gold into the sling.

"Higher!" Alcamenes screamed. "It must clear the knot!"

"We're cleared!" Agoracritus went on to mutter, "He thinks he's the only one who knows how Phidias—"

"Higher! I know how Phidias wanted this done."

"He never meant it to be done at all!"

"I suppose he didn't tell you that he made the gold removable in case we needed it to pay for a war."

Pericles brought his hand to his forehead. If Alcamenes and Agoracritus couldn't get along on this, they'd never complete the marble figures for the temple's pediment, the great triangular section under the roof that would hold marble figure of the Olympian gods.

What impressive control Phidias had over these strong personalities. His skill as a sculptor lay as much in that as in his knowledge of the materials and his novel ideas.

"He's a patriot!" Agoracritus screeched.

"He's a thief!" Menon yelled.

"There's none like him," Alcamenes said.

On that they could agree. The memory of Phidias just might keep them united long enough to finish the work.

The workmen struggled to bring the bloused piece to rest within the sling.

"It's taking so long," Hagnon said.

"That's a heavy section, nine talents."

The piece leaned upright against the cords. Wouldn't Phidias have wanted it moved flat? He couldn't know everything himself. It was up to the sculptors.

But when the pan tilted slightly in its descent, the gold rubbed against the cords. Some could rub away—and change the weight!

The piece swayed in the sling, carrying its ropes with it.

"It's not centered," Pericles said to Hagnon.

Hagnon rested a hand on Pericles' shoulder.

With the next quarter turn of the wheel, the sway was wider than before.

Pericles had intended to remain quiet. "Stop! The gold will upend the sling if it topples forward!"

"You're not in charge, Pericles," Lacedaemonius said.

"Adjust the ropes!"

The wheel made another quarter turn. He was angry. The ropes holding the gold were clearly slack.

Agoracritus called out, "Catch hold of the gold!"

But halfway down to the scale, it was out of reach.

Hades! If it falls, it will bend at the very least, Pericles thought. The edges will be crushed, the pleats flattened. Could Alcamenes rework them to the form Phidias had intended? If not, could Agoracritus?

"Stop the wheel!" Alcamenes said.

The gold leaned heavily against the lip of the sling. A dangerous amount of shining yellow metal showed above the leather, like a baby standing in its cradle.

The tallest ladder was wheeled forward. Agoracritus, with heavy coils of rope around his shoulder, climbed to the level of the knot of Athena's gown, just below the gold in the sling.

"Throw the rope from above so it won't knock the gold forward," Pericles called out.

"He's at the top of the ladder," Hagnon said.

Holding the coil slack in one hand, Agoracritus swung the rope back and forth with the other, broadening his arc, readying his toss. Then he stopped and drew the rope to him.

Pericles peered upward.

Agoracritus knotted the rope's end and set it in motion again.

The knot carried the rope higher than before, but the risk was greater in that, if it fell short, it would dislodge the gold by its weight.

Agoracritus hauled in the rope and over-tied the knot, thickening it. That heavy head could kill a man. Yet Agoracritus knew his craft. Pericles remained silent.

Again Agoracritus started the rope swinging, leaning outward from the ladder to guide it on its curved path. With each swing, the knot swung higher and came nearer the gold.

The knot swung just above the gold.

"Now," the crowd murmured.

"Quiet," Pericles said.

The heavy knot swung above the gold again. More light showed between the gold and the knot.

"Now."

"Now," they repeated with the next swing.

"Now."

But Agoracritus wasn't ready.

Suddenly he stretched out from the ladder like a worm from a twig. He swung the rope, and when it reached its peak—"Now!"— Agoracritus let go and it plummeted, releasing the coiled slack. Antigonus caught the knot a yard from the marble floor of the temple and guided the rope backward so that, when it settled against its outward swing, it came to rest flat against the sheet of gold. The gold held steady. Kept in place by the rope with the heavy knot leaning against it, the gold remained upright for its descent to the scale.

"You've won the prize, Agoracritus," Simon called out.

Everyone applauded.

"A wreath for Agoracritus!" Pyrilampes said.

Phidias would never have tempted such danger.

"The scale balances at nine talents," Squirrel announced.

Nine talents is the weight of the bloused drapery," the secretary reported to the magistrate.

"You know this is a waste of time," Pericles told Hagnon.

"It's not a waste of time to prove no gold has been stolen."

He was right, yet as more and more of the gold plates were removed, Pericles felt that the investigation was not only tiresome but pointless. The wood frame over which Phidias had laid the gold plates was revealed. What was hidden came to light. It was indecent. Pericles averted his gaze.

A tall, narrow piece from the hem of Athena's skirt rested in the scale pan, like bark stripped from a tree. It weighed three talents.

The last gold to be weighed was the round exterior of Athena's shield showing the battle of Amazons and Greeks.

"Phidias sculpted himself and Pericles," Menon said loudly. "There's the two of 'em!" But as this was the last piece, concentration was intense and no one paid attention to Menon.

"Here are the eleven talents that make the forty-four." Pericles tilted his scroll for Hagnon.

"What a waste," Lacedaemonius muttered. "I could pay one thousand good workmen for a year with that."

"The scale balances at eleven talents," Squirrel said.

"Eleven talents is the weight of the shield's gold," the secretary reported.

"Record eleven talents for the shield piece," the magistrate told the auditors.

Pericles strode forward purposefully.

"There are forty-four talents."

Hagnon caught Pericles' cloak.

"Let the magistrate figure the numbers, Pericles!"

"No gold is missing." Pericles breathed deeply for the first time in several days. Caught by the pulls on his cloak, he moved in a circle like a stone swung on a rope. He nodded to the men he passed so they would realize before the magistrate announced the number that he had won—that way, they would share his sense of victory.

CHAPTER 43

The Parthenon in Moonlight

When Pericles had spoken to the Athenians at the dedication of the gold and ivory Athena, he had thought that Phidias would complete the sculptures of the Olympian gods for the Parthenon pediments soon, but the marble sculptures did not advance as quickly as he wished. He had passed his sixtieth year and sometimes he feared he might not live to see all that had been planned for the Parthenon, though he did not mention that to Aspasia since thoughts of his death pained her.

What if a large, armed conflict forced an interruption? The Athenian allies seemed ever more inclined to rebel, ready to forget the defensive guarantees and economic profit the alliance brought them, and daring to think they could prosper and defend themselves on their own. Furthermore, Corinth, ever jealous of Athens' commercial dominance, was striving to incite Sparta into a new war against Athens. The Peace Treaty between Sparta and Athens set rules for avoiding war—it did not turn Sparta into friend. Pericles had maintained the Athenian fighting force at a high level of readiness, fostered the dominance of the Athenian navy and garnered a large gold reserve on the Acropolis against the likelihood of rebellions and the possibility of war.

He had not, though, anticipated the accusation of theft of gold and ivory against Phidias and the sculptor's escape, which left the sculptures of the Parthenon pediments in the hands of apprentices and assistants. Could these younger men complete the Parthenon sculptures with the surpassing excellence that Phidias would have brought to them? Pericles doubted it. Phidias was generous in his teaching. Pericles had seen him demonstrate the use of chisels, rasps, hammers, files and drills. But could Phidias teach his gift from the gods that made him the greatest sculptor among the Greeks? Pericles sought reassurance in Phidias' assertion that the figures would truly be his creations because he had thought about them first—his mind had given birth to them. "If you believe Anaxagoras that Mind is the power of intellect that sets the cosmos in motion," Phidias had said, "believe me about this." But marble is a material substance, not power of intellect. It was hard to believe him.

Finally, though, Pericles witnessed the last scene of the planning, design, and building of the Parthenon, a drama that had been as suspenseful as any ever played in the theater of Dionysos. Working over several weeks, the sculptors had hoisted the marble gods of the East Pediment high into the aether (plus the chariot horses of the rising Sun and the setting Moon), situated them against the wall of the pediment, and doweled them securely into the floor. Then they lifted off the pulleys, chains, ropes and scaffolds, liberating the Parthenon. The gods settled into place.

Or did they?

Gazing upward at the sculptures after the protective equipment had been removed, he saw something he did not like. Or thought he had. Or doubted he had seen anything troublesome at all. But as he feasted and celebrated the completion of the Parthenon with Aspasia that evening, he found that the joy he expected—that he *deserved*—eluded him. Toasting the sculptures of the East Pediment, drinking the wine, he wondered if Philemon had diluted it with too much water? His next cupful wasn't any better, nor the next.

That night, as happened when, rarely, he drank too much wine, he couldn't sleep. Instead, frowning at the ceiling, he strained to remember the entire array of the marble gods he had seen when the sculptors had exhibited them at ground level before raising them into place. Certainly he had been pleased, even thrilled. It had seemed to him that the sculptures captured the surpassing power and beauty of the gods who dwell on Mount Olympus. Phidias had been right: the sculptures were his. What, then, had bothered him today? He would like to discuss it with Aspasia but—he looked to the side—she was asleep.

He looked at the window: the olive tree he and Aspasia had planted years ago had branched beyond the frame; the leaves were bright. He rose and went to the window. The sky was filled with a creamy light, like the night he'd first loved Aspasia in her little room. With this much light, he'd be able to see the sculptures. He reached for his cloak; he'd awaken Philemon to carry his torch. He moved quietly so as not to awaken Aspasia; she might not understand why he wanted to go out. Well, she'd understand if he explained but that would take time.

"You're going out? In the dark?"

He finished tying on his boots. "To the Acropolis. I must see the sculptures, and tomorrow that new alliance will keep me in the Assembly all day."

She sat up, her arms around her knees. "You won't be able to see much."

"I long to set my eyes on them."

"I'll come, too." She hadn't had an adventure for years, not since her son was born.

"You'd want to do that at night? I didn't think a woman—We can see the Chariot of Xanthippus, too, my father's dedication, I've wanted to show that to you. Hurry, the clouds may change."

Torches converged. Lanterns flashed at their faces. Aspasia tightened her veil. Sentries stationed at the entrance to the Acropolis knew their General from all the Athenians and didn't ask for an explanation. Unlocking the man-sized door in the tall metal gate, they let Pericles, Aspasia and Philemon through, sending additional guards as an escort. The men took the opportunity for a close look at Aspasia but, respectful of Pericles, they held their tongues.

Midway along the roped path through the construction work on the new Entrance Building, Pericles stopped and peered to his left. He leaned over the rope, straining to see into the still unroofed chamber that would one day hold paintings of Athenian victories— for now it was cluttered with scaffolds and shadows.

"I'll go over this with my architect in daylight."

Ahead the Parthenon sat confidently on the Acropolis. It was a building certain in the knowledge it was right.

High above was the West Pediment that told the story of Athena and Poseidon contesting for votes to win divine dominion over Athens and Attica. In Athens, even the gods sometimes have to stand for election—the Athenians had elected Athena. Those sculptures had been in place over a year so, without breaking stride, they headed east, catching the scent along the way of newly planted rose bushes. A patrol had alerted the temple guards, who raised their torches. To anyone looking from below, the Acropolis must have seemed to flicker with excitement.

Reaching the east end, Pericles and Aspasia climbed a few steps up the altar and turned to face the building. Their eyes traveled up the fluted columns, past the sturdy capitals that crowned them and beyond the carved pattern of triglyphs and metopes all the way to the vast, triangular pediment that depicted Athena's astonishing birth from the head of Zeus. The pediment was no longer the desolate colony he had imagined the day they had dedicated the gold and ivory Athena. It had become a cosmos thickly populated by gods, those nearest the center witnessing Athena's birth with amazement and passing the divine news to those farther from the event in waves of transmitted excitement. The gods jutted out fully into our world; their splendor emerged from the hazy moonlight as if formed of it.

Looking for an error, Pericles saw perfection. All the gods were larger than natural men and women and Zeus sat taller than the rest. If he were to rise from his throne, he would crack through the pediment's overhang. The god of the Greeks was handsome. Pericles examined the thick, curling hair, the shadowing brows, the straight nose, full lips, and muscled torso—not that of a youth but of an older athlete. "Notice, Aspasia, Phidias has carved his biceps bulging as he grips his thunderbolt."

Aspasia nodded. "It's very natural."

Pericles remembered the smack on the rump Phidias had given to a horse he was polishing to a fine finish. "To him, his marble sculptures were alive."

"It's hard to know how Phidias could—" her hands curved as if drawing a loaded bucket from a well—"pull life from stone."

I like to carve. I give it a little each day. Pericles heard Phidias'
voice from years ago, when he'd been working on the sculptured frieze
of Athenians installed below the pediment—hard to see tonight in
the shadows. "He was a stone carver, Aspasia."

Tomb makers were stone carvers, Socrates, for instance, was a
stone carver but—she shook her head—Phidias was no mere stone
carver. She had herself posed for one of his bronze statues of Athena.
"Still, of course, Phidias' great works are in bronze and gold while
these on the pediment are only stone." Since Pericles looked as if he
disagreed with her, she added, "Though they are beautifully carved,
and grand and impressive, for stone."

"It's a matter of Mind, not material. Looking at our marble Zeus,
I can imagine the majestic god Phidias will create for Olympia." His
curved fingers tapped his lips. "In gold and ivory."

He rarely spoke of it but Aspasia knew that Pericles was
disappointed, even bitter for having lost a gold and ivory statue by
Phidias to another city. How to soothe his sadness? "Men come from
all the world to see our Athena! And she's right behind those bolted
doors." He said nothing so she added, "Twenty-six cubits!"

She was kind. Taking her hand, he looked up and squinted.
And then he saw what had thinned his wine and kept him awake—
what he had been looking for while hoping not to find.

"It's the throne."

What was he talking about?

He swung up his arm, bowstring-taut from shoulder to finger.
Following his gesture, her eyes landed on the center of the pediment.
Her hand went to her chin. "What about the throne?"

"There's an error. Don't you see it?"

She did not like to appear slow but . . .

"Look closely, Aspasia. The back of the throne faces out toward
us but the seat faces sideways. It's not as in nature."

Now that he'd pointed it out . . . "I think it may be the shadows.
It will vanish like a nightmare in daylight."

"No." He had not fully understood the imperfection in daylight,
but he had seen it. "Phidias made a mistake."

Shadows cracked Pericles' moonlit face—the furrow between
his brows, the grimace of his mouth. She went to work. "The reason

is that Zeus has to sit to the front in his throne because he's a majestic god, but also, since he just gave birth to Athena from his head, naturally he twists around to see her. Phidias made the throne follow him because it wouldn't look right for Zeus to be sitting on the edge of his seat." She eyed Pericles; he seemed to be listening intently, so she went on. "And since he's twisting, he's forming a spiral. And that's what a vortex is—a spiral in motion. Think of it, Pericles, there's Zeus, creating the vortex! It's just the way we planned it with Phidias and Anaxagoras!" That time years back, when Anaxagoras had read from his writings and she had learned that sculptures could hold ideas—something like books.

That was when Pericles' cynical son Xanthippus had said to Phidias, "You can't mean that just by twisting his torso Zeus becomes that cosmic vortex you're always talking about." But Aspasia's pale friend, Dion, had hammered in the nail: "Zeus will be ordinary Zeus for ordinary people, and he'll be Mind, the power of intellect, for those of us with true understanding."

Pericles studied the wayward throne. "The truth is that no one has ever made a chair—or a throne—with the back facing one way and the seat another. It's illogical. As I feared, the apprentices—"

Aspasia shook her head. "Phidias ran out on us for some last details but the designs were his. And look—he draped Zeus' cloak to cover so much of the throne that you can hardly see it's illogical. No one will notice. Anyhow, there are always compromises."

Always compromises. True. And she was right that no one would notice. Even Aspasia hadn't seen it. And it had taken him weeks. Although . . .

She yearned to erase his frown. "No matter what Phidias creates at Olympia, Zeus will never appear mightier than he does here, in the very center of our pediment." She turned her head to speak into his ear. "As mighty as Pericles."

He glanced around. Philemon was chatting with the guards at a respectful distance.

"He *is* Pericles," she said.

"Anaxagoras' idea is that I am Zeus, not the other way around."

"What's the difference?"

"There's less hubris to Anaxagoras' way of saying it."

"I still don't see a difference."

He smiled.

"Zeus is in the center of the cosmos as Anaxagoras teaches, and *you* here in Athens are at the center of the world," she said.

"*Mind* is at the center—that's what I like about Anaxagoras' teaching."

"Zeus is Mind, and if ever there was a man with force of intellect, it's my Pericles."

They looked up at the sceptered god.

"For all the teachings of philosophy," Pericles said, "the Greeks still see him as a king, father, storm god, wielder of the thunderbolt."

"They also see him as unfaithful and philandering."

"And cheating and vengeful."

"Untrustworthy."

"Partial as a ruler."

"Altogether unworthy for a god," Aspasia said.

"Homer was wrong to depict him like that and the rest of the Greeks have followed him in it. Anaxagoras has taught us a better way to know him."

"It's Homer's poetry," she said. "It puts a picture in your mind. 'Zeus the son of Cronus bowed his craggy dark brows and the deathless locks came pouring down from the thunderhead of the great immortal king and giant shock waves spread through all Olympus.'"

"Our Zeus is giving birth to intelligence for all the world—that's more important than 'deathless locks.'"

"I love the way the story of the Birth of Athena brings together many thoughts—it reminds me of the various colored threads in my weaving that make one color." Her chin was on her hand. "The Birth of Athena is such an unusual subject—I've never heard of it on any temple—I sometimes wonder how you and Phidias ever came up with it."

"Didn't Phidias ever tell you his little joke?"

"Joke?"

"He was describing to me all he wanted to convey by showing Athena's birth—that many-colored weaving you spoke of. I thought his idea was perfect for our temple, but I was displeased because

465

the subject is old-fashioned. Phidias came up with a new argument. He said that I'd have a companion in Zeus of the Large Head—he carried Athena, like a mother but inside his head instead of his belly, up to the time she was born. By the time he gave birth to her, his head was huge."

She regarded Zeus, regal but decidedly surprised, his eyes on Athena springing away as a child must one day leave its parents. "I remember, but that was just . . . " *A joke into marble . . . into a god . . . into cosmic . . . ?*

He watched her face as he did on those rare occasions that they spoke of the overlarge size of his head. For once she looked genuinely amazed, not just agreeably so. Her fingers crossed her lips. She needed time to take it in.

"Phidias was smiling, tried to put it forward as a joke, but it wasn't a joke to me, nor to him. You know, Aspasia, this large head of mine is a burden—on the neck." He tried slipping *that* in as a joke. But it was burden on his soul, and Aspasia knew it.

"It's very hard when we compare ourselves against the perfection of the gods, yet we do it all the time—their images are everywhere."

"Never mind the gods. It's hard to have anything so peculiar about oneself that it stands out in the world of men," he said.

"I've noticed that but, if you think of it, everyone has something peculiar—at *least* one thing."

"Not everyone. For example?"

"I've heard Herodotus had a deaf son."

"I've never seen him."

"Take your friend Sophocles. He's rich, intelligent, and handsome but has such a small voice he can't perform in his own plays."

Pericles nodded. "I think Alcibiades is going to lisp forever."

"We're born with things like that." If after so many years she revealed the secret of Silky's child, born with a twisted foot, she might seem untrustworthy, so she said, "Remember Dion—the gods forgot to paint him."

"You're perfect, Aspasia."

This wonderful man—he'd forgotten, for the moment, how she'd made her living. "Not everyone would say so."

He himself had thought her too thin and bony at first, but he knew that's not what she meant.

Aspasia looked up at Zeus' well-painted craggy dark brows and deathless locks. With his idea, born of their discussion years ago, Phidias had turned the—yes, undeniably ugly—burden of Pericles' overlarge head into the finest of things by carving Zeus giving birth to Athena from his head. She felt a little jealous of Phidias who, in making the burden of his head easier for Pericles to tolerate, had accomplished what she could not. But artists were magicians whereas she did what she could.

"So then, have I convinced you that the birth of Athena, the goddess of wisdom, belongs on our pediment?" He was smiling.

"Wisdom is at home here. That's why all the philosophers come—it's why my father set out for Athens."

"The wisest ideas originate here—democracy, I think, above them all."

"And now you've carried democracy all the way to the Black Sea."

"To the south coast, but not yet to the north."

Excitement did not rob Pericles of his accuracy—she loved that in him.

"It will reach the north coast—in time, everywhere."

His arm around her shoulder, they beheld the scene together.

"That's why Phidias made the news of Athena's birth beam outward from god to god," Pericles said. "Wisdom is spreading."

"All the way from the rising Sun to the setting Moon." Aspasia's finger traced the broad arc from one corner of the pediment to the other. "A new day is dawning."

"If we stay out longer, it will indeed be dawn."

With the light, Athens became noisier. Already below them, men were moving toward the Assembly hill. There was a commotion at the entrance to the Acropolis.

"That will be Damon and Hagnon, come to get me for the Assembly."

"It seems the news that Pericles is on the Acropolis is also spreading."

The gold light of the rising sun touched the top of the pediment like a crown. They watched it first illuminate the heads of the marble figures and then move lower—the way Aspasia wove her tapestry, it occurred to Pericles.

"Everyone says you and Aspasia reign here as Zeus and Hera." Hagnon breathed deeply after the fast climb. "I see it's true."

"It's late," Damon said.

"Are you pleased?" Hagnon gestured toward the pediment.

"We must hurry," Damon said.

"I'm somewhat pleased." He looked back at Aspasia. "We'll see the chariot another time."

The sun glinted on his helmet. After a moment she felt the same rays touch the back of her neck and then warm her shoulders, like his arm looped across them.

"And Pericles—" Another thought had occurred to her. *Since the rising sun and the setting moon surround Athena's birth, wisdom spreads over time also and*—But he was already descending the hill with his friends and to call out was unseemly. She would tell him tonight.

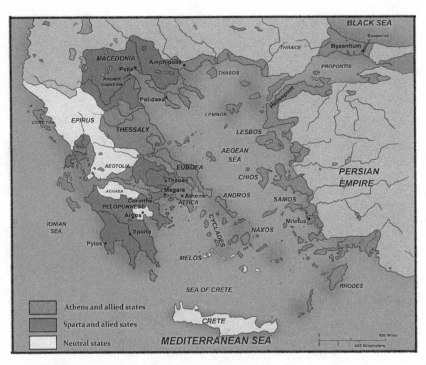

Map of Greece and Aegean region, 432 BC: Spheres of Influence

CAST OF CHARACTERS

(Characters who appear in more than one context.)

Agariste: Pericles' mother who died a long while ago.

Agoracritus: A young sculptor at work on the Parthenon; apprentice to Phidias.

Alcamanes: A sculptor at work on the Parthenon; apprentice to Phidias.

Alcibiades: Younger son of General Cleinias and his wife Deinomache. When Cleinias is killed at war in Boeotia, Alcibiades and his brother, Young Cleinias, become wards of Pericles and his brother Ariphron.

Amycla: The Spartan nursemaid of Young Cleinias and Alcibiades.

Anaxagoras: The philosopher who theorizes that Mind is the dynamic and creative force in the universe.

Andocides: A general and trusted supporter of Pericles whom Pericles places in control of Athens during the long siege of Samos.

Anticles: A general at Samos and political ally of Pericles.

Antigonus: A helmsman on Pericles' expedition to the Black Sea who aids in weighing the gold.

Antipatrus: An ardent Samian democrat who aids the Athenians in Samos.

Archestratus: A young political ally of Pericles.

Ariphron: Pericles' older brother.

Aristocleia: Pericles' wife, mother of his sons Xanthippus and Paralus; earlier married to Hipponicus, she re-marries him after her divorce from Pericles.

Aspasia: The hetaira (courtesan) from the East Greek city of Miletus whom Pericles falls in love with and who bears his youngest son, Young Pericles.

Calliope: Pericles' sister; she lives at his country estate in Cholargos.

Cleandridas: A Spartan; the uncle and advisor of the young Spartan king.

Cleinias: Pericles' kinsman, a general killed in war in Boeotia, leaving behind his wife, Deinomache, and their young sons, Young Cleinias and Alcibiades.

Cleon: A young political opponent of Pericles, a tanner by profession.

Cratinus: A comic playwright who ridicules Pericles and Aspasia in his plays.

Damon: Pericles' political advisor, an arch democrat.

Deinomache: The wife of General Cleinias who loses her mind when her husband is killed in Boeotia; mother of Young Cleinias and Alcibiades.

Demodicus: A ship captain who knows the waters from Italy to the Black Sea.

Dion: Aspasia's friend, a pale bookseller with an interest in playwrights and love of theater.

Douris: A farmer; a councilman who presides over the investigation of the theft of gold.

Dracontides: Priest of Athena's Old Temple, hostile to Pericles and the Parthenon temple.

Euangelus: Pericles' steward who manages his estate, a slave, possibly the father of Philemon.

Eucleia: Daughter of Teisander, promised to Pericles' son Xanthippus.

Euripides: The playwright; he has not yet matched the prestige of the somewhat older playwright Sophocles.

Euryptolemus: Cousin and friend of Pericles' son Xanthippus.

Glaucon: A young commander of Pericles' tribe who competes with Pericles for influence and beats him in an election for general from their tribe.

Hagnon: A general and strong supporter of Pericles who participates in the siege of Samos.

Herodotus: A historian, author of the *Histories*, friendly to Pericles and his circle.

Hippodamus: The city planner who, like Aspasia, came to Athens from Miletus in East Greece, and has designed Athens' port city, Piraeus.

Hipponicus: Aristocleia's first husband whom she re-marries after her divorce from Pericles.

Hygiaenon: A youth who is training for the pentathlon at the Olympic games.

Hypanis: An entertainer in Piraeus loved by Hippodamus.

Ictinus: The architect of the Parthenon, lover of Silky.

Lacedaemonius: A political opponent of Pericles; son of Cimon who was an important general, no longer living, whom Pericles had prosecuted for betraying Athens.

Lampon: A seer with close ties of family friendship with Pericles' family; influential with Apollo's oracle at Delphi.

Lysicles: A young political ally of Pericles.

Melissus: The leader of the Samians with whom Pericles deals in ending the siege of Samos.

Menon: An older sculptor at work on the Parthenon.

Paralus: Pericles' second son, born to Aristocleia.

Pericles: Statesman, general, leader of the Athenian democracy, lover of Aspasia.

Phidias: The major sculptor of the Parthenon including its gold and ivory cult statue of Athena, with overall charge for the artistic design and organization of the Parthenon project.

Philemon: A young groom in Pericles' household, a slave, possibly the son of Euangelus.

Phormio: A general who participates in the siege of Samos; he becomes an outstanding naval general.

Pleistonax: The young Spartan king, nephew of Cleandridas.

Protagoras: The philosopher, an expert in politics, law and education.

Pyrilampes: An Athenian diplomat with ties to Persia and an interest in peacocks.

Rhodia: The owner of Silky's brothel.

Silky: Aspasia's friend, a hetaira (courtesan), lover of Ictinus.

Simon: A bootmaker whose shop is near the boundary of the Agora; a friend of the barber Xenon.

Socrates: A young philosopher, not yet well known.

Sophocles: The playwright, author of *Antigone*.

Squirrel: An agile workman on the Parthenon who leads the charge up the scaffold trying to breach the walls of Samos.

Teisander: A supporter of Pericles whose daughter is promised to Pericles' son Xanthippus.

Thucydides: Pericles' arch opponent in Athenian politics; leader of the conservative wing of the Demos (the voting Athenian populace).

Tleson: The jailer in Athens.

Tleson (II): The son of Tleson the jailer who sails in Pericles' expedition to the Black Sea and takes a land allotment to settle in the region.

Xanthippus: Pericles' oldest son, born to Aristocleia. Also the name of Pericles' father, General Xanthippus who died a long while ago.

Xenon: A barber with a shop in the Agora; friend of the bootmaker Simon.

Young Cleinias: The older, cognitively challenged son of General Cleinias and his wife Deinomache. When Cleinias is killed at war in Boeotia, Young Cleinias and his brother, Alcibiades, become wards of Pericles and his brother Ariphron.

Young Pericles: Pericles' and Aspasia's son; the youngest of Pericles' three sons.

Zoe: Aspasia's maid, a slave, who helps raise Young Pericles.

SOURCES

Almost all characters in *Pericles and Aspasia* are based on persons whose existence is known through classical texts. For some there is rich evidence for their lives and personalities and for others fragmentary information; most but not all are named in classical literature. Pericles had a sister but her name is unknown; I named her Calliope. Since the name of Pericles' wife is unknown, I named her Aristocleia; her early connection with Hipponicus, her divorce to marry Pericles and their divorce which led her to remarry Hipponicus are attested although the details are controversial. I gave the name of Deinomache to the wife of Cleinias and mother of Alcibiades and Young Cleinias. The character of Dion was inspired by mention of a pale man who sold books under a tree in a corner of the Agora. The elderly aristocrat who propositions Aspasia in the Agora was suggested by the anonymous author, called the "Old Oligarch," who wrote a treatise critical of the Athenian democracy, *Constitution of the Athenians* [Pseudo-Xenophon]. Squirrel was suggested by an account of Pericles' grief at the death of a worker who fell from the heights of the Parthenon. The named characters that are wholly invented are: Zoe the maid, Aspasia's friend Silky, Rhodia the brothel owner, Xenon the barber, Hypanis the Piraeus dancing boy, Pericles' servant Philemon, Demodicus the ship captain; boys at the palaestra including Hygiaenon (pentathlete), Lycaon (long jumper), Euergides (javelinist), Teisander's son Epilycus and Xanthippus' wrestling opponent Stephanos; the Chian democrat Antipatrus, Castor who loves Hygiaenon at Samos, Antigonus the helmsman, Tleson son of Tleson the jailer, Tleson the jailer, and Douris who presides over the investigation about the gold.

While there are many sources for the life of Pericles among Greek and Roman authors, there are few for Aspasia. As is often emphasized, in evaluating a source and assessing its usefulness, many factors that can shape a point of view have to be considered including the purpose of the text, its form, its context and its likely bias. The lapse of time between when an author writes and the individuals written about provide all the more opportunity for facts to be lost and misleading views—including celebrity gossip—to be solidified into a tradition. It is no wonder that controversies abound, given the complexities. To write *Pericles and Aspasia*, I have read the classical sources and rich scholarship on the history and culture of Athens in the fifth century BC and on the lives of Pericles and Aspasia, seeking to sort out the biases, gossip and lacunae and searching for the factual and emotional nuggets of truth.

Selected sources for the life of Pericles (c. 495–429 BC) found in Greek authors:

The historians Thucycides (c. 460–c. 401 BC), an Athenian citizen, and Herodotus (484–425 BC) were Pericles' contemporaries and by all indications had seen him in action and may well have known him personally. Thucydides' Books 1 and 2 concern the history of Greece and Athens during the period of *Pericles and Aspasia*. See *The Landmark Thucydides,* edited by Robert B. Strassler, a newly revised edition of the Richard Crawley translation, The Free Press, 1996. Thucydides expresses his view of Pericles' character and method of leadership in Book 2.65, *The Landmark Thucydides,* p. 127.

Herodotus, born in the Greek city of Halicarnassus, spent many years in Athens. His *History* is a source for the history of Greece and other nations before and during Pericles' lifetime. See *The Landmark Herodotus,* edited by Robert B. Strassler, a new translation by Andrew L. Purvis, Anchor Books, 2007. In Book 6.131 of his *History,* Herodotus outlined Pericles' illustrious ancestry culminating in the marriage of his father Xanthippus with his mother Agariste, and recounted her dream during pregnancy of giving birth to a lion, shortly after which she gave birth to Pericles; *The Landmark Herodotus,* p. 483.

During Pericles' political life, the comic poets Cratinus (c. 519 BC ?–c. 422 BC) and Hermippus (active mid-430s-early-410s BC) used Pericles' policies, his person, his relationship with Aspasia, his association with Zeus and his "Olympian" persona as grist for the comic mill. Since their plays have not survived, what is known of them has been gleaned through fragments and references in works by later authors. Cratinus, in his play *Chirons,* aimed his satirical arrows at Pericles' dominant position in Athens—as well as his overlarge head—and at Aspasia. See *Fragments of Old Comedy Alcaeus to Diocles,* edited and translated by Ian Christopher Storey, Loeb Classical Library, 2011, pp. 386-391.

Many plays of the Athenian comic writer Aristophanes (446–386 BC) have come down to us. A youth during Pericles' lifetime, he composed his comedies after Pericles' death. In his *Clouds,* he alludes to Pericles' "necessary expenditures," a bribe he paid to the Spartans to forestall an attack on Athens. *Aristophanes: Clouds. Wasps. Peace,* translated by Jeffrey Henderson, Loeb Classical Library, 1998; *Clouds,* pp. 126-127. In *Peace,* Aristophanes alludes to Phidias' theft of gold and Pericles' fear of involvement in the scandal. *Aristophanes,* same citation as above; *Peace,* pp. 502-505. In *Acharnians,* Pericles, "that Olympian," is seen as starting the Peloponnesian War in revenge for wrong done to Aspasia. Aristophanes, *The Acharnians, the Clouds, the Knights, the Wasps,* translated by Benjamin B. Rogers, Loeb Classical Library, 1986; *The Acharnians,* pp. 120-123. For an engaging discussion, see *Pericles On Stage, Political Comedy In Aristophanes' Early Plays* by Michael Vickers, University of Texas Press, 1997.

Xenophon (c. 430–355/354 BC), writing in a satiric vein similar to that of Plato's Socratic dialogues, depicts Pericles as falling awkwardly into a verbal trap set by Alcibiades about a subject Pericles knew well: the nature of law. See Xenophon, *Memorabilia,* translated by Amy L. Bonnette, Cornell University, 1994, pp. 13-14.

Plato (427–347 BC) used his extraordinary skills as a writer to ridicule and otherwise demean the Athenian democracy and its great representative, Pericles. For example, in Plato's dialogue *Gorgias,* Pericles is depicted as having corrupted the Athenians and thereby was "not a good statesman." *Plato: Lysis, Symposium, Gorgias,* translated by W. R. M. Lamb, Loeb Classical Library, 1953; *Gorgias,*

Yvonne Korshak

pp. 492-499. Elsewhere in Plato's dialogues, Pericles' wisdom is undercut by his being blamed for the ineptitude of his sons. Plato, *Charmides, Alcibiades 1 & 2, Hipparchus, The Lovers, Theages, Minos, Epinomis*, translated by W. R. M. Lamb, Loeb Classical Library, 1927; *Alcibiades* 1, pp. 154-157. In the dialogue *Phaedrus*, while, with some hedging, Pericles' natural gift for oratory is acknowledged, its high-minded character is attributed to someone else—the philosopher Anaxagoras. Plato, *Euthyphro, Apology, Crito, Phaedo, Phaedrus*, translated by Harold North Fowler, Loeb Classical Library, 1914; *Phaedrus*, pp. 546-547. For Pericles in Plato's dialogue *Menexenus*, see sources for Aspasia, below.

In his *Athenian Constitution*, Aristotle (384–322 BC) provides information about Pericles' legislation requiring that for a child to be an Athenian citizen, both parents had to be Athenian citizens. Aristotle places Pericles within the development of the Athenian democracy and cites his introduction of payment for jurors. See Aristotle, *The Athenian Constitution*, translated by Frederic G. Kenyon, Compass Circle, 2020, pp. 37-39.

Diodorus the Sicilian (90-30 BC), drawing upon good earlier sources, recounts the history of Greece and Athens in the years surrounding and during Pericles' lifetime, including the role Pericles played in the period. Diodorus Siculus, *The Library of History*, translated by C. H. Oldfather, Volume V, Books 12.41-13, Loeb Classical Library, 1950, pp. 2-25.

Early in the second century AD, Plutarch (46–after 119 AD), born in Boeotia, Greece, composed the only biography of Pericles from the classical world. Plutarch wrote from a broad base of knowledge of the authors who came before him and, while he admired Pericles, he included hostile accounts. He was a remarkably judicious author and indicated what of the material he incorporated into his work he considered doubtful or of little merit. His depiction of Pericles needs to be approached with a critical mind-set and analysis but is invaluable. See Plutarch's *Lives*, translated by John Dryden, edited and revised by Arthur Hugh Clough, Digireads, 2018; *Pericles*, pp. 171–199, 216-217. Plutarch in his *Lives* also wrote about Pericles in his life of Cimon, pp. 538-539, and in his life of Alcibiades, p. 218.

Athenaeus of Naucratis (?170–223 AD) included in his *The Learned Banqueters*, (*Deipnosophistae*) fragments of texts by earlier authors, Stesimbrotus of Thasos (c. 470—c. 420 BC), Antisthenes (c. 446–c. 366 BC), and Clearchus of Soli (active c. 320 BC), regarding the personal life of Pericles and Aspasia, most of which can be discounted as scurrilous gossip. See *Athenaeus*, edited and translated by S. Douglas Olson, Books 12-13.595b, Loeb Classical Library, 2010; Antisthenes, Book 12, pp. 110-111; Clearchus, Stesimbrotus and Antisthenes, Book 13, pp. 404-407.

While Pericles' life is well attested, little is known with any certainty about Aspasia (? c. 470–? c. 400 BC). By all indications, she was born in the Greek city of Miletus (today in Turkey), her father's name was Axiochos (conventionally Latinized to Axiochus), and she was well-educated. In context, her education was a rarity since, in Athens of this period, women were not educated, including women of the highest classes who lived in almost cloistered seclusion, their participation in religious festivals and events serving as a kind of escape valve. Aspasia arrived in Athens sometime in the 440s BC where she made her living as a hetaira, a courtesan (hetaira from the Greek word for "companion"). Pericles fell in love with her, they lived together, and she bore him his third son, named Pericles. After Pericles' death in 429 BC, Lysicles, of Pericles' circle, became Aspasia's protector, and she may have had a son with him, but Lysicles died soon after. She probably died around 400 BC. She seems to have carried on an intellectual salon and probably did engage in philosophical discussions, including after the death of Pericles. Plato indicates that she was known for her rhetorical compositional skills and use and teaching of the Socratic method. On the other hand, it is plausible that to some extent, Socratic irony, and Plato's hostility to Pericles and the democracy may lie, in part, behind this aspect of her reputation which Plato may have appeared to promote as a way of undercutting the reputation of her consort, the great democrat— Pericles. One may well feel that all these uncertainties are frustrating. Isn't there anything else *certain* about Aspasia? I think we can be sure of this: she was highly intelligent, forceful, and intellectually stimulating; otherwise Pericles wouldn't have loved her. Aspasia made an impact on her times and on history: she performed the rare feat, for the period, of making herself a part of what was essentially a "man's world."

Selected sources for the life of Aspasia (c. 470-c.400 BC) found in Greek authors:

The early comic poets Cratinus and Hermippus targeted Aspasia in her connection to Pericles. Cratinus, in his play *Chirons*, alluded to Aspasia as Pericles' ". . . Hera, a dog-eyed concubine." See *The Poets of Old Comedy Alcaeus to Diocles*, edited and translated by Ian C. Storey, Loeb Classical Library, 2011; Cratinus, *Testimonia and Fragments*, pp. 390-391, and generally for *Chirons*, pp. 386-391. Aristophanes' *The Acharnians* refers to Aspasia with vivid vulgarity and, since Pericles is accused of starting the Peloponnesian War to revenge a wrong done to her, Aspasia becomes the root cause of the war, in that like Helen of Troy. See Aristophanes, *The Acharnians, the Clouds, the Knights, the Wasps*, cited above for Pericles' sources; *The Acharnians*, pp. 122-123.

In Plato's dialogue *Menexenus*, Aspasia is said to have taught Pericles the art of public speaking, as well as having taught Socrates and other men, and to have composed Pericles' speeches. Beyond that, Menexenus, Socrates' interlocutor, repeats from memory a speech and—a further tour de force—a speech within a speech that he had heard Aspasia deliver. This dialogue has contributed to the tradition of Aspasia as a wise woman conversant with philosophers. On the other hand, although Aspasia is given a lofty role in the dialogue, Plato's uses demeaning and sexually laden tropes of the comedy tradition hostile to Aspasia that may not be immediately apparent today but would have easily sprung to the minds of Plato's contemporary audience. From other points of view, it appears that Plato, who hated the democracy, is denigrating the great democrat and great orator, Pericles—not only is he under the thumb of a woman, he did not even compose his own speeches. How sly of Plato to use Aspasia herself to undermine Pericles! See Plato, *Timaeus, Critias, Cleitophon, Menexenus, Epistles*, translated by R. G. Bury, Loeb Classical Library, 1929; *Menexenus*, pp. 332-381.

The characterization of Aspasia as a woman conversant with philosophers derives also from Xenophon (c. 430-355/354 BC); he, like Plato, was close to Socrates. She is a skilled matchmaker in Xenophon's *Memorabillia* and an expert on good relationships in marriage in his *Oeconomicus*. See Xenophon, *Memorabilia. Oeconomicus. Symposium. Apology*, translated by E. C. Marchant, O. J. Todd, revised by Jeffrey Henderson, Loeb Classical Library, 2013; *Memorabilia*, pp. 156-157; *Oeconomicus* pp. 412-415.

Writing centuries later, Plutarch was a thoughtful, serious author, and his biography of Pericles is a good source for the little that is known about Aspasia. Plutarch records many anecdotes about her, including salacious ones from the comic tradition, but expresses doubt about their trustworthiness, leaving it open to others to reject them on face value, to reinterpret them, or to search for evidence about Aspasia that, with the benefit of analysis, may lie behind them. See Plutarch's *Lives*, cited above for Pericles' sources, pp. 187-189; pp. 193-194.

As noted with regard to Pericles, Athenaeus of Naucratis, writing in the third century AD, includes in his *The Learned Banqueters*, (*Deipnosophistae*) fragments of texts by much earlier authors of the fifth and fourth centuries BC, Stesimbrotus of Thasos, Antisthenes, and Clearchus of Soli—seven hundred years later and Athenaeus was repeating the same old gossip: Pericles evicted his wife in order to live with Aspasia (incorrectly said to be from Megara), and gave himself over to pleasure, squandering his money on her. See *Athenaeus*, cited above for Pericles' sources, pp. 110-111; for the idea that Pericles started the Peloponnesian War on Aspasia's account, see *Athenaeus* same citation, pp. 404-407.

Madeleine M. Henry in her *Prisoner of History, Aspasia of Miletus and Her Biographical Tradition*, Oxford University Press, 1995, presents thoroughly researched, insightful, richly nuanced and thought-provoking discussions of the sources for Aspasia's life, viewed from a feminist perspective. After examining classical sources, Henry continues on to trace and analyze conceptions of Aspasia in the western tradition to the late 20th century, including accounts of Aspasia in fiction, non-fiction and the visual arts.

A marble portrait herm in the Vatican Museum with Aspasia's name inscribed on the base is probably a Roman copy of an unknown Greek sculpture (illustrated by Henry, Figure 1.1, page 18). The inscription leads one to hope to set eyes on Aspasia's face but the date and authenticity of the sculpture, as well as of the inscription, and whether the inscription is intrinsic to the statue or was added to enhance its interest and value are uncertain. As commentators have noted, the face is not individualized and is void of personality.

QUOTATIONS

Epigraphs

Pindar's ode: *Nemean 6*, in *Pindar's Victory Songs*, translated by Frank J. Nisetch, The Johns Hopkins University Press, 1980, p. 256. Reprinted with permission of Johns Hopkins University Press.

Michael Chabon, *The Amazing Adventures of Kavalier & Clay*, Random House, 2000, p. 325.

Chapter 1

Sophocles, *Ajax*, translated by R. C. Trevelyan, in *The Complete Greek Drama*, Vol. 1, edited by Whitney J. Oates and Eugene O'Neill, Jr., Random House, 1938, p. 320.

Sappho, "Raise high the roofbeam, carpenters . . . ," translated by author. For Greek text with English translation, see *Sappho and Alcaeus, Greek Lyric I,* edited and translated by David A. Campbell, Loeb Classical Library, 1990, pp. 136-137.

Helen's magic potion: Homer, *The Odyssey*, translated by E. V. Rieu, revised translation by D. C. H. Rieu, Penguin Books, 2003, p. 46.

Chapter 2

Herodotus' description of the Babylonian custom of sacred prostitution, read in part by Herodotus in Chapter 2, is in Herodotus *History* 1.199. *Herodoti Historiae*, Libri I-14, Oxford Classical Texts, 2015, p. 117, translation by author. See *The Landmark Herodotus,* edited by Robert B. Strassler, translated by Andrew L. Purvis, Anchor Books, 2007, p. 107.

Chapter 6

Homer's account of the encounter between Odysseus and Nausicaa that Aspasia reads to Pericles is in *Odyssey* Book VI. Homer, *The Odyssey*, translated by E. V. Rieu, Penguin Books, 1960.

Chapter 8

Aeschylus, *Agamemnon*, translated by E. D. A. Morshead, in *The Complete Greek Drama*, Vol. I, edited by Whitney J. Oates and Eugene O'Neill, Jr., Random House, 1938, p. 181.

Chapter 9

The quotations from Xenophanes and expressions of his ideas are found in Greek with English translations in G. S. Kirk, J. E. Raven and M. Schofield, *The Presocratic Philosophers*, 2nd ed., Cambridge, 1983, p. 179.

Chapter 10

The song Pericles sings: *Sappho*, translated by Mary Bernard, University of California Press, 1962, p. 41.

Chapters 13 and 31

The quotations of Anaxagoras' philosophy in Chapter 31 are found in Greek with English translations in G. S. Kirk, J. E. Raven and M. Schofield, *The Presocratic Philosophers*, 2nd ed., Cambridge, 1983, p. 363. Anaxagoras' expression of his ideas in Chapters 13 and 31 are drawn from pp. 363-366.

Chapter 26

The vineyard in Homer's poem about the Trojan War: Homer, *The Iliad*, translated by Robert Fagles, Penguin Books, 1991, p. 485.

Chapter 29

Sophocles, *Antigone*, translated by Robert Fagles, in *Sophocles, The Three Theban Plays,* Viking Press, 1982, pp. 63, 64, 68, 76-77, 82, 97.

Chapter 43

"Zeus the son of Cronus . . . ": Homer, *The Iliad*, translated by Robert Fagles, Penguin Books, 1991, p. 95.

ACKNOWLEDGMENTS

Ever since William Whipple's ninth-grade Ancient History Class, I have been fascinated by the classical world, and I have since been fortunate in encountering teachers particularly stimulating in the literature and the art, archaeology and culture of classical Greece. Among these are J. K. Anderson, Peter von Blanckenhagen, Clairève Grandjouan, Evelyn B. Harrison, Eric A. Havelock, Elbert Lenrow, Kenneth S. Lynn, W. K. Pritchett and Ronald Stroud. I am grateful to Professor Anderson for leading our University of California, Berkeley excavation at Old Corinth, Greece. My thanks to Professor Havelock for alerting me to view Plato and his influence with a wary eye. I offer my appreciation to Professor Harrison whose reconstruction of the positions of the figures of the Parthenon's East Pediment, "Athena and Athens in the East Pediment of the Parthenon," published in the *American Journal of Archaeology* in 1967 (Vol. 71, No. 1, pp. 27-59) stimulated my interpretation of meanings of the Pediment, presented at the Annual Conference of the College Art Association of America, February 1988, *Abstracts* pp. 32-33.

A world of scholarly books, analyses, articles, lectures and presentations at professional meetings lies behind this book. Though these are far more than I could ever name, I have a keen appreciation and awareness that they form the fabric of my understanding of the ancient world.

Peter Gelfan, Karl Monger and most recently Peter Rader have provided editorial assistance. Thank you for all you have taught me and for propelling me forward.

Anthony Boas, Barbara Eisold, Richard Garner, Lawrence Hartmann, Ann Ruben. Robert Ruben and Karin Schwartz have read the book all or in part and have provided illuminating comments and critiques. The book has benefited significantly from suggestions by members of the Lotos Writers Group: Diana Benet, Peter Friedman, Stephen Greenwald, Paula Powell, Henrik Petersen, Norman Poser, Robert Ravitz, Edward Schiff, Gloria Shafer and Renee Summer. My husband, Robert Ruben, has read the manuscript several times, always challenging me with questions that lead to clarifying the meaning of situations. Barbara Eisold, Alice Howard, Stephen Kates, Joanne Pugh, Andrea Webber and Harriet Zuckerman have provided helpful consults on aspects of design. I am grateful for Nancy Boas' persistent encouragement, bibliographic assistance and generosity of spirit.

My loving thanks go to members of my family, A. J. Ruben, Ann Ruben, Emily Ruben-Long and Karin Schwartz who, busy as they are, have taken time to give essential technical help "on the spot."

The steady confidence in this book of my daughter, Karin Schwartz, has sustained me. My husband, Bob Ruben, has been at my side throughout the writing of the novel, unfailingly providing whatever might be needed, from editorial acuity to computer assistance, from reassurance to inspiration.

Yvonne Korshak

The Sword of the War God, a sequel to *Pericles and Aspasia*, will appear soon.

Printed in the USA
CPSIA information can be obtained
at www.ICGtesting.com
LVHW041638301123
765068LV00001B/43